# THE ICE MOVES FOR NO ONE

## THE DUSKINGR SAGA
### BOOK ONE

ARLO Z. GRAVES

QUILLS & COSMOS PRESS

# DEDICATION

*This book is for Lillian Csernica, who stepped into a low point of my life and said: you can do this. Who believed in The Ice Moves for No One first. Who met me in a liminal space and told me yes, you can, yes, you will. I would not be a writer without you. Lillian, this book is for you.*

*This book is for David LaFrance, who met me where I was with a smile, always a smile. Who demonstrated a level of compassion, fairness, and kindness that goes unmatched. Who modeled for me the value of self-worth, integrity, and the pricelessness of decency. I would not be where I am without you. David, this book is for you.*

# CONTENTS

# PART THREE
## THE ICE MOVES FOR NO ONE

# PART ONE

## THE DUSK TRIALS

CHAPTER

# ONE

I step into the sweltering spotlights and dusty sand of the arena. It's so bright, I can't see the audience, but I can hear them. They roar like the tide. I hold my battle axe, Gevit, across my body, the Zahlek script on her handle worn to near oblivion. Old and battered as she is, her double blades shine in the glare.

My opponent walks into the ring resplendent in his mesh uniform. The Lamplight Petroleum logo blazes down his flank. He holds a flanged mace. I wonder if he too carries the weapon in honor of his ancestors, or just for show.

The referees walk us around the arena for the pleasure of the audience and then position us facing. My opponent hands his mace to his coach and accepts the tournament-safe buckler and short sword. The blade is edged, but contoured for superficial cuts, not to cleave, to sunder, or impale. We're not here to kill, we fight for first blood.

I hunger for that blood. Every drop I draw leads me one step closer to who I was born to be.

Bringing Gevit to my face, I kiss the flat of her blade before letting a referee take her. I watch my adversary's coach adjust his straps and test his tournament weapon for balance and sharpness. He wears the logo of one of Ruhnsvalla's biggest companies. I face him in a compression bra and kneepads meant for dancing. I wear the runescript of Tophinghua, the Dread Hurricane, painted down my bare arms and legs in black ink.

The ref hands me a matching buckler and short sword, and I recite a silent prayer. *Tophinghua be with me. Ice of my ancestors, blood of the storm, be with me, Mother. May your ferocity guide my blade...*

I bought my fiberglass helmet from a thrift shop. It covers my ears, and I can hear my own breath rushing in my head. *Mother, I am your daughter. Every drop of blood I draw, I draw for you.*

The referees step back. The voice of the announcer blares over the loudspeaker: "AND FIGHT!"

My opponent and I circle, size each other up. Our clothes cover little of us, our strong, honed bodies on display. He stands over six feet tall but so do I. My meaty arms hold my weapons steady and my latissimus muscles strain against the compression bra. I am a roadmap of my training, a testament to every early morning swim and late-night sparring session after work. I have built myself for victory.

*What are you?* My birth mother asked me once.

*This*, I think. *I am this.* A warrior. A victor. A daughter of the Dread One.

I wonder for a moment, if my birth mother ever thinks of me.

My opponent lunges in and I meet him. The crash of our bucklers jolts through us, blades flash. I slip away and fall into a low stance. He has years of experience in the tournament circuit, and that comes with a salary, a career, and confidence. I see an obstacle. I work part-time on a fishing boat and live with roommates in a postage stamp apartment. We're both selkies, so winner of this match will be offered a sponsorship and trainer for the upcoming Dusk Trials. There's no way around it, I don't care how good he is or who pays his bills, I am going to beat him. That sponsorship is mine. The Fury of the Dread One is mine, and She will not be denied.

My opponent strikes again, feigning low and jabbing high. I roll around the quick flash of steel, anticipating its path while keeping myself low, a small target. Strands of my long black hair stick to my sweaty neck.

Our match proceeds and our excitement transforms into exhaustion. My thick thighs tremble with fatigue as I dance out of reach. We are evenly matched, more so than I wished. So be it.

I wade into his defenses, flicking out with my blade and shoving the buckler into his sword arm, backing him off balance. My arms shake with the effort.

My opponent turns his stumble into an attack, but I block in time, just in time, catching the blade on my buckler. The audience gasps. I hear the announcer babbling, running his mouth about risks and advantages and my comparative lack of professional experience. "SHE'S GOOD, SHE'S SCRAPPY, BUT WILL IT BE ENOUGH?" I tune him out. Has he ever bled? Has he ever sacrificed? He is scenery. He is a distraction. Right now, he is irrelevant. *Focus.*

*Let me be enough,* I pray.

Sweat glistens on our bare arms and legs, it drips into the dust as we circle once more. The spotlights overheat the arena, our veins stand out on our muscles, our hands grip the handles of our weapons.

Again we step in, we entangle, and we withdraw. My steps feel heavy, my breath rasps, insufficient to fuel my muscles, and my heart hammers in my ribs. I feel my body grow dull through the fire. I can't take much more of this, but neither can he. We are exhausted, chipped down by four days of matches that brought me and this man in his Lamplight Petroleum logo here, and that is perfect. This is where the worthy rise in the flames of conflict, and the unworthy fall to ash. Sooner or later, one of us will misstep, one of us will parry too late. It will not be me.

He doesn't have to take the bus home tonight and be up at dawn for work tomorrow. He doesn't need to win the sponsorship tonight. I do.

My arms shudder as I block the blade and dance around him. I know I do not have much time left. I make my move.

I catch his blade on the buckler, but I accept the blow. The blade slides close, too close. I feel the flat of the steel brush my belly. All he'd need to do is turn it. *Fuck...*

I lock my shield arm over the man's wrist. If I miscalculate, or hesitate, I've handed myself to him, sacrificed myself.

But the startled white rims of his black selkie eyes tell me all I need to know. I twist, I drag him forward with his own momentum, over my shin, I pull him to the sand floor of the arena and wrench his arm behind his back.

My opponent thrashes and bucks but I push my knee into his back. I slice a shallow, diagonal cut down his shoulder.

Then I step away, stagger away, breathless and dizzy, expended. I lean on the wall of the arena, against an advertisement for Spindel soda pop, and wait for first blood to fall.

The referees swoop in like buzzards in bright yellow vests, holding my opponent and I apart until his bright blood splatters to the sand.

"Blood!" calls one of the referees and the crowd explodes. Cameras flash, the announcer booms. I let my head fall forward as I catch my breath.

"AND THE ROOKIE TAKES REGIONALS!"

As his trainer hops into the arena with gauze, my opponent uses a hand up to get to his feet. Our eyes meet and he nods. I nod back.

Then, a referee pulls me into the beam of the spotlights. The buckler and dinky short sword are removed from my grasp and the heavy, deadly weight of Gevit returned to my hands. When the referee holds my arm aloft, when the crowd thunders, I lift Gevit above my head. I roar in triumph.

*Tophinghua, I claim first blood in your honor!*

Because I didn't just win Regionals. I won a sponsorship in the Dusk Trials. I won an honest shot at my dreams, to become who I am meant to be. I tear the thrift store helmet from my head and shake my black hair free. Tophinghua's blood runs in my veins. I am indomitable.

A feral, joyous grin stretches my face. I throw back my head and howl. The Dusk Trials are the only obstacle left between me and my future. Just another fight. Just another game.

My name is Aalgur Thalon. I am a daughter of the Dread One. And I am going to win.

CHAPTER

# TWO

My heart sings as I race through the underwater obstacles, diving down to grab concrete weights from the bottom and then speeding to the surface, breaching my sleek body from the water. I heave the weight onto a floating platform and dive again. My flukes pump the water like the wings of a bird. I am a sea lion, black and fast as a harpoon. I sail through the metal hoops suspended over the racecourse and hit the water, nose first. My best friend, Kip, a ringed seal, races to stay on my tail.

The underwater portion of the Dusk Trials, the Gauntlet, isn't live, of course. Not yet. The more challenging features won't be added until closer to race day. But in the meantime, selkies like us are free to use it for practice. After the last set of hoops, Kip and I crash into the water and bob up like corks.

Six months ago, we both took to the podium in the Regional Armed Weapons Tournament and now, we have but six short days left until the Dusk Trials begin.

Kip and I swing our pinniped bodies through the kelp as we return to shore. He swims fishlike with his rear flippers while I use my big, black fore-flukes like wings. Water passing over my whiskers paints a picture of the world around me, seeing what my eyes cannot. The fish, the weeds, the parts of the Gauntlet, I feel them around me, and see them in my mind.

*What are you?* My mother asked, ever shocked to have birthed a sea lion pup.

What am I indeed.

Selkies swarm the course, leaping through hoops and tossing concrete weights onto the floating platforms from their mouths. I watch for a moment. The weights are a new addition to these Trials. I wonder what they're for.

Two fluffy little pups slide up onto the platform, all big eyes and curious whiskers.

A pair of racing selkies hurl their weights up, nearly squashing one of the pups. Bristling, I dart for the platform. Right before I reach it, I shift my body back into a human enough shape to speak. I become an awkward in-between creature, mostly sea lion with a human bust and face.

"HEY!" I bark at the offending selkies before they can dive. They stop and size me up. I show them my teeth. "Be a little careful, huh? The course is open. As in: open to *everyone*."

The offending selkies slip away without comment, slinking under the water and away from me. I turn to the wide-eyed pups. "Hey, this isn't a great place to play. Assholes abound." I nudge them back into the water and steer them north. "Why don't you head up to Coven Cove to play?"

One of the selkie pups shifts her shape into that of a pudgy, sweet-faced girl. "We want to see the Dusk Trial champions. We want to compete someday too!"

I smile but nudge both kids away from the ruckus. "You'll be great at it. But until you're a bit bigger, you've gotta keep from getting squished by idiots like us."

The girl dips her chin. Her human-ish shape begins to morph back to that of a harbor seal. "You're not an idiot."

"Heh, debatable. He sure is though." I splash water in Kip's direction. "Run along now. I'll see you next Dusk Trials, yeah?"

"Yeah," mutters the girl. She and her friend dive away, heading north as suggested.

Satisfied, I revert to my full sea lion form and continue to shore. Kip spits water at me along the way.

In the shallows, Kip and I curl our streamline bodies beneath us, call our thyir, and change our shapes.

We selkies used to move the ice and the ice moved us. We are descendants of Tawkthalon and her thyir, her magic of ice and bone, still shimmers inside us. But as generations pass, the gift of the sea leaves us. Each year, fewer and fewer of us are born with pelts, our thyir weakens. And now, the ice moves for no one.

Or so the saying goes.

I take a breath of air as I fully change shapes, as my insides stretch and my joints pop. The thyir in the water flows through my bones, cold and cleansing. We cannot shift on land, only in water. Only with the thyir connecting us to the sea.

The shift feels like stretching your shoulders after sitting for too long, like flexing right out of one body and into another. My black sea lion pelt splits open. The fur peels back from my skin, leaving behind a sticky residue over my thick muscles.

The shift takes effort and energy, it costs us. But it shouldn't hurt. Which is why Kip gives me a look when I stumble and groan.

"Step on an urchin, Thalon?" he asks.

My joints grind, like they have sand in them. I stand with my hands on my knees, catching my breath.

"You'd like that, wouldn't you? For me to get tetanus right before the Trials," I quip.

Kip holds up both hands, boyish grin at the ready. "Hey now, I said *urchin*."

That grin hasn't left him since the day we met, since the day I offered him a hand up in the school yard after chasing off a pod of asshole older kids. At twelve we swore an oath to each other beneath the moon on Coven Cove.

*We train together. We fly together. By Brosk and the Ingvu, we'll crew the Duskingr together...*

I shake off the discomfort. "I'm just a bit sore, I think." I crack my neck, then my jaw, making sure my teeth have lined back up straight.

Kip bounces an eyebrow. "By all means, stay sore."

"Someone should put signs up on the Gauntlet or something. Kids are gonna get smooshed."

"We didn't get smooshed."

"We didn't have those concrete weight things ten years ago," I point out.

"Fair. Not sure what that's about, but whatever. Kinda fun."

With my pelt free, I kneel to wash the residual slime from my body and pull my long black hair into a bun. Kip washes as well, shaking out his light hair. I quickly forget the moment of discomfort.

With our practice run over, we stand shoulder to shoulder, knee-deep in the tide, facing out to sea. We bow our heads, offering silent gratitude to the water, our way of life. As selkie folk, we are born of the water, of the sea, and know to always give thanks for our thyir and our second skins.

First, we hold our hands over the water, palm down. "In honor of Brosk," we whisper together. Then, we turn our hands over and press them to our hearts.

"For the honor of the Dread One," I add in a hush. I do not dare speak Her name aloud. Kip glances at me, he dares not speak of Her at all.

I must though. I need Her to remember I am of Her bloodline.

*Tophinghua*, I say her name in my mind, *Mother*.

Ritual complete, Kip and I walk out of the sea toward the coastal city of Vatska. A ferry of spectators pulls up to dock, regular humans by the look of them, with their cameras on lanyards, floppy hats and button up shirts printed with flowers and animals. Excellent fodder for the knickknack shops. Gulls shrill overhead in the gray sky as the tourists file down the gangplank, joining a handful of reporters in snappy suits. Fingers immediately point at us and cameras raise. Some people avert their eyes and blush, others stare as Kip and I raise our hands in greeting. Perhaps we are the first selkies they've seen.

We are also nude aside from our pelts and do nothing to hide it. The taboo of nakedness never really caught on in a city with so many selkies, but it sure does give the tourists a thrill.

Kip and I are both brawny and mature at twenty-five, tall and broad shouldered, especially by human standards. I'm leaner, my muscles round and powerful, breasts an afterthought. Where Kip is beige with ash blond hair, I'm tanned, my hair and eyes black as a moonless night, my features strong and chiseled. As we walk, I make sure my pelt hangs open enough that none of the gawking tourists miss my contoured abdomen. It is, after all, a fashion show of sorts. We're spectacles to them and we're unashamed. Kip even stops to flex for a photograph.

"Look, look! Selkies!" squeals a teenager. She holds a bottle of Spindel soda in one hand and waves a Dusk Trial booklet with the other.

I wave back, teeth bright, smile huge.

The girl squeals and flails her arm in the air. "Azoto! AZOTO! You're my hero!"

My smile sours into a snarl. I turn all the way around to see Azoto and Rawl strutting out of the sea behind us.

Rawl's animal form is an elephant seal. His human shape isn't much different. He's built like the child of a refrigerator and a tugboat and is just about as smart. Azoto makes a striking counterpoint to him, as if she keeps him around just to have something coarse and blunt for visual contrast.

Azoto Seppanen saunters out of the water and tosses her wet brown hair over the fur seal pelt on her shoulders. She smiles at the excited girl and waves. Every sway of her thick hips, every curve of her lips is deliberate and rehearsed as reporters begin snapping photographs. She's short, all rounded edges and jiggling flesh, all part of her trap. Azoto swims and fights with a ferocity few can match, or so I hear. And with the sponsorship of the entire Seppanen family behind them, Azoto and Rawl are favored to place high in the Trials.

Azoto poses, wet and glistening, for the newspapers. Her narrow black eyes find mine. We stare holes into each other until Kip takes my elbow and pulls me along. The teenager tries to hop the railing of the gangplank to get Azoto's autograph.

"I have to rinse off and clock in." Kip hooks a thumb over his shoulder to Shanty's Chowder Shack on the wooden wharf. "Step on some more urchins, won't you?"

I shake my head and keep walking. "Catch you later."

The sand becomes a dirt path leading up through the ice plant to the paved streets and sidewalks. The rolling green Blackberry Hills set the backdrop for Vatska with its quaint wooden houses, metal roofs, and garden boxes. The sweet, quiet neighborhoods cluster around a giant black temple to Brosk, the God of the Sea. To the north, huge hangars, adorned with the carved heads of sea monsters, rise from the airfield. To the south, a sprawling industrial metropolis clutters the skyline, remnants of the stronger selkie tribes from centuries past. Many of the handsome buildings sit empty now. The decennial Dusk Trials are the continent of Ruhnsvalla's biggest sensation. Perhaps they'll rekindle a bit of life in the once thriving city.

I take the road along the bay lined with inns. Even a week out from the Dusk Trials, the streets throng with tourists and vendors. There have never been huge corporate sponsors before. I hear this year will be the biggest Dusk Trials ever held.

I make my way around the schools of tourists, idling cars sputtering out smoke and more tourists juggling corndogs. I tune out the chaos. I see only the arena.

The Dusk Trials are only held once a decade. In the interim, the stone arena serves as a venue for markets, trade shows, or carnival grounds. It transforms now, hung with banners and fit with a mooring mast. It looms on the edge of town, a gatekeeper of my future, my fate.

I stop on the sidewalk, staring up at the arena. How many people can it hold? A hundred thousand? More?

I turn, and my gaze travels down Scallop Avenue. A humble wooden house sits at the end. I still remember the smell my salty wet footprints left in the doorway. But that door is closed to me now.

I turn my back to the little wood home and look up at the stadium. Last time I watched them transform the stadium I was but a pup of fifteen, full of dreams. Now, I am a beast in my prime, a force of reckoning.

This is where heroes are made or broken. This is where the new sailors of the Duskingr will be chosen. My stomach twists a little.

It's finally here. After ten long years, the Dusk Trials are here. I am here.

I take a last look at the cozy old house and walk on. Nothing there can hurt me anymore. Nothing there can stop me.

# THREE

"Crank them in, pups! We aren't bobbing for apples here, crank in the nets!" Cortland, captain of the trawler the *Golden Cormorant*, and my boss, spits over the railing. He takes a drink from his bottle of Spindel, swirling it around so the plastic beads inside make the sugary soda foam.

I climb the ladder on the rear of the ship, pelt still adhered to my skin for warmth but back in my semi-human shape. It's a comfortable in-between: woman shaped but covered in sea lion fur to the neck and dark rubbery skin from the knees and elbows down. Aside from sharper teeth, my face looks human.

"Weak catch today, Thalon," says Cortland.

When I began working on the *Cormorant* five years back, Cortland had been bright and chipper. Now his pep is faded into suspicious sneers and endless lectures about not wasting time because time equals money, and if you're leaning you could be cleaning.

I grunt and shuffle to the towel rack. Today's shift felt longer than it had any right to. My rubbery, webbed feet make a squeaking sound on the deck. I'd trade jobs if I could, but it's hard to find one that pays enough for rent while still giving me the time to train. My sponsorship didn't pick up the slack like I'd hoped.

I worked a summer at a fish market once. But I can't show my face there again...

I grab a towel. "The fish aren't schooling. Lot of sludge eels though."

"How many fish you eat down there?" Cortland watches fish gulp and struggle in the net.

I roll my hair in the towel. "Two."

"That's the merchandise, Thalon. Since you've eaten, skip your break and help the boys get the goods processed."

I say nothing, watching the human crew maneuver the crane. I say nothing, because if I open my mouth, I will scream. But I help, and then I swab the deck. I stay out of the human crew's way, avoiding eye contact. We're friendly enough, but as the only selkie on the *Cormorant*, I don't exactly get invited out for beers at the end of the day.

As I finish up and the *Cormorant* makes port, Cortland approaches me with a leather book. "How many days you taking off for the hoopla, Thalon?"

My rubbery hands squeak on the mop handle. Cortland stares at the book and I stare at him. He smells slightly sweet, almost like cotton candy but with a hint of vinegar beneath. My nose wrinkles. I won't be coming back after the Trials.

"Gonna need you to come in the first three days of the week." Cortland's eyes dart to mine, then back to the book. "You know how the seasonal workers are. And if the pickings are as slim as you make them out to be..."

I breathe out through my nose, keep my expression blank. "Fine. But when I move into the rookery, that's it."

"That's it," Cortland echoes. He walks off without another word. He cracks into a fresh bottle of Spindel, chugging it with his back to me.

I hop the railing onto the dock. My left leg buckles and I squawk.

I rub my knee and thigh, sucking air through my teeth. Maybe I really have been training too hard. Another week and I can put this whole chum bucket life behind me. Cortland, the *Cormorant*, my closet bedroom, leave it in the dust. Wave bye-bye as I fly away. Six more days.

I limp to the Temple of Brosk from the docks. Sunset burns pink and orange against the wispy clouds. My heavy canvas coat buffers the gnawing ocean wind. Even with the coat and my fur, I still shiver. The ancient, thatched-roof temple looms over the village like a black, gaudy cake. The Temple is meant for people like my parents, people descended from the Ingvu but born without pelts, born as humans. It offers them a connection to the old ways they can't find in the sea itself.

I used to enjoy attending services in the Temple of Brosk. The priests sure know how to work people up for the holidays. The Temple lost me when the sermons turned to talk of Tophinghua. Specifically, insisting that Brosk the God of the Sea creating Tophinghua in his own image made her male by default.

"*She* is a literal *god*." I clearly recall standing on a bench in the temple as a child. "If a god can't remake Herself in Her own image, what's the point of being a god?"

After that, my parents sent me dance classes instead, to learn the ts'kmet. To put all that energy to good use, they said.

At the Temple now, the sunset glows like bourbon through the courtyard. Bronze statues of Brosk and his five Ingvu attendants stand in two rows of three on either side of the path. Krescean, Volier, Ryshvarad, Zandruik, and of course, Her. They crew the *Naudeleid*, the ice ship, and shepherd souls lost at sea to their resting place. Their faces smolder in the light.

I honor each of them, but I stop to incline my head to Tophinghua.

Tophinghua, the Dread One, Storm, and Strife, patron of warriors. So fearsome and so feared is She, we do not speak Her name lest She turn the eye of Her hurricane upon us. She stands over me in human form, storm cloud hair frozen in a wild dance, shoulders broad as the mountains. Whoever made the bronze statue wasn't brave enough to give Her breasts.

The statue looks down at me. My heart swells with pride. My pelt, my blood, my magic descends from Her. It was Tophinghua who crafted a pelt for the human girl sacrificed to Her. Tophinghua, who breathed thyir into the young girl's lungs. And it was that girl, Tawkthalon, who mothered my people so long ago.

It was her blood that birthed me. As all selkies are, I was born in my animal form. My mother cried when she saw me, which she reminded me of when I made her especially cross.

When I grew into a plump armful, a priestess came from the Temple to un-pelt me for the first time.

My mother drew my wet pelt from the water, pulling it close to herself and away from my chubby human limbs. *Does she have to keep this? She's still so young... she won't even remember...*

When I became a toddler, my mother hid my pelt from me if I misbehaved. *I can't stand the sounds she makes when she's like that*, she said. *Barking and squawking. And it's not like she'll remember...*

I remember.

Tears well in my eyes and I swipe them away. I look into the bronze eyes of the statue. "I am Your daughter. Yours."

The statue, of course, says nothing.

Arms full of groceries , I waddle my way through a labyrinth of pop-up tent shops selling everything from sports drinks to Dusk Trial commemorative key chains. One booth even sells the little glass-faced boxes that talk to the ether. Of course, on this side of the Svall, the boxes can't connect to the repeaters on the Otherside, rendering them all but useless. Especially for the price point. I can't even afford lox today.

Not all Otherside gadgets and technology are useless to us

though. Before my parents had me, a device came through the Svall that allows doctors to look inside the body without cutting it open. Most of the time though, the Otherside spits out gadgets, gizmos, and trash, so much trash. Supposedly monsters come through too from time to time, but they're not from the Otherside, they're from the Svall itself.

I hike my bag of groceries higher in my arms and wade through people, bumping them gently out of my way like buoys. This will be my third time seeing the Dusk Trials and second time competing. This time it feels different. This time there are sponsorships, brochures, and betting. There must have been betting before, but this year, official booths stack up on hotel steps and around restaurants. Tourists in suits pour over spreadsheets, money trades hands. Betting and soda. I can't turn my head without seeing bottles of Spindel and smelling the cotton candy stink of it. Spindel Co. is one of the big sponsors this year, so I shouldn't be surprised.

In fact, this is the first year sponsorships are required, not just a bonus. I competed for the first time as a gangly little thing of fifteen and paid my way with the summer's newspaper delivery money. If Kip and I hadn't placed in Regionals, we'd be stranded at low tide.

"Thalon! Thalon!" My head snaps around as Kip bounds through the crowd, still in his apron from Shanty's Chowder Shack. He reaches me and hisses in my ear. "The Duskingr's here! Let's get on top of the Ivory Inn before the tourists notice...!"

I squeal and nearly drop my groceries as we make a beeline for the four-story Ivory Inn, the tallest building in this district of Vatska after the Temple of Brosk.

Racing through the double glass doors and up the red carpeted stairs, we bolt through a knot of tourists, past an angry bellhop and into the stairwell. We whoop and holler like pups playing Pirate Trove.

From the roof, I squint into the darkening sky. There she is! The Duskingr! I swallow as my stomach flips.

The rigid sided airship blots out the bloody remnants of the sunset as she sails in from the sea, silent as the wings of an owl. Her fin rudders move as she begins to bank. The lights of Vatska illuminate the visages of beasts etched into her black belly.

Screams and shouts go up as tourists start noticing the Duskingr from the open-air market. Her streamline shape gives the ship the air of a shark, deliberate and fierce. Streams of people flock into the street, cameras flaring, jostling to catch glimpses of the airship as she casts her shadow, prowling over Vatska. Out over the bay, several Sky Navy airships tail her.

The Duskingr pivots to face into the wind and begins her descent over the arena. My hackles raise, my breath lodges in my throat. There are six Duskingr in total, as many of our gods come in threes or sixes, serving as sentinels along the Svall, protecting us from the Otherside. This ship's name blazes in red Zahlek runescript down her flanks. Neither Kip nor I speak Zahlek, a dead language from long ago. Still, the blazing red angles of the runes bring a flutter to my heart and an icy chill to my belly.

Which Duskingr is this? I wonder. *Machtesh? Kullkesh? Ursul?* One of the others? Her shadow eclipses two full blocks as she passes overhead. Her gun turrets catch the lights of the arena below.

"Look at the guns! The Duskingr have guns?" I holler, bouncing. The Duskingr aren't warships, they're realm ships. The guns glint along her gondola like folded viper fangs.

"I don't know! How cool!" yells Kip.

We scream and bounce like popcorn kernels on a skillet. I forget the guns. "She's here! She's really here!" Dignity has left us.

The ship drops anchor to the arena's mooring mast, and slowly, so slowly, comes to rest on the berth along the far side of the arena. Crimson spotlights blaze on. They sweep the sky and tilt to illuminate the Duskingr. A thundering cheer rolls up from the throngs in the streets.

We whoop too, fists pumping. My groceries spill at our feet. Kip and I leap up and down, kids again for a moment, eyes bright with joy and hearts brimming with wonder. I accidentally step on an onion.

Tiny figures file from the ship and walk the rim of the arena.

Kip and I go still and cling to each other. The Duskingr is here, and that is her crew. In a few short days, will I walk among them?

I smack my hand on Kip's starched sleeve and point. "There they are! That one's the Illuet!"

Though we can scarcely make out the bug-sized figures filing along the rim of the arena, I recognize the Illuet by her elaborate mask. The High Priestess wears a mask of leather and bone in the likeness of Kvellsett, the Coyote Woman. Antlers sprout from her head. Her robes drift around her in a flow of burgundy and shimmer, her identity, like the duties of the Duskingr, a mystery to me.

A retinue of three attendants in half masks follow the Illuet as her long strides carry her around the arena. Each Duskingr sails under the command of an Illuet—a huldra priest—and a selkie captain. The crew consists of huldror who have trained in kvell and selkies powerful in their thyir. The best of the best. We're taught young that huldror kvell and selkie thyir can damage each other. Yet somehow the crewmen must live and work together in ship's quarters. I even heard a fable that selkies and huldror once dueled side by side in Dusk Trials of legend. How? I haven't a clue. The Duskingr keep their secrets close.

I will learn soon enough, though. Those secrets will be mine.

"Hollow people," mutters Kip, eyes narrowing at the huldror. "Thyir-breaking hollow folk. Look at them. Strutting in like they own Vatska..."

I give him a look from under my eyebrows. "You sure you're up for calling these 'thyir-breaking hollow folk' your coworkers?"

Kip huffs air out his nose. "I'm up for calling myself a Duskingr sailor."

I open my mouth to rib him some more. Excitement pulses through me and my comment fizzles as four selkie warriors walk out next. Other crew and members of the Duskir Parliament exit last but

I couldn't care less about them. The Illuet leads the procession to the side of the arena where she pauses to lift a hand to us. The captivated audience erupts.

Even from our perch atop the Ivory Inn, we can see the tufted tail at the hem of each huldra's robe. As Kip said, the huldror have hollow backs, like ceramic figurines, or so the legends go. Like all huldror I've seen, these sailors cover themselves completely in ceremonial attire, doing nothing but whetting my curiosity. Do they have spines? Lungs? Hearts? I've never met one in person.

These people will decide my fate.

*No, they won't*, I remind myself. I make my path, choose my fate. This is simply the game I must play.

Turning, the Illuet leads her huldror down hidden stairs into the secrets of the arena, the Duskir Parliament follows behind them. The selkies keep waving and pumping weapons in the air while the crowd goes bonkers. They too depart, the spotlights blaze over the Duskingr a final time and switch off. Withdrawing her anchor, the Duskingr lifts off and becomes part of the darkness.

My hands reach inside my coat to feel my plush fur, the fur given me by Tophinghua. I was born for this.

"Are you ready?" asks Kip.

I stand in my spilled groceries. The ship fills my eyes. "Are you?"

CHAPTER

# FOUR

I duck the swing of Kip's sword and slice out with my hand axe. The practice blade leaves a line of chalk across his flank.

"Seagull sucker!" spits Kip. He swipes at the chalk. Spinning the hand axe, I slip it into the hook on my belt and lift the battle axe off the rack of wooden weapons.

"About the axe..." Lexija's voice cuts through the clatter of wood, shouts of aggression, dismay, and victory. Our trainer strides around one of many sparring circles to Kip and me. She walks like a snow plough, moving people out of her path with the wedge of her gruff presence. Our sponsor, Anton Gill of Gill's Goods, trails after her.

"Did the final head count come in?" I ask.

"Yes. Five hundred and sixty-two in total. A walloping one-hundred-and-twenty-eight will move on to the Blood Spire tournament after racing the Gauntlet... talk about feeding the spectators. But about the axe..."

"What about the axe?" I ask, resting the practice weapon blade-down on the grass. A stiff, briny breeze snarls my black hair around my face. I know about the axe, I know what Lexija is going to say.

Lexija takes the practice weapon from me and hangs it back on the rack. "This is the Blood Spire, not the Crack Open a Suit of Armor Spire. The tournament's a fight to *first blood* and a double-bladed battle axe is *not* the best way to do that."

"I'm good with the axe." I scowl as Lexija thrusts a spear into my hands.

"I know you are. You're good with a lot of weapons. But for fights like this, the axe just isn't it. I'm less mad about that one." She indicates the hand axe on my belt. "But you need range. Reach. Speed. I've tossed Gevit around. That clunker's *heavy*."

I spin the spear and jab the butt into the belly of our grain-sack dummy.

"Yes, good," sighs Lexija.

"I'm finally allowed to use Gevit in combat." I shake the spear a little. "I've *never* gotten to use her in live combat…"

"And for good reason! That thing could take an arm off! Plus, it's slow, and with the blade safety guards you'll get, it's going to be even slower."

"You know what Gevit means to me." I dip the tip of the spear in chalk and face Kip.

"Yes, I do. It, excuse me, *she*, was handed down through your mother's line… she's important. Pose with her in pictures, but—YES! That's more like it!" She yells as I block Kip's sword and stab him with white powder on the rebound.

"Yikes!" shrills Kip. "Step on a few more urchins, won't you?"

Lexija claps her hands once. "See how much faster that is? And it's got the range you'll need. Tawkthalon Herself carried a spear into battle, you know."

I don't have the spear of Tawkthalon. I have Gevit. I huff.

"Regionals are an entirely different game, Thalon. Pocket change. Well, you and Kip got Anton's attention, and now you've got me, but regardless. The Dusk Trials are life altering. Especially *these* Dusk Trials. People are going to fight filthy in the arena."

*I can fight filthy*, I think.

"Spear's the smarter choice." Kip grabs a towel and wipes his face.

I scowl at him. He placed sixth in Regionals. Somehow, we both ended up with the grocery store sponsor. I suppose that's because the other four folks on the podium with us were human.

"This isn't the moment to be sentimental," Lexija continues. She hands me a bottle of water. "No one else out there is going to be, and if they are, they're going to lose. It's also not a solo game, Thalon. You're not a one-woman army. You don't have to be. We're a *team*."

I knock the butt of the spear around Kip's ankles. "You're telling me this goofball's my brother-in-arms?"

"I'm saying we all are, Thalon. What was the point of winning a sponsorship if you fight me tooth and nail at every turn?"

I suck air through my teeth. "I'll consider it." I crack open the bottle and drain half before passing it to Kip.

"Following off of that..." Gill clears his throat. "Are you absolutely certain you wish for your patron in the Trials to be listed as..." He gives his binder a nervous glance. "The Dread One?"

"Not you too. And yes." I gather my tangled hair into a bun. The snapping wind from the sea hits my sweaty clothes. I shiver.

"Ah well. I wanted to make certain." Gill keeps staring at the open binder in his hands, thinning hair whipped wild. "The final decisions need to be in this evening..."

"She's my patron." I put the spear back on the rack.

"She's also considered, by some..."

"By *many*," adds Lexija.

"Considered a fell omen. Bad luck. Ill fate..."

I fold my arms. "She's also the God of War and Victory."

"There's only one other competitor crass enough to wear the sigil of the Dread One..." Gill pokes something in his binder with his pen.

"Well, there you have it. Someone else has taste." I lift my canvas coat from the edge of the weapons rack and shrug into it. No sense shivering in the wind if we're going to have this argument again.

"Kipper, you've chosen Volier, yes?" asks Lexija.

"Yes," Kip bobs his chin. "Volier, the Driving Wind. Good old dependable."

He flashes me with his sweetest smile. I stick my tongue out at him.

"How old are we?" asks Lexija. "Forget the one-woman army, army of idiots is more like it."

Gill keeps tapping the binder with his pen. "Aalgur, I respect your faith in Her but, if you make it into the Blood Spire, which we have complete confidence you will... the reporters are going to have things to say about wearing the Dread One's sigil..."

"So? She's important to me, and it's me who has to live up to Her reputation." I stare at Gill's face as he stares at the binder. I'd practiced my responses to their various arguments.

"Very well. Aalgur Thalon will wear the sigil of... the Dread One..."

"Make sure you spell Her name out for the pamphlet." I tap my finger on the top of the binder. "Don't want Her thinking I'm fighting in honor of some other Dread One."

"No... of course not," concedes Gill. He flips a page over. "I put the deposit down for your tournament armor this morning, pending you both clear the Gauntlet."

"No boob armor." I tap the binder again. Kip snickers. "No boob armor for me anyway, but maybe make sure Kipper gets some."

Gill traces his pen around something written on the paper. "I put those exact words in the order for you. So, if your armor has um... is unacceptable, take it up with them, Thalon." He closes the binder. "Thalon, Kipper, best of luck. Make sure to get plenty of rest. The gods know you've trained enough."

"Thank you, sir." I dip my head. Kip does likewise.

Lexija waits until Gill begins picking his way back across the practice field before pointing to my jacket and the rack. "Trained you might be, some fine tuning still won't hurt. Kipper? Trade out that sword for a one-hander and a shield. Thalon, spear."

Biting back my opinions, I dip the spear in chalk again. She does have a point that we will need to switch weapons to keep advantages. But she will also have to accept I'll be fighting with Gevit whenever possible. She might call it a team effort, but in the arena it will only be me and my adversary.

Bringing the spear to the ready like a two-handed staff, I fall into my stance as Kip faces me. He is good, quite good. I grin. I am better.

Something warm stirs in me, a snag in my belly. My skin pimples in a chill. Turning, I find the Illuet herself towering over us. A security detail flanks her. They do not carry swords, spears, or axes. They carry rifles, brass and steel gleaming in the rising sun.

We competitors go still, watching the small parade. The Illuet turns a slow, pensive circle, observing us. Her white coyote mask glints with gold, jasper, and bronze. Pieces of reindeer antler comprise a headdress worn over her hood. Living antlers stick out of it, too. Her dusky brown robes shimmer with iridescent purple in the blazing dawn, covering her completely. No visible tail, no feet. She keeps her arms folded together inside her sleeves, hands a mystery. She must be seven feet tall, eight with the antlers.

Kip leans sideway, mouth beside my ear. "Are those rifles for her protection or ours? You can *feel* a huldra's nasty kvell if they're too close…"

"Oh, come on. Like you'd know." But I do feel something. A shiver passes through me.

"She's here to watch…" hisses Lexija. "Be ready."

The Illuet's masked gaze falls over me and I am not ready. I feel her hidden eyes trace over my body, taking a measure of my worth. Kip goes pale and ghostly beneath her scrutiny. I hear him take a shaky breath. Again, something in me shifts. I feel unsettled, unmoored.

One by one, the Illuet considers us as the sun rises behind her. My heart pounds in my ears and sweat trickles down my spine. The handle of the spear becomes slippery in my hands.

The Illuet gives a single, definitive nod.

"Fight!" orders Lexija.

* * *

I SHIVER IN MY COAT AS I WALK TO THE DOCKS, STILL RUFFLED BY THE encounter with the Illuet. Her presence left me feeling loopy, slightly nauseous even.

A deep, rib-rattling rumble catches my ear. Flutelike music plays over it. The first gargantuan trucks pull off the road and rock over potholes. Where a normal long-haul truck takes up a lane on the road, the Karrvoss rigs span two. Colorful flags and banners cover each truck and open pipes along the trailers sing in the wind. The children follow the trucks to an empty lot. The Karrvoss Caravan has arrived.

The Karrvoss Caravan circles the country of Ruhnsvalla, traveling up and down both coasts and crossing the Duskheim Mountains.

A graying fellow in mutton chops descends the ladder of his turquoise and silver rig.

"Hansel Fransel!" I wave.

Road weary and baggy eyed as he is, the old driver still chuckles when he sees me. "There she is, Eel Guts!"

We shake hands. I always stop myself from going in for the hug, unsure if we are to that level yet or not. Hans, whose name is neither Hansel nor Fransel, was a friend of my father's once. The familiar scent of cloves and tobacco greets me as he pats my back.

"Better late than never. By the stars and currents, Hans, the Dusk Trials start in *six days*. Think you cut it close enough?"

"Ay-ep," Hans sighs, pushing unkept hair back from his friendly face.

For an old guy, he's oddly beautiful. Like the rest of the Karrvoss Nomads, tufts of fur turn his eyebrows and ears into dreamy wisps. Transparent scales shimmer on his cheeks and neck. His eyes shine with more colors than they should, always drifting towards the distant mountains. The Karrvossians worship the Mountain. It is their sacred task to always cross it, to honor the Mountain. They call their god the Boreackt. They say she brought them to Ruhnsvalla long ago. That's as much as I know.

An unfamiliar strain tugs around Hans's eyes. Shadows lurk on his cheeks.

"Hans?" I ask.

"Ay-ep... it's been a trip, that's for sure. Wasn't sure we'd make it on time. Some new distribution company's buying up the roads down south. Really throwing a wrench in things. Between that and the wildfires, we had to take some detours."

My nose wrinkles. "You can buy roads?"

Hans just shakes his head. Other Karrvoss Nomads climb down from their rigs, oddly quiet and subdued. Normally, the Caravan brings the party. Today, they might as well be a funeral procession.

"How are things in Poppy City?"

Hans's eyes lose their shine. They are the eyes of a man who followed the will-o-wisp too far into the bog. "Katch," he says. "New fancy drug. Eating the place alive."

Shaking his head, Hans offers me a thermos of hot, strong coffee.

"That's over there and we're over here. You ready for the Dusk Trials, kid? I've got a wager on the line saying you'll make top ten."

"Just top ten?" I joke, taking a sip of the offered coffee.

"Ay-ep. Sure you'll do just fine, kid. Now, unless you want to help me get the goods unloaded, I'll catch you around."

The silence of the Caravan chills my spine. No songs, no jingling of festival bells. Whatever happened with the roads, the wildfires, the Katch, whatever is happening in the world beyond Vatska is changing the Caravan.

I shake my head. I can't dwell on this right now. I need to focus on the Dusk Trials. I can't fix the world, I can only save me.

* * *

By the time I drag myself home from a double shift on the *Cormorant*, I'm fighting a throbbing headache. My knees weaken at the smell of freshly baked bread drifting from the open window of our apartment.

Our little gray apartment building with its shed roof sits a few streets over from the tourist infestation. Tourists holler from their tent clusters like drunk crows. Slogging up the steps, I drape my coat on the outside hanger.

"Basil flatbread with sheep's cheese and bison sausage." Wavern points a ratty oven mitt at the steaming tray. "Boots at the door, Thalon."

"You are a god, goddess, and blessed face of the divine." I kick off my deck boots and pull spritely little Wavern into a side hug before shoving a slice of melty goodness into my mouth. I puff out the steam. "Hot, hot, hot…"

"Oh yeah, and it's hot, dumbass. Guess you don't store your brains in your biceps."

"I love you too, Wavern," I slur through molten cheese.

Wavern is Kip's partner, not mine, but since Kip works at a chowder shack with access to home cooked meals, he doesn't appreciate the little nerd enough.

"Do you know what happened to Flake?" asks Wavern. They point to one of two tanks of baby eels on the kitchen counter.

"What's a Flake?" I bite into a fresh slice and fan my mouth. The cheese sizzles like lava.

"Yeah, it's still hot. And Flake was one of my control cove eels. I can't find him."

I hold up my hands and shake my head to show Wavern I still have no idea what they're talking about.

Making an audible sound of frustration, Wavern points to the eel tanks. Little purple larvae worm around in the muck. Wavern takes the pencil out of their messy bun and scribbles a note on a clip board. "Flake was important…"

I eat more flatbread, too hot or not, watching Wavern trace a green-tipped finger over the glass tank and grumble. No one really knows what Wavern is. I've heard folks call them a troll, goblin, and elf, to which Wavern always responds with a shrug.

Wavern enjoys cooking and doesn't mind sharing. They could be three squids in a frumpy sweater. They feed me, what do I care?

"I saw the Illuet today. She came by the dawn practice." I rub the back of my neck, then my temples, not sure where the headache originates. "She's at least seven feet tall. Kip almost pissed himself."

Wavern doesn't look up from their notes. "But he's *totally* not a racist or anything. Maybe I should grow a tail. That'd teach him."

I snort. "Thanks for dinner, Wavern. This was the best part of my day, honestly."

"Good," they reply, still not looking up.

"I'm going to shower and be in my room sharpening weapons if you need me."

"Good."

Stealing one last slice of flatbread, I do as I said, washing in the shower made for someone half my size and heading up the narrow staircase to my cubby. I keep it tidy and organized, my sea glass and other trinkets lined on the windowsill or hanging on the wall beside the altar. The altar, a plank of carved driftwood, depicts the Zahlek bindrune for Tophinghua and a wheel of stars. Thirteen stars form a circle, curved lines between them creating a spiderweb or mandala. It almost resembles a compass of sorts. Though to where, who can say?

The high, pitched ceiling of the cubby let me build a loft with a sitting space beneath. I settle into the cushions and stare at Gevit, my old battle axe, on the opposite wall.

I don't take her down to sharpen though. I lie back and try to rub the ache out of my neck. I stare at the poster for *Divine Jubilee* on the underside of the loft. If I unfocus my eyes, I can still hear the songs, still smell the popcorn and replay the sounds of laughter and screechy carnival attractions. That night feels like a different life. I don't have time for that sort of thing now, or who I went there with. I can't even remember the last time I danced.

I jolt to attention at the sound of Wavern chiding Kip, demanding to know what happened to Flake.

"To what?"

After the eel description, Kip laughs. "An eel? I probably ate him."

"You... you..." A pause. "Why him specifically?"

"Because he was biggest. Pretty tasty too. Good cove eel is hard to come by these days..."

"The Dread One take you, Kipper! I've told you and I've told you, this is important!"

"And also delicious!"

I can tell Wavern's mad because they go quiet and refuse to leave the communal space, eventually edging Kip into their shared room by force of spite.

Shaking my head, I sit up and reach for Blitz, my little hand axe, and the whetstone. I'll get to Gevit later, when this unreasonable headache goes away.

"Thalon." Wavern opens my door with a steaming mug that smells like hot, mushed up plants. They set it on the ground next to me, green toes gripping the painted wood floor. "It tastes like ass, but it will take care of your headache."

I blink. Wavern never ceases to blindside me with intuition.

"I like the taste of ass." I drink some, my mouth puckering. "Never mind. This is some rank ass..."

"Listen. When the whole Dusk thing is over, before you fly off on the blimp into the sunset, do you think you could swim up to Coven Cove and harvest me some more eel eggs?"

"For a pot of fish head stew?"

"My pleasure."

"Then you have yourself a deal. An eel deal, pal."

"Thanks, Thalon. If I could go in the water, I'd get them myself..."

"It's not a big deal. I can supply my personal chef some slimy grimy eel eggs."

"Or, conversely, sucker punch my darling Kipper if you catch him snacking on the science." Wavern bounces an eyebrow.

"Heh." I sip more tea, rank or not. "Might be able to arrange that…"

"How's your head?"

I assess and snort in surprise. "This swamp water of yours worked *fast*!"

Wavern's job at the apothecary pays off in spades. They nod and walk back down the stairs. "Good. Have a nice sleep, Thal."

Feeling more like myself, I set Blitz aside and lift Gevit from the wall. I cherish her weight, power, and history in my hands. I bring the blade close to my face to smell the metal. I drag a nail down it to hear the musical note.

I look into my own black eyes in the blade. The eyes of my ancestors. Warriors. Shapeshifters. I may not carry the spear of Tawkthalon, but Gevit will do just fine.

CHAPTER

# FIVE

Out on my morning swim, I watch a Lamplight Petroleum boat patrolling the course of the Gauntlet. I bristle my whiskers. Suppose that means the course is closed.

Diving down into the kelp forest, I snap up a squid in my jaws before heading to shore.

I feel thyir in me and in the sea, magic of ice and bone. It beats with my heart and tingles in my flukes.

In the shallows, I call on my thyir and shift. A snag catches in my back, and I fall to my hands and knees. Spitting out the squid, I gasp and whimper. My spine pops and grinds. When the shift finishes, I stay on my hands and knees, shaking. The squid makes an escape. I squeeze my eyes shut against rising nausea.

The pain fades and I catch my breath. When I stand, I feel hollow and flimsy, and the sudden wind off of the sea sets my teeth chattering. I decide to stay in my in-between shape for extra warmth. Shaking off, I bundle myself into the coat I left on the beach.

It takes a hot cup of tea from Shanty's to start feeling like myself again. I roll my shoulders. The joints grind and click.

Thoughts of sand in my bones get smacked out of my mind as I round a corner and come face to perfect, alluring face with Azoto Seppanen. She's printed on the cover of *The Coastal Post.* The headline reads: "Hometown Princess and Darling of the Community Sweeps Us Off Our Feet."

*Are you fucking joking...*

Azoto grins, flawless sun kissed skin, natural highlights painting her chestnut hair, flight goggles resting atop her head.

Snatching the *Post,* I flip the pages to see more images of Azoto... *and printed in color...!* My blunt claws wrinkle the glossy paper and I hiss through my teeth. A full-page spread shows Azoto posed in a ridiculous lace gown beside the Seppanen family airship hangar. Poised and soft as a doll. The photograph above the article shows her nude from behind walking into the sea, hips full and round, back casually muscular, hair tumbling in the wind. My claws bite a little deeper.

I skim the article, face hot. It's an interview. I flip another page to find Azoto staring right into my eyes, mouth frozen in a laugh. I know exactly how that laugh sounds, low and rolling, her professional laugh.

I read a little.

"Coastal Post: With your pilot's license and experience flying for the family business, do you anticipate actually flying a Duskingr one day?

"Azoto: (laughs) the most important thing, the reason for participating in the Dusk Trials at all, is to represent Vatska on the Duskingr. The Seppanen family has dedicated itself to preserving and protecting the sacred traditions of the selkie and huldror, thyir and kvell. It's the goal of the Seppanen family to make sure we remember where we came from as we move forward.

"CP: And how would you do that, if you place in the top twelve and continue on to crew one of the mysterious Duskingr?

"A: I believe our best course is to work together, to take steps towards unity. Long have the huldror and selkie folk seen ourselves as separate, as descendants of opposing magical and spiritual

TRADITIONS. AND YET, WE MUST WORK TOGETHER TO CREW THE DUSKINGR…"

Azoto, everybody's darling, spouting her nonsense about unity. Selkie and huldror crew the Duskingr in equal numbers because one side or the other would blow their ballast if those numbers got jostled. None of us are going to fix that.

A wounded, restless resentment rises up and I fight to squash it back down. I remember when the Seppanens didn't personally participate in the Dusk Trials. It would have looked like they were sticking their fingers in too many things, as such an influential family in Vatska. They sponsored athletes, but participation was always kept off the table. I clench my jaw until it pops.

Realizing my claws have torn angry little holes in the magazine, I place it back on the rack and hope no one notices. I take a few deep breaths to steady myself. I could fight Azoto in the Blood Spire. I try not to speculate on the possibility of us both placing in the top twelve. With any luck we'd end up on separate ships.

The foghorn drones a loud, melancholic note. I massage my neck and jaw. They both hurt, my shoulders too. Rubbing my eyes, I continue to the docks and the *Cormorant*. I give silent thanks that I only work the morning shift today.

* * *

"SHIFT'S DOUBLED," CORTLAND GREETS ME. "GET CLOCKED IN, YOU'RE netting sludge eels today."

"*Sludge eels*?" I sputter. My stomach tightens in anger and a bit of unease. "You can't sell sludge eels…"

"Did I stutter?" Cortland cracks open a bottle of Spindel. It foams over, reeking of chemical strawberries.

I peer into the dark water of the harbor. "Why the eels?"

"Driving out the other fish, invasive turds." Cortland takes a swig of the soda. "We've all gotta do our part."

No one else is doing a part. It'll just be me down there in the water, and the sludge eels bite. I have a red scar on my hand to prove it. Nasty thing got infected, too. I don't need that before the Dusk Trials.

The thought of the writhing, purple-gray eels combined with the headache makes me ill.

"I'm really not feeling great today, Cortland," I try honesty. "If there's other work on the *Cormorant*, please let me do it. The Gauntlet's almost here, and I need to be at my best..."

"I don't have any other selkies, Thalon. You're the best, and we need you."

* * *

SADLY, STROKING MY EGO DOES THE TRICK AND I CHASE SLUDGE EELS.

Hours later, a hissing, vile mass of mud gray serpents twist on deck. I lean on the metal rail as my head throbs. It feels like a thorn stabbing behind one eye, and my stomach sloshes around every time the *Cormorant* rolls in the water.

The sludge eels have gotten out of hand over the past few years, clogging up the Erling River mouth. We're not sure why our waters entice them, but it's a rare sight now to see a local cove eel, like Wavern has. The sludge eels have even infested the brackish Erling wetlands. I'll have to go up the coast to get Wavern their eggs.

An eel squirms out of the net, snapping at me. I kick it overboard. The effort makes my head pound, and the frigid wind whips through my thick fur. We seal folk used to move the ice. Now, I can't even handle a crisp breeze.

"You slacking on the clock, Thalon?" Cortland hollers across the deck.

I glare at him and slink inside the cabin. I don't know why he wants the eels, or how he'll profit.

The wind rattles through the creaking ship and crawls into my bones. Even hunkered in the boiler room, I can't chase it out. I huddle in my fur and a towel, hands held as close to the boiler as I dare, sniffling from the cold and frustration. I'm so tired and so sick of slogging on the *Golden Cormorant.* So sick of the rattling, rusty winches and barnacle crusted hull. Sick to death of Cortland and his "take pride in your work" speeches.

The problem is, I do take pride. If I didn't, I wouldn't have herded eels all day. I wouldn't have spent years training for the Dusk Trials either. I stare into the boiler and listen to the ship creak. Azoto's professional laugh, smile, and oiled, gleaming ass spin round and around in my throbbing head.

No, if I didn't have so much pride, I wouldn't be here at all.

* * *

As soon as the *Cormorant* moors, I punch out and dive overboard.

I make it halfway to the beach before realizing I forgot my coat and boots. *Seagull sucker.*

Doubling back, I shift my body into its mostly-girl shape and cling to the ladder on the side of the *Cormorant.* I breathe through a bout of dizziness and grating bones. The smell of sludge eels hits me and I retch a little, grateful I skipped lunch for once. What in Brosk's name is the matter with me?

Eyes squinted, I begin to climb the ladder but stop as I hear Cortland and someone else talking on deck above me.

"—satisfactory haul, yes…" I catch a snatch of a masculine voice I don't recognize. "Good for you, good for us…"

I pull myself up another rung, mouth twisting into an indignant scowl. So, Cortland does have some deal for the eels.

Wind sends the nets' and chains clanging and I miss part of the exchange.

"—That's a small fortune for a trawler," remarks the stranger. "I dearly hope you can pay it when it comes due. But, we'll be able to make use of this rust bucket if not."

Cortland's snarly laughter cackles. "I'm not one for making stupid bets…"

"I see," replies the mystery man.

I blink. Cortland's placed the *Cormorant* on the line? What line?

A swell washes over me. When it subsides, I shake the water from my ears and strain to hear the conversation again.

"To Aalgur Thalon, may she make me a wealthy man." Cortland's voice carries a smirk.

"To Aalgur Thalon, may she leave you in ruins," replies the voice and the conversation drifts down the gangplank and onto the dock.

I freeze, heart in my throat.

Cortland is betting... on *me*? Sliding from the ladder, I tread water. Cortland *believes* in me. Enough to place the *Cormorant* down as collateral? I stare at the barnacle crusted hull in awe. He is wagering his entire livelihood... on *me*.

In a bit of a haze, I clamber up on deck to fetch my coat and boots, rolling them in a waterproof sack for the swim before slinking back into the sea.

My boss, my slimy, conniving boss with his yellowed teeth and never-ending Spindel... believes in me.

An unexpected glow spreads through me like Midwinter mead. I float in it, bask in it. As much as this job's been a thorn in my ass, I won't let Cortland down. I'll change both our fates.

They'll see. Everyone will see.

CHAPTER

# SIX

I blink, and the last few days before the Dusk Trials vanish. Suddenly, it's happening, it's now.

"Racers make ready! On your marks!" the ancient megaphone booms over the crowded beach and streets.

I stand on the shore naked. My sea lion pelt hangs loose from my shoulders. Five hundred and sixty-one other selkies crowd the beach with me, our racing numbers painted on the backs of our pelts.

I face the Gauntlet with nothing but Wavern's ass-flavored tea in my belly and my heart in my throat. Despite the chilly morning, I sweat, teeth chattering, hands shaking. Hulking, muscular bodies press around me, the best of the very best from every corner of Ruhnsvalla. Even Kip has become a stern-faced stranger. As tall and fit as I am, looking into the horizon of my fate, I feel miniscule.

Spectators pile boats along the Gauntlet course, filling the pre-dawn with excited chatter. Not that they will see much, most of the race stays beneath the water. Still, they hold flags, cameras, and bags of kettle corn. Kiosks of sponsors line the beach, each with trainers and medics at the ready. I scan the faces for Hans.

The imposing Illuet and her attendants make a row of dark robes along the railing of the chowder shack. Their security detail holding tourists ten yards back down the wharf. They bring an unsettling stillness to the Gauntlet, like a retinue of masked owls whispering mysteriously to each other as we peasants perform for them. A small airship circles overhead with cameras trained on the course.

*Breathe,* I remind myself. *All you have to do is swim...*

The shot of the starting gun hits me like a punch to the stomach. I sprint into the water and dive. My bones grind as I call my thyir, but I don't care. Hundreds of bodies hit the water with me. Muffled chaos presses on my ears.

Instincts kick in and I charge forward. The moment I have flukes in place of arms, I launch into the race. Many contestants struggle to shift, and I leave them at the beach.

Thyir swells through me, my tether to the sea. I ride the thrill of it as I dive. As I reach the first concrete weights on the bottom, I realize there aren't possibly enough for all of us competitors and grab the closest one in my teeth.

As I angle for the surface, I recognize Azoto and Rawl up ahead, a fur and elephant seal respectively. Both lift their weights like feathers to their landing stations.

But I, too, am strong. Grasping the weight in my mouth, I speed for the surface. Once there, I toss the weight onto the wooden platform where the pups almost got squished. I'm still not sure why this task got added to the Gauntlet, but that's a problem for future Thalon.

Air fills my lungs, and I exhale as I dive again, angle for the surface, and sail through a hoop above the water.

A red flag on a buoy guides me through a turn, and I focus on speed, sailing through the water. My powerful flukes propel me as I close the distance to Rawl. One, two, three strokes and I leap from the water, overtaking the enormous form of Rawl and plunging into the next turn. In the distance, I see the finish line waiting.

I'm in the Gauntlet, it's happening. I'm doing fine...

A seismic boom unsettles the water. Suddenly I'm spinning. A wave of heat hits and I'm torn out of the world.

* * *

I entered my first Dusk Trials at fifteen having never been hit by a fist or a weapon.

"Momma, Pappa, I entered! I entered!" I squealed as I ran into our cozy home on Scallop Avenue. I waved my receipt around like a trophy.

"That's exciting!" Momma smiled at me, cheeks warm and pink. Pappa smiled too. They seemed so happy, so glad for me.

At least, I thought they were excited for me. Two months later, after I had been hit by both a weapon and a fist in training, I learned the truth. The day I signed up was the day they found out I would be a big sister.

I clapped my hands over my mouth and bounced off the floor. "A pup! A pup!" It felt like a gift made just for me.

Instead of swimming sprints, meeting in the practice fields, or even attending the communal ts'kmet dance circles, I haunted the library, reading book after book on selkie children. When I was a baby, my mother had to call someone from the Temple to peel me from my pelt for the first time. I hoped that when the time came, they would let me do the honors for my new sibling.

The day of the Gauntlet arrived. So did the baby.

"It's today... it's coming today," Momma gasped.

"But it's the Dusk Trials..." My voice got lost in the bustle of nurses and midwives. I ran down the street, through the fog, to the edge of the sea. I showed an official my paperwork and they painted a number on the back of my pelt. The only familiar face I remember was Hans. Hans came to cheer me on.

I swam, I lost, I sprinted home.

"She's beautiful... she's perfect... oh, Aalgur, come see her..."

Momma called to me, drunk on painkillers. I smelled the tang of blood in the room. A sister! I had a *sister!*

When Momma showed me the wrinkled pink sausage on her chest, I looked between her and Pappa. "What is that?"

"She's a baby, Aalgur." Momma stroked the tuft of sparse black hair on the infant's head.

"Where is her pelt?" I asked.

"She doesn't have one, Aalgur." Pappa petted the child as well.

It felt like the ceiling fell on me. I tried to breathe, and only little huffing sounds came out.

"Come here, Aalgur," whispered Momma. "Here. Hold her, Aalgur. You're a big sister now..."

The midwife lifted the spongy, naked creature and placed it in my arms. I didn't even mourn what could have been. I fell in love with her, with Ashling.

"I will show you the sea, little sister," I promised her. "The ice of our ancestors, blood of the storm."

* * *

The water hits my body like a slab of concrete. I float for a moment and sink.

My head rings like a gong. *What are you, what are you...* Momma's voice whispers through the dark water.

I snap back to my senses with a snort, bobbing like a cork to the surface. The bright gray sea buzzes with yipping and barks; selkies in distress. I turn looking for course flags, panic clawing through me.

*What happened? Which way do I go?*

Aha! I spot a red flag in the distance and speed for it. I do my best to anyway, my flukes feel like plastic kayak paddles, stiff and unwieldy. The underwater signs directing us along the course become alien symbols as I lumber past, and I almost miss a hoop.

Another deep, bone-crushing boom shakes the water. My rear flippers tumble over my head as a wave of heat tosses me like a pelican flinging a sardine. This time I keep my bearings though, aiming for the narrow tunnel leading into the final hoops. Pumping my clumsy flukes for speed, I then tuck them to my sides. I slide into the narrowing metal corridor and jet out the far end.

Red flickers in the water around me. I turn towards it, thinking it's a race flag. The red flickers on my other side, then beneath me. I fan my flukes to slow myself and squawk in alarm. It's blood.

I have no time to think, no time to wonder. The final hoops jut from the water up ahead and I charge for them. And then I am flying, airborne, dawn breaking over the Blackberry Hills before I plunge into the water across the finish line. Wooden platforms wait for us, and I slide onto one. Officials take hold of me and record my number.

"Number one-oh-nine placed forty-third!"

My first thought: *I made it...!*

My second thought: *... forty-third?*

"Thalon! Thalon! You made it!" Kip paddles to me in his nearly-human form.

I try to shift and get stuck halfway between shapes. His webbed hands help me sit up. I can't breathe, I can't think. The white, bright sun cutting through the fog smothers me.

"We made it, Thalon! We both made it!" My mind struggles to keep up with Kip's chatter.

"I got sixteenth... Azoto and Rawl..."

"You... beat me?" I slur. My face feels numb.

"Just lucky, I guess. Been minding my feet of urchins..."

More pinnipeds land around us, a gong sounding for each finisher.

Then a siren begins to whine. Strobing red lights blaze atop an emergency vessel as it pulls away from the dock and speeds for the course. Red bubbles to the surface of the water. Deep, dark red...

"Thalon... are you okay? You don't look so good..." Kip helps me into the water for the swim to shore. Race officials in neon vests wave their arms and bleat on whistles.

"I'm fine... I'm fine..." I am not fine. Everything feels too hot, too bright, too cold, too sudden. My bones crunch as I assume my fully aquatic shape for easier swimming.

It's over. Just like a bad dream, the Gauntlet is over. And then we stagger up on the beach to uproarious applause. Why does it feel like I'm watching the world through a telescope? Why does it feel like I missed half of it?

I catch a glimpse of Wavern screaming and waving from atop Shanty's Chowder Shack before Lexija catches us and drags us to a recovery tent.

Normal Thalon would swell with pride as people thump hands on my back. But I feel wrong, fundamentally. The sea sways, the glaring bright beach tilts, and I fall to my hands and knees. I choke, puking my guts out in front of the gods and everyone.

"Oh, my gods, Thalon, are you okay?" someone gasps, Kip, perhaps.

I face plant into the sand. Then I open my eyes to find myself flat on my back, staring at the glaring white ceiling of a medical tent. Someone in a green apron sticks a needle into the crook of my elbow to draw blood.

"Aalgur? Aalgur? Can you hear me?" Another green apron leans over me and a pink glove moves back and forth in front of my face. "Can you follow my finger? Aalgur?"

"Yes..." I croak, unsure how I got here.

"No, she's tough as nails," Lexija chatters, voice pitched high and breathy. "I would have known if she was sick... nothing was the matter with her *yesterday*..."

The matter with me?

"She likely got hit by one of the steam jet obstacles in the course," replies the medic leaning over me. He turns his attention to me. "Aalgur? How are you feeling?"

"Nerves, could be nerves." Lexija rattles on, as if trying to talk me out of whatever I'm experiencing.

"Aalgur?" The medic shines light into my eyes.

It stabs my brain. "My head..."

"She was vomiting and disoriented..." Lexija paces. "She's never like this..."

"Aalgur? Did you take anything before the race? Any pills, any liquids..." prompts the medic.

"No," I croak. "Yes... Wavern's tea..."

"What's a Wavern?"

"It's just an herbal painkiller," snaps Lexija.

"How long have you been taking it?"

"A... week. My head's been... headaches..."

"Headaches for a week, and now vomiting?" The medic leaning over me and pops something into my ear and frowns. "Selkies run a bit hot." He glances over his shoulder at someone else, then back at me. "Aalgur, is there any chance you could be pregnant?"

Lexija's breathy voice smolders down into a crackling hiss. "Oh, so help me, if you've gotten yourself with pup, girl... If you and Kipper have been sneaking around..."

"What!" I rasp, disgusted. My insides crawl. "I haven't... haven't slept with anyone..."

"When was the last time you had sex?" asks the medic.

I try to do math as the flapping white room rocks back and forth. We aren't on a boat, are we? No... that's a sand floor, we aren't on a boat. "A... a while ago. More than six months..." I can't bring myself to reveal the truth. I haven't shared a bed with anyone in years, and even then, she couldn't get me pregnant. "I'm absolutely not pregnant."

"Alright... well, test her anyway." Instructs the medic and turns back to me. He continues questioning me about alcohol, drugs, parties, and other potentially fun things I haven't touched with a nine-foot spear.

"You probably just got a bit concussed out there in the Gauntlet. Here's some painkiller. I'll be back when your blood work's processed." A fresh needle inserts into my arm and soon a warm, fuzzy oblivion washes over me.

My eyelids sag. What is going on...

Lexija jolts to her feet beside me and grasps the hanging curtain. She's not fast enough. I see the stretcher. I see a face. A teenage boy. His empty black eyes stare into me.

Frozen in an asymmetrical fusion between handsome boy and harbor seal, his supple body lurches as paddles are placed on his chest. Splotches of dark red blood muddy the sand beneath him. The medics shock him again, but his eyes keep staring, unblinking and dull. They roll him over and I see the raw meat and splintered white bone of his femur. His leg is gone.

Lexija curses and yanks the curtain closed, hiding the boy from view. But she cannot hide the sounds. Not the calm voices talking through procedures. Not the long, wailing sound of a heart monitor flatlining. Not the sound of a voice, quiet and resigned, stating: "Elren Johanson. Nineteen. Six thirty-eight in the morning..."

He is dead. The Gauntlet killed him.

"Lexija?" I moan. The medicine has smothered the pain, but I feel woozy and misplaced. I reach for her, for comfort.

"You're fine, Thalon." Lexija pushes me back down on the cot. "You'll be moved into the arena rookery as soon as the doctor gives you the all clear. There're tubs. Take a hot bath. You did good out there today...."

My body shakes. "He's... dead..." The name "Elren" seeps through my mind like a blot of squid ink. He died, just now. Next to me...

"And you're not." Lexija paces. "But the gods damn it, Thalon. If you're pregnant..."

"She's not pregnant." The original medic returns to my curtained cubby. "No drugs, no poisons, though, there are signs her body is fighting an infection. Tourists brought a lot of flu with them. That's likely all that's going on, that and a shakeup during the race. As her impromptu medical professional, I advise you pull Aalgur Thalon from the competition."

"What?" I squawk.

"What?" demands Lexija. "You just told me she has a cold and a bonk on the head. People have come through the Dusk Trials with... with limbs missing!"

The doctor looks at the clipboard in his hands, jaw flexing. "She has a low-grade fever, overactive antibodies, and signs of a concussion. I must advise you to pull her out."

"No!" Lexija and I say together.

"Then that is all I can offer for now. I will have the prescription for antivirals sent to the arena. Feel better, Aalgur."

I wait until the doctor steps from the tent. "You can't pull me out, Lexija!"

"Not planning on it."

I lie back, unable to catch my breath. Thoughts bounce around in my skull and slip from my grasp. I'm sick, I got hurt... *a boy died.* "I need to... tell Kip..." I croak. I need to tell *Azoto*, too... I lift my arm. It's still a fluke.

"Kip's already on his way to the arena." Lexija's voice carries a crisp edge. "And now we've got to worry about you coming down with some gods-forsaken tourist flu... What luck..." She rubs her eyebrows. "But no, you'll have to be a hell of a lot worse for me to pull you."

I barely hear her. A selkie died today, participating in the sacred Trials of our ancestors. Tears slide off my face as I stare at the ceiling. I need to pray for him. I should offer prayer to his chosen patron. "The kid... Elren... who was his patron? Do you know?"

Lexija picks up her ledger from the sand and flips through it.

"Johanson... Johanson... Elren..." Her voice crackles out like static on the radio, the crisp edge falling away.

"Who?" I ask.

Lexija closes the ledger and turns toward the curtain. Is the body still right on the other side? Separated between life and death by a single sheet of flimsy cloth?

"He chose Her," says Lexija. "The Dread One."

# SEVEN

The wheels of a stretcher screech with sand as medics take Elren's body away.

My breath sticks in my chest and my eyes seep tears. There should not have been explosions in the Gauntlet.

The medicine fogs the world. That and exhaustion fade me into a misty gray nothing.

From the emptiness, I step into a strange place. Tall black shadows surround me. Are they trees? In the distance, waves whisper against a silver beach. A rumbling stirs the quiet night. It reminds me of the Karrvoss trucks, so deep and seismic. A chill travels through me. It is a deep voice. The voice sings in a language long forgotten.

Ahead, a campfire flickers, blues and greens and violets. A shadow looms over the fire, tending the flames and singing. I walk and walk and never seem to get closer.

Then I am in the tent again as voices chatter around me.

"Malfunction in a steam jet," someone says.

"Totally unprecedented," adds another.

"An unprecedented tragedy. Inexcusable."

"We must mourn the loss and continue..."

I slip back to the beach, too worn out to listen. The singer looms over me. Brosk. He's Brosk, I realize, God of the Sea.

I look up into the hulking darkness. His head turns to face me. Starlight gleams behind his polar bear teeth as He grins. Smoke floats from His mouth on His deep, resonant voice.

*Aalgur Thalon...*

I startle awake as Lexija shakes my shoulder. I sit up on the cot. The sun hangs low over the fog. Out on the beach, the Anchor of Brosk casts a dark silhouette against the apricot sky. The priests must have moved it here from the Temple. The anchor glitters with candles and folded paper prayers. My heart sinks like a ballast stone into my belly.

"Thalon. Glad you got some sleep. How are you feeling?" asks Lexija, sweaty and rumpled.

I take stock of my body. I still feel loopy, a bit drunk. I recall the doctor's warning. "I'm fine. I could eat..."

"Great! Sounds like a big improvement!" Lexija stands to the side as a medic in a green apron measures my vitals and signs my release papers.

The dimply medic gives me a warm smile. "Sorry it took so long to send you on your way, Miss Thalon. There were more injuries than we anticipated. Here's a top off on pain meds. Good luck tomorrow." She and her colleagues then begin folding my cot.

I have one arm and one fluke, but at least I have two human legs. I chew the pain pills and grimace at the bitter taste. Lexija helps me up, wrapping me in a wool blanket.

"Transport is here. You'll be able to use the bath in your room to put yourself back together." She marches me up the beach to an idling vehicle waiting on the street.

I look over my shoulder to the Anchor of Brosk. I offer my hand, first palm down, then palm up, and last, pressed over my heart. "May the currents guide you home, Elren," I whisper.

"Come on, Thalon, you need to get cleaned up and put right. Then food, then bed. What a day. Some Karrvossian vagrant tried to get to you while you were passed out. Yikes."

"Hans?" I wrinkle my nose at the word *vagrant*.

"Could've been. We had him escorted back to the truck camp. No need to worry about him, the Karrvoss bums are forbidden entry to the arena."

I have no time for affront. Lexija pulls me into the low, red car with blacked-out windows and three people in snappy black suits. I blink at the rifles across their laps, but slide in beside Lexija.

"Why are there... these people?" I ask. The car pulls away from the curb.

"Protection against foul play," remarks Lexija, as if such a thing should sound perfectly ordinary to me. As if I am someone like Azoto Seppanen.

"I don't remember this from the last Dusk Trials..."

"Yes, well, things change, Thalon."

The word *understatement* bounces around inside my skull. Understatement, understatement... Vatska blurs around me as my head grows heavy and then...

Then I see the stadium. My hackles stand at attention.

Rolling gray clouds drifting over the Blackberry Hills set the backdrop for the limestone arena. The Duskingr floats above it. Black smoke rises from the arena like the caldera of a volcano. It must be for show, but it gives the illusion of fire, of danger. Spotlights inside the arena, hazy in the drifting smoke and jarring red. Two crimson pillars of light stabbing into the bloated clouds. Red like the emergency boat, red like illuminated blood.

The car pulls up to a flock of suited security officers bearing bolt-action rifles. I step out. My body feels like a lumbering shell with my thoughts vaguely attached inside. I turn a circle and get pushed along by Lexija. I feel like one of the wind-up automatons from the *Divine Jubilee* production, lurching and jerking wherever the conductor bids me.

Lexija puts a firm arm around my shoulders and marches me to the guarded doors in the side of the arena.

A deep bass rumble washes through me, teeth-rattling, dire music, and long, haunting notes overlain with a *shkk shkk shkk* like blades swiping over whetstones. My hackles raise at the sound of the music. I crane my neck to see the spears of red light painting twin bloody moons on the clouds overhead. I hope it's the medicine, not nerves, but I can't stop trembling. I am feeling better, a lot better. Probably the medicine.

"Let me see…" Lexija lifts a key from her pocket, a rectangular card of metal with notches stamped in it. "Two-thirty-eight."

The hallway arcs around as we walk. I know it's an oval, but with no windows, it feels endless. We pass bolted exit doors and clusters of rooms. We pass more black suits and rifles, trainers and medics, but no competitors. A cart of swords rolls past, blades clamped in plastic guards so they can't cut too deep.

"Here's you." Lexija stops at one of the rounded metal doors and inserts the key. She grunts as she pushes the hefty door inward. "Pretty nice digs."

The creamy, rounded marble room is almost as large as our apartment's first floor. A cozy bed sits against the opposite wall from a giant window of wavy glass. It looks out across an empty cavity beneath the arena floor. Lights glow in hundreds of other windows.

"Arena's old, but we've got modern electricity." Lexija motions to the orangish lamps on the walls. She opens a door beside me to reveal a full bath with a huge soaking tub. "There's a hydrothermal spring beneath the arena, so endless hot water. Abuse it. Let me just find your medicine and you can get yourself put back together into something less monstrous…"

I stay in the doorway as Lexija searches through items left for me on a mahogany cabinet. Gill's Goods has left a basket of snacks and Spindel soda.

Bending down, Lexija opens the icebox. "Here they are."

She tosses me a bottle of pills. A red Zahlek bindrune stamp bleeds over the instructions. I suppose it means the medicine has been approved by Parliament for the competition.

"Have some food, take your flu-be-gone, get rest." Lexija returns to me. "Weapons are on the wall, food is stocked. You're all set."

I shuffle in, sniffing the cozy cave smell and mild musk of sulfur from the taps. The glass window is large enough for me to sit in but gives only a distorted view of the subterranean space beyond. Clusters of orange lights let me know where other competitors are staying. One orange blob is Kip. One is Azoto.

"Can I go check out the arena? Can I see Kip?" I push salty hair behind my ear.

"No," Lexija states. "Contestants are to remain in their rooms until collected by a trainer, medic, or Parliament personnel. There is no contact permitted between contestants. If you need anything, knock on the door. Security is patrolling."

The arena suddenly seems so much smaller. I feel smaller still, a mouse trapped in a circular maze.

"Don't give me that look, Thalon. You'll be fine. Enjoy the peace and quiet." Lexija gives me a thin smile. The smile fades, replaced by grim grooves beside her mouth. "Thalon. If you're unwell, I *can* pull you..."

My head snaps to her. "Absolutely not."

She dips her chin. "Then take care of yourself, I'll see you tomorrow."

"Say hi to Kip for me?" I take a step towards her. "Tell him he stinks, from me...?"

"Sure, Thalon." Lexija lets herself out. I hear the locking mechanism inside the door clank.

I inhale and exhale. I place a hand over my heart and the other on my belly and repeat the breathing. I sit and then fall backwards onto my luscious brown bed.

"Gevit!" I gasp. Bouncing back to my feet, I snatch her from the hanger above the bed. "What did they do to you?"

A plastic security guard covers Gevit's double blades, rendering her unbalanced and awkward. The fur stands up on my back.

"This is fine. It's fine," I assure myself. I test her skewed balance. "It's just for safety... don't want to be chopping off arms or anything..." I try to swallow but my mouth has gone sandy and dry. This is how it will have to be, I suppose. "Ahh, seagull sucker..."

Returning Gevit to her place of honor beside Blitz, I read the pill bottle in my hand. *Take with food.* Inside the icebox I find fragrant hard cheeses, berries, and pink slivers of lox. I gobble up the lox, sitting cross-legged on the floor and balancing the tray on my fluke. I moan a little, licking my fingers clean twice. With its market price, I normally only get lox at Midwinter and Midsommer. Maybe for the Day of Dusking, if I'm feeling wild with my cash.

Taking a pill, I crack into a bottle of mineral water. I get into the fancy crackers next, my body making up for the lack of meals today. Hydrated, brined, and continuously burping, I waddle into the bathroom. I claw into a bar of pink soap just to smell the rose essence.

I fill the tub, watching the hot water gush and spin in the stone pool. Once full, I slip in and shift first into a sea lion, and then into a woman. The shift grinds my joints and everything in me that can pop does. Then it's over and I hang my pelt on the hook to dry. I try every single bath product before crawling out and opening the dresser drawer to see what has been provided for clothing.

A heavy plush robe. I snatch it and cocoon. I find black undergarments and a new pair of boots with shin guards. Opening the next drawer down, I lift out my metal helmet and try it on, appreciative of the noseguard and simplicity. We're allowed horns and plumes on our helmets... more things to catch weapons on. Then I reach my armor and lay each piece out on the bed to admire.

Admittedly, the armor doesn't cover very much, as we are meant to cut into each other. But Gill came through. The chest and shoulder portion has no boob contours, just a practical, fitted chest plate, spine guard, and some neck protection, painted with the Gill's Goods logo. I trace a finger over the spiral hurricane motif and compass of stars sprayed over the heart.

A light garment reminiscent of stretchy chainmail goes on first to theoretically protect the organs, at least from slashing and stabbing. It won't do much if I get crushed.

I get gloves, thigh guards and a loin cloth, all with silver and red accents. I'll essentially be fighting in a bikini, boobs or not. We all will. Sticking my hand into a glove, I flex it.

The armor fits, I try it all on and shake my butt around in the bathroom mirror. Without Kip to clown around with though, the novelty wears off fast.

I return the armor and open the last drawer in the dresser. I lift out a flat wooden box which unfolds in three sections to reveal an altar inscribed with Zahlek runescript and the Anchor of Brosk, an intricate sigil of tusks and bones. The drawer contains a candle, dried herbs, a length of thin rope for knot meditation, and an abalone shell for offerings. There is also a box of dried ink for adorning myself for battle.

I pause as I stare at an object beside the ink. A small, humanoid shape covered in a black cloth, like a death shroud. Like the dead boy in the tent. A twist tightens in my belly as I take the corner of the cloth and roll it back. It reveals a spiral of storm-cloud hair, and an impressive physique draped in the pelt of a leopard seal standing on a compass made of stars. Tophinghua.

They left Her covered so as not to draw Her attention.

I feel a bit hollow as I place Her in front of the foldable altar. I set out cheese as an offering—I ate all the lox—and light a candle. The light of the flame shifts over the little statue's wooden features, distorting Her expression from impassive to twisted and cruel.

I stare at Tophinghua, She stares at me. I should talk to Her, but no words come, so I switch on the little desk radio.

A deliberate, almost accusatory voice speaks from the box.

"*—An unprecedented tragedy today in the Gauntlet as Vatska mourns* *the death of Elren Johanson of Tannenburg, who tragically lost his life in a water jet malfunction.*

*"With me now is Hermon Sokolov of Lamplight Petroleum Works. Mr. Sokolov, does Lamplight have any words for the community tonight?"*

*"Yes, Kelpie, thank you."* A droning, familiar voice, an anybody sort of voice. *"Lamplight Petroleum mourns with you tonight. People are talking, something about Johanson having chosen the Dread One as his patron..."*

*"He is not the only one to do so, Mr. Solokov. In fact, a contestant with Her as patron has moved on to the Blood Spire. But a total of thirty-eight participants sustained various injuries during the course of the Gauntlet this morning. I fail to see how choice of patrons played a role..."*

*"Yes, yes. Most unfortunate... Lamplight Petroleum will be providing support and relief to those injured and their families..."*

I switch the radio back off and rub my temples. Elren's family lived in Tannenburg, on the eastern side of the Duskheim Mountains... Will his family receive a letter announcing his death? Will someone take an airship to inform them in person? Or will they hear the news through this radio broadcast?

Listless, I pace around the room before cracking open a bottle of Spindel. The smell of chemical strawberry and cotton candy syrup brings a grimace to my face, and I crank the lid back on. Turning the bottle in my hands, I see the words, *contains naturally occurring vitality enhancers,* in the ingredients after caffeine. The colorful plastic beads inside glint, fizz the soda up, but don't come out the mouthpiece. They swirl like schooling minnows.

I pace a bit more and sit to stretch out some of the stress of the day. It hardly feels real. It doesn't feel right. No one should have died.

Restless, I fetch the box of ink to paint myself. Like my prescription, the box carries the red stamp of approval from the Duskir Parliament. Sitting, I open the instructions.

After mixing the dry and wet ingredients, I dip a brush in the thick paste and paint memorized Zahlek runescript down each arm and down the outsides of both thighs, as I do before each battle. I then go to the bathroom mirror, and stain my lips, chin, and cheeks with the stars of the Dread One.

All of us warriors will do this. We will wear our heritage with pride as we step into battle. My runescript, though I cannot read it, traces my maternal line all the way back to Tawkthalon. The first selkie.

"I am your daughter," I whisper. I raise my eyes to the wooden statue. "I am Aalgur Thalon of the line of Tawkthalon. Tophinghua, Mother of thyir, magic of bones and skin. You who remade Yourself in Your own image, I am Yours. I am Your earthly daughter..."

For a moment, I am sixteen. I stand on the bank of the Erling River, holding Ashling's tiny hand in mine. *I will show you the sea*, I said. *My blood is your blood, Her blood is ours.* I blink and the blank eyes of Elren Johanson look into me. I feel my body tossed like a scrap of chum in the Gauntlet. I rest my forehead on the floor.

"I carry myself and my weapons into battle in Your honor, Mother. Lend me Your strength. Let the roll of Your thunder and the bite of Your lightning be my teeth and my claws..."

I pray to Tophinghua. I pray She sees me. I pray I am enough.

Prayer finished, I dip my hands and feet into the ink and let it set before washing all of it away. It leaves my hands and feet stained gray-green and the runescripts vividly black. I braid my hair and curl up in the window.

I press a greenish palm on the wavy glass, imagining one of the many orange dots across the arena to be Kip. Has he already painted himself? Prayed to Volier? Did he feast on lox too?

I tap my finger on each orange dot from a window. Every dot represents someone I have to beat, something I must overcome.

Closing my eyes, I try to picture my first victory, my first blood. Instead, I imagine Hans as security pulls him away from the medic tent. *Vagrant*, Lexija called him. I wish he was here with his strong, spiced coffee. I wish someone was here.

If Ashling was here in Vatska now, would she watch me fight to crew the Duskingr? Would watching me fight mean anything to her at all?

*Don't think about her.*

My forehead thunks against the glass. Even with all the injections and pills, a creeping pain gnaws at the back of my skull.

I thought it would feel different to stay in the rookery. I thought I would feel proud, strong, ready. Instead, I feel alone.

CHAPTER

# EIGHT

I adjust the buckles on my armor for the fifth time and pace around my limestone room. Lexija woke me up with breakfast and the order to be ready by nine for the Exposition of Champions before the Blood Spire begins.

I pace a sweaty figure eight. Somehow my skimpy inner thigh armor feels more naked than simply being naked. It's exposure in a different way. Consumable. Bouncing my helmet in one arm, I force myself to eat one bite of food every time I pass the platter, even though it feels like sawdust in my mouth.

*It's alright. I have time. Sip some tea, have a bite of fish, Thalon...* I reach for the fork.

The lock clicks and Lexija stalks in. "Take the armor off, Thalon. No Exposition."

"What, why?" I stand with my helmet in both hands, unsure what to do with myself, knocked off balance by the change in plans.

Lexija stalks to the dresser and eats a slice of bread herself. She shakes her head. "We lost five competitors during the night...Some sort of foul play... Their matches will be byes now."

"*Lost?*" My voice shrills.

"No one died." Lexija lowers her voice to a hiss. "But there were some copied keys and people got hurt…"

"Kip wasn't…"

"No. He's fine. Get comfortable. Eat as much as you can. I'll be back in a few hours when they figure their shit out."

I still stand there holding the helmet as Lexija grabs a slice of fish and stalks back out. The door locks closed. My eyes slide to the food. I should eat. I feel punchy from either the pills or the stupid tourist flu and know food should help. Sinking onto the bed, I unbuckle the armor piece by piece. The thought of one more bite makes me feel like retching.

A knock on the door startles me and I snatch Blitz just in case.

The door cracks open and a man in a black suit nods to me before placing a bundle on the floor. "A gift for Miss Thalon," he says, and locks me back in.

Sweat slides down my sides from my armpits and my hands tremble. *Don't be a coward,* I scold myself, slinking closer. I relax a little as I see the Parliament bindrune of approval fastened over various parts of the odd bundle. If it's foul play, it came from the top.

The largest parcel appears to be a coat bag. And atop that rests a silver shoebox with a golden slip of paper tucked into the ribbon.

I poke the side of the box with Blitz. When nothing happens, I break the bindrune seal and unfold the golden card, reading the lavish script within.

Miss Thalon,

You will be collected and escorted to the sponsor's suite at promptly eleven o'clock. Please accept these items for the encounter.

No signature. I turn the card over and then open the box. Strappy black high-heeled shoes. My eyebrows skew and I click my tongue in confusion. High heels? Surely not. I then carefully unfold the garment bag to reveal an immodest black dress.

Holding the dress up to my front, I take note of the asymmetrical hemline adorned in red fringe. Wrapped in tissue, I find a silver clasp for holding my pelt over my shoulders like a stole.

My eyebrows skew the other way. I rifle through the packaging, looking for anything meant to harm me. Nothing. I hold up the dress again. Did Gill get these for me?

What sort of encounter should I expect right after the Exposition of Champions got cancelled?

The clock beside Tophinghua tells me I have thirty minutes to get ready. I would have chosen a suit for myself. I don't even own a dress, let alone one made from such supple fabric or sewn with such fine stitching. I sit on the edge of the bed, holding the dress. The last time I wore something like this, something so celebratory, was when we flew up the coast to see *Divine Jubilee*... That dress had been blue.

That was also the last time I shared a bed with someone, the last time someone's hands and mouth and body lit me aflame...

I shake my head and step into the dress. I cannot afford to dwell on things long past. I have to stay focused. No one can win my fights for me.

* * *

The dress flatters my hard-earned body. The overall lack of fabric shows off my wide, rounded shoulders and thick thighs. Black Zahlek runescript blazes on my exposed skin. The silver clasp pins my pelt at the shoulder.

A knock sounds on my door and then it cracks inward. I expect the anonymous black-suited security and do a double take at the imposing woman waiting outside my door.

The woman nods to me. My height, similar build, her uniform leaves her arms bare to show off the prominent muscle. Black hair like me, braided over one shoulder and the same strong nose. Her short, thick eyebrows and broad upper nose bridge tell me she's a selkie too. Are we related somewhere up the family tree? We could be cousins. Or sisters.

A bronze nameplate on her chest reads: Capt. VZ

"Aalgur Thalon?" The woman greets me with a low, confident voice. She cuts an impressive figure in her black and gray uniform. She extends a hand to me. "You can call me Valmut. Or just Captain."

Is she a *Duskingr* Captain?

"Yes. I'm Aalgur Thalon..." My voice fries. Nerves flutter through my stomach. A Duskingr Captain! I've never seen one up close, not even as a little kid. As elusive as double rainbows, they hide in the sky.

Nodding, Valmut holds out an arm to indicate I should follow. I declined the high heels, and my Blood Spire boots make a soft scuffing sound on the floor. In case of trouble, I would like to be able to run, thank you, not break my ankles.

I can't help myself. "You're a Duskingr Captain?"

"That's right," replies Valmut.

My voice pitches up into a breathy simper. "What's it like? On the Duskingr?"

Valmut chuckles. "Oh, you know. Patrol the Svall. Pick up goods that come through." She slides her eyes to me, grin sly. "Fight monsters."

"Wow..." *She's too cool... stop talking, Thalon...*

Captain Valmut leads me up the flight of stairs and past the entrance to the arena. I catch a glimpse of black-suited security personnel scurrying around the enormous floor like swarming flies. Each carries a bolt-action rifle. The red spotlights glare into the gray morning sky, blinding crimson beacons staining the coastal fog.

I get little opportunity to ogle the sheer number of firearms before Valmut ushers me through another door and into a torchlit stairwell leading up, up, up. We enter a third interior hallway and travel halfway around the stadium before Valmut uses a key card to open a door in the wall. She holds the door for me and steps through with a smirk. Her silence sets a shiver between my shoulders. What is she leading me into?

We enter a spacious cavern overlooking the entire stadium

through clear glass windows. To one side, a glass Duskingr sits as centerpiece atop a lavish spread of food. No, not glass... an ice sculpture. Piles of treats surround the ice airship. Sliced raw tuna belly, blood-red cherries, orange wedges, roe and cheeses and deviled quail eggs, each as small and perfect as a gemstone. A table of sparkling decanters from deep orange bourbon to shimmering green absinthe sprawls beside the food. A row of Spindel soda bottles sit front and center, seven different flavors in buckets of ice, like champagne.

"Aalgur Thalon." A polished voice purrs from the desk beside the farthest window. An elegant older woman stands to greet me. "That's a name, isn't it? *Aalgur.* When first I read it, I imagined a boy. Aalgur. But here you are. Quite the young woman, aren't you?"

I stand still, hands folded, unsure what to say. The woman behind the desk makes a tall and narrow stem in a gown of deepest green and choker of plump, rounded pearls. She uses the transcontinental radio accent. It reminds me of Azoto and I feel slightly trapped.

Tightly pinned auburn curls cap the woman's head. Her gray eyes pick me apart. "Please, Miss Aalgur. Help yourself to refreshments. You will find moon wine, fresh Adelaide cherries flown in last night... you may have whatever suits your fancy."

"I'm alright," I stutter. I make myself take a breath, smile, and relax my posture before my lats pop my side seams.

"Very good, Miss Aalgur. Please take a seat." The woman motions to a chair across from her as she sits back down.

Valmut makes herself a Spindel with rum and takes a chair to the side, close enough to join the conversation if she fancies, far enough to keep to herself if she chooses. The easy boredom with which she sets her lips on the glass, the casual cross of her legs and elbows resting on the table... That's what I want. Proud, confident, powerful. Frightening. Our eyes meet and she gives me a half smile. I want to be like her.

She must be ten or more years older than me. I must have competed against her as a teenager.

The sounds of footsteps pull me out of my head. I glance over my shoulder to see a black suit help himself to a drink as well. Five guards stand along the wall, rifles over their shoulders.

"Edyta Gadvig." The woman behind the desk introduces herself. "President of Headwaters. We specialize in distribution." Gadvig takes a small drag on an ivory cigarette holder and rests it on a volcanic glass tray. Smoke meanders from the ember. Gadvig's gray eyes scan me, this time from chin to belly, what she can see of me over her desk.

Sweat slides from my armpits into my precious, spindly dress. I wait, keeping my expression neutral as my sweat sticks my butt to the leather seat.

"We enjoyed watching you in Regionals, Miss Aalgur. As unprepared as you clearly were, you overcame it, overcame the best training money can buy. Your skills do not go unnoticed. We would like to see how your first two matches go. Depending on how you perform, we may have an offer for you."

"An... offer?" I repeat back.

"Indeed. For sponsorship, Miss Aalgur. We may offer you resources to aid your performance and recovery during the tournament. And after that, should you be assigned to a Duskingr, a winner's salary will be banked in your name."

I blink, eyebrows askew. "A salary... Ma'am?"

"Well, think of it more as a retirement plan. When the Dusk Trials come to an end, four sailors from each ship, two of the sea, two of the mountains, will hang up their uniforms from their twenty-year tenure. And what do you think they have to show for those years, Miss Aalgur?" She pauses, leaving room for me to answer.

Valmut is the first sailor I have ever seen up close. "I don't know, ma'am," I say.

"Honor, Thalon." Captain Valmut clicks the ice in her glass. "But honor can't put a roof over your head or food on the table. Toiling away your youth on a meager trawler, selling your body for sport... denying yourself the comforts of companionship for one, minuscule chance at honor... But what will that honor get you, Thalon? What will wait for you when your time on the Duskingr runs out? The Duskingr pension? Part-time income. That's all the service can pay. Sure, it used to get you better mileage. But in today's economy? The economy twenty years from now?"

I squeeze my hands together under the desk but say nothing. My skin feels hot. I never thought of the money...

Gadvig picks up where Valmut stopped. "Consider it an investment in your service to the country of Ruhnsvalla."

She watches my face, my ribs as I breathe, leaving me naked and exposed. How much do these women know about me? How did they find out?

"It seems unfair, doesn't it, that one family should live in such luxury at the expense of those less fortunate."

I find my voice. "You... do you mean the Seppanen family?"

"Whoever I mean, would you not wish such comfort for yourself, but through your own means and merit?"

The question hits me like a fist. "Yes, ma'am. I... would."

"And would it not interest you to, how to say it, put a certain member of a certain family in her place?"

The hairs on the back of my neck prickle and my hands clench tighter beneath the desk. How could she know? *Oh...* Dizziness presses on the back of my head... *Oh gods, it didn't make the paper... did it? How else would she know about... that?*

"Miss Aalgur?"

I nod. "Yes."

"Then, show us what you're made of, and we will discuss an accord."

"Why?" I manage. "Why would you pay me to do... the job I'm trying to do anyway?"

Gadvig smiles her elegant smile. "The work of protecting the nation of Ruhnsvalla is the work of Headwaters, Miss Aalgur. The rest, we may discuss in time." She stands and I stand too, hoping the black fabric of my dress hides the sweat marks.

Valmut remains seated. "How long have you been training for the Dusk Trials?" she asks. She looks into her drink instead of at me.

"More than ten years, Captain. It's... all I want to do."

Gadvig takes a drag from her cigarette and breathes out fragrant blue smoke. Her eyebrows raise a hair.

"It shows." Valmut leans back in her chair, resting her shin over the opposite knee. "You clearly take pride in your body and skills. Punch down those doubts and fears and show us what you can do. I see a lot of myself in you, and I know I could deliver a Regional level performance again. As many times as I needed to. And so can you."

*You see yourself in me...* I feel a bit breathless.

Gadvig tilts her head. "Do what I know you're capable of, and we will speak again. Good day, Miss Aalgur."

"Good day, ma'am."

"Thalon." Captain Valmut sets both boots back on the floor and extends a card to me between two fingers.

The card has her photograph on one side; assured, stoic, regal. On the back I read an address for the Ikthvar air base in the Duskheim Mountains. Her name is not listed.

"If you need anything," she says.

"Thank you, Captain."

Security leads me back to my room. My head feels like it's filled with fluff.

Does Captain Valmut truly see herself in me? *Me?*

*People were impressed,* I tell myself. *They saw what I can do and are interested. They see me, they see my worth.*

*Valmut...* my heart flutters.

*She sees that I'm good,* I remind myself. *That I'll be an asset. That I'm enough.*

As the excitement fades, the headache returns. I swallow my pills and kneel before Tophinghua in gratitude. *I'll show them I'm worth it. I'll make them proud.*

I don't feel so alone anymore.

# CHAPTER
# NINE

I put my armor back on and sit on the bed. I try to eat more, but the smell of the broiled cod makes me gag. It's nerves. I rub the back of my neck, trying to loosen it up.

Lexija charges through my door yelling: "Grab your stupid axe, girl!" We half march, half run, to the stairs, black suits on our heels. "Stupid show runners decided you're up *right now*."

My armpit sweat sticks my biceps to my sides as we hurry down a long stretch of hallway. Other competitors appear with their trainers and guards. Some smirk, most look like a stiff breeze could make them piss their little loincloths.

Lexija seems to know where to go, as she leads me through a door and up a dark stone staircase into a hall much like the rookery below.

"Parliament declared each fighter must have a one-to-one escort. Gill has Kip," explains Lexija.

She guides me towards the noonday sun streaming through enormous stone arches. Dire, intense music plays from inside the arena, almost a dirge.

I am about to walk out into the first day of the Blood Spire. An icy knot tightens in my stomach.

We step through the door into the blazing bright afternoon.

The stone bleachers reach into the sky, overflowing with loud, faceless masses. I choke a little on my own spit at the sheer numbers. I have never seen so many people... at least not so many people looking at me.

Looking at us, by the gods, there are so many of *us*. Perhaps it's just an illusion created by the addition of security and handlers, but the interior of the stadium seems to crawl with people. Matches have already started in two separate rings.

*I don't have to beat them all... It's just me and my opponent... I don't have to beat them all...* I search the floor of the stadium for familiar faces, Kip, mostly. I lock eyes with the hulking beast of Rawl in his sea anemone braids. His smile splits his face into an animalistic leer. I snarl back. At least he's wearing the same skimpy thigh armor as me.

My eyes rake the seating, searching for Valmut. I spot the Illuet instead, unreadable in her Kvellsett mask and surrounded by security.

Lexija leads me to a tent inside the wall of the stadium. She drags over a rack of weapons. I hear a shriek and blood sprays into the air. Applause follows.

Lexija jerks me around to face her. "Remember, girl, fight smart, not hard. You can switch weapons, but only three times a match, and you're only allowed two at once and a shield counts as a weapon. To call pause, make a "T" with your hands, like this..."

"Who am I fighting?" I wobble as Lexija jerks and tugs on my buckles and straps. The ghost of Gadvig's voice floats through my brain, something about the first match, especially the first match...

"Not a clue. Give the axe back."

"I... I want to start with her..."

"Gods, you're insufferable... Fine." Lexija spins me around as a garish loudspeaker announces: "AALGUR THALON, RING TWO".

"Godspeed, girl." Lexija snaps open the security strap on Blitz's scabbard, angles me for Ring Two, and slaps my half-naked ass.

"ERIK LEIVARA, RING TWO," booms the announcement voice.

A flash of motion from Ring One catches my eye and I hear the punishing crack of a whip. A whip! We can use whips?

"Huh!" I grip Gevit in both hands, breathless as I step into the blood-red circle. The spotlights blind me. The whoosh of my own breath deafens me.

Erik Leivara bellows as the audience cheers. More than a few people up in the bleachers seem to know who he is. Taller than me, broader than me, I take note of his powerful but tight movements, the way his eyes flick over me like I'm not worth his time. He carries a one-handed sword, and a dagger on his hip. Lifting his eyebrows at me, he spits on the floor and steps into the ring. In my career as a tournament fighter, we've never crossed paths.

"Ready!" hollers the referee. "And fight!"

I've fought enough floor-spitters to anticipate his aggressive charge. I dart out of the way. Rather than engage, I sink into a low stance, Gevit held across my body as protection. I dance out of Erik's way three times before he catches on and falls back into a stalking stance. We circle each other, watching for tells, anticipating the next action. Erik bares his teeth at me, growling, intimidating. I return the gesture.

And then Erik makes a "T" with his hands and walks off. I blink.

Erik reenters the ring with a nine-foot spear.

When I remain where I am, the referee yells: "And fight!"

The moment *fight* leaves the referee's lips, Erik stabs for my belly. I swing Gevit up to parry...but it was a fake out. Erik yanks the spear back, completes the rotation, and slams the metal capped butt of the weapon into my chest plate.

The impact spins me off balance. I stagger, hopping and scrambling as the spear stabs for my thigh. I block just in time with Gevit's handle but the impact jolts up my left arm. I gasp as pain shoots through my arm, my neck, my hip. It's so hot, so deep, I stumble.

"Call out! CALL OUT!" screeches Lexija.

I block, stagger, and "T" my hands.

Lexija drags me out of the ring. Erik's trainer towels him off and offers him water, which he spits in my direction. The crowd roars approval.

"No more axe." Lexija pries Gevit from my shaking fists and hangs her on the rack. Blitz ends up in my left hand. "Shield!" Lexija pulls my arm through the straps of a disk shield. It's light, some sort of hard plastic, easy to move.

"Where's your head at?" demands Lexija.

I stutter. Blitz shakes in my hand. My left arm burns all the way up through my jaw and into my teeth. I sway.

"Doesn't matter. You know the drill, Thalon. Get that spear away from the seagull sucker and shove it up his ass if you have to."

I nod. If I speak, I'm going to throw up.

"Take a breath, Thalon. Good. Take another. Trust the process, believe you're the beast. It's real simple, spear, ass, victory... got it?"

I nod again.

"Good. And use some of that ts'kmet footwork, won't you?" Lexija shoves me back into the circle.

Erik grins and cracks his neck.

"And, fight!" bellows the referee.

Erik charges, going for the kill. I roll to avoid the spear.

Lexija is right. Spear, ass, victory. When Erik thrusts the spear at me, I throw my shield arm over the shaft and brace my wrist beneath it. Before Erik has time to yank it away, I charge the length of the spear, slamming the front of my helmet into his chin.

Erik's head snaps back, spit flying. I slice Blitz's dainty razor edge down his veiny arm. Blood spurts over me, over him, over the ground, and onto the referee as she leaps onto the scene to see who the blood belongs to. The audience boos.

The referee steers us apart. I gasp and double over. My insides feel molten, lungs on fire and stomach in my throat. But I've been here before, too tense, too worked up, and breathe through it as the referee lifts my arm into the air.

Erik yells, then bellows. He bellows again, eyes bulging, frenzied, spit spraying from his mouth as his trainer pulls him back and away from me.

"I'll kill you! I'll kill you, filthy welp!"

"ERIK LEIVARA HAS BEEN ELIMINATED! AALGUR THALON MOVES ON!" booms the announcer.

Erik keeps screaming and thrashing. Four black-suited security officers drag him away. I look up just long enough to read the logo on the back of his armor. *Headwaters*, it reads.

Lexija pulls me to the tent and pours water onto a cloth to clean off the blood. "The gods drag me to the abyss, girl, you let that go on far too long..."

* * *

"LEXIJA... CAN I GET SOME MEDICINE FOR MY HEAD?" I GRIMACE AS I PEEL the helmet from my soaked and tangled hair.

"I'll have something sent down, sure. Sure," Lexija huffs as she marches me back to my cave hole. "You've taken your antiviral for today, right?"

I nod.

At my door, Lexija spins me around and smacks my cheek a few times. "Hey. Look alive. You just won your first match in the Blood Spire. Catch your breath and hang this asinine relic back on the wall where it belongs." She shoves Gevit into my arms.

* * *

A BOTTLE OF PARLIAMENT-APPROVED PAINKILLERS ARRIVE IN MY ROOM. I take some and pass out on my bed, armor on. I wake up with sweat-matted hair and unreasonably rank armpits.

"Up! Second match!" Lexija claps her hands.

"How did Kip do?" I ask. We head for Ring Two again.

"You know I can't answer that," replies Lexija. She fits me to the disk shield and Blitz again.

"Hey, did I hear a whip earlier? Whips aren't allowed in Regionals..."

Lexija indulges in a gratuitous eye roll. "It was. It's been a whole clusterfuck, or so I hear. I guess whips weren't explicitly *excluded* in the Dusk Trials rulebook. Anyway, you're up!"

My name rumbles from the loudspeaker and I step into the afternoon sun. A quick, wiry boy with a short sword and dagger combination faces me. I can tell just by the speed and bounce of his steps his animal form must be an otter.

I assume my stance, low and guarded, reading his steps, the shift of his weight... The boy runs right in, slashing for my arm. I'm not entirely sure what happens next. I blink, and blood trickles down the boy's leg.

"Ah! Urchin sucker!" yelps the boy. "Damn it..."

My temple throbs. Black shadows follow my vision as I turn. Did we even fight? I offer the boy a hand up.

"DO NOT TOUCH YOUR OPPONENT OUTSIDE OF COMBAT!" yells one of the referees. Two other refs jump in to separate me from the equally startled kid.

A referee hoists my arm aloft and the crowd cheers.

I shake Blitz in the air and the cheers thunder. It's not important how I got here, it's important that I won. Pounding Blitz on my shield, I hold my arms out and roar, for my own entertainment as much as theirs.

* * *

"I don't know, Thalon, that first match, oof!" Lexija shakes herself. "That last one felt much more like you. Very smooth. Keep that energy going, will you? Leivara nearly gave me a stroke."

I smile but I feel… off. My head still hurts, sure, but something's not as it should be. The flow of thyir through my body feels hot, dry. Stupid tourist flu.

"You're through the two elimination rounds, so tomorrow you'll start in the thirty-two-person bracket. There are so many contestants, they're doing consolation rounds instead of automatic boot in the butt from here on out. Plus, gotta give the crowd what they paid for, huh?" She chuckles and unlocks my door. "Well, Thalon, good night. Soak in the tub. Gorge yourself. You did good today, girl."

"Thanks, Lexija." My smile skews into a grimace. "Hey, did you really think I'd slept with Kip?"

Lexija shrugs. "I don't know. Why not? I don't know what you're getting up to. You're cute, he's cute…"

I roll my eyes as Lexija shuts me inside. Sleep with Kip? The Dread One take me. I hope he's doing well. I hope I get to see him again soon. Cute or not, I could do with a dose of his boyish grin.

* * *

I wish I could sleep, but my head buzzes and my muscles throb, especially my left arm. I lie on my bed like a bloated whale corpse. I feel worse by the hour, the pain in my head an ice pick behind my eye, my stomach far too caustic to eat any of my fancy food. A tiny, insane voice in my head wishes I was simply pregnant, like Lexija had feared. That, I could get fixed. This? I don't even know what's broken and the medicine is proving a weak salve.

A gentle knock rouses me from my mushy thoughts. I knock back and startle when Gadvig herself opens the door. Two security guards and a young man in a pinstriped suit flank her.

"Might my assistant Blake and I come in a moment, Miss Aalgur?"

"Yes! Please!" I sputter. I wrap my robe around myself and kick my dirty laundry out of sight. "I was resting...it's a bit of a mess in here..."

"Not to worry, Miss Aalgur." Gadvig gives me a perfect, ironed smile. Ironed, starched, pressed. "You fought well. We are impressed."

"Thank you, ma'am." I straighten my posture to look as healthy as possible.

Gadvig slides a hand to Blake, who places a crisp blue folder in it. "Inside you will find Headwaters' offer, Miss Aalgur." She places the folder in my hands.

Opening it, I trace my name penned beautifully into the contract.

"This ensures sponsorship from Headwaters, Miss Aalgur, and everything that entails."

I skim the paper, only half seeing the words. My mouth feels dusty.

"Should you be assigned to a ship, this assures your legally binding support from Headwaters and all of the privileges therein."

"And...what do I provide in exchange for...for these privileges?" I murmur.

Gadvig smiles again. "Your loyalty, Miss Aalgur. And your dedication to fair trade and access of goods."

My finger floats down the first page. Flourishes pop out at me, carefully underlined sums of money. Even dull as a stick from the drugs, the money leaves me breathless. I could move up the coast if I wanted, where crystalline water washes over white sand. I could buy my own cottage. Would I live there alone, swimming and lying on the beach as I please? Or would I drape my pelt around a companion? My fingertips hover over the numbers, remembering how lips once felt on my neck.

I flip through the other five pages. The phrase *Temple of Brosk* catches my eye, but I return to the first page.

"Simple technicalities and safety measures," purrs Gadvig.

The money shines in my eyes. Staring at the contract in the royal blue folder, I glimpse a future I have not dared imagine.

Fair trade and access to goods?

I have no argument against that. Gadvig slips a pen into my fingers. My hand trembles as I sign my name. A moment later, Blake closes the folder and slides it beneath his arm.

Gadvig opens a clutch, beaded with pink pearls, and lifts out a tiny bottle of black glass. "Your records show you are being treated for a flu. It is a shame to see you unwell, Miss Aalgur. You have worked hard to be where you are. You deserve to enter the ring with the same edge as your adversaries." She offers it to me.

"What is it?" I ask.

"A simple energy shot. Drink it if you are feeling unwell. You will find the effects most excellent."

I turn the bottle in my hand. It bears Parliament's seal of approval.

I try to keep skepticism from my face. I'm no stranger to energy boosts and, aside from a basic kick of caffeine, find them of little use in a fight. Still, I nod my gratitude. "Thank you, ma'am."

Gadvig dips her chin to Blake and they both move to the door. "No, Miss Aalgur, thank you. I anticipate a fond relationship with a capable young woman such as yourself. You may find our interests align in more places than one. Rest now, champion."

As soon as the door closes, my straight posture crumbles and I sink to my knees before my statue of Tophinghua.

*Please*, I press my forehead to the floor. *Please help me win.*

The Headwaters logo on Erik Leivara's armor flickers through my mind. I ignore it. I don't need to worry about it, I just need to win.

*Please...*

# TEN

I dream of my childhood home on Scallop Avenue. Chubby toddler Ashling stands at the top of the stairs. She teeters, about to fall. I yell for her but I cannot reach her. I'm in my room.

I reach for the doorknob of my room but can't turn it. I'm a sea lion. I have flukes in place of hands. I ram the door with my body. I have to get to her before she falls.

"Stop this!" scolds Momma. She smacks her hand on my door. "Stop this right now, you stupid animal!"

*I'm not an animal*...I try to say. I am a sea lion, and I cannot speak human words. I cry and whimper and bark.

Momma's voice whispers in my ear: *What are you?*

* * *

I awake with a start. I take a breath and moan. My body aches and my head throbs. My joints grind like they have grit between the bones.

"Ah...gods." I'm hot, dry, and yet I can't stop shivering. I stumble into the bathroom and the light from the lamp stabs through my eye. I lean on the sink, fighting not to throw up.

Eyes closed, I feel my way out of the bathroom and smack the door to the hall with my hand.

Someone outside replies. "Miss?"

"Medic..." I croak. "Please...headache..."

"Right away, Miss."

I slide down the door and curl up. The stone floor cools my burning neck. I press the heels of my hands into my eyes and groan. My stomach rolls like I'm in a wind-tossed airship. I've never felt this sick before. Not like this. Every injury I've ever had smolders. The dislocated jaw, the twisted knee, the time the net chains hit me in the ribs on the *Cormorant*...

I dig my fingers into the back of my skull. Tears leak down my face.

I've had the flu before. This isn't the flu. The Illuet appears in my mind. What had I felt when she looked at me on the practice field? Could her kvell have hurt me like Kip said? Why would she do that?

I hardly realize when my door opens and a medic takes my vitals. She questions me and I slur answers. Pressing a bottle into my hand, she instructs me to drink it, then leaves.

I do as instructed. The liquid tastes fruity, floral. I'm unconscious by the time I reach my bed.

* * *

Lexija lets herself in. "You look hungover."

"I'm not..." I walk beside her up to the arena. I feel like I'm using a stranger's body.

"I got a memo that you had some kind of migraine now, that they gave you the good stuff. You've got to kick this flu nonsense in the ass, Thalon."

I nod. I take a long drink from the coffee in my hand. Yesterday slowly returns to me.

"Lexija, have you met a retired Duskingr sailor?"

"No...I haven't."

"Are there any here?"

"Not this year."

"They...used to come to the Dusk Trials...when I was five, they...I think they signed autographs or something..." The memory of dark uniforms fuzzes in my head. "Why aren't they here?"

"Above my pay." Lexija smiles. "Those answers are for fancier people than me, Thalon. I'm past my Dusk Trial days. I'm just a coach."

I wonder where they've gone. I drain my coffee. I can worry about that later.

"AALGUR THALON!"

My name booms from the loudspeaker as Lexija does a final fit check on my armor, tightens my chinstrap, and pushes me toward the ring.

I walk to Ring One to an uproar from the audience. Captain Valmut stands in the front row. When our eyes meet, she salutes me. I straighten and square my shoulders. But then my eyes track over to the Illuet. She's in the front as well. The black eye holes of her mask turn to me. I cringe a little but lift my chin. *You don't scare me...*

Well, maybe a little.

"BRYR KLASHEK!" roars the announcer.

My opponent walks out to face me, holding her sword aloft. Smaller than me but equally muscular and steady on her feet, she carries a shield and short sword.

We face each other, her expression calm, focused, locked on me.

"Fight!" yells the referee.

Bryr and I take our time. Her, I recognize. We've fought a couple of times over the years. Every step she takes is efficient, each duck or parry calculated in anticipation of her next move. I catch her blade and flick it away; she blocks Blitz, then parries again.

Back and forth, we move in together, locked, step, step, a flurry of blows, an intricate dance, much like the ts'kmet. And then we break apart. No one has an advantage yet.

My chest burns, sweat runs into my eyes. Bryr darts forward and I meet her, metal clashes, one, two, three, and we spring apart to regroup.

My belly burns. Each gasp I take wheezes. *Breathe, rest, recover...* I tell myself. But I get worse. The stadium sways, Bryr turns splotchy and I "T" my hands.

Limping to Lexija, I let her towel me off and pour water over my head. "You're doing great. She's good, but so are you. And you've got stamina. Outlast her. Outlast her and then out dance her. Wear her down and come in hard..."

I half hear the advice. My body craves energy and yet the thought of eating nearly makes me retch.

I pull my hair into a tail and strap my helmet on. "I'm ready. I've got her..." I step back into the ring.

"AND FIGHT!"

We circle. I focus on her, not on how bad I feel. We snap together like the hammer of a rifle, trade blows, and spring apart. Bryr lunges, feigning high and jabbing low. I catch her blade on my shield and toss it back. My blade sweeps around, I feel it connect, then I double over in agony.

My shield caught her blade just wrong, in the perfect way to wrench my shoulder. Pain erupts in splotches of flaring red and purple, clouding my vision. The pain consumes my entire arm, my neck, my jaw, my spine.

I "T" my hands as best I can as I stagger back to Lexija. I fall to my knee pads and curl over my arm. I can't speak, I can't breathe. Numb to my surroundings, I clutch my arm and whimper.

"Medic! Medic!" Lexija hollers.

Next thing I know, someone has my elbow pads off and moves my arm. I gasp, my vision darkens.

"Thalon. Just breathe. Breathe, Thalon." Lexija pats my cheek and turns my chin toward the arena. "You cut her! You won! Get up, you have to be declared victor!"

I can't think. I see the sun spark off Blitz as the referee thrusts my hand into the air. I don't remember walking back out.

Next comes a flurry of motion and voices. The world sloshes around me, inside me. I come back to my senses vomiting coffee into a trash bin.

A medic uses rough paper towels to wipe my mouth. Two other medics help me limp into the hallway. I'm still holding Blitz and a shield. Lexija is gone.

They take me to a beeping, flashing medical ward. Someone takes my weapons and pries off my sweaty armor. Someone else gives me an oxygen mask while two more medics read my pulse and move my shoulder.

A woman kneels in front of me. "No broken bones... soft tissue seems alright. What hurts, Miss Thalon?"

What doesn't hurt? I can only shake my head. My teeth chatter and I shiver.

"I've got her file," announces a voice. "She came in with the flu. Then it says a migraine last night. Not uncommon with the flu. Thalon? We're going to give you some medicine for the pain and nausea and let you recover."

"My arm..." Tears drip down my face. It burns, a deep, hot ache in the bones.

"Yes. It will stop soon." The medic gives me a bottle of the same floral liquid as last night. I drink it and sigh as cool relief fades the agony away.

* * *

Back in my limestone room, I sleep. I wake up somewhat recovered. After forcing myself to eat at least a few bites of fish, I kneel before Tophinghua.

*Why is this happening, Mother? Why am I sick? Please help me get through this... I just have to get through this. I just have to win...*

And then what?

A black suit startles me from my prayers by opening my door. A man in pinstripes and pocket watch chain stands behind the guard.

"Aalgur Thalon?" asks the man..

I lumber to my feet. "The one and only."

"Excellent. Time for your newspaper photos. Follow me."

"I look like..."

*...Ass*, I finish internally.

"Not to worry. The makeup crew will fix you up."

Pinstripes doesn't talk, so neither do I. I focus on walking, ignoring the chain mesh riding up between my butt cheeks. The medication's left me sluggish and clumsy. Pinstripes motions me into a bright studio abuzz with conversations.

"Gracious, Willits," sighs a young man in winged eyeliner.

He looks me over, rubs his face, and motions me into a chair. Four people attack my long, loose hair and prime my face. They talk to each other, treating me more like a mannequin than a person, but that's fine. It gives me time to rest.

"There. Presentable," declares the makeup artist after an hour's work. He motions for me to stand in front of a neutral-colored screen. "Over here, doll. Give us a pose."

I look down at my hands and feel naked. "I don't have Gevit..."

"This is just a mug shot, you've got all you need. Now give us that pose, girl!"

I straighten my back and glare at the enormous camera.

"No... no, doll. Not *I want to rip out your intestines and wear them as a scarf.* This is for the fans. Give us *fighting fuck toy*."

"W-what?" I sputter. Two people take hold of me and help me pose.

The strobe flashes and I squint. Each flare stabs through my eye and into my brain. The team twists my waist, angles my shoulders, and sticks out my butt. My knees tremble and I let it happen.

*Where's Thalon?* I ask myself. Where's the ham ready to bask in her own glory and put on a show? Where's the girl who walked out of the sea and posed nude for a boat of tourists? *Where in the depths am I?* My left arm twitches. Looking down, I see faint red dots between the painted runes. *What's happening to me?*

"That'll do. All done, doll." The artist pulls me away from the screen and writes my room number on a tag.

"First prints go the papers, of course, but we'll have collector's cards sent to you later."

I rub my arm. What are those marks? "Collector's cards?"

The artist pulls me to the door and hands me off to Pinstripes. "Yes, yes. You're all getting them. All of you who made it this far. Immortals. Lose now, you'll still be on a card forever."

# ELEVEN

Twilight paints the sky violet over the arena. Dramatic black smoke rises around the red beacons from vents, transforming them into glowing fingers of a god. The tectonic music rattles in my chest and the Duskingr and Sky Navy ships circle like barracudas.

The two sparring rings have been replaced by a single red circle. Orange spotlights blaze into it from four sides.

Lexija pulls me over to hiss in my ear. "If you place here, you're almost guaranteed a spot on a ship. Top three get a bonus, but I hear it's nothing special."

I carry Gevit with me again. She may not be the perfect weapon for this sort of tournament, but I need her. She reminds me that long ago I had ancestors just like me. Ancestors who would understand me. She reminds me who I fight for.

Lexija keeps hissing. "Be smart, move smart. You've been ill, don't push it, don't show off. Keep your distance, read your opponent. Play to your strengths. Frustrate them, wear them down, toss a rock at them and give them a bloody nose if you have to... From here on out, there will be consolation rounds... even if you lose this match, it doesn't mean you're out of the running…" Lexija reaches for Gevit but stops. "You will be formally announced. You can hold the axe for that…"

I leave my energy shot in our prep tent and buckle on my helmet.

"FIGHTERS AT THE READY!" booms the announcing voice.

Nodding to Lexija, I step into the arena. A spotlight falls over me, plunging me into a bright tube of solitude. It washes my surroundings away. *I am a daughter of the Dread One*, I remind myself. Her blood is my blood. I step into the crimson circle and lift Gevit above my head. The stands explode with ravenous applause.

"IN HONOR OF THE DREAD ONE, GOD OF STORM AND STRIFE, AALGUR THALON OF VATSKA!"

I shake Gevit and roar. My teeth flash, muscles shining with excited sweat. I revel in the cheers, drinking them in. I let them burn the ache and pallor from my body. I am here, I am Her daughter… And then I am left blinking and blinded as the spotlights sweep to my opponent.

I squint, eyes adjusting. A huge shape manifests in the light.

"IN HONOR OF BROSK HIMSELF, RAWL KANE OF VATSKAAAAAA!"

My fists tighten on Gevit. Rawl. I am going to fight Rawl…

Rather than cheer for the monstrous man in his anemone braids and spiked mace, the crowd starts up a chant: "RAWL! RAWL! RAWL!"

Rawl throws his head back on a neck nearly as thick as my waist and laughs, milking the crowd.

Across the arena, his beady black eyes find me. Tusks jut from his bottom jaw as he grins.

"FIGHTERS! CHOOSE YOUR WEAPONS!"

"Reach!" Lexija takes Gevit, thrusts a spear into my hands. She hooks Blitz to my belt. "If he tries to take the spear, let him have it, Thalon. Run back here and get something else. You aren't fighting him, you won't beat him in a fight. You're outsmarting him. Use all three of your breaks. For the love of the gods, don't let him tangle with you. Don't block, don't parry, get the fuck out of his way!"

Lexija isn't joking. We are different creatures entirely, Rawl and I. I might pass as human to someone who doesn't know how to spot the selkie eyebrows and nose. Rawl however, keeps his gray complexion, his tusks, and his size. The Kane Clan has long served the Seppanen family as bodyguards, as warriors before that, symbiotes of a sort. Facing Rawl, I have no doubt he sees me as little more than an inconvenience, a squishable mouse to kick out of the way with the side of his boot.

"Remember, don't fight him," hisses Lexija. "Outsmart, outlast, survive..." She squeezes my shoulders and shoves me into the arena.

Rawl holds a spiked mace and a shield nearly as tall as I am. His eyes flick to me, the hungry eyes of a shark. He inclines his head. I bare my teeth and hiss.

"MAKE READY! AND... FIGHT!"

I crouch low in my stance with my spear crossing in front of me, waiting to see how Rawl will move. I expect him to be slow, to lumber. He charges like a raging train. I yelp and dive away. Tumbling over the shaft of my spear, I bounce to my feet.

Rawl charges again. His huge, thick body moves with unprecedented grace. I scramble and Rawl skids to his knees. He sweeps my feet out from under me with the rim of his kite shield.

I fall and bounce and land face down in the grit. Splotches of color dance in my eyes. I lash out with the spear, panicked and stabbing blindly. *I have to end this...* I push myself to my feet and charge him. I do exactly what Lexija told me not to.

I jolt to a stop. Rawl locks my spear beneath his arm like I did to Leivara. Next thing I know, I am flying through the air.

I crash into the ground. I bounce and tuck into a roll. Using my momentum, I leap to my feet, ready to run, ready to stab... and my knees buckle. I crash into the sand with my left arm pinned beneath me. Pain blooms through the shoulder, my head, my spine. I grunt. I can't get enough air to scream.

I kick myself over and "T" my hands. Then I lie there. I can't get up on my own. I can't hear, see, or think.

"Thalon!" Lexija pats my cheek and I spit sand onto the floor. I'm back in our tent. Lexija holds a bag of ice against my shoulder. My arm hangs limp in my lap. Did I black out again?

"Thalon? Are you with me? Hey, Thalon..."

Air hisses through my teeth. I can't move my arm. "The bastard... broke my arm..."

"Nothing's broken, just a little strained." Lexija tries to assure me. "I sent the medic for a sling, we'll strap it down."

Two people in green aprons appear and strip my upper armor. My whole body shakes as cold night air hits my wet skin. The medics tape my shoulder. I sit inert, a doll in their hands.

A medic speaks to Lexija. "She's injured and her chart says she's sick. We advise your athlete forfeit."

"No," I grunt. I use my good arm to snap some armor back on. "I'm not forfeiting!"

"Thalon..." Lexija helps me strap in.

The medics try to strap my arm across my belly. Pain cuts through me. "Stop!"

"Can you move your left arm?" asks Lexija.

"Enough," I grunt.

"Use this thing." Lexija unsnaps Blitz from my belt. "You have good aim, throw it at him. He's good, Thalon... and he's fresh."

All I hear is fresh and good. I stumble and use the weapons rack for balance. The pain in my arm is white hot and molten. I'm going to pass out or throw up or die.

"Thalon... you don't look well..." I hear honest concern in Lexija's voice. It stabs into me like a sliver under a thumbnail.

"I'll beat him," I rasp. "I'll beat him..." And I walk back into the arena.

"WE'VE SEEN THALON STRUGGLE IN HER MATCHES," announces the loud, radio voice. "WINNER OF THE REGIONAL OPEN WEAPONS CHAMPIONSHIP, THALON ISN'T BRINGING HER

WINNING GAME TO THE BLOOD SPIRE. DOES SHE HAVE WHAT IT TAKES TO DRAW FIRST BLOOD ON SUCH A FORMIDABLE FOE?"

"SHUT UP!" I scream into the red, smoky haze of the sky. "SHUT UP! SHUT UP!"

"AND... FIGHT!" yells the referee.

I don't have time to catch my breath after screaming. Rawl charges. He's traded out the shield and mace for a two-handed staff with a small blade on each end. I run. I try to anyway. I take two steps and land on my face in the sand. Did he trip me? Did I trip myself? The audience gasps. I roll away before the staff can tag me.

I stumble to my feet. The sounds of the stadium fade in and out like a broken radio. The staff swings for me, and I duck. It spins back around and clips me in the chest plate, sending me sprawling into the dirt.

I "T" my hands and Lexija helps me walk out of the arena to a chorus of disappointed groans and cheers for Rawl.

"Rawl! Rawl! Rawl!"

I catch my breath and go out again. I stay low, as low as I can crouch on my trembling legs. I try to remember the steps of the ts'kmet, how I would slide to my knees and spring into the air, and dance around my partner on weightless steps. Now, my chest heaves for breath, I move as if I'm knee-deep in mud.

The shaft of the spear catches me across the belly. It throws me back into the stone barrier. I "T" my hands. I can call no more breaks. Back with Lexija, I hold my stomach and wheeze. Lexija applies icepacks on various parts of my body as I shiver. She gives me water but all it does is make me throw up.

"Thalon..." Lexija rubs my back. She hands me the little glass bottle from Gadvig. "Try a sip of this... I'll see if there's anything they can give you. Just to get you through..." She leaves me shivering in a puddle of sweat.

I fumble around with the bottle, eventually biting through the wax seal and pulling out the stopper with my teeth. The thick, molasses-colored ooze inside tastes of cotton candy and mildew. I almost throw up again. But I drink it. I doubt it will help, but I need any edge I can get.

I sit with my face in my shaking hands. I feel like a hard-boiled egg with its shell shattered. I might still have all my pieces, but they're held together by little more than membrane and mucus.

Warmth spreads through me and I stop shaking. Then, I can take a full, luxurious breath. I flex my left hand, then the arm, it works again. *What?*

I stand and stagger, but a grin spreads across my face, or perhaps a grimace. I hone in on Rawl across the arena. I take a step towards him, then another. I carry nothing but little Blitz. My heartbeat speeds up, or perhaps the world slows down. Inside me, my thyir crackles and sparks like a match dropped into a pile of dry leaves.

The referee turns toward me. He moves in little jerks, like the image in a flip book.

"ANNND... FIGGGGHT....!" he drawls.

Rawl looks at me. The staff lifts and then lowers, ready to strike. I follow the motion with my eyes. I see the shift of his weight through the creases in his thigh armor, the sway of his teeny chain mesh loincloth. But huge beastly Rawl and his double-sided staff are so slow. I spring to action.

I run, duck, roll, spring. Rawl's bladed staff follows me but I slip behind him. Blitz glints in my hand and I fling her for Rawl's exposed thigh.

The shaft of the spear barely blocks the spinning axe, deflecting her to the side. Rawl bellows, lumbering to face me. I slip behind him again, leaping the sweep of the staff as easily as skipping rope. I use the spear shaft to pull myself, hand over fist, into Rawl's defenses.

He tries to shake me loose. I bounce off the sand, growling and shrieking as fire burns in my veins. My overheated mind has room for one thought: *I am Aalgur Thalon and I am going to win!*

Throwing me to the ground, Rawl aims a kick for my belly. I spring, wrapping around his meaty leg as it crushes into me, absorbing the blow. Grasping his boot in both hands, I sink my teeth into his exposed calf and bite down...

Rawl bellows and I fly from his foot. I anticipate my spiral through the air and catch myself on my hands and toes. Locking eyes with Rawl, I spit his blood across the floor.

Confusion rises from the crowd as the referees run to the spray of blood. There is no doubt, red spurts from Rawl's leg and his trainer swoops in with gauze.

I throw back my head and cackle, then crow. Tophinghua is with me! She came for me, Her daughter, bringing me to life with Her fire.

I fall to my side. Beneath the orange spotlights and blazing red beacons, I laugh. I laugh until I sob. Blood runs down my chin and chest. It takes two referees to drag me away.

# TWELVE

I pace my room, still laughing. Rawl's blood stains my chin, I can still taste it. I want to kneel, to offer my gratitude to Tophinghua, but sitting still makes my skin crawl.

Frustration twists my guts. I need to fight... I need to claw and tear and bite and... I slam my fist into the wall. Knuckles pop. I shake my hand and whimper, desperate and alone.

For a moment, I am back in the house on Scallop Avenue. I taste blood. Ashling wails and I look down to see her tender little arm between my teeth. Momma and Pappa loom over me in shock and horror.

I crumple to the floor in my little cell beneath the Blood Spire arena. I have become the animal my parents always feared.

In the spell of Gadvig's energy shot, I lose my place in time. One moment I pace, the next I sit on the floor surrounded by food wrappers. I've eaten a pound of lox, a brick of cheese, and a bowl of cherries, pits and all.

The fire in me fizzles, replaced by aching skin and bruised bones. I wake up in the wee hours of the morning with clawed talons of agony squeezing my skull.

My arm screams, twitching and shaking. My head throbs, my feet ache and I can't seem to get enough air into my lungs. I skip again in time and find myself curled on the bathroom floor. The room spins and I vomit thick, red slime. I can't tell if it's Rawl's blood, mine, or simply cherries. Whatever the case, I call for a medic and receive another tiny bottle of floral liquid painkiller.

This time, it only dulls the pain. I lie on my bed, alternately sweating and shivering. Red-hot barbed wire burns from behind my left eye, down my neck, through my shoulder to my fingertips.

*I'm hurt...* I think. *I'm sick, I'm so sick...*

I wish someone could be with me, could sit with me. I wish someone would tell me everything will be okay. No one comes. I am alone again.

* * *

MY SENSE OF TIME IS FIXED WHEN I WAKE UP, BUT I AM NOT.

I can move my aching left arm again, but red splotches have appeared around the painted runes. Bruises, I think at first, but when I touch them, I feel little bumps. The same sparse rash covers my chest and belly. My knuckles and toes feel itchy and stiff.

Putting on my armor proves to be a struggle, my swollen hands hardly close, but I manage it, then call to a black suit to bring me hot tea. A quick inspection in the mirror reveals a single pink blotch on one cheek, easily passed off as a blemish. I look down at myself, the rash is hidden. I can't let Lexija see it. I can be disqualified for communicable skin conditions. I can't afford to deal with that. Not now.

After the tea, I kneel before Tophinghua to pray. Instead of gratitude, a sob leaves my mouth. The tears don't stop once they start and I weep, a pathetic, worthless creature. The harder I try to stop, to stop shaming myself in front of Tophinghua, the harder I cry.

*I am Your daughter...* I remind myself. Snot runs from my nose as I look up at Tophinghua. *Am I worthy?*

My door opens without warning and I startle, knocking Tophinghua askew and catching her before she falls. I scramble to my feet and snarl through the snot.

A small figure slips through and pushes the door closed. A small greenish person wearing gloves and a bonnet around their hair.

"Wavern?" I croak.

Wavern pulls me into a fierce hug and I start sobbing anew.

"Thalon... what's going on with you?" Wavern rubs my back then holds me at arm's length. "You've been a complete mess out there. I got into your records, did you get hurt in the Gauntlet? You don't have a flu, by the way, not sure anyone told you, but the test turned up negative..."

I take in Wavern's greenish smock, bonnet, and sterile gloves. I can smell disinfectant on them. "Are you... did you get on the medical team?"

Wavern rolls their hazel eyes and sits on my bed. "After the explosions in the Gauntlet, I might have gotten a little... creative. It's taken me a little extra work to get access..." Wavern jiggles a key card and identification badge. "But I did it."

A grin threatens the corner of my mouth. I sniffle. "Of course you did."

"Of course I did. But listen, these Dusk Trials? Something's going on. I'm not sure what yet, but you should see the airships parked behind the stadium for the sponsors... it's unreal, Thalon. The wealthiest of the wealthy are here."

"But... why?" I use the corner of a blanket to wipe my face.

Wavern shrugs and bounces up and down. "Not sure yet. Spectacle, obviously, but people are getting hurt. I mean *hurt*, hurt. Blade guards are flying off. People are losing fingers and eyes right, left, and center. The first night in the rookery, five contestants from Adlervik got assaulted in their rooms. By assaulted, I mean stabbed. All of them were sponsored by the Seppanen family."

"Kip...?" I ask. I bite my lip.

"Kip's gone undefeated, I visited him last night..." Wavern holds their key card in one hand and bounces it off the opposing palm. Their eyes wander away from mine. "He's berserk out there, Thalon... He nearly decapitated someone. He accepted a sponsorship... a good one. From Headwaters, the distribution company..."

My breath hitches. "I took a sponsorship from them too..." I whisper, as if afraid the walls might hear.

Wavern scowls and clicks their tongue. "I don't get it... I don't understand what they get from the champions... it makes no sense..."

"But listen, you're not right, Thalon. You've been off your game since...since last week, haven't you?"

"I started getting headaches at work... Cortland put me on doubles..."

"Something's wrong, that's for certain." Wavern's eyebrows lower. "And what in the depths was that with Rawl? You *bit* him? Psycho."

I shrug, fresh tears spilling over. I shake my head. I don't know how to explain how displaced and splintered I feel.

"Well, you won." Wavern shakes their head. "But you're a wreck and it shows, and I don't want to see you get hurt out there."

"I'm almost... I'm almost there, Wavern..."

"I know. And I know I can't stop you... but there's foul play and... oh!" Wavern's back straightens, eyes huge. "All of the athletes who got bloodwork... they're all testing positive for some chemical I don't recognize, and the Parliament waved it through as noise in the tests..."

"What chemical?" As if I know squat about chemicals.

"Not a clue. But I mean, it's almost *everybody*, Thalon. It's something you've all been exposed to..."

"Kvell?"

"Not a chemical." Wavern takes my hand. Then their nose scrunches. "How long have your knuckles been swollen like this?"

"Since... this morning... I might have punched something..."

Wavern's scowl deepens. "Thalon... you're getting hurt out there... I've never seen you like this. This event is rigged..."

"Wavern…" I whisper. I nod to the radio clock. "Lexija is going to walk in here any minute…"

Wavern hops up and snaps each glove. "Good thing I've finished my examination. Diagnosis? Disaster. I'd get you out of this if I could, Thalon."

I smile. My face hurts. "You can't, Wavern. But I'm glad to see you. I'm so glad to see you…" My shoulders start shaking again.

Groaning, Wavern pulls me into a last hug. "Get your shit together, Aalgur Thalon."

Sniffling, I nod. Wavern slips out the door, unsuspected by the black-suited guards.

* * *

By the time Lexija leads me to the arena, I can hardly walk.

"I see you're feeling that fight with Rawl," she remarks. She doesn't look at me. She seems distracted.

I'm feeling more than that but keep it to myself. All I have to do is get through this fight. One move at a time.

"FIGHTING IN HONOR OF THE UNSPEAKABLE STORM, AALGUR THALON OF VATSKA!"

I limp into the arena. The glaring spotlights make my stomach churn. The spotlights rove to my adversary and my world goes cold as a winter night.

He steps into the light, tall, broad, confident. His ash blond hair feathers out of his helmet. He does not react. He looks at me as if I am a stranger, an obstacle.

Where is the boy I met in the schoolyard? The scared little pup I stood over and defended from a group of bullies. Where is the skinny twelve-year-old I sat with on the beach in Coven Cove and swore an oath to the gods?

*We train together. We fly together. By Brosk and the Ingvu, we'll crew the Duskingr together…*

There is no trace of that boy on my opponent's face.

"FIGHTING IN HONOR OF VOLIER THE NORTHWIND, KIPPER ARNFINS OF VATSKAAAAA!"

"Kip?" I whisper. *No, please, no.*

"ANNND, FIGHT!"

Kip walks toward me. He carries a short sword and a dagger on his hip. I watch him approach. Tears well in my eyes and I blink them away with a snarl. *Get it together, Thalon. You know how he fights. You know you're better.*

Kip lunges and knocks me off balance.

*You've trained together for years. You beat him in almost every fight...*

Kip doesn't make eye contact. He treats me like we've never met. White hot rage surges through my chest. I bash him with my shield and slice with Blitz.

It works, I back him up a step. I know his weaknesses, he always leaves his flank open...

I slash for the exposed skin of his upper thigh. My blade hits air. I stumble. Kip's big fist closes around my wrist. He wrenches my axe arm overhead and back. I try to hit him with the buckler but he torques my arm further. My shoulder pops.

"Kip..." I rasp.

Kip says nothing. A slick line whips across my thigh and he lets me go.

I stumble and trip, catching myself on my hands and knees.

Blood trickles down my thigh. I feel blistering heat and bone chilling cold. My lips are numb. Kip spits into the sand and grins.

The referee thrusts Kip's arm aloft. He strides from the arena without a backwards glance.

# THIRTEEN

"How could you make me fight Kip?!"

"You think I set that up? Sit the fuck down, Thalon." Lexija slams the door of my room behind her.

"How could you..." ...*make me fight my best friend.* I limp around my room. Instead of sitting on my bed, I kick the mattress.

Kip's eyes haunt me. He didn't even seem to care that we had to fight each other.

"I don't have time for your shit, Thalon. You fight who you fight, and Kip handed you your ass. Deal with it."

I hug myself and sob, loud, hideous sobs.

"Thalon!" Lexija stomps her foot. "You're already in the top twelve. You already made it on a ship. Slurping painkillers like soda even. I don't have time for a tantrum. Cool the fuck down!"

I wonder what that would feel like, to cool down. My body can't remember. With my eyes screwed shut, my teeth chatter and my stomach ties itself in knots. Kip beat me.

I clench my fists. I'm burning and shivering. My mouth waters and my sweat turns cold.

My mother's voice pounds in my head with every throb of pain.

She looms over me the day I accidentally bit Ashling. Her face is a mask of loathing. *If we'd known the gods would give us you, I'd...*

She later apologized. But the wounds had already been cut.

"S-sorry..." I stutter. My knee buckles. I can't even hobble into the bathroom and I throw up on the floor.

"Drag me to the depths, Thalon! What's wrong with you?" Lexija wets a cloth and hands it to me to clean my face.

I shiver and moan. Lexija unbuckles my armor and pulls it off. "What's this on your chest? Is this a rash? How long have you had this? Thalon? You need a doctor. Real doctors." A long, terrible pause. I can hear her swallow. "I'm pulling you out."

"No!" I lock my hand around her wrist. "No. You can't."

Lexija stares me down. "You can't fight like this."

"I have to."

"You don't. You can't. And frankly, I need to give my time to my winning fighter."

The words hit me like a fist. I sputter but nothing coherent comes out. After six months of training, am I nothing more than a paycheck to her?

"You said... we were a *team*, Lexija."

"Like you know the first thing about teams, Thalon. Now look. I'm calling the medics. You took your shot. This thing's not worth your life."

"*You have no idea what my life is worth!*" I shove her hand away and push myself back from her. Hot tears streak my face. I don't fight them anymore. I'm too tired to choose this battle. "I have to finish the tournament. I have to..."

"Alright... alright..." Lexija straightens up and rubs her eyebrows. "You have a point... you don't want an illness DQ, that could move someone else up to take your spot on the ship. Here's what you're going to do. This will be your last match, right? Walk out there, let your opponent cut you, walk off. It's a loss, it will mean you won't get a chance at a bonus... But you're not holding together for one more fight."

I weep, face twisted and blotchy. "I've worked my whole... my whole life for this, Lexija... I have nothing else..."

"That's not really my problem, Thalon. I need to go coach Kip now. Put yourself back together as best you can." Just like Kip, she leaves me without a second glance.

I lie on my side and sob.

*What are you?* whispers my mother's voice. *You're an animal. A stupid, vicious animal. A beast. If we'd known the gods would give us you, I'd...*

I cry until I can't anymore. And then I lie there, staring at the wall.

My door opens a crack and closes again. I turn just my head to look.

A single black bottle of Gadvig's energy drink waits for me.

* * *

"Remember, Thalon. Walk out there, get cut, walk back." Lexija tightens the strap of my helmet and places Gevit in my hands.

I nod. I can hardly hold Gevit. I can hardly stand.

The announcer calls my name and I limp into the arena. I squeeze my eyes shut until the spotlights move from me to my opponent. The audience shrieks like a cyclone.

"VATSKA'S OWN WARRIOR PRINCESS, AZOTO SEPPANEN!"

She steps into the spotlight, golden highlights in her unbound hair, a sway to her bare hips... gratuitous, jiggling boob armor. My insides turn ashen at the sight of her.

Azoto pumps a coil of leather in the air and roars for the crowd, a creature I never dreamed she could become. I do nothing. I am a husk, a shell. Gevit weighs so much, I almost drop her. A snap like a bolt of lightning jolts through me as Azoto cracks her whip. A whip! Metal barbs spark at the end of the leather, fangs of a supersonic snake.

"AND... FIGHT!" hollers the referee.

I "T" my hands and stagger right back off.

"Thalon! Thalon, what are you doing, don't be stupid..." Lexija shakes my shoulders.

I almost fall right then and there. Picking Gadvig's bottle off the weapons rack, I open it with my teeth and swallow the sweet, sticky tar.

"I'm fighting her," I say. I walk back out. The arena begins to slow. The sweet warmth of the drink spreads through me. I draw on that stolen strength and lift Gevit above my head.

Does the crowd cheer? Are they silent? I can't tell. My world has narrowed to Azoto Seppanen.

Azoto steps within range and snaps her whip at me. I take my chance and swing with Gevit. The tip of the whip spins tight around the shaft, I sweep the battle axe around. Grasping the whip in my swollen fists, I yank it from Azoto's grip and snarl.

Both Gevit and the whip clatter the floor, my proud old battle axe far too heavy for me now. I snap Blitz from my hip as Azoto draws her dagger. We begin to circle. Her black selkie eyes watch me. Her soft lips part as she breathes.

Instead of speeding me up like expected, the drink removes my sense of time. Where before a roar of flames filled me, now I find myself unable to move my body through the slow-motion world. Azoto flickers, in front of me one moment, to the left the next. Blank spots clutter my mind.

I put my foot down and can't feel the ground, like my leg's fallen asleep. I shift my weight and wobble. My left arm tingles. The exposed skin turns red and blotchy before my eyes.

Elren Johanson's face takes over my mind, his staring, sightless eyes. *I'm next*, I think.

Azoto slashes and I block out of instinct. The impact of steel-on-steel splinters through me like an earthquake. I gasp, staggering away from her. Azoto's black eyes follow me. The girl who could never decide between the pink or the yellow ballgown is gone, replaced by a stranger, a hunter out for my blood. Just like Kip.

Azoto blinks as she watches my numb, hobbling steps. She can see my pain. She can also see her victory. I hear murmuring from the audience, a grating of insect shells in my head. Sweat turns my long black hair to limp kelp around my face. Blitz shakes in my stiff fingers.

*Tophinghua, please...* I beg. But I know deep down, the God of Storm and Strife shows no sympathy for the weak.

Azoto's face sets in grim determination. She wades in, confident of her win. And yet, she hesitates, measuring me with her eyes, adding me up.

"Thalon?" murmurs Azoto's low, soft voice. Is there concern there?

I see her naked ass in the magazine, her frozen, professional laugh... Then, from long ago, I hear her real laugh, snorting and shrieky with mirth. I remember her fingers on me, in me, and the plush press of her lips on my skin.

Azoto slashes for my exposed arm.

I do the only thing I can think of. Rather than meet her weapon with mine, I slide to my knees and slip around her. It takes every ounce of Thalon to flick Blitz backhanded and up before she can block.

The slide, the spin, the strike, they take the last from me.

My blade connects, for the briefest of moments. Then I see only blinding white and the ominous, smoky red of the spotlights overhead. The stream of thyir inside me splinters into a thousand agonizing shards.

*Get up,* I order myself. *Get up. Don't give in. Tophinghua! Tophinghua, I need Your strength. I need to get up...*

Arms pull me into a sitting position. Someone screams like a dying animal. It's me, my voice screams.

Azoto supports me in her arms. Azoto holds my face in her rough gloves.

The megaphone thunders: "DO NOT TOUCH YOUR OPPONENT OUTSIDE OF COMBAT."

"Don't you tell me what I can and can't do!" hollers Azoto. "Get a medic. Get a fucking medic!"

Then, softer, her voice low and calm. "Thalon, no... come back... Thalon, what's happening? Come back..."

Behind Azoto, I see shadows of referees, of Lexija, of strangers. The rim of the stadium makes an oval in the sky. The spotlights stain the clouds bloody, luminous red. The Duskingr leers.

Darkness reaches up from beneath me and pulls me down, down, down.

I don't know if I drew first blood or not.

# PART TWO

BROKEN GIRL

# FOURTEEN

I wore a blue buckskin dress beaded with bits of whalebone. We shrieked with glee as the ground fell away below us. The sky opened and the world spread wide and yawning below. Propellers hummed as the dirigible angled over the ocean. I was twenty years old.

"I can't believe your father let us fly without a Kane." I ran a lap around the empty ship cabin and stopped behind the pilot's seat. I leaned over Azoto's shoulder.

"This isn't my first flight to Adlervik you know," countered Azoto. She wore over-the-ear headphones with a mouthpiece, for speaking to other ships and ground control. We climbed so high we could see the globe of the world, a droplet of water and dirt spinning through eternity.

Azoto raised a finger in my direction, pushing the headphones off an ear. "Father knows we're taking the *Cloudberry* to retrieve his shipment from Bonnybrite Farms for Mum's priss priss dinner party. What Father doesn't know..." Her gloved hand reached into her aviator's jacket and withdrew a pair of metallic copper tickets.

"No!" I shrieked. "No! You got them!"

"*Divine Jubilee.*" Azoto puckered her lips into a perfect plump bow.

The tickets glimmered. They felt heavy and priceless in my hand. "Your parents are going to *murder* you!"

Azoto lifted her shoulders. The golden highlights in her deep brown hair flickered in the sun. "Then I'll die happy."

Grinning so hard my cheeks hurt, I leaned over the pilot's seat. Our mouths met with nothing but the blue sky and blue sea around us. The kiss deepened and I could taste mint on her tongue.

Once, in a sky-blue dress on a blue-sky day, I had everything.

* * *

Ceiling tiles pass overhead as they roll me down a hall on a stretcher. Voices drone, people ask me questions. I can't understand. I'm in a hospital, that's all I know.

Strong hands sit me up and bend me over a pillow. I see a needle, a huge, gleaming needle. *You won't feel this*, they say. They slide the needle into my spine.

I feel it. I feel metal slip on my vertebra. The pain happens to me. I am powerless against it.

They lay me down, more needles pierce me.

*There's swelling of the brain and spinal cord. It's hard to say what caused it.*

They leave me in a room with no windows. Faceless shadows come and go, holding my useless hand or pushing my limp hair from my clammy face.

I float in a gray nothingness, neither living nor dead.

* * *

I met Azoto Seppanen because my parents didn't know what to do with me. A Priestess of Brosk made the introductions when we were little more than toddlers. We grew up together. Selkie girls against the world.

The best summer of my life, we worked together in the Seppanen fish market. It's technically illegal to employ children in Vatska, so Luka, Azoto's older brother, paid us in ice cream vouchers.

Throwing fish by day, passing ice cream cones back and forth by night, Azoto and I learned of our people's proud history as ambassadors of the sea. The Seppanen family worked hard to keep it that way, I learned. On weekends, Luka took us into the sea to teach us to hunt, to sing underwater, and to play a pirate game passed down from our ancestors.

Azoto and I learned other things. Secret, sacred things that happened between ice cream and when she bid me good night at Scallop Avenue before a Kane came and picked her up in a car. Like how it felt right to link our fingers together and feel the warmth of each other's hands. Like how we'd lie together on the beach in our pelts after hunting fish, using each other's body as pillows. Like how the orange of a sunset burns differently in a selkie girl's black eyes, or how soft her skin becomes when the seal pelt peels away.

* * *

"We're here!" Azoto landed the *Cloudberry* in Adlervik's central airfield atop a natural coastal hill, and let the ground crew guide the ship into a hangar. As soon as we reached the edge of the tarmac, we clasped hands and ran screaming into the enormous capital city.

We dashed through the shadow of the sandstone Parliament palace. *Divine Jubilee* lured us in with flashing lights and carnival music. Signage guided us to the underground playhouse and into another world of dancing animal automatons and low, sultry lights. A song played that night. It still haunts me.

Rides creaked and jangled, bells dinged as people won prizes, and buttered popcorn perfumed the air. But nothing could distract from the song.

That song, that pulsing, jarring, jumping song, it got into our blood like wine. We ran together to the dance floor. Spare kneepads lay in a pile for the taking, and we each grabbed a set. The song told a story, a fable of an ancient worm traveling down the river from the mountains. The story was important, it meant something to the people who brought *Divine Jubilee* to life. But at the time, it was meaningless to me. Only the music had meaning. It told me to dance.

Sweet heady smoke from fancy cigars twirled with us as the music pushed and pulled us through the ts'kmet. Toe, toe, heel, heel, we kicked out our legs and tapped the sides of our feet together. The dance threw us into the air and sent us skidding to our knees in wild displays of strength and agility. We pressed closer, legs hooking around legs, thighs sliding past thighs, chest to chest and cheek to cheek. We gave ourselves completely to that night and that music.

Then it ended, as all things do. We walked back to the airfield, Azoto's jacket over my shoulders, the scent of her soap and lotion clinging to my skin.

Back in the sky, I watched a flicker of green and blue in the far away dark. It formed a ribbon across the sea, shifting and swaying.

"Is that the Svall?" I pressed my hands to the window.

"Yes," whispered Azoto. "The home of the gods. The veil between our world and the Otherside. All the realms, really." She turned to me, brows lowered in mock offence. "Honestly, Thalon. *You've* competed in the Dusk Trials. You should well know this."

"Yeah well, I've never seen it for myself."

"Look into the Duskheim Mountains..."

I looked. The same blue and violet glowed deep in the wolf-jaw spires of the Duskheims. "It's in the mountains too?"

"Yes. They say it follows the water. The Svall always leads back to the sea. It crosses the continent to the south, too, sometimes. If there's a Svall Storm."

The glow of the Svall danced in the distance, eddies of blue and green fire.

"I want to see it closer..." I tucked my feet beneath me and leaned on the dash.

"That's the job of the Duskingr," replied Azoto.

Only the Duskingr traveled the Svall, I knew. I paid enough attention to know that. They used to sail through it. To other worlds, other times, long ago when we could move the ice. Even without the ice of our ancestors, the Duskingr were still the only ships that could approach the Svall. Anything else that got too close got pulled inside and sent to the gods knew where or when.

We sat in reverent silence for the rest of the flight. When we moored, Azoto took my hand and pulled me through the streets of Vatska.

"Where are we going?" I asked.

Azoto chuckled but said nothing. She led me down incoherent streets until we reached the Temple of Brosk. Then she pulled me through the pylons, into the deep and quiet dark.

"What are we doing?" I began.

Azoto shoved me to my back and pinned me to the sand. "I'm peeling that dress off of you, is what we're doing." Her hot breath stirred my hair. Her fingers undid the whalebone buttons.

As selkies, we saw each other's naked bodies daily. This time was different. By slivers of moonlight, I traced the curves of her supple body with my eyes. She shed her top, then her pants. No matter how many times you see a girl naked, when her hands touch you, when she nestles her warm weight atop you, it changes you.

We are creatures of thyir, capable of changing form. That night, the magic in our bones cast a different spell.

"I love you, Aalgur Thalon." Azoto's black eyes held the moonlight. "And I'm sick of calling you my friend."

I blinked, mind blank.

Azoto's soft hand slid over my belly. We kissed, long and wet and warm in the sand. I was twenty, she was twenty-one. We burned bright with thyir and other forces of nature. Her touch brought a glow to my belly as easily as if I had been a lamp in her hands.

"It can be like this, you know."

We kissed more and her fingers searched out other places. My calloused hands fumbled over her smooth shapes. She knew more about what to do than me, how to make a woman incandesce. She ignited my body, I gladly let her. She was a woman of magic, a sorceress. I was just a girl in the sand.

"We've danced this dance for years, you and I, Thalon," she whispered, low and husky in my ear. "I wish to take you as my wife."

"Yes…" I breathed. In that moment, the whole world made sense. "Yes…"

For a night beneath the Temple of Brosk, I was wanted. I was loved.

* * *

A week before the Midwinter festival, Azoto flew us back to Adlervik for dinner at the Cypress Inn. She wore her fur seal pelt fastened over one shoulder. I again wore my blue buckskin, but my pelt as well this time. Perhaps we would switch pelts tonight. I dreamed of the moment Azoto would place hers around my shoulders and claim me for her own, forever.

Instead of a warm fur, Azoto set a folder on the table between us. "We have to go over the prenuptials." She rolled her eyes. "You know how my family is."

I swallowed the blob of bread in my mouth, coughing out crumbs. "There's paperwork?"

"And that's all it is, paperwork." Azoto opened the folder. A pen lay at the ready in the crease.

The Seppanen crest shimmered in deepest green at the top of the document. I placed a finger on the text as if trying to hold it still. The words made no sense to me. I poked a sentence as if trying to squash an ant. "I must forgo all claim to Seppanen properties and assets?"

"Yes, but does that really matter? We will have everything we could ever need…"

I read the last paragraph three times before I looked back to her. "You won't allow me to compete in the Dusk Trials?"

Azoto picked up a slice of bread, turning it around in her fingers. "It's a conflict of interest. Seppanen family members don't compete directly. We offer boons to competitive hopefuls. It can't look like we're trying to get our people on the Duskingr. Even if we are."

An emptiness yawned inside me. "You want me to give up my dream?"

Azoto inhaled a long breath. "A pipe dream at best. And if you did win? Twenty years of your life."

I took a deep breath and read a bit more. To gain access to wealth and assets, Aalgur Thalon would need to be ordained a Priest, or complete tenure as a Duskingr sailor. I leveled my eyes on her. "But you're telling me I can't do that. You won't let me fight."

Azoto's exhale gushed with ire, like bellows in a furnace. "You aren't listening. You would never have to leave. The Duskingr would take *twenty years* of your life. We will have everything we'll ever need, Thalon. You and me. Us. *You don't have to prove anything*. You can live... you can quit that disgusting trawler job..."

"I have to..." I pressed my finger to the line on the contract about the Dusk Trials. I felt dizzy. "*I have to*."

I could feel Azoto's face grow hot across the table. "The gods damn it, Thalon, you don't have to be so damn proud!"

"Don't." My tears choked me. I stood from my seat. People around us stared and Azoto laughed her smooth, professional laugh to dismiss their curiosity. As if to say: *There's nothing interesting to see here*. Shame burned me as I let Azoto and everyone see me cry.

Knocking into my own chair, I stalked outside, to the balcony overlooking a ragged coast. Gray foam churned beneath me. I unfastened the brooch holding my pelt and tugged at my buttons with shaking fingers. When they didn't come free, I twisted my fists into the neck of the dress and tore it off myself.

"Miss?" asked a confused server.

"Thalon, stop! You're making a scene!" Azoto hurried onto the balcony.

I glared at her, stripped nude. The entire restaurant craned their necks to see the drama.

"Will I ever be what you want? Am I not enough?" I turned away from her, mind already made up.

"Damn it, why won't you choose us, Thalon?" Azoto's voice haunted my footsteps as I reached the rail, as I climbed up. "What do you have to prove?"

I dove into the water, I let my true form take me down, down, into the darkness.

What indeed.

* * *

DYING IN A HOSPITAL, MY MIND VENTURES OFF ON ITS OWN. IT WANDERS from a charred forest out onto a beach awash in starlight.

In this place, blue fire glows. It moves through a silken dance, like the Svall. I struggle closer, body clumsy, heavy, useless. I fall to my knees, unable to stand. Hand over hand, I drag myself across the sand, to the fire and the warmth.

The shadow of a man-beast blackens the stars above me. The beads in His braids and locs clack as He stirs the fire.

"Brosk..." I whimper. I drag myself closer, arm over arm. "Please help me..."

His lava eyes turn upon me and His mouth of polar bear teeth grins. Starlight shines from the back of His throat. The Brosk at the Temple is peaceful, a fatherly shepherd. This Brosk stokes the fire with the mast of a damned ship.

Brosk's voice rumbles, deep as tectonic plates. Hot coals fall from His mouth onto the sand. "Children of the land, children of the sea, cleaving yourselves in two, as you have split yourself in two, little one."

"What?" I croak.

"Child of Tawkthalon, you have felt Her, my daughter. The blood of the storm flows through you, and yet you cleave yourself in twain."

"No," I whimper. "I fought for Her. I lived for Her…"

Smoke rises from Brosk's nostrils. "And yet you deny Her, little one."

I can crawl no further. I lie in the sand and weep. "I would never deny Her…"

"Then see Her. You must see all She is and nothing less. You fell in battle with Her name on your lips. Her fire dies in you."

"Please," I beg.

"The ice moves for no one. Not anymore, child of Tawkthalon." Brosk holds a hand, palm down, over the fire. He turns the hand over, closes it, and presses it to His hairy chest. Then He begins to lumber away. A coat of sewn together animal hides drags in His wake.

"Brosk!" I weep. "Brosk… please help me…"

Brosk turns back to me. He leans over me, so tiny and pathetic in the sand. Embers fall from His mouth. He places a giant claw against my sternum. Something inside me twists and writhes.

"I am," He says, and shoves me backward into the sand.

I wake up alone in the dark. Tubes dangle from my arms like parasitic worms.

CHAPTER

# FIFTEEN

I come back to myself again through a heavy fog. My toes wiggle, then my fingers. My mouth tastes moldy. I squint my eyes open.

"There you are." Wavern sets a clipboard aside and reaches for my hand. Tubes hook into my hand and elbow. Above me, bags of fluids drip.

My eyes move from Wavern to the battle axe lying on the side table.

"Gevit?" I ask. My voice rasps like an unoiled door.

Wavern shrugs. "Don't look at me. You're the one who asked for her. You're high as the Duskheims." Wavern fetches me a cup of water. They hold it for me so I can take a sip.

The water makes me cough. My eyelids grow heavy, so very heavy. "Did I... draw first blood?"

Wavern exhales a long breath. "You've been in the hospital for two weeks. *Two weeks*, Thalon. You've had a spinal tap. Turns out your brain's in your skull after all and it was swollen. The Dusk Trials should be the farthest thing from your mind."

The words mean little to me. My eyes close, too heavy to keep open.

"Oh, she's awake?" asks a voice, a nurse most likely. Hands move parts of me around like a puppet. "Aalgur? Are you in pain?"

"Mm-hmm," I manage. I can't tell her what hurts, though. I am a continuum of pain, it seems.

Soon though, a warm fuzziness dilutes the pain, like waves pushing sea scum up the beach.

I reach for Wavern's hand. They take it and give it a squeeze. "Azoto came to sit with you a lot. Azoto Seppanen. She stayed right up until the last second before shipping out. Seems really nice, actually. I eat some of my words about trust fund kids and all that."

Tears slide down my cheek. I drift away with Azoto's honest smile in my mind. The memory of her silly laugh lulls me to sleep.

* * *

SEVERAL DAYS PASS BEFORE THEY LET ME LEAVE THE HOSPITAL. NURSES MAKE sure I can walk more than a few steps before fatigue crushes me. They make me walk the length of the hall before unhooking me from all my tubes. My left hand twitches and jerks.

"You've been quite ill, Miss Thalon." A doctor stops by to discharge me. "You had swelling around your brain and spine. You're doing great though! All things considered, you're doing splendidly."

"Why?" I whisper.

The doctor looks at her paperwork. "We couldn't find a definitive cause. But you're already up and walking. Give yourself a few weeks and you'll be right as rain!"

Wavern helps me out of the sickly hospital gown and into my own pants, shirt and arena boots. They then bundle me in my heavy canvas coat, and we wait for the ferry.

"Where are we?" I croak.

"Adlervik. The Seppanens flew you up. The hospital here has

better equipment, being next door to Parliament and all. Again, I eat my words about trust fund kids."

I shiver, even in the coat. I have no memories of the illness except for the needle. I can see the needle when I blink. I shiver harder.

When the ferry docks, Wavern helps me over and lets me lean on them. They hold Gevit for me.

The lapping wavelets outside the window lull me. My eyes flutter and I snap awake with a gasp when I see a stranger squinting at me.

"What?" asks Wavern, placing a hand on my arm.

I tilt my head. The stranger in the window tilts her head, hair matted and greasy. The wan, gray face, the hollow cheeks and black, haunted eyes... is me.

Wavern makes a pillow with their coat and motions for me to lie on the bench seat. "You've been on some heavy drugs. Why don't you try to get some sleep?"

* * *

WAVERN LETS US INTO THE APARTMENT THAT EVENING. THE WOODEN STATUE of Tophinghua leers at me from the counter. "You're... you're not afraid of Her?" I ask.

Wavern places my medications on the counter beside the figurine. "She's a force of nature, Thalon. Nature is powerful. Nature can be devastating. That doesn't mean we need to live in fear of it." They pick up the statue and walk over to set Her beside me on an end table. "She also literally re-carved herself when Brosk made Her wrong the first time. So, an absolute legend."

I turn Tophinghua just enough so She's not glaring at me. Settling onto the couch and curling up, my eyes rove around the room. Without Kip's belongings strewn around everywhere, the apartment feels sparse, naked.

"I'm sorry about Kip..." I look away as tears spring to my eyes, unexpected and unwelcome. I am not sure who my words are meant for, Wavern, or me.

"It was time." Wavern puts a kettle on the stove. "He was pretty, we had fun, he ate my eels... Now, I can get my research together to present at Adlervik University. Besides, I saw a different side of him in the Dusk Trials..."

"I used to worry he wouldn't make the cut... in the Blood Spire..." Tears spill over now. My shoulders shake. What did he feel when he cut me in the tournament? When he walked away without a backwards glance. Did our friendship mean nothing to him? "He beat me..."

"Thalon... you're just going to make yourself feel worse." Wavern takes a seat beside me. They wrap me in a quilt. Leaning over, they grab something off the side table and hide it in their sweater.

"What was that?" I ask.

Wavern pauses before passing the envelope to me. Opening it, I see my own face grinning back at me. AALGUR THALON OF VATSKA, reads the card. It lists my fighting stats. The woman on the trading card is a stranger to me. Painted, posed, aglow with life. But her eyes are haunted and sick. She knew she was sick. I can't bring myself to look at the other competitors and set the cards on the end table.

Wavern breathes out a measured breath. "I don't want to get your hopes up... There were a few days we weren't sure you'd be leaving the hospital... But someone from the Duskir Parliament will be coming in two weeks to see if you're ready to ship out. You're ranked twelfth among the new sailors. There's a thirteenth champion on standby if you're not well..."

"I'll be well," I state. "I'll be ready."

The kettle whistles. Wavern gets up to pour the tea, returning with steaming mugs.

"You can start by having some tea, a bit of food, and putting yourself in bed, Thalon. You look, respectfully, like a corpse."

I take the tea and do just as Wavern says, holding the mug in my good hand. Corpse I may be, hope spreads through me. A most delicious drug.

* * *

MY FIRST WEEK HOME, I DO LITTLE MORE THAN SLEEP. I WAKE UP NOW AND then and watch Wavern feed their eels and take notes on some Otherside device. By the start of week two, I use scrap paper to make a countdown sheet, crossing off days until a Parliament member comes to collect me. I set daily goals such as: "walk around the block," and "cook my own meal." Pain shoots through my left arm from shoulder to fingertip if I move it, so I wear it in a sling. I hobble around like someone three times my age, bent and shaking.

On the day with the goal "walk around the block," I walk all the way to the Temple of Brosk and back. I almost faint on my doorstep.

"You shouldn't push yourself. They literally have no idea what made you sick in the first place," Wavern scolds me.

"I know, I know." I drink my hot drinks, take my painkillers, and fall back asleep. I'm going to get better, I have no other choice.

One frigid late autumn morning, I set out with the intention of speaking to Hans. He bet on me, after all, and I didn't come through.

The foghorn drones from the lighthouse and leftover tourist trash skitters in the wind. I hobble to the open lot where the truckers camp. Some oil puddles and axle grease are all that remain of the Caravan for now. They will not return until around Midwinter.

Taking a seat on a log, I rest my forehead in my hands. I hope Hans is alright. I hope he didn't bet too much on me.

*Cortland...* I inhale a sharp breath. A stab of pain shoots through my shoulder. Cortland bet his ship... *But I placed. I made it...*

Nonetheless, I bundle tighter in my wool sweater and limp to the docks. By the time I reach the docks, I feel like I've hiked to the Duskheims.

I sink onto a bench beside some seagull shit. I hug myself and groan as the familiar headache throbs behind my eye.

"You alright, Miss? You sick?"

My head snaps up to see an angler in his waders. He keeps a safe distance from me.

"Recovering," I reply. My voice sounds like a broken whisper. Clearing my throat, I try again. "Is the *Golden Cormorant* at dock? Do you know?"

"*Cormorant*? Naw. Left a week ago." The angler kneads his hands together as he looks me up and down. "You'll catch your death out here, Miss."

"I'm fine," I snap. I stand to my full height. A wake from a passing ship rocks the dock and my brain goes mushy. I hold onto the railing to keep from losing balance. My cheeks burn.

"You need to get inside, Miss." The angler keeps his cushion of distance between us. "You have somewhere to go, don'tcha?"

"Yes," I growl. Shame burns through me as I turn and limp home. I am one of the twelve winners of the Dusk Trials. I wonder if he would treat me differently if he knew.

*It doesn't matter if he knows,* I remind myself. *Only four more days, and I never have to worry about any of this shit ever again.*

* * *

"I'm hoping we can get you as warm as possible before you throw yourself into that freezing water. A piece of an iceberg washed into the harbor yesterday, Thalon. An iceberg!" Wavern plies me with a hot, savory drink. I get myself wrapped in my pelt, my coat, and then a wool blanket over everything. Wavern even got me wool slippers. I shiver anyway.

The hospital took more out of me than I realized. Two weeks hooked to saline and two weeks on the couch have left me stripped to the muscle and bone. The points of my hips jut out, shadows fall beneath my clavicles and ribs, beneath my sleepy, dull eyes.

But today is the day, so into the sea I must go.

We amble down to the shore. Amble is all I can do. A bleak autumn drizzle beads on the wool blanket. It makes my face ache.

"Ms. Gadvig." I straighten up in surprise.

Gadvig turns to face me, flanked by two men. The men are

strangers to me, I haven't the faintest idea which one of them might be part of the Duskir Parliament. A third, younger man waiting off to the side gives me a nervous finger wave. He holds a pelt, he must be the back-up selkie.

I look up and down the beach, half hopeful, half in dread, but I do not see Valmut. Had I wanted to see her? Do I crave her support or am I ashamed of her seeing me like this?

"Miss Aalgur." Gadvig looks me over from head to slippers. "You gave us quite a shock in the Blood Spire, fainting as you did. We hope you are healing well."

I nod. I hope Gadvig doesn't notice how skinny and weak I look.

Gadvig turns to face the water, arms folded behind her back. "All we need to see is that you can shift. That your thyir is strong." Gadvig holds a hand toward the surf. "When you are ready, Miss Aalgur."

My teeth start chattering before I've even touched the water. I try to swallow and find my throat dry. *I just have to shift. Then I can get out and get warm... then I can lie down by the heater... All I have to do is shift and it will be over... I'll be free...*

"You alright?" Wavern whispers as I hand them my clothes.

The tightness around Gadvig's mouth has me on edge, the gray of her eyes as cold as the fog. The spare selkie shifts his weight from foot to foot and blows warm air on his hands. At least I'm not the only one who notices the weather. The two other men do not react at all.

"I'm alright," I whisper back. Am I though?

Clenching my jaw and forcing my aching spine straight, I step out of the slippers and walk to the water. After a brief ritual to Brosk, I step in.

The frigid waves hit my bare thighs and steal the breath from my lungs. The ice of the water digs into me like thorns. I force myself deeper. My chest convulses and I gasp for air. Black shapes cloud my vision as I push my weak, feverish body into the sea.

Gadvig and her associates wait on the beach, impassive as I glance over my shoulder, three crows in blue winter capes.

*I am the force to be reckoned*, I remind myself. *Tophinghua, I am Your daughter... let me serve You. Let me serve the Duskingr in Your honor...*

I breathe in, I exhale, I dive under. The ice-cold water shocks me. I inhale it, a wave drags me out. I suddenly can't touch the bottom. The sea rolls me, tumbles me. I struggle and thrash to the surface where I cough up salt water. I hold onto my pelt in one fist and kick to keep my head at the surface. My body is not my own, as if my soul has been placed in some pelt-less weakling. Expelling the water from my lungs, I grit my teeth and shift.

Nothing. The next wave rolls me, dragging me farther out to sea.

I flounder, sputtering for air, legs pumping and burning in the freezing water. I call on my thyir, my strong, steady flow of thyir, and shift.

The flow, the song of thyir in the water and my bones snaps. I bob up into the gray morning in the wrong body.

This time, I don't scream. It takes every ounce of strength and will to swim back to shore and crawl up the dry sand, skin over bones, teeth clacking.

Spare Selkie helps me in. Water soaks his clothes. He picks me up and sets me down beside Gadvig and her men.

"Thalon..." Wavern's voice sounds distant, as if filtered through a radio. Their hands bundle me in the wool blanket and separate me from my wet pelt. My body shudders, out of my control.

My vision blurs. Gadvig's meticulous leather shoes appear before me.

"We are sorry, Miss Aalgur Thalon." She does not sound sorry to me.

I look up and watch one of the men hand Spare Selkie a blue folder and pen.

Gadvig bends at the waist and sets a hand on my shoulder. "Without your thyir, you will not receive the benefits of a Headwaters sponsorship. We can see you are not fit to crew a Duskingr at this time, Miss Aalgur. Do take care of yourself."

"No…" I plead. "No, no… give me time… another week…"

Gadvig turns and walks to the sleek red automobile waiting on the street.

Wavern tries to lift me. "We need to get you home. Need to get you warm…"

Already on my knees, I sink to my elbows, press my forehead to the sand, and wail. Up on the road, the rich engine turns over and I look up, sand crusted to my tears. I watch everything I ever wanted, everything I thought I was, drive away.

# CHAPTER
# SIXTEEN

*On darkest night by firelight, the Ingvu hear your prayers.*
*Take off your skin and dance with kin, shed your worldly snares.*
*Fair Ryshvarad with eyes so blue, He sees your worries through and*
*through.*
*Let Zandruik set your fears to rest, She'll take to Brosk your dear request.*
*But the Dread One, let Him sleeping lie, beneath the blackened winter sky.*
*Let the Storm eternal slumber take, speak not His name, lest He wake...*

"Her," I mutter. I scrape uneaten food from a plate into a bin. Grabbing the next plate from the ever-growing tower, I repeat the process. The cheerful Midwinter carol sings over the radio. I try to ignore it.

The warm, deep winter bustle of Shanty's Chowder Shack clatters around me. I clear tables and prep plates for the dishwasher. Cinnamon bundles hang in the windows and thorny wreaths sparkle with tea lights. The smell of spiced chai makes my heart ache.

Or, maybe my heart just aches. The rest of me sure does. Two months have passed since my release from the hospital, and I've hit a plateau.

I plop a bus tub on a table and inhale slowly through my nose. Some kids cracked open their Spindel bottles and scattered the plastic beads all over the mashed potatoes. I pick them out one by one with a fork and hiss air through my teeth.

"Thalon, please clean table six so we can seat the seven top." The lead server takes over the Spindel disaster for me.

Grabbing an empty tray, I pick my way over. Crackling fire in the hearth, merry voices on the radio, smiling families, and festive spirits. I navigate slowly through it like a ship over a submerged reef. Something went haywire in my brain after the Dusk Trials. I walk into chairs, tables, and people, not entirely aware of where my own body is in space anymore. I limp. If I do too much, my left arm starts twitching.

I clear table six and waddle the bus tub behind the bar. The first hefty soup bowl I lift out slips from my fingers and cracks in half on the floor. Chowder splatters my boots.

"Thalon." The lead server, Wilk, gives me a look from across the room. "Thalon, your shift's up in ten. Go ahead and clock out. Don't forget we're closed for the holiday. Use the time to rest, won't you?"

*Yeah, yeah,* I think as I scoop broken ceramic into the trash. *Rest. A lot of good that's doing me.*

Outside bloated, thunderous green clouds hang over me as I limp off the wharf. Holiday cheer spirals around me; wreathes and bells, little effigies of the Ingvu dangling from lamp posts. Sentimental voices on the radio harken in the season of family, gratitude, and togetherness. I stare at the ground as I walk, trying to ignore it.

When I reach the apartment though, the warm briny smell of fresh baked sourdough warms my heart just a little. I let myself in and prop my boots by the door just in time for Wavern to slide a tray of round, deep golden loaves onto the counter.

"No touchy." Wavern bounces a finger at me as the smell reels me in like a fish on a hook. "These are for the fish-head stew, which comes after the eel eggs."

"Ah right. The eel deal." I sink onto the couch and pull my hair out of the bun I wear at work. The memory of Gadvig's fancy car driving off crushes down on my shoulders. I haven't tried shifting since then, not even in the shower, but Wavern still insists they need me for the eel eggs.

Fancy stationery catches my eye from the trash bin. I can see the letterhead stamped with the Anchor of Brosk.

"What are the letters from the Temple?" I ask.

Wavern uses their foot to crush the contents of the trash down to the bottom. "Just... you know, those 'we're so pure and generous... please give us money,' things. Don't worry about it."

Wavern plops down onto the couch beside me and sets a slice of steaming bread and melting butter in my hand. "Here, a down payment." Wavern twirls an orange plastic keychain shaped like a star between their hands. "I appreciate it, you know. I can't hold my breath like you can and I just... sink. I'm denser than I look."

Thalon of two months ago would rib Wavern a little about being dense. All I do now is eat my bread and try not to think.

Wavern pats my back and hops up. "When you're ready, Thalon. I've already got the jars prepped."

* * *

The typical Vatska fog rolls up Coven Cove from the gray, steely water. Limestone cliffs cup the cove and charred bonfire pits pepper the sand, remnants of beach parties and other festivities. To the south, the wide mouth of the Erling River meets the bay. The unsettled green of the threatening thunderstorm growls along the horizon.

I shiver in my coat and wool slippers.

"Don't like, dillydally in there." Wavern hands me a jar and gloves. "It's egg season, there should be plenty. Grab some and get out so we can go home and cook you alive in hot stew."

Exhaling a heavy breath, I strip and hand my clothes to Wavern. I offer my palms briefly to Brosk and trudge into the frigid water.

"Seagull sucking... shit-cicles!" I squeal through my teeth at the breathless bite of the water. Was the sea always this cold?

Sooner I'm done, the sooner I can leave. Reminding myself I have to hold my breath in my human form, I gulp air and duck under. Bubbles fill my ears and I paddle with clumsy strokes down to the reefs. Sardines flicker silver and rainbow glints of Spindel beads wink from crevices. Gods, those things are everywhere.

A peace folds around me. I close my eyes and realize, I feel like a stranger here, in this place I once called home. Out of instinct, I reach for the thyir in the water. It's there, dancing out of reach, just beyond my fingertips. My bones ache in the cold.

Spotting a patch of slimy eel eggs, I scoop them into the jar and flop back to shore.

"Excellent! Good, you got a good sample." Wavern pats my back and rubs me down with a towel before smothering me in my coat. They hold up the jar of eggs and jelly against the sky. "An eel's a deal, friend. It's fish-head stew tonight!"

* * *

"Well the gods drag it all to the depths..."

I open my eyes from the couch to see what has Wavern in such a tizzy. My bread bowl of stew sits on the end table next to Tophinghua, mostly untouched. The swim left me too tired for much appetite. What a miserable selkie, can't even collect on an eel deal, of all the stupid things.

Wavern spins themselves away from their microscope and drags their hands down their cheeks. "So much for *fucking* controls..."

"What?" I ask when Wavern begins typing with fury into their foldable Otherside device.

"It's nothing you did, don't worry..." Wavern rotates on their spinning stool and squints into their microscope. "It's just... damn it. The eggs are corrupted. It's like our cove eels are interbreeding with the sludge eels now... That's the only thing I can think that would make the eggs like this..."

Stinking, slimy sludge eels swim through my mind. My nose wrinkles at the memory of their stench. Lying on the couch, listening to my friend grouse, I'm far more concerned about Wavern's impending departure to the university in Adlervik than eels. After Midwinter, we'll be parting ways and I hate it.

"Maybe they're contaminated," I say.

Wavern's head snaps to me, green-streaked hair bouncing. "What was that?"

"You know, contaminated. Like how Spindel beads are all over the reefs. Maybe there's something dirty in the water... I don't know, Wavern. I'm not a scientist." I'm not an anything anymore, am I?

Wavern blinks at me and then leans over the Otherside device. Their green fingers tap with furious intent. "Something in the water... something in the water..."

*  *  *

I dream of my childhood home on Scallop Avenue. My bare feet sneak down the wooden staircase.

"I don't know if..." Papa speaks in a hushed voice to Momma. "Aal." He smiles when he sees me.

The bundles of cinnamon, the tiny paper lanterns and tray of treats on the table tell me it is Midwinter, Kindling's Eve. A leather-wrapped gift waits for me. I am twelve years old.

Momma unties the leather thongs. "This thing was meant for... someone like you, Aalgur. It's just been collecting dust in the basement. We haven't really known what to do with it..." She pushes it toward me.

My heart thuds in my ribs. The leather opens to reveal a double-bladed battle axe. Remnants of runescript ghost over the blades and handle.

"It was called Gevit... in Zahlek that means thunderstorm, or something like it…" says Momma. "It's been passed down for centuries now. To the selkie women. The daughters of Tawkthalon."

"It's… mine?" I whisper. I lift the heavy, awkward axe in my soft little hands.

My childhood home explodes in a shower of sparks. Brosk leans over me, huge as the sky.

"Daughter of Tawkthalon! You deny Tophinghua?" thunders Brosk.

He reaches both hands over me as if to grab me and tear me in two. But then He turns His hands over, closes them, and brings them to His chest. Lava drools over me from His glowing mouth. I startle awake, drenched in sweat and clutching my throat.

"Brosk again?" asks Wavern from the kitchen, elbow deep in eels.

I cough but otherwise say nothing. Rolling my back to them, I let the tears spill across my face. I was a daughter of Tawkthalon once. A daughter of Tophinghua. What am I now?

* * *

THE EEL EGG RETRIEVAL TOOK A HEAVIER TOLL THAN EITHER I OR WAVERN anticipated. I doze on the couch, getting up only to use the toilet, shower, or pick at food when a bit of hunger surfaces.

"You're coming tonight, right?" asks Wavern, several days into my sofa era.

"Coming where?" I croak.

"Tonight's the Burning Tree. Kindling's Eve? Midwinter? Ring any bells…?"

I scowl. "Today's Midwinter…?"

"Believe it or not, time still passes in the right direction." Wavern brings me a mug of hot mulled cider. "We'll go together. It'll be fun. A little fun would do you good."

* * *

I find myself squished between teenage girls and Wavern in the field we used for training grounds just a few short months ago. Not far from here, the Illuet once watched me fight. I had an entire future waiting for me then.

Hunched in the cold, I sniffle, not feeling any of the fun Wavern mentioned. An enormous pyre looms beside a small, festive stage. We call it the Burning Tree, even if it looks nothing like a tree. It's built from a broken ship's mast and adorned with offerings. A string quartet plays cheerful holiday music.

"Oo, this is so fun!" squeals one of the girls. "I've never seen them light the tree on fire before! Back home they just put electric lights on it!"

"You're in for a treat!" encourages Wavern.

A scowl etches into my face. What am I doing here?

I don't have time to ponder. Three priests of Brosk in fur-lined coats and crowns of walrus tusks climb the steps onto the stage. They form a crescent around the microphone. "Good evening and Blessed Burning of the Tree!" They greet us.

The priests talk at unnecessary length about keeping the fire of the Burning Tree alive in our hearts the whole year through.

My mind wanders off. I wonder if they're celebrating Kindling's Eve on the Duskingr. I wonder if Kip or Azoto are thinking of me.

"And now, as master of ceremonies, please give a warm welcome to Lars Seppanen!" The priest places the microphone back on the stand and bows the Seppanens onto the stage.

The crowd cheers, of course. Lars Seppanen, Azoto's father, claps as he walks on, waving and smiling his perfect magazine-cover smile. A representative from *The Coastal Post* snaps a photo of him and his wife, Hannahlesh. They hold up little brown fluffballs, a litter of Seppanen grandchildren, no doubt, and pose in front of the ship mast pyre. The family, which also includes the two grown sons, Jalmari and Luka, their wives, and some of the older but well-behaved grandchildren, take seats in the middle of the stage while an elderly Kane woman minds the fresh little pups. Two other hulking members of the Kane Clan join the stage, a man and a woman, bigger even than Rawl. They wear silver clasps fastened on their braids and their bottom tusks are buffed ivory white. They lurk at the back of the stage like stone giants. Wherever Lars Seppanen goes, his chum, Brenntavoni "Bently" Kane is never far. Tonight, I see the back of his gray head at the front of the audience.

Lars Seppanen keeps smiling and waving at the crowd, eyebrows raising and teeth sparkling as he pretends to recognize people. He finally steps up to the microphone. Unlike the priests of Brosk in their ceremonial garb, Mr. Seppanen wears a stylish, high-waisted suit and capelet, short black hair mussed just enough and not a tad more. For a man in late middle age, he carries the trim, youthful good looks only money can buy.

"Oh my gods, Daddy Seppanen's *so hot*," giggle the teenage girls. The way they say *Daddy* makes me want to stab them in the throats with a screwdriver. Wavern cackles.

"Welcome Vatska friends and travelers!" beams Lars in his transcontinental radio voice. Taking the microphone off the stand, he strolls right up to the front of the stage to address us.

"This has been a hell of a year, hasn't it? Just two months ago we celebrated the Dusk Trials and the choosing of seal folk to serve the Duskingr alongside our huldror brethren..."

*Brethren?* My nose wrinkles. Kip would have something to say about that. Well... Kip's an asshole. Not a citable source, as Wavern might say. I can't believe him... I still can't believe him.

Lars says something else, but I don't tune back in until he starts in about the tradition of the Burning Tree. I'm too busy seething about Kip.

"It's easy to take for granted where our stories come from. Sure, the Burning Tree might be a fun holiday tradition, a worthy excuse to drink mead and eat smoked salmon..."

*I bet you eat smoked salmon every damned day, Daddy Seppanen...* growls my mind.

Lars holds up a somber finger. "But it is important to remember what it stands for. The Burning Tree represents Brosk's fire, ever blazing in the Svall to guide us. It represents the turning over of the clocks of the world, a moment to not only look to the future, but to give thanks for the past. And it also represents the forces of nature that move and guide our world: thyir, kvell, and the Svall itself, always in a careful dance with one another."

Lars walks one step at a time across the front of the stage, leather shoes so supple, they've never seen dirt. "As we prepare ourselves for revelry, I am reminded of the story of the Ingvu, Ryshvarad. We all know the story of how a young and naive Ryshvarad bound himself to the soul of a dead human boy, simply because he coveted the boy's good looks, only to be shackled by the burden of the boy's grief, essentially tethering himself to a mortal life. In doing so, he learned humility, patience, and the value of the life we often take for granted."

Bold of Lars Seppanen to speak of humility with his personal airship, the *Cloudberry*, moored in the background.

"As Ryshvarad learned these values through his own folly, so too must we of Vatska and beyond. As the tides shift, our inaction becomes a deliberate step away from the paths of our ancestors. Unity, community, and cultural preservation are values we must choose, and choose again, and keep choosing, lest they slip away forever." Something akin to genuine worry tarnishes his perfect smile. "We must remember: We are more than one.

"And so, with those thoughts in our minds, I invite you, friends and family, to join me in igniting the Burning Tree of Vatska and welcoming in a season of both reflection and change."

Everyone claps as expected and Lars wrangles his whole family to light the torch. They hold it up to the fuel-soaked pyre until the flames leap into the black sky.

Still on the back of the stage, the two lumbering Kane brutes make sneaky hand gestures at each other and chuckle. I wrinkle my nose at them. Smug shits.

I'm not sure what Lars's speech was about. Likely some stunt to butter up *The Coastal Post* for his upcoming campaign. Long has Lars coveted a seat on the Duskir Parliament, but as neither a Selkie Chief nor a Huldra Illuet, his efforts garner little attention. Not that Selkie Chiefs are more than relics, but Lars still isn't one. For the best, to be sure. As if the Seppanens need more influence.

Still, my eyes drift to the *Cloudberry*. Did they really fly me up north to the hospital?

Hannahlesh, in her white fur gown and icy blonde hair, picks up the microphone. "Chai and mead for everyone! And please join us for singing, dancing, and games!"

While I want nothing to do with either singing or games, I do let Wavern drag me to the mead.

As Wavern and the teenagers pour mead in giddy abandon, my head ratchets toward the stage. Rollicking music begins to play. Laughing people step into line, guided by the wordless melody. They link arms for the ts'kmet. Their feet kick, toe, toe, heel, heel. The fast-paced dance spreads through the crowd like a communicable disease. Most folks stick to the basic steps, but a few young folks throw in the jumps and knee skids like Azoto and I used to.

The dance gnaws at me, pulling me by the heart. My feet remember the ts'kmet. I allow them a few steps, a little kick... Why shouldn't I enjoy the night?

My knee crunches and pain stabs through my hip all the way up through my ribs. I grasp the edge of the mead table to keep from falling.

*I can't dance*, I realize. My leg trembles. *I really can't dance anymore.*

Unaware, Wavern laughs and cheers with the squealing girls. Before anyone can get the bright idea to overpower me into festivities, I steal an entire bottle of mead from the refreshment table. I limp as quickly as possible to the Temple of Brosk to drink it.

* * *

Why did Azoto Seppanen enter the Dusk Trials? With half a bottle of honey wine in my stomach, my fuzzy brain decides to stew on Azoto. I haven't been drunk in years and have no tolerance. I don't care. How could being drunk be worse off than I am? I sit in the sand beneath the Temple and lean against a support pillar.

But Azoto... yes, the hussy. Bare-shiny-ass-in-a-magazine Azoto. What could she possibly hope to gain from entering? And after all the talk of conflicts of interest, ha! I hope she's broken every perfect nail.

I take a long drink of sweet, spicy mead. There's no good reason other than to beat me at my own game. That's the only reason I can think she'd join: to humiliate me. I barely remember that she brought me to the best hospital in Ruhnsvalla.

And she did, she beat me at my own seagull sucking game. I hurled myself over the railing of that stick-up-the-ass restaurant five years ago. I suppose this was her way to get back at me.

"Cheers to you, 'Zoto." I hold the bottle aloft and take a long swig for her.

Between my bad leg, shit balance, and alcohol, I lean on fences and walls, crawling along like a starfish to get home. By the time I arm-over-arm my way back to the couch, the righteous anger at my ex melts into a smothering melancholy. Azoto's face fades to Kip's. He walked away without a backwards glance. Did our friendship mean nothing to him?

Corking the bottle, I stash it and curl up in my pelt. I run my hands through the plush, oily fur. I couldn't even dance the ts'kmet tonight.

I stare into the kitchen wall. In the glow of the eel tank, I see Elren Johanson's dead black eyes staring back at me. Just a kid with everything to live for. If I'd known where I'd be today, I would have gladly and willingly taken his place.

# SEVENTEEN

Midwinter passes as quickly as it came. The ashes from the Burning Tree get raked up and the *Cloudberry* stuffed back in her hangar.

Back in Shanty's Chowder Shack, I pretend like I care about my work. Wilk won't put me on serving yet, but I try to look as friendly and approachable as possible while busing tables. If anyone recognizes me from the Dusk Trials, they don't show it, talking around me as I reach for stray utensils.

I load my tray with glassware from an empty table and heft it to my shoulder. It feels steady. I smile, glad to feel my muscles work a little. Then, the whole thing crashes over the empty table beside me. Colorful drinks splash outward like fluids in a crime scene.

"Thalon! Gods damn it, Thalon..." Wilk spins to me. Guests lean back in their chairs and whistle at the wreckage.

"Ohh, that sucks," whispers someone.

"Is she... alright?" whispers another.

"It's alright. It's fine. Go take five." Wilk points me to the back and flags over the other busser.

I hunch over in the back of the prep kitchen, eyes closed. As tall as I am, in my corner I'm small, skinny, and gray. I sniffle in shame. Sometime later, Wilk lets himself in.

Wilk flings his gloves into the trash and pulls up a crate beside me. "You're looking pretty awful, Thalon."

I keep my eyes on the floor. "More so than usual?"

"Somebody asked if you're contagious."

"It's not contagious." I snuffle snot back up into my nose and rub the twitchy pain in my arm.

"Well, you've got the next few days off..."

Ah yes. To help Wavern get packed and on the ferry to Adlervik.

"Before you come back, I'm going to need you to get a doctor's note, just to make sure..."

"I've been to the clinic a million times. They can't do anything for me."

Wilk presses his lips into a hard line. "Thalon. I don't want to sound mean about this, but if you can't get it together, you're not going to be able to keep working here."

My hands clench. "I need this job..."

"Then go get that note. Maybe they'll be able to help this time. You do look terrible."

"Thanks," I mumble.

* * *

I MAKE IT THROUGH THE REST OF THE SHIFT IN THE BACK AS A DISHWASHER. By the time I hobble off the wharf, my spine feels fused from standing so long. Around me in the dim gray evening, Vatska's community volunteers have already stripped down the Midwinter decorations. Without the pops of color and cheer, the city feels desolate.

I hobble in the direction of the apartment, hood up, eyes down. I think about losing the job at the Chowder Shack. I can't even cut it as a busser. My stomach clenches. The Midwinter Burning Tree blazes in my mind. To the depths with work, I can't even dance anymore. Will I ever dance again?

A smell hits my nose like a slap to the face. Sticky, oily cotton candy and rot... my mouth waters.

A car honks at me and I shuffle out of the street. I sniff the air like a hound. My heart picks up and my eyes rake the store fronts. Where's it coming from? I follow the smell right up the steps of the Ivory Inn and into the smoky parlor. The last time I was here, I ran up three flights of stairs like a caffeinated pup to watch the Duskingr arrive. Today, just the stairs to the parlor leave me wheezing.

A few rough sailors lean around a billiards table while a cluster of even rougher looking folks my age pass a small, black bottle between them.

My eyes follow the bottle as it moves from mouth to mouth, the viscous liquid clinging to their tongues. I barely see their yellow teeth and sallow complexions, I remember time slowing down just for me, I remember the fire burning up my pain and clearing my head.

"You need something?" asks one of the group, a man with hollow eyes and nervous, spidery hands. He wears an expensive, high-waisted suit, now beleaguered with stains and frayed threads, complete with a rumpled pocket square. He lifts a fresh, sealed bottle from his pocket and gives it a shake.

My voice sticks in my throat. My body remembers those hands, those eyes, the jaw once frothing in blind rage. "Erik Leivara?"

"Who's asking?" Erik looks me over as if assessing the palatability of sidewalk bacon.

I go still and smooth my expression. My stronger right leg takes a partial step to better distribute my weight. My hands hover around chest level, ready to snap up in defense.

Erik is changed. His suit coat hangs loose on his frame and his eyes dart, expression caught between wary and jovial, grinning yellow teeth and blank, desperate eyes. But he's still strong, still nimble, still capable. I am crippled. His parting words to me ring in my head: *I'll kill you! I'll kill you, filthy welp!*

My stomach twists. "I am. I'm asking..."

"Look, I'm not in the market for *friends*." Erik puts extra stress on *friends*. "Go look at someone else like that." I can smell the dark liquid on his breath.

I point to the bottle hanging loose in his fingers. "Where did you get that?"

Erik snorts. "Don't shake me down, skank. This is the last of the shipment." He places the glass bottle on the edge of the billiards table. I can see the unbroken wax and a remnant of the Parliament bindrune seal. My heart throbs in my throat.

"I... I need that." I reach into my pocket for my wallet. "I'll buy it from you..."

"Dealer won't take too kindly to resales," says Erik.

I go still. "Dealer?"

"Wait... I know you." Erik takes a step around the table.

A chill grips my chest and I steady my balance.

Erik's expression twists, his lip curls over his stained teeth. He speaks in a whisper. "Aalgur Thalon. You... you *bitch*. You took *everything* from me. Everything..."

*Run,* pleads the voice in my head. *Run away, you can't even bus tables, he's going to tear you apart...* I snarl my teeth instead. "What did you fucking call me?"

"I had the deal of a lifetime... I was *set*. And you..." Erik telegraphs his intention from his bared teeth, through the rotation of his torso, and along his arm as he doubles it back. He's fast but the swing is obvious and open, aimed at my face.

I duck the fist and charge into him. My hands hook around the backs of his thighs, my momentum lifts him from his feet and crashes him into the billiards table. I hear his spine crunch.

But I crunch too. My shoulder pops, little zings of electricity zap through my left arm. I'm a moment too slow as I disengage.

Erik's fists twist into the front of my coat and he throws me off him with a yell. My weight lands on my left leg and it buckles. I scramble to catch myself but bounce off the garish wallpaper. The wall doesn't give, it hits me like a streetcar, and I land on my hands and knees.

Erik dives for me and I scramble. My limbs feel thick and heavy, the breath I gasp burns my lungs and stomach as the deep, bone-rotting fatigue of my endless sickness begins to take hold. Riding the sudden, blinding wave of fear, I launch myself across the billiards table.

"I'll kill you for real..." Specks of spit fly from between Erik's teeth.

Erik's comrades back away, hooting and chuckling. "Skank's gonna get it now..."

I misjudged my leap and land half on, half off the green felt table. I yelp as my ribs crush against an unforgiving ball. I reach out, fingers blind and searching...

Erik claws his way over the table like a rabid badger and kicks me the rest of the way off the other side. I hit the floor with a thud, legs awkward in the air. A ceiling fan spins lazy circles through the cigar smoke above me. I roll as Erik lands, shoving myself away with my legs.

I bump into one of Erik's chuckling cronies and tear the cue stick right out of his grasp. Staggering up, I whip the cue across my body like a spear or staff. It feels agile in the smoky air, fast. Now we're talking.

Red flashes over my vision as Erik's fist connects square with my jaw. I balance for a moment, thoughts wiped blank. The triumphant cue slips from my hands and clatters away. I don't feel myself fall. I do feel Erik's steel strength latch onto me and heave me onto my belly. I feel his fist twist into my long, loose hair. He wrenches my head back, back. My spine arches, my hands grab for anything, any bit of him. He pulls my head farther than it should go, exposing my throat.

A glint of metal catches my eye. A knife? He has a knife?

Is this it then? For one moment, I stop fighting. I'm so tired.

"That's enough of that!" a voice bellows through the haze.

The hand in my hair tightens.

"I said, that's enough!"

The hand lets go. Erik's weight leaves me as three of his friends haul him back and away.

With nothing supporting me, I lie on the floor with my face between my elbows, coughing and choking. Blood flows from my nose. I sputter it out of my mouth.

A fist grabs the back of my coat and drags me toward the door of the inn. I get my feet under me before the Ivory Inn employee hurls me into the street. I stumble and slip to my hands and knees, cutting my palms on the asphalt.

"I tolerate you Katch junkies but fighting's a hard limit."

Katch? "I'm not..." I croak. I cough and spit blood on the pavement. The Ivory Inn rocks, or maybe it's my vision rocking.

"I see you again, I'm calling the police!" The employee yanks the door closed.

In the street, I cough and shiver and wipe my bleeding nose on my coat. My body trembles. I push myself up to a sitting position and for a moment, I'm not sure I can stand.

But I have to. I have to get home.

With my mostly uninjured right hand, I grope around the inside of my coat until my clumsy fingers close around a black glass bottle.

* * *

"Gadvig gave me Katch! It was Katch!" I slur as I stagger into the apartment. The backswing of the door sends me crashing to my hands and knees all over again. Fresh hot blood plinks to the floor from my nose. "Ow! Gods damned seagull sucking, cod coddling... mollusk mothered..."

"Is that life I hear?" Wavern hurries in from their room, arms teetering with books. "You look..." They balk and drop the books. "Krescean's sake, Thalon! What happened to you?" Grabbing my arm, Wavern hoists my much larger frame onto the couch. They fetch wet paper towels to clean my face and press an icepack to my swelling jaw.

"Were you... you weren't in a *fight*, were you?"

A pause. I don't deny it.

"You were *fighting!* Thalon, my gods. I know you're sick, but do you have to be an idiot to boot?"

I cough phlegm and blood into a wet wad of paper towel. Wavern rubs their temples, muttering, then stoops to clean my blood off the floor.

"There's potpie soup, if you can even eat it with your jaw knocked halfway off the map like that..." Wavern looks up from the blood smear on the floor. "What do you mean Gadvig gave you Katch?"

I use my feet to peel my boots off and kick them toward the door. I lift the black glass bottle. It shakes in my unsteady fingers. "This is the same exact shit. Same exact bottle... still sealed shut... and this one still has a scrap of the Duskir Parliament seal..." I cough some more and hold it a little closer to Wavern. "This is what she... gave me in the Blood Spire. When I bit Rawl..."

Wavern scowls at the bottle and holds it against the light. "You're *sure* this is what Gadvig gave you? Gadvig, like Headwaters Gadvig?"

"Yes." I press the ice to my jaw. I hope it just feels crooked. Safe in my own home, an aching, nauseous fatigue seeps through my muscles. I fight to keep my eyes open.

Wavern gets out a magnifying glass and takes the bottle into the bright kitchen. "You can kind of see the Duskir Parliament seal...got a little bit stuck on there still. I'll need to do a chemical analysis... but that'll have to wait until they let me into the university... There's *no way* what Gadvig gave you was Katch..."

Sludge sloshes through my mind. "What about... I remember you said everyone's bloodwork was weird?"

"It was. Pretty much everyone's. But as far as I could tell, only a few of you got the rabies juice. Still. This puzzle just keeps getting weirder and weirder." Wavern rolls the bottle in their hand. "It's okay if I take this, right?"

My body remembers how that goo burned away the sickness in my bones. Will I ever feel that good again? I hesitate a moment too long for my own liking. "Take it."

Wavern tucks the bottle into a box. My breath catches.

When the bottle disappears, I rest my head on the arm of the couch and close my eyes. Tears slide across my swollen face.

Wavern plops beside me and rubs my back. "You're going to be okay when I leave, right? I should stay that extra day to make sure you get moved into the work-share house alright... Make sure you don't get into any more fights."

My jaw trembles. "No. I don't need help..."

"We all need help sometimes, Thalon. You've helped me tons."

"Oh?" I force my eyes half open. "Name one time."

"Well, well..."

"Ha..."

"Well, I'm stacking up points in my favor, like those punch cards at the ice cream parlor. Ten dinners, one free help from Aalgur Thalon. Oh! You get things off the top shelves for me. You open jars!" Wavern claps.

I shake my head. "Save that Thalon punch card for me, will you? It gives me... something to shoot for."

"Yes! A goal. You're a girl of goals. A project might really lift your spirits. I hope the Werkhaus can give you that again. And keep you out of... how *did* you get in a fight anyway?"

"Oh, you know. I'm just so charming."

I force myself to sit up. It makes me feel woozy and faint. Wavern's hand still rests on my back. I reach up and take it, holding it in mine. "You've been wonderful, Wavern. I mean it. I don't know what I would have done without you. You're a good friend. Scratch that from the records: You're a *great* friend."

"And you're pretty great yourself." Wavern tucks up their knees and pulls their knit sweater over them. "I'm... really worried to leave you. I know you're working and stuff but..."

"You have to take those eels to the big science people."

Wavern squeezes my hand. My eyes drift close again.

"I wish I could have gotten to know you better, the real you, I mean," Wavern mutters. "Whatever kind of girl you were before you buried the bitch under Dusk Trials and despair. She's in there. I know she is. But you're going to have to be the one to dig her out. For you and for the people I'm sure you'll meet. I've got shit to do."

"I hope you do it, Wavern. Whatever you're doing with kitchen eels. I hope it's all you've hoped for."

Wavern blows air through their lips. "I suppose we'll see."

We sit in silence for a while, watching the heaving rainclouds sweat outside.

Wavern takes a breath. "Thalon?"

"Hm?"

"Don't give up, okay?"

"Okay," I say. I place my hand on Wavern's back now. I don't know how to tell them, in some ways I've given up already.

* * *

The next day I see Wavern down to the ferry station and wave them off. There they go, boxes full of kitchen eel notes. When the ferry sails out of sight, I let myself crumble and cry. The currents will likely never cross our paths again. Wavern was right. Had I not buried myself in the Dusk Trials until I broke, we could have been better friends.

But those weren't the choices I made. I chose pride.

A fluting, jangling music catches my ear. Yellow headlights shine in the distance. The Karrvoss Caravan rolling in. Ducking my head, I limp for home as quickly as I can. Shame aches in my chest. My cheeks burn. I can't look Hans in the eye. I don't need another reminder of how terribly I failed or how many times I've lost.

# EIGHTEEN

I lived in Vatska's Werkhaus with Kip after my parents moved to Poppy City. Rainbow signs yell greetings at passersby and boxed garden plots abound. Carrying my belongings in my arms and selecting a bunk almost feels like a homecoming of sorts, except I catch an abominable cold. During my interview with the Hausmeister the next morning, my words croak through my swollen throat. The bruised jaw doesn't do me any favors either.

"We will grant you a grace period of three days to recover." The rotund and jolly Hausmeister lets me know. "And I can see in your intake paperwork you are partially disabled and low skilled, so your assignments will be narrowed to Animal Care, Kitchen Duty, or Custodial. Please sign up for shifts beginning this Nadeltag."

I sniffle and stare at the giant chalkboard wall calendar where the other residents have scrawled their nicknames by tasks. The Werkhaus isn't a free stay. Residents, mostly older teenagers or early 20-somethings, can work off the fees with chores. I chalk my name in next to POTATOES, LINENS, and CHICKENS for Nadeltag. Other tasks such as ACCOUNTING and INVENTORY have little gold anchors beside them. They're only for skilled workers. A little mental math lets me know quite a bit of my Shanty money will go to cover my room and board.

With my head feeling like it's inside a fishbowl, I hobble back to the dorm I share with five giggling girls on winter holiday. I keep my altar and Tophinghua figurine in my pack, so my roommates don't feel threatened. Gevit and Blitz lie beneath the bunk, wrapped in blankets, for the same reason. Wrapping myself up, I lie down facing the wall.

The words *partially disabled* and *low skill* bounce around inside my skull like the billiard balls in the Ivory Inn. *I'll kill you*, says Erik. *Take some pride in your work*, says Cortland. I stare at the blank wall until I drift off.

* * *

MY COLD LINGERS, SETTING DOWN ROOTS IN MY LUNGS AND TURNING INTO A thick, rasping cough.

Life in the Werkhaus goes just about as well. On one of my hen house excursions, my leg and arm glitch out in tandem and I end up wearing the basket of eggs.

The Hausmeister pulls me into his office. "Thalon, I know you're in a rough spot, but you're not going to be able to stay if you can't meet the weekly fee."

"I know. I'm sorry." I cough into my sleeve.

"Our prices are the lowest they get, Thalon. And collecting eggs. How did you manage to mess up collecting eggs? How did you get every single one of them *on* you?"

I hobble to the showers in defeat. Aalgur Thalon, daughter of the Dread One, wielder of Gevit the Thunderstorm... Incompetent Omelet.

I imagine how much Kip would get a kick out of this. My momentary smile falls off my face. Kip defeated me in combat. Kip's on a Duskingr now. Kip was... I guess I never really knew the real Kip. I rub my jaw, a reminder that Erik defeated me in combat, too.

I lean on the shower wall and cough until I choke myself. I'm supposed to start back at Shanty's tomorrow... I'm going to need that damned doctor's note for real.

* * *

I catch a trolley to the South City clinics before my shift. The old buildings stand mostly empty. The Dusk Trials didn't save their business. The majesty of South Vatska isn't lost on me, stone palaces and mead halls from the selkie tribes of old. Relics now, crippled husks like me.

Stone stairs lead beneath the street to limestone nooks from five, six hundred years ago. Cavern pubs and bakeries from when the selkie folk thrived in Vatska. Beautiful hand-hewn travertine spaces have become laundromats and health clinics.

At least I don't have to wait long to be seen.

"Aalgur Thalon?" A nurse calls me back. He measures my height against a wall chart before waving me onto a scale. "You're underweight for your height, are you eating enough?"

"I don't know." I keep my gaze on the floor as he leads me to a windowless room. An electric lamp buzzes on the wall beside a faded oil painting of the Duskheim Mountains. He checks my vitals.

"You're in today for...?" He hovers a pen over his clipboard.

I stifle a cough. "I need a note for work."

"I see. And, do you have a file with us, Aalgur?"

I nod.

"Alright, well, sit tight and the doctor will be with you shortly."

I sit on the crinkly paper of the examination table, staring at my wool trousers and work boots. My left hand lies across my lap. Now and then the fingers move on their own. I hack into my elbow.

"Aalgur Thalon?" A short woman with a tender voice and a zillion tiny braids walks in with a knock. "I'm Dr. Belkis, I don't think I've met you before, but I have your file. How are you feeling?"

"Like hot garbage." I twist a strip of paper between my fingers.

Dr. Belkis's brows bow together. She reads through my file, turning a paper over. I wonder what it says about me, how many layers of Aalgur Thalon are on each page. "It says you've been to this clinic four other times?"

"Yes, I'm not getting better. I'm like this *every day*. I mean… I have a cough now, but I'm… I'm not recovering." I rip the strip of paper in two.

"And aside from the arm, the limp, the headaches… what other symptoms are you experiencing?"

"I'm tired." I exhale a long breath. "I'm so tired. This is the third cold I've caught this season. My thyir's broken…"

"I can't speak to that." She makes a note. "But… the vomiting. Are you still experiencing that?"

"Not as much, no."

"I'm concerned about how much weight you've lost from your pre-Dusk Trials physical…"

I shrug again.

"And Aalgur, what do you do in your down time? What do you enjoy? What are your hobbies?"

"I don't really have any. I'm not really… good at anything."

Her brow crease deepens. "Do you ever feel hopeless?"

"Ha." The chuckle ends in more coughing. "I can't shift. I can't catch food for myself, my thyir is *gone*… How would you feel?"

Dr. Belkis scratches something in my file and sets it aside. She assumes a softer posture. "Aalgur, I think you might be experiencing depression. It's perfectly normal, especially after such a frightening illness. It's nothing to be ashamed of, but you should seek treatment."

It takes me a moment to catch up, then I blurt: "You think I'm depressed? You think *depression* made my arm like this? You think *depression* took my thyir? If this shit was all in my head, I'd have kicked its ass the same way I have everything else… by the raw power of spite. But I've been doing that… and all I'm doing is getting sicker."

"None of your tests have shown anything conclusive. You should be well, Aalgur."

I clench my teeth so my jaw doesn't shake. "Well, I'm not."

Dr. Belkis lifts a piece of heavy stationery. "I'm going to write you a prescription for the cough and sign you out of work for the week at least. Come back to see me after that. We'll get you into therapy."

I blink. "No, I... I need you to sign me *into* work. I need to work, I need the money..."

"I don't feel confident sending you back in this state, Aalgur."

Cold tingling spreads through my shoulders. I look at the floor as she passes me the sick note. I'm not even fit to bus tables, part time, at a fucking chowder shack...

Belkis looks on the last page of the file. "Aalgur, have you been contacted by the Temple of Brosk?"

I shake my head.

"May I let them know you have moved residence? They have a new program for young selkies."

"Go ahead." I stand and wrap up in my heavy coat.

The doctor stands too. "There might be community there for you."

"Sure," I say.

* * *

BACK AT THE TROLLEY STATION, I TEAR UP MY GET-OUT-OF-WORK PASS AND shiver. In North Vatska, I pick up my cough medicine and take a shot glass of it. Chemical cherry. Gag.

I last a valiant thirty minutes at Shanty's Chowder Shack before I walk smack into a table and send Spindel and ice cream floats crashing over a mother and three children.

"THALON!" Wilk pulls me into the back by the collar. The dusty air sets off my cough. I choke and wheeze until tears streak my cheeks.

Wilk grimaces. "Thalon... you didn't get that doctor's note, did you?"

I shake my head.

"Thalon, you're not alright. You're especially unfit for food service. You're a good worker but I'm going to have to cancel your shifts until you're... presentable."

I want to argue. A part of me wants to toss him across the room. But he's right. I hate it, but I'm a mess. The most Incompetent Omelet.

By the time I slink back to my bunk at the Werkhaus, I can hardly limp up the steps. Sinking onto my bunk, I grope around beneath until I find my leftover Midwinter mead and drink a few swallows.

I lie awake as my roommates giggle their way in and out of the room on some adventure. My body aches from the cold, the fight, the sickness in my bones. Rolling, I reach under the bunk for Gevit.

I slide her out and unwrap her. A few pocks of rust pepper the blades in her disuse. I buff them with my sleeve. *You and me both, Gevit.*

Elren's eyes stare back at me from the dim metal, and I place my hand over them. He was the only other contestant who took the Dread One as his patron. In that moment, I know what to do. I know my options. Mind made up, I search out one of my giggly roommates to see if she has any makeup she's willing to sacrifice.

On the beach, by the light of my campfire, I paint Zahlek runes down my arms in liquid eyeliner. The statue of Tophinghua glares at me in the dancing light.

"It's all I could get." I apologize. A plastic bowl stolen from the Werkhaus serves to hold Her offerings. I fill it with leftover mead. Around the fire I draw the runic hurricane and wheel of stars. In the light of one small fire, Coven Cove feels dark and devoid of life.

"Tophinghua." I offer my hands, palms up. I kneel before the statue and the sea. Storm clouds blanket the horizon.

"I am Aalgur Thalon of the line of Tawkthalon, Mother of us who change our skins, protector of pups, slayer of betrayers. Tophinghua, I am Yours, of Your line, God of Storm and Strife, Valor and Victory. Ice of my ancestors, blood of the storm..." My voice breaks. I pause to wipe my eyes.

Pulling my long black hair over my shoulder, I use a pair of borrowed scissors to cut it. I cut it right at the back of my head and lay the thick hair across the mead bowl as an offering, a piece of myself.

"I carry myself into the sea in Your honor, Mother, that You may see me and know that Your line yet lives. As You once reshaped Yourself in Your own image, may You shape me once more in the image of Your daughter. Mother, I would never deny You. Let me be Your daughter again."

I stand and fold my coat, leaving it atop bath towels beside the fire. I moan as the scalding cold of the ocean rushes past my feet. Tears stream down my cheeks. Here, I speak directly to Brosk. "You said I deny Your daughter. Tell Her I am here. Tophinghua, I am here. Mother." I lift my eyes to the storm clouds now. "Let me become whole again. As You once joined Tawkthalon to the pelt You sewed for Her, please rejoin me to mine..."

I wade in past the breakers. I gasp and flinch as the cold shocks me. It crawls into my bones and joints and mind. It slows my movements and my thoughts.

Wrapping my pelt around myself, I slide into the inky black pain of the sea. What used to be my home now brings only torment. The hungry sea pulls me out, out into the depths.

The thyir in the water taunts me. I force my shape to change, but nothing happens. Blind in the dark water, I tumble, a confusion of fur and arms and feet. I can feel the ice of thyir all around me, a song with no words, a promise of ancestors lost to time. I reach for it, and it dances away.

"Tophinghua! I am here..." Saltwater chokes me and pushes me under. My ears roar as a wave crushes me down.

And in the crashing of the surf, I hear Her voice reply: *You do not see me, Aalgur Thalon... you do not yet see...*

I give up. Already dying in the freezing water, I stop swimming, stop fighting, the sound of my sobs lost in the roar of the surf. "Then I offer myself to You, Mother. Please accept my sacrifice..."

A wave grabs me like a fist. It throws me down. My back cracks against the seafloor. I scream silently and forget to be brave or bold or strong.

The wave lifts me and hurls my body onto the shore. Shells cut my palms and knees. I choke up seawater. My pelt slips from me and I pin it to the sand with my fist before the sea can drag it away.

Naked, un-pelted, and nearly frozen, I gasp air into my burning lungs. My new short hair sticks to my face. Lightning strobes on the horizon. The electricity sparks across a yawning crescent, as if leaping between the teeth of a grinning mouth.

"Will you not accept my sacrifice?" I weep.

Twin orbs flash in the storm clouds like a pair of moons. Lightning crackles in Her sneer.

*"NO."*

* * *

Numb, I crawl up the beach and lie beside the fire. I want to cry but can't. I simply shiver. I dry myself with numb hands and dress again in human clothes. Then, with slow, agonized steps, I return to the Werkhaus.

My roommates have long since gone to bed. I drop the remaining eyeliner beside the girl who loaned it to me, and limp to the shower.

No quantity of hot water can warm me. I return shivering to my bunk. No thoughts cross my mind, no *what next?* Nothing. Truly, there is nothing left for Aalgur Thalon.

An envelope waits on my pillow. AALGUR THALON, it reads. My fingers fumble to turn the envelope over, but when I do, I read: TEMPLE OF BROSK, GOD OF THE SEA. BE WELCOMED.

# CHAPTER
# NINETEEN



I don't know what happened to the daring fringe dress from Gadvig. For all I know she took it back while I was unconscious. I do the best I can with what I have. Trousers, suspenders, and my canvas coat, with my pelt thrown atop everything, even if it's useless. The clothes fit loose, almost like hand-me-downs, I'm such a sickly twig. There's not much I can do with my new chopped hair.

I limp across Vatska. The low winter sun is brilliant after last night's thunderstorm. My breath steams. I move in a daze, the experience at Coven Cove pressing down on me.

The dark wood Temple towers over North Vatska. Seagulls pinwheel overhead. Fashionably late by five minutes, I struggle to open the heavy wood and iron door.

Inside the blue and green stained-glass hall, rows of tables dressed in mesh runners form three sides of a square. An anchor tapestry hangs above the altar. Nearly two dozen people mingle with each other, eating from heaping plates of food on the burl end tables.

The men have on trousers and coats or traditional leather formal wear while the women sparkle in dresses. There doesn't seem to be an option between boy and girl, so I lurk over to the coffee station by myself. Everyone wears their pelts over their clothes. Am I the only one who lost my thyir in the Dusk Trials?

Despite how hollow I feel, my stomach growls when I smell the delicate slivers of lox. I grab a plate and fill it with lox, cracker bread, sliced cheeses, and a blob of roe the size of a scoop of mashed potatoes.

A fork dings against crystal, and the selkies shuffle to their seats. Unsure how anyone knew what "fork ding" meant, I find a seat in the back corner away from everyone.

"Thank you all so much for coming, champions!" A woman I recognize from Kindling's Eve addresses us with a luminous smile. "My name is Priestess Signe, and before we get to the presentation, we invite you all to eat and enjoy yourselves! Scoot a little closer to a friend!" She stares right at me.

I focus on my plate, shoving a whole spoonful of roe into my mouth. The morsels pop between my teeth. My left arm twitches, so I hide it beneath the table.

Glancing around, I notice details I missed at first: the man up the table to my left wears an eye patch. A girl in a green dress only has one hand. I see scars, amputations, and a familiar hollowness in the black selkie eyes. All of these people got injured in the Dusk Trials too, I realize. I had no idea the Temple would look out for us. I had no idea I would ever be included among the crippled.

*Is that what I am now? A cripple? A disabled adult of low skill? No wonder Tophinghua refused me. What could an Incompetent Omelet possibly offer Her?*

I don't have time to drown in self-pity. Priestess Signe hooks a confused young man out of his equally lonely chair, marches him past a string of empty plates and shoves him beside me. We lock eyes and he shows me his teeth, more grimace than smile.

"Go on then, introduce yourselves!" urges Signe.

"I'm Thalon," I blurt. I bristle, uncomfortable with an uninvited person in my bubble.

"I'm Jess," replies the boy, equally stiff. He picks at his plate. I notice he's missing several fingers. So much for those stupid blade guards. He wears a black pelt, the fur coarse and dark like mine.

"You're a sea lion too?" I ask.

"I... I am. Stellar... from Movaska originally..." He doesn't look at me.

"I'm a western sea lion," I reply. "The Stellars up in Movaska... they do a lot of granite mining... quarrying... something like that, right?"

"Granite for construction, right. I'm not involved in that though... I've been working at a bar at night so I could train... got kind of stuck in Vatska after needing..." He shows me his hand.

"That sucks porpoise ass," I say. I mean it with my whole heart. Jess snorts. His expression shifts as if trying to remember how to smile.

Lifting my left arm out from under the table, I hold it so Jess can see it twitch.

"Gods in the waves, what's the matter with you?" Jess scoots sideways. "Are you sick? Is that contagious?"

He might as well have picked me up, chair and all, and thrown me through the stained-glass window. I stare into my roe, jaw trembling. Weren't we comparing scars?

"It is," I growl. "It's blood worms. You can get the eggs just by being too close... got 'em off a poisoned blade in the Spire. Once you know you're infected, it's too late..."

Jess picks up his plate and walks down the tables to sit with a group of harbor seals. A quarter of me wants to laugh: the idiot. The rest of me fights back tears. I hide my arm under the table again. I hope the Temple's offer doesn't involve being around other people. I hope I can go be a crippled low skill omelet by myself in peace.

I shove more roe in my mouth and gag as I bite into something hard. Retching a little, I spit up roe jelly and a hard orange bead. Several people, Jess included, stare at me. Their utensils hover in midair.

"Plastic!" I hold up the bead and roll it between two fingers, still coughing. "Spindel garbage is getting into everything, right?"

One by one, the other selkies look back to their plates. "Blood worms..." I hear Jess hiss.

I make a mental note to cough on him before we part ways. We eat for a few minutes, undisturbed. I'm starting to relax when Signe and three other priests file onto the podium and wait for our attention.

"The Dusk Trials have been especially challenging for this generation," Signe begins, reciting her spiel from memory. "The Dusk Trials are a celebration of our proud heritage of thyir and our rightful representation on the Duskingr... training for success should not mean our most promising young people are left crippled in the cold."

Ouch. But not a lie.

"Across Ruhnsvalla, the selkie way of life is, to be blunt with you, dying out. In a few short generations, we may not see children born in pelts. Or if we do, they will be the outliers, the outcasts..."

I grip my sick arm beneath the table. *Some already are.*

"Should Ruhnsvalla lose selkies, who will crew the Duskingr beside the huldror? They already outnumber us ten to one, if not more.

"That's why it's so important that you, you strong, brave young men and women, be cared for. Without you, our future will fade away."

I poke around in my roe for Spindel beads. *Now we're talking.*

Signe smiles, hands balled into hopeful fists. "And so, with the generous donation from Spindel Co., the Temple of Brosk is pleased to offer you shelter, security, and comfort. In return, we ask that you choose mates among your peers and bear our future's pelted pups!"

I sputter the roe across the table. My wet coughing is the only sound.

The other selkies look around at each other, murmuring. Brows furrow, forks clatter on dishes. I gag on my own spit.

"You will be provided rooms in the Clifton block," Signe continues. "All medical costs, including fertility treatments, and maternity care will be covered. You will receive a stipend for food, clothing, and entertainment. And, best of all, should healthy, pelted pups be born from these unions, the parents will receive two years wages each and the option of keeping and raising their child or leaving it in the care of the Temple.

"Too many forces work against the selkie folk," Signe forges on. "Far too often, promising young selkies choose not to marry, or choose barren unions..."

I feel the force of her gaze leveled specifically on me.

Something inside me snaps like a rubber band, tight against my lungs. I stagger to my feet. I look directly at Priestess Signe. "You're telling me, that in order to get support, as a crippled competitor, I have to be the Temple's whore?"

Someone gasps. Whispering and snickers follow.

"This is a gift!" Signe insists. Her hands make soothing motions on the air. "To bear pelted pups... this is the highest honor of Brosk, father of us all!"

"Brosk carved the Ingvu out of sea garbage!" I stutter, backing away. "This... this isn't in honor of Brosk! This is... this is..." I don't actually know what it is. "This is stupid! And insulting!" My voice catches and the word *insulting* ends in a sob.

Rage strengthens me, straightens my spine and stills the tremor in my hand. But shame and sorrow cut me deeper. Realizing I can't keep myself from crying, can't tamp it down, I shove out my chair, use it as a crutch to turn myself around, and limp for the door.

*Brosk would never want this for me, never want this for any of us...* My hot tears splash on the black wooden floor, the floor under which I gave myself to a girl. *I am Tophinghua's daughter... descended from Tawkthalon. I am made exactly as the gods intended...*

I grip my twitching arm to my chest and squint my eyes shut. I stumble into the sunlight. Did the gods also intend for me to live a broken, partial life?

"Aalgur Thalon! Miss Thalon!" Priestess Signe hurries after me. She places a hand on my bad arm and holds me in place.

"I can't! I won't!" I blurt, swiping rage tears off my face with the back of my hand.

"Dear child, there's no need to be so upset." Signe guides me into the shade of the roof. "You're Aalgur Thalon, aren't you? You're the poor soul who nearly died from the spine sickness. Please listen. We would send you wherever you needed to go for treatment."

"They literally don't know what's wrong with me!" I hiccup.

"Aalgur, dear, you're hurting. We can see that. We understand what a hole the Dusk Trials have left in so many lives...but Aalgur, think about it. You're already five and twenty years, are you not? Living alone in the Werkhaus. With us, you'll have a home, a family... financial safety..."

I am weak. I pause.

Signa continues. "We won't be choosing partners for you, any of you. No, we'll be hosting parties, dances, chances to get to know each other, possibly even to find love. Aalgur, even if you don't, should you bear a pup for Brosk, you can leave it and go live whatever sort of life you choose after."

I breathe in and breathe out. I smell the brine and hear the seagulls squawking in the low winter sun. "Any life I'd choose has already been taken from me," I say.

Signe holds on as I try to pull away. "Consider the gift you would offer your gods and your people…"

"So, I am only worth the ability to breed. To make more selkies. I, in the eyes of the Temple, have no worth at all."

Signe keeps talking, soothing, trying to coax me back. If only I could see my own potential, she rambles.

I don't hear much more. "No," I state.

Signe inhales through her nose. Her eyes lose their wrinkles of sympathy. I notice a blue file folder in her arms for the first time as she opens it. She flips pages. "This is your signature, is it not?"

I blink at the familiar scrawl. "It… is. Is that my Headwaters contract? I broke that fucking thing. They've withdrawn all support."

Signe licks her finger and folds a paper back. She reads aloud to me. "'I, the above signed, hereby grant the Temple of Brosk, in partnership with Spindel Co., Lamplight Petroleum Works, and Headwaters Distribution, use of my person and abilities at their discretion, in the event I do not rank top twelve in the Dusk Trials or am otherwise incapable of fulfilling my duties. I understand that I may be asked to offer blood, tissue, or other aspects of myself at the Temple's discretion. I understand that failure to comply can and will result in arrest, a fine, and assignment to a cause of the Temple's choosing. I agree that I have read and understand these terms.'"

The glaring winter day wobbles around me. I wobble too and catch myself on the Anchor of Brosk statue. Sweat breaks out on my back and hands and the inside of my mouth turns to sandpaper.

Signe's eyes crinkle with compassion again. Her hand still grips my arm. "Come to us with love and hope, Thalon. Don't make this harder than it needs to be."

I draw on my long years of combat training to blank my expression and steady my shaking limbs. My lips stick to my teeth as I speak. "I'll think about it."

Warmth returns to Signe's face. "Wonderful, that's just

wonderful," she coos. "Everything will work out. You'll see! Just give it a chance, give yourself a chance." Her hand squeezes my arm and she lets go. "I'm so happy for you, dear."

I show Signe my teeth, a smile, a leer, and back away from her. When I'm certain she isn't following me, I change course to the empty lots, to the Karrvoss Caravan. I smell the open grill pits and marinated meats the truckers like to cook.

Tents and awnings strung with chain lights and colorful flags make a festive haven against the winter chill. I hurry for it, as fast as I possibly can. The chiming of bells reach my ears, I inhale a desperate breath and sob it out. *Where is he? Where is he?*

Truckers and locals mingle, merchants, prostitutes, I couldn't care less. I listen for the familiar *ay-ep*, look for the graying mutton chops. *There!*

"Hans!" My voice squawks. "Hans!"

Leaning over a grill with a poker in his fist, Hans shoves his goggles up into his hair. "Eel Guts! Bless the gods, you're alive!" He drops the poker and runs to me.

We collide and my knees give out. I'm choking, I can't get air.

"When they flew you off in the airship, I thought..." Hans rambles. He pins me against him. He's hugging me, holding me up. I hug him back, as tight as I can. My hands grip his leather jacket. Cloves and tobacco fill my nose.

"I have to get out of here..." I dissolve into tears. He holds me tighter, his gruff hands on my back, mutton chops bristling against my cheek. "I'll do anything. Please... please get me out of here."

# TWENTY

"It's a bit of a pickle, Thalon. A pretty big pickle. Koshkarl's got his rules about hitchhikers and tagalongs... and for good reason." Hans takes the coffee pot off the grill. He sprinkles chai spice over the top from a tin that looks like it's been through war, and adds cream for me.

I hunch around the mug and pull my hood over my head. Warm spices, sweet, earthy coffee... I close my eyes and try to push Signe from my thoughts. I can't do it. The coffee shakes in my hands.

I sip so my mouth isn't bone dry. "Yes, but you know me, Hans. You worked with my father... and Cortland."

"Ay-ep." Hans settles back and lights a cigarette off the grill. "Koshkarl doesn't know you though's the thing, Thalon. Neither do they." He nods in the direction of the other Karrvossians. They peek at us from the shadows of the camp. Scales sparkle here and there and eyes glint.

I shrug. "So?"

"Well..." Hans clears his throat and swirls his coffee around before replying. "You fell in battle wearing the sigil of the Dread One.

And yet, here you are, still kicking. You're a little bit cursed as far as they see it, Thalon."

*You have no idea*, I almost say. "That's asinine," I say instead. My nose scrunches. "I thought you worshipped the Mountain."

"Ay-ep... The Boreackt brought us here. We are the people of the Mountain. That doesn't mean we don't respect the Hurricane. The Hurricane welcomed the Boreackt when She settled here to rest. We know Her might, even if She's not our god. And Koshkarl makes the rules."

I glare down the sides of the trailers to the trucker cluster, trying to spot Koshkarl.

"He's in town." Hans leans forward to dust ash from the cigarette.

I rest my mug on my thigh. I can't let this chance slip by. "So, what does Koshkarl want?"

"Ay-ep... we're in the market for a fish vender. Should have broken contract with Cortland last year, to be honest... And now he's made for the hills."

Shame sinks like a stone in my belly. "It's my fault he's gone... I was his only pelted selkie... and I haven't been able to swim..." I can't bring myself to mention the bet, in case he lost the *Cormorant* because of me... I can't bring myself to learn what Hans must have lost, either.

"You? Bah." Hans swipes the notion from the air with his cigarette, painting smoke between us. "Cort's been cutting corners every which way he's able. You're the boots on the ground type, or, well, fins in the water, I suppose. But Cort also brokers our shelf-stables for the eastern leg of the circuit, to the landlocked communities and such. Supposed to give us locally canned, smoked, dried. Supposed to be fresh, clean, and all that. Koshkarl's got a hunch old Cort's been buying in bulk from Gill, removing labels, and selling to us at a premium."

I scowl. "Huh?"

"Ay-ep. And as far as the *Cormorant* goes, whatever's happened to her isn't your fault either, Thalon. We all suspect the mangy ferret's been taking hits of Katch. That's brain rot, is what it is. His downfall is his own responsibility. Too bad though, looks like we'll be partnering with a company all the way up in Adlervik." He looks over his glasses at me. It is a deliberate look. He expects me to figure something out.

I straighten up. "Adlervik's a long drive."

"Ay-ep."

The cogs slide into place. A thrill of excitement grips me, followed by a wash of dread. "What if I could make an introduction? What if you could get a competitive contract here in Vatska? Do you think that could convince Koshkarl to let me hitch a ride? I just need to get out of Vatska…"

"No promises, kid." Hans snubs out the butt of the cigarette and squints at me. "What kind of connections can a deckhand swing?" His voice rings sly. He already knows damn well who I know.

"I know someone," I say. The dread sits in my chest. "We haven't spoken in a while… so no promises from me, either. But… let me see what I can do."

"Ay-ep. Seen what you can do, kid. You're a hell of a fighter when you're not fainting in the arena. Don't shake 'em down too hard for us, huh?" He chuckles.

My shoulders hunch and the shame spreads over me like a pox. "I hope you didn't lose too much on me, Hans. I've let so many people down…"

Hans cackles, a jolly laugh. He slaps his knee. "A case of beers and smokes? Eel Guts, it sure drained the old under-seat coin stash, but I think I'll recover."

"Ah!" I smile, weak with relief. Just a case of beer and cigarettes, Krescean bless it. Here I thought I'd wrecked his life.

Hans keeps chuckling as he refills my mug. "Now, before you go getting into back alley fights over smoked mackerel, tell me about this Spindel soda pop funded pup factory… that's a tale I've not heard before…"

* * *

I wish this was a back alley brawl. Even as a crippled, incompetent omelet, I'd take fists over this any day.

For once, my head doesn't hurt. I still feel like puking as I look up at the sleek sign for Seppanen Fish and Cannery.

*Don't be an omelet.* I try to talk myself up at the door. *Literally the very worst thing that can happen is: He can say no.*

Reminding myself that it's this or the Temple's bonkers baby-making scheme, I set my jaw and push through the door.

The receptionist smiles and stands as I enter the clean, fog-gray waiting room. Old ship wood and rope accents lend a nautical note. "Right this way, Miss Thalon. Mr. Seppanen is ready to see you."

I follow the receptionist's floor-length skirts down a carpeted hall. While the cannery must take up most of the building, I can't smell nor hear evidence of it aside from a distant, hydraulic hum.

A framed newspaper on the wall draws my eye and the urge to puke doubles. Azoto, Rawl, and Kip stand before the Duskingr in gorgeous new uniforms. Kip smirks, arms crossed, a mean, confident version of the person I thought was my friend. Azoto stands with her arms folded behind her back, deadly serious. Rawl towers behind Azoto like a bodyguard.

The City of Vatska Celebrates Three New Sailors! yells the headline.

*Why did you do it?* I mentally ask Azoto, ignoring Kip. *Why did you enter the Trials?*

"Right in here, Miss." The receptionist lets me into a bright office. Windows overlook the wharf and shoreline. Mashed potato clouds float by, painted pink by the low winter sun.

A large photograph of the *Cloudberry* graces one wall. Photos of a woman with twin boys and two plump pups greet me from a wooden desk.

"Miss Thalon, as I live and breathe." Luka Seppanen stands and offers me his hand for an unnecessarily firm shake. "To what do I owe the pleasure after... *five years* without a word?"

Luka absorbed his father's effortless good looks and his mother's curvy body shape or perhaps just their aestheticians and trainers. I give him a tight smile and take the offered seat. I *could* ask why Azoto entered the Dusk Trials. That is not, alas, why I'm here.

"I wanted to inquire about making introductions." I sit straight and keep my left arm hidden in my coat. "I have a friend in the Karrvoss Caravan and they're in the market for a supplier of preserved fish. There's a good offer up north in Adlervik, but if something comparable might be worked out..."

Luka cuts off my practiced monologue with a raised hand and cocked brow. "Bold of you to walk into my office and request a business meeting, Thalon. Bolder still, considering how dramatically, how *publicly*, you humiliated my sweet baby sister."

I bristle. The gall.

"You broke 'Zoto's little heart. And then you avoid hide and hair of the whole family for years. Literal *years*, Thalon."

I soften my jaw just enough so not to growl. "She broke my heart first."

Luka folds his arms and gives me a hard, cold look. "Whatever happened between you, it doesn't excuse your actions."

Angry words pile up in my throat. Oh, how I want to lean across the table and take him by that snappy collar. And yet, he's not wrong. My pride turns my insides molten. I swallow vile words and thoughts. "I know. I'm sorry."

Luka tilts his head half a cog to one side. "I am afraid I missed that. Did Aalgur Thalon say she was sorry?"

"I'm sorry!" I spit. I swallow my ire like bile. I stare down at my right hand. It leaves a sweat shadow on his desk. It trembles now, too. "I'm sorry. I... acted like an asshole. I was an asshole. I *am* an asshole."

Luka raises his brows a few more hairs.

"There were... things... that hurt me, but I hurt her too. Making a scene like I did... it was an embarrassment. But I could have apologized. I could have asked for forgiveness. And instead...instead I've been a gutless coward, avoiding someone... someone who cared about me." My eyes flick to the *Cloudberry* on the wall. "Someone who *cares* about me."

I knew I might face shame walking in here today. I did not anticipate the sorrow. "She stayed with me in the hospital, you know. Before she left on the Duskingr." I swipe quickly at my eyes with a sleeve and blink them clear. "She is, by far, a better person than I."

Luka drums his fingers on the desk, first one way, then the other. "If I did not know you, Aalgur Thalon. If I had not pup-sat you and played Pirate Trove with you that summer you and 'Zoto made a complete mess of my market, I would call you a convincing actor. I would congratulate you on your performance and send you on your way.

"But I am well aware you can neither act nor lie convincingly, and it is reassuring to see you have, in spite of yourself, grown up. At least a little."

My mouth puckers as if I bit into a lemon, but I keep it shut. Heat spreads up my cheeks.

"I wish I could tell her I was sorry," I admit. The sorrow overbalances the injury to my pride. "She still cares about me. And now she's... gone away."

"Now she's gone away," echoes Luka. A blink-and-you-miss-it shadow crosses his eyes, then they return to cocky and intense. "This Karrvoss Caravan, we haven't done much business with them before. With whom would I be speaking?"

I do my best to switch gears, not nearly as fast or smooth as a Seppanen in that regard. "That would be... that would be Koshkarl. Earl Koshkarl. I think he's a priest of the Mountain or something..." I meet his dark gaze with mine, strengthening my words as I continue. "The deal in Adlervik is a decent match. I'm simply inquiring into other possibilities."

"Much of Adlervik's supply comes from Headwaters' offshore imports," muses Luka. "I assume that will be who supplies them. At least until Headwaters replaces the Caravan altogether."

I swallow. Is Headwaters planning to do that?

"The Seppanen family prides itself for quality, transparency, and tradition," continues Luka, citing the brand slogan. "Which means, of course, we cannot offer the lowest price possible."

I wait to see if he has an answer for me, or not.

Luka reaches into his drawer and scrawls numbers onto an appointment card. "I am a busy man, Miss Thalon. Do make sure your friend Koshkarl arrives on time." He slides the card to me.

I take it in my steady right hand.

"A decent match in Adlervik is still two hundred miles up the coast no matter which way you slice it. So, we will see just how good of a match it is."

I stand as smoothly as possible. "Thank you, Mr. Seppanen."

Luka stands as well, fastening a button on his coat and shaking my hand once more. "Miss Thalon."

I turn to go.

"Oh, and Thalon?" Luka calls after me. He gives me a sly grin. "It was nice to see you."

# TWENTY-ONE

"Ay-ep. You know, Eel Guts, you might've considered the Temple's offer a little harder. Comfortable place to live? Stipend? Shucks, kid, I bet if you'd shopped the room a little, you'd have found a nice young man who's got himself a boyfriend. Could'a been roommates. Gamed the system a bit before anyone caught on."

Sitting on the passenger side of the huge, warm cabin, I watch the drab winter forest of the Blackberry Hills pass by. I sip a thermos of spiced coffee. "They're *forcing* people to... you know. And I just... no. Absolutely not."

Hans shakes his head. "It's a weird look, I'll give 'em that. Dipping the ol' toe in eugenics. Ay-ep. I've been sayin' it. Big companies are taking over."

I sit with my socked feet tucked up on the seat. The musical pipes on the sides of the rigs whistle and sing. We left this morning and are still stuck in the Blackberry Hills. The road follows the Erling River and I swear we've rounded the same corner six times.

The coastal fog burned off some miles back. I feel displaced without it. The winter sun casts deep shadows, highlighting the thick, dry underbrush and dead leaves. The whole place feels asleep, stagnant. We didn't get a lot of rain or snow yet this season. The landscape holds its breath.

We reach the first clear view of the Duskheim Mountains at sundown. The rolling Blackberry Hills taper into a wide valley, golden with dry hay. The land is flat and then the Duskheim Mountains erupt right from the prairie. We're on a plain, rolling hills to our backs... And then the view crashes into a wall of stone. I hadn't expected the mountains to be so abrupt.

The flatlands don't look very wide, but it takes over an hour to reach the foot of the mountains. When we do, a murky blue night closes off the plains.

Ahead, a road winds up into the Duskheims and into the swallowing dark.

Hans pulls his rig into a gravel parking lot and climbs from the cabin. I watch a dozen other Karrvoss Nomads follow suit. They work in teams, opening their trailers and hauling out scrap wood.

"Bonfire!" announces Hans.

I help set up as best as I can. We're near a village and I watch folks meander in ones and twos to mingle with the camp. They bring goods and stories to trade.

Hans passes me a plate of food. "Been out this way before, kid?"

I shake my head.

"Ay-ep. You're in for an experience."

We enjoy a simple, quiet dinner. No one talks to me besides Hans. I'm fine with that, the drive wore me out. The shadows of the Duskheim Mountains cut a jagged hole in the starry sky.

That night, Hans opens his last trailer and makes me a nest among packaged bulk clothing. He sleeps in the cabin, on the fold-away cot behind the seats. He makes sure I have whatever I need before patting the side of the trailer and leaving me to rest.

I lay awake to the song of crickets, trying not to think of Signe and her threat. I'm not sure what good I'm worth, but I know it isn't that. Anything but that.

* * *

WE PACK UP AND ROLL OUT AT DAWN. YESTERDAY FELT HOPEFUL. CLIMBING into the giant old beast of a truck and setting off into the unknown felt like a fresh start. Now as the truck lumbers up switchback after switchback, I feel queasy and exhausted.

I sit wrapped in my canvas coat, rubbing my neck as the familiar headache creeps in. Maybe hitching with a band of nomads is as crazy and desperate as it sounds. Maybe I'm crazy and desperate.

"You okay there, Eel Guts? You're looking a touch carsick."

I pull my hood up. "I'm fine."

"We'll be stopping in a few miles to hook into the cables. Say something if I need to pull over. Would prefer not to be cleaning biscuits and gravy out of the ol' upholstery."

I sigh, unwilling to admit I do, in fact, feel ill.

Good to his word though, Hans slows and then stops the trucks at the base of a mountain spire. The closer we get, the bigger the Mountain becomes. I figured they'd get smaller but nope. It's like, the higher we climb, the taller they get. A metal trough draws a straight line several thousand feet up the steep, barren stone. Wheel grooves to either side have polished the stone like glass. To the right of this, a machine system fills a cavern in the mountain. Stooped old Koshkarl unchains and then unlocks the cavern, revealing gigantic cogs and weights inside. It appears to extend all the way back into the mountains. Miles? Tens of miles? How big is this machine?

"Is that the Boreackt?" I ask.

Hans lights up a cigarette and takes a ponderous drag. "Ay-ep. That's the Mountain Herself. Whole thing's the Mountain, actually."

"Who built it?"

"The Mountain came as She is from lands unknown. She brought us with Her, stopped here to rest. Been here so long, She built up the continent around Her, the Ruhnsvalla you know."

"Yeah but... who built Her?"

Hans shrugs. "Who builds any god?"

I climb out of the truck and look up. The mountains are so big, too big. The machine inside rumbles to life. The sound does something to my stomach. A twist and tingle between awe and dread. The Boreackt is immense. Could She have come from another world, like Hans said?

The first rig begins to strap into the cables that lead up the slope.

I slide my eyes sideways to Hans. "This is safe, right?"

"Ay-ep. Never done wrong by us. We take care of Her, She takes care of us. We place our trust in the Mountain."

I get a good whiff of heavy lubrication oil. "How old is this thing? Best estimates are fine."

"Old as the land, old as the sea, tempered by glaciers and wind..."

"Alright. How long ago did the Mountain arrive here?"

"Oh... hundreds of thousands of years, I'd reckon. More, perhaps. The Mountain arrived before time as you figure it."

"Hundreds of *thousands*?" My voice squeaks. I hope Hans just can't count. I hope this is spiritual creativity speaking. I look into the cavern at a clockwork cog. It's as big as the Werkhaus.

Hans props his fists on his hips and squints at the cable. "Ay-ep."

"Who keeps it running?"

"Us. The people of the Karrvoss Caravan. It is our sacred journey to cross the Mountain, to honor the Mountain with our passage and care. She gets most of what She needs from the earth, but we give Her anything else She may want. Whatever the Boreackt needs, we supply. The Boreackt always sees us over."

"So... we're just going to tie the truck to that *literal ancient artifact* and let it drag us up the mountain?"

"Ay-ep."

I stand next to Hans. Smoke belches from the spire like a volcano. "So... if the Karrvossians take care of the Boreackt... there aren't a lot of you. What will happen if there are even less?"

"That's the question," replies Hans.

The smoke thins, heat rises on the air as the engines settle. Hans motions me back into the truck and we wait our turn. Koshkarl gives us a hard look before queuing up at the cables. I get the impression he still sees me as cursed. He's not wrong.

I watch the Karrvossians work. They work with huge cables, as big as my wrist, securing them to the chassis of the truck with giant carabiners. Emergency fail safe cables then fasten to other places on the chassis. Each driver checks, and then double checks the security cables.

A sloping road leads up and into the guide trough, so the trucks and trailers ease onto the mountain without crunching together. At the very last moment, the front wheels secure into a rolling metal plate that moves along the trough. I guess it keeps the wheels straight. I hold my breath as three drivers check the cables of the first truck, give it an "all clear," and the driver hops in. Gargantuan gears thunder and slowly reel the truck to the mountain like a fish on a string.

I keep holding my breath as the truck reaches steeper and steeper angles, forty-five degrees or more in places. The hitches groan, wheels spray dust as the driver feathers the brakes. Then, off it goes, trekking a slow, deliberate line up the side of the mountain.

Hans, confounding in his disinterest, cleans mud from the tread of his boot. "Ready, kid?"

* * *

"Whoops." Hans catches an unsecured coffee cup as it sails from the dash.

I stare straight ahead at the dash sticker that reads: put it in gear, dummy trying not to think about the cables holding us up.

I just start to relax when we reach the top. The cable pulls the truck onto a flat landing. The truck rolls to a stop. Hans hops out without a care in the world to uncouple us. He walks to a little building in the side of the cliff. Taking out his lighter, Hans goes through some sort of ritual, scattering cloves from his pocket. He leaves something, perhaps as an offering.

"Too bad you can't hook the truck in backwards." I throw out, resting my feet on the dash. "Bet the view's amazing."

"Oh, you can. I like to do it at the second cables though." Hans pulls onto the gravel road and lights a cigarette. The pipes on his rig sing as we get up to speed.

"There's more Boreackt?"

Hans chuckles. "More than you'd believe, kid."

* * *

HANS MEANT IT. THE SECOND CABLE HOOKUP DIDN'T LOOK TOO IMPRESSIVE from a distance. Now that we're at the base, I have some clarity. I feel like a flea staring up at it, a tiny, witless little flea, easily blown over the edge by a swift mountain breeze. The cables are miles long.

I huddle inside the truck cabin as Hans hooks us in. A few months ago, this would have set my blood pumping, my heart singing. I would have thrived. Now I feel like a woozy shell.

The truck starts moving backwards.

"HANS! Hans, what...!" I scramble around the cabin like a cat in a bathtub.

"Ah, shucks, Eel Guts." Hans peels paper off a stick of cured meat with his pocketknife. "Wouldn't think a Dusk Trials champion would be such a scaredy-cat. Sheesh, weren't you going to crew an airship? As in: a ship in the air? In the sky, all high up like?"

"I'm not scared!" I shout. The truck jolts backwards, and I squeak. The trailers slide up the slope in the rearview mirror. Then, a new sound comes out of me, a sound I'd almost forgotten I could make. I laugh, then crow, as the cabin slides up the mountain.

"Look at it." Hans's voice softens in awe. "Never know the next time you're going to hold the world in the palm of your hand, eh?"

The laugh gets stuck in my throat by unexpected tears. From here, the Duskheims spread out on either side of us, a shattered jawbone thrust up from the earth. Snow clings to the spires like plaque on teeth. Below us, the Blackberry Hills have become no more than gopher mounds, the Erling River a puny thread. Night creeps in from the east and the first stars sparkle.

Stars sparkle on the dash, too, a faint silver aura. I place my hands on them, tracing the wheel of stars. "Hans… these are the Dread One's stars…"

"Ay-ep," Hans opens a panel on the dash to reveal a scattering of Zahlek bindrunes beneath, illuminated by the same distant starlight. "I told you. The Mountain and the Hurricane have a pact. Some say they were lovers even."

"Lovers? Mm, skeptical."

"Fine, they were roommates."

I snort. "Where did you buy your truck, Hans?"

"Buy? We don't buy them. This old girl's been passed down to me from the old days of dusk magic. We keep 'em up to date, working well, but some of these old parts come from her first form, from when she was built to drive to anywhere or nowhere. Like the Duskingr." Hans closes the panel and brushes the faint stars with his fingers. He pulls a pair of beers from the under-dash cooler. Cracking them open, he passes one to me. Holding his beer, he gazes over the world below. "Ay-ep. We gotta enjoy this while we can."

"What do you mean?" I rest my feet on the dash and sip the beer.

"Welp, some folks want to put a train through the Mountain. Faster transportation and all that. They want a tunnel, so I hear. But you can't put a tunnel through a god. Not sure why folks can't see that."

Hans toasts the stars on the dash with his beer. "We built the Duskingr too, you know. Us Karrvoss folks from the world beyond the horizons. Our ancestors built the world. Now, we're an inconvenience."

I turn the bottle of beer in my hands, watching condensation drip to the floor. "I had no idea about the Duskingr."

"Ay-ep. We're caretakers of the old machines. But like the old magics, we're fading away."

Hairs raise on my neck. "Don't say that, Hans…"

"Not saying it won't make it untrue, Eel Guts. Us Karrvossians, we're not meant for this place, not really. Long ago, we crossed the Mountain just to cross it. Why do you think we're haulers? We're not allowed to wander anymore. Everything costs money. Nothing can be enjoyed just 'cause it's there. Our Mountain reshaped the world, and now we can hardly afford to honor Her."

Hans makes a vague motion to his left. "There's farms going up in the Erling River watershed. Don't know what that's about. Hoping it can be a Not Hans Problem."

"Do the farms get in the Caravan's way or something?"

"Not directly. Not yet. Can't help but feel we're in *their* way though."

"Did there used to be more Karrvossians?" I ask.

"Oh, like you wouldn't believe, kid. Trucks stretched far as the eye could see, singing in the wind, free as the sky."

Smoke hovers on Han's breath. The scales on his cheeks gleam in the fading light. "Say, you think about hitching over the mountains to Poppy City? Now that we've got you, we're stuck with you. Koshkarl's not gonna leave you on the side of the road, curse or no curse. Hospitality rules the road. We've climbed the Mountain together, you're Karrvoss in soul.

"You could see Ashling and your folks. Bet they'd be happy to see you..."

"No." I shake my head. A lump jumps into my throat at hearing Ashling's name. My fingers squeeze Valmut's card in the pocket of my coat until it creases. "No. I'm just getting away from Vatska. That's where I need to go. Anywhere but west... or Poppy City. East, north, south..."

"South," begins Hans.

"South by the side of the Road.
North and East and the dry harvest feast
West marked by needle and lode.

"Up, we climb higher, down we descend
   By engine, by smoke, by wheel and spoke
   As the Mountain once roamed, so too in the end.


"Dark of the sky, the forest in embers
   The Mountain endures
   The Mountain remembers."


Hans finishes his poem and clears his throat. "You know, they say when you cross the Svall, you never know when you'll end up or when you'll get back. The Svall takes, the Svall gives, but we cannot control what, where, or when."

I tuck up my knees and wrap my arms around them. "Cross the Svall?"

"Ay-ep. How d'you think the Boreackt got here? Watched someone do it once, an old trucker hoping to return to Karrvossha. Didn't even get too close to the ribbons. It just reached out and took him, vanished him away into oblivion. Beautiful thing. Still see it in my nightmares."

* * *

THE CARAVAN CAMPS TWO NIGHTS ATOP THE BOREACKT BEFORE CONTINUING. I mostly sit in the camp and watch the truckers joke and banter, unsure what to do with myself. All this way on top of the world, I begin to relax, knowing Signe and Gadvig's disgusting contract can't chase me down up here. I'm free. Free to do what? Well... that's a bridge I'll have to burn when I get to it.

On the third day atop the Boreackt, the nomads slowly pack up and we depart around noon. The sway of the enormous truck still makes me queasy, but I'm getting used to it. The warm, cozy cabin keeps the chill of the mountains out of my bones as we turn east, lumbering down into U-shaped valleys with glacial green streams.

We pass thousand-pound bears fishing in the rivers and moose grazing among the pines.

Hans makes us tuna sandwiches for lunch, and we munch as the trucks wander along the twisting spectacle of the mountain road. A whole world exists up here, a whole world I never conceived. I always drove myself to crew a Duskingr, I never took the time to imagine the places I might see.

Sandwich finished, Hans balls up the paper wrapper, tosses it over his shoulder into the sleeping cabin, and cranks up the radio. A bouncy, thrilling song about airship racing comes on and Hans leans my way to force eye contact.

"What...?" I begin, unable to stifle a chuckle as he lowers his UV goggles.

"Uh-oh, DJ Hans is in the house!"

"Ah gods..."

The lyrics start and Hans sings along. I shake my head and sigh, but my foot starts tapping on the dash in spite of myself.

By the second verse, Hans plays drums on the wheel as he sings. As the chorus approaches, he shoots me finger guns. "To you, Eel Guts!"

I can't help it, I burst into song along with him. My singing voice sucks, I'm garbage at pitch, but like when we climbed the Boreackt, I find myself laughing.

The bridge comes on and Hans uses his knees to steer so he can shred his air guitar. I bray like a donkey until tears well in my eyes.

We scream the final repeats of the chorus together. "FLLLLYING TO THE...."

The radio whistles and screeches.

*"WE INTERRUPT THIS BROADCAST WITH A SHOCKING REPORT!"*

"Stones spare me, here we go," mutters Hans, taking the wheel with his hands like he almost can't be bothered. He reaches to change channels.

*"This is Kelpie Live reporting from Parliament. In an unprecedented turn of events, an accident has occurred on the Duskingr Ursul!"*

Hans adjusts the radio for a clearer signal instead of tuning away. We both go quiet.

*"In a freak training accident, four new sailors have fallen to their deaths over the South Sea! Two huldror, two selkies!*

*"This is breaking news. I am receiving their names this moment! Four young sailors, dead and gone in the service of Ruhnsvalla!"*

Hans's brows lower. "Fallen? Into the sea?"

*"And here it is, gentles all, our four brave and valiant sailors! Willawesk of the Shonoda Shrine. Hildergulda of the Ingfalla Shrine. Rawl Kane of Vatska and Azoto Seppanen of Vatska. Let us come together to remember their bravery and sacrifice."*

I forget how to breathe; I forget how to think. A spear thrusts into my chest and all the way out through my spine. An invisible spear tearing open an unseen wound.

Azoto.

I reach for Hans, my fingers dig into the sleeve of his leather jacket.

"P-pull over..." I gasp.

The truck slows and rumbles to a stop on the shoulder. I fumble with the door and fall out, landing on my hands and knees. I can taste vomit in my throat but can't throw up. My lungs scream but I can't breathe.

Azoto.

Hans leaps out. Gravel crunches as he slides down beside me. He holds me, he talks to me. I can't hear him.

Azoto's professional smile laughs from the page on a magazine. Her true smile looks up at me as we walk on a sunset beach. Her small hand holds mine as I lie, more dead than alive, in the hospital.

Azoto.

I'll never see her again.

*Am I not enough?* is the last thing I asked her.

And just like that, like a drop of rain into the ocean, she is gone.

CHAPTER

# TWENTY-TWO

"And now we are seeing *Duskingr* Captain Zynk return the pelts of Azoto Seppanen and Rawl Kane to their families. The pelts are folded and adorned with gold ribbons. The Captain presents them to the families on folded Ruhnsvalla flags. The young soldiers fell in the line of duty. They will be remembered, immortalized.

*"But what happened? How did four young sailors meet their deaths over the bleak ocean?"*

Reporter Kelpie speaks in a somber voice over the radio. Hans switches her off.

"Ain't gonna bring them back, kid," he says. "Just gonna make you hurt."

I lean against the passenger window, an inert object as Hans pulls the truck over with the rest of the Caravan for the evening. He leaves me there with the heater running, for well over an hour.

I don't move. Where would I go? What could I possibly do?

She's gone, she's dead. I'll never get to say I'm sorry.

The Karrvoss Nomads have long since set up fires and laundry stations by the time Hans returns. He holds a small wooden box in his hands. Inside I can see wax, paper, and corn husks.

"Come on, kid. We can't fix it. We can't make it better. But we can do what's right for them."

When I don't move, Hans comes around to the passenger side and opens my door, steadying me as I stagger out. My whole body physically aches, the sickness in my bones mirroring my broken heart.

Hans pulls my canvas coat around me and guides me upriver from the laundry stations. "Come on, kid. It's right we do this."

* * *

"This is the Shastaar River. It joins with the Erling, it returns to the sea."

Hans and I kneel together on a small rug on the riverbank. He helped me make a paper boat and dipped it in wax. A pair of cornhusk dolls lay within the boat, cradled in paper prayer petitions.

"As you make this journey, we walk with you, children of the sea," Hans begins. He scatters cloves over our tiny campfire and sparks flutter. "As the threads of you fall loose in Fregnym's tapestry, let Kvellsett lift you into Her basket and carry you over the mountains. May She carry you into the land of sunset. Rest until you are ready to be woven once more..."

"I didn't realize you... know how to pray to our gods..." It's the most I've said since the radio announcement. My voice feels raw.

Hans lays a bundle of herbs inside the little boat. "We Karrvossians know the gods, Thalon. The Mountain brought us here to be part of your world." Lifting the boat, he places it in my hands.

I do nothing but hold it as the light grows frigid and dark.

"You need to say it, Thalon. She is a part of you. You need to say goodbye to Azoto."

My face crumples and the tears finally fall. Taking a deep breath,

I set the boat on the bank. I hold my hands over the water and close my eyes. I feel the water in my mind, let the heavy slowness of it push through me. I stay still and breathe until I can imagine the song of my ancestors flowing through it, the ice we used to call. Even though I cannot use my thyir, I feel a shimmer of it. I hear a whisper of the song it used to sing to me. We used to travel the Svall but now the ice moves for no one.

Hans is right, I need to say something. I have no power in my voice, and so I whisper. "Azoto Seppanen, Rawl Kane, they were Your humble servants, Brosk. Lift them from the dark waters and place them on the deck of the *Naudeleid*. Warm them beside Your fire, Brosk, and share with them Your song. Grant them happiness and comfort and let those who they leave behind find peace."

I turn my hands over, close them to fists, and place them against my heart. The thyir in the river shivers but I cannot touch it, not anymore. I lower into a bow and cry.

I cry for Lars and Hannahlesh who lost their only daughter. I cry for Jalmari and Luka, who lost their baby sister. I cry for the Kane Clan who lost a brave, strong warrior. And I cry for myself, for the different paths I might have walked, for the bridges that I burned. My tears fall into the Shastaar River. Someday, my tears will return to Vatska.

I lift the paper boat and kiss each doll. "To the sea we are born, to the sea we return." I place it in the water.

When I let it go, a part of me goes too. I could have been so different. I wish I had. Now, it is too late. I watch the boat bob away until the night gulps it down. "May the currents cross our paths again, Azoto. Someday."

Hans, kneeling beside me, whispers the end of his prayer. "Dark of the sky, the forest in embers, the Mountain endures, the Mountain remembers."

Tears clog the back of my throat and I cough. It feels obscene, that she should die while a sickly thing like me still lives.

"Come on, kid," Hans helps me up by the arm and leads me back to the light of the camp. "What needed doing is done. Time to get out of the cold."

* * *

"WE CLIMBED THE MOUNTAIN TOGETHER, THALON. WE'RE FAMILY NOW."

I stare out the window and into the wall of stone beside us. A seemingly endless, gaping canyon yawns on our other side. The mountain road has become a gauntlet, funneling us off into oblivion.

"You can stay with us, long as you need," Hans continues. "Not even ol' Koshkarl will have anything to say about it..."

I keep staring out the window.

Hans inhales. I can hear the concern on his breath and I don't care.

A V opens in the wall of stone, affording me a flash of a green glacial valley below. A wooden sign passes, and my head moves so I can follow it with my eyes. Ikthvar Peak Air Base. Seven miles.

Hans notices. "Ay-ep. Haven't been there in a while. Parliament's not having us bring the shipments for the Duskingr anymore..."

Silence smogs up the air in the truck cabin.

"Say, you remember how you got the nickname Eel Guts?"

I shake my head. My heart, my lungs, and my stomach feel like cement. The truck slows as we enter a pass where half the road is supported by metal I-beams, a precarious little wedge of road teetering thousands of feet above a crevasse.

Hans chuckles and cracks the window to light a cigarette. "Let me tell you. The origin story of Aalgur Thalon getting in over her head..." He doesn't start the story. He leans over the wheel, squinting down the road.

The cigarette fizzles out in Hans's hand before he can take a drag on it. Up ahead, the other trucks come to abrupt stops on the half bridge, half road. The road makes a sharp curve, the wall of the mountain obscuring our view of the first two trucks.

"Ay-ep, must be some rocks came down." We wait, the truck idles. Hans relights his cigarette.

A stooped old figure hobbles our way in earnest. Koshkarl. Up ahead, I catch a glimpse of figures opening the trailers of a truck. They don't move with the leisure of the Karrvossians, but with stiff proficiency. Even from all the way back here I identify crisp black suits and bolt-action rifles.

Koshkarl reaches us and Hans opens the driver's door. "Headwaters checkpoint," he says. "Making sure we're not hauling contraband or whatnot."

"Sons of biscuits," spits Hans.

"More than that," Koshkarl takes a step up the ladder and lowers his voice. His colorful eyes look across Hans to me. "They're lookin' for criminals. Folks on the run. Seals who have broken deals and the like." Patting the side of Hans's rig, Koshkarl swings himself down and turns back to the front of the Caravan. "Jus' sayin'."

Hans and I stare straight ahead, watching black suits pull crates of dry goods out of a trailer and cut into them.

Signe's face flashes through my mind. My skin crawls. "They'll make me go back... Please don't make me go back..."

"They can do a lot worse than that..." whispers Hans. A steely fury fills his otherworldly eyes as he watches the suits slash open cereal and jerky. "These aren't their mountains, these aren't their roads..."

Seven more black suits step into view, all of them armed.

Panic claws through me, clogging my throat and tangling through my mind. "*'I understand that failure to comply can and will result in arrest, a fine, and assignment to a cause of the Temple's choosing.'*" Signe's voice whispers in my ear, reading Gadvig's contract. "*'Cause of the Temple's choosing...'*"

Hans keeps his gaze straight ahead. I map his face the way I would an opponent in the ring. The tufts of fur on his ears shiver though there is no wind in here. He holds his jaw tight, teeth gritted, nostrils flared. He knows something about the black suits that I don't. They frighten him.

Eyes still fixed ahead, he says, in the most casual tone: "Get your things, kid. It's an easy walk to the air base. They can fly you where you need to go..."

I open my mouth but say nothing. Up ahead, one of the black suits holds his rifle across his body, not aimed yet, not threatening yet. But close.

"Move, kid!" orders Hans.

I snap back into myself and begin stuffing my pack. Hans leaps out and runs around a trailer, returning with food supplies. I slide Blitz through my belt, heart thudding in my ears.

Pulling me so the trailers obscure me from view, Hans leads me back down the road and onto the trailhead. I hold my breath so the idling fumes don't make me cough. When a thicket of birch trees creates a visual barrier, Hans relaxes a little. He helps me secure Gevit to my pack and get the whole thing on my back.

"Weather's an absolute gift. This trail here'll get you there in a couple hours..."

I'm not thinking. I'm stuck on a carousel of *I just lost Azoto, I can't lose Hans.* "I won't let them hurt you..." I croak.

Hans huffs. "They're not gonna hurt me kid. Got all my paperwork in order, not movin' anything that shouldn't be moved..."

I grasp at anything I can, mouth dust dry. "Why can't I just... hike around the checkpoint? Meet you on the other side...?"

Hans shakes his head before I even finish. "It's cliffs as far as the eyes can see, Eel Guts. Thirty, forty miles to walk around. You'd be campin' in the cold. Bastards put their checkpoint right where they can control the end of the road.

"But it's not the end of the road. You're going to hike to the base and hitch a ride east or south." Hans fumbles a notepad and pencil from his pockets and scribbles. "If you can't find us, write me in Poppy City or Caldera. We've got post boxes there. We go north first, so if you write, you won't hear from me till after

Midsommer, got it?" He tucks the paper into the pocket of my coat.

I try to swallow. "What if... what if the people in black suits are at the base?"

"Parliament controls the Duskingr. Your people crew them. You've got better odds at the base than me trying to smuggle you through the checkpoint... they'll catch you there for sure, and then we'll all be had. Now, it's just a little walk. Just a little walk on a pretty day." Hans squints into the pine and granite landscape.

The spines of the Duskheims spread into the eastern distance, the span of them unfathomable to me. We selkies don't often leave the sea and as far as I am concerned, the mountains go on forever.

We stand at a trail head, the end of one road, the beginning of another. Hans straightens my collar and pretends he's not upset. The edges of his colorful eyes crinkle. "You're gonna be just fine, kid. Don't you worry about us."

Standing here, more or less alone at the top of the world, I am lost. I feel like a broken joke, a pelt-less shell of a person with shattered thyir and a rejected sacrifice on her conscious. I fell in battle with the sigil of the Dread One on my chest. I'm a fugitive and the woman I once loved is dead.

"It's all good, kid," says Hans again. "Take your time. Air's thin. It'll sneak up on you if you're not used to it."

I nod. The words mean little to me. In my pocket, my hand crushes Valmut's card. She had been with Gadvig. I have no way of knowing if she will be my savior or my doom. I have no way of knowing if she'll be at the base at all.

Hans pulls my hood up as the wind rises. "Don't let the world knock you down, kid."

*Too late*, I think.

Hans draws me into a hug. I breathe in the scent of cloves and tobacco. He holds me fiercely, then, he lets go and pats my arm. "What do you want me to tell your folks if I run into them in Poppy City?"

My guts squirm. "Nothing. Tell them nothing about me. Please."

Hans steps back from me and lifts a hand in farewell. "Find us. If you can't find us, write us and I'll find you. May the gods walk with you, Aalgur Thalon. May you walk in peace and power having climbed the Mountain, and the currents take you where you need to go."

# TWENTY-THREE

Alone, I begin my slow walk down the trail.

A Thalon from the past would find herself enraptured by the sweeping stone spires carpeted in pine, birch, and lush shrubs. The crisp, arboreal breeze spinning down from the glacial peaks would have brought a skip to the step of old Thalon. But I am not her.

Tears cloud my eyes as I trudge down the path and my face twists. If I had only been able to shift, would I have been assigned to *Ursul* with Azoto? If I had been there, could I have saved her? If I can find Captain Valmut at the air base, will she help me or hand me to Gadvig? And what then? Lowering my chin, I walk as fast as I can.

My head starts to spin and I find myself breathless, gasping. Each foot drags unseen anchor chains. The sign at the trail head said the air base was only seven miles. Only seven miles. I can walk seven miles.

The path leads around a spire and then between two, so that my view switches from overlooking the Blackberry Hills and the far-off glimmer of the sea, to the troughed valley between peaks. We'd been traveling south the past few days before the narrow, hazardous road veered east. As high up as I am, the spires of the Duskheim Mountains still reach higher.

A black stain crosses my path. I stop and poke it with the toe of my boot. Is it grease? Oil of some sort? It spreads into the weeds and bushes on either side of the trail. Soot would mean people… I squat down to get a better look and stand right back up at the acrid smell. I almost gag and quickly hop over the black stain and hurry on my way. Whatever it is, it's gross and I can't be bothered.

*You're doing fine*, I tell myself. *It's already been a couple of miles, you'll be there soon.* I focus on how good the shower will feel. I hope the air base has showers.

*You're doing fine.* My heart pounds in my ears, my short hair sticks to my cheeks.

*You're doing fine…* I squint my eyes against a hot, building headache. The pain offers the single boon of distraction from my losses. Crying and sniffling makes it worse. *Focus.*

I walk for hours. There's no way I haven't gone the seven miles. Seven miles isn't far. And yet, I get nowhere. The sky turns purplish. *You have plenty of time before it gets dark*, I assure myself. And then the darkness settles in.

A thick band of stars across the sky provides my only light as I slog along the trail. I stumble on roots and pebbles. Each stumble shoots pain through my hip. I need to stop, I realize. My knees shake and my head pounds. Hobbling out from a stand of trees, I see stars beneath my foot. My stomach drops and I fall back on my ass, assuming I walked out on a ledge of some kind. But then, the stars ripple. I'm on the shore of a lake.

Catching a relieved breath, I crawl the last few steps to the edge of the water and scoop a handful into my mouth. I spit it right back out again.

"Seawater?" I sputter. Scooping another handful, I sniff it. The deep salty musk of the open ocean. I shake my hand off in confusion. "Seawater?"

Seawater or not, my brain starts to go fuzzy. I pull my pelt from my pack. Bathed in the songs of foreign insects, I feel alien. I shiver as the coyotes yip to one another, alone and pathetic. With my second skin and my coat to keep me warm, I have no more energy to plan or mourn. Unconsciousness takes me out like an assassin.

* * *

I dream of whale song.

No... I squint my eyes open and find myself bathed in blueish green light. I sit up. My body aches, my left arm trembles, and my toes feel frozen. This is not a dream.

The fluting, ethereal calls of humpback whales roll through the valley and echo off the granite cliffs. My skin prickles into gooseflesh. *Guess you have brain damage after all...*

Beams of blue and green light shine onto the surface of the lake and I look up, expecting to see the moon. Instead, I see the light fading into the sky like the spotlights of the Dusk Trials arena. I stagger to my feet in terror and awe. The light originates from inside the lake, from deep down.

My breath sparkles on the air, blue with the flickering light coming from under the water.

Minute by minute, my hackles settle, and my heart slows. Sitting against a pine tree, I listen and watch. Did there used to be ocean here? Could whales have been trapped? I can't imagine some other way they got to the top of a mountain range. Humpbacks certainly weren't flown in by airship. And what about the light? I heard somewhere gas can glow, or something like that. This can't be the Svall... can it?

The lake sings and the light dances, but whales never surface. Every so often, I catch a glint of orange light down in the forested valley, but it vanishes as quickly as it appears.

I intend to stay awake and watch the lake, but fatigue pulls me back to the ground. The whale song folds me into dreams.

* * *

I WALK THROUGH BLACKENED TREES. GRAY SAND CLINGS TO MY FEET. A bonfire smell burns my nostrils, letting me know it's not sand at all, but ash.

Through the black trees, the moon hangs low and yellow. Then a second moon appears. Eyes.

My feet slow, growing clumsy. I look down to see ice covering my boots. Frost crackles over my knees, my thighs, freezing me to the ashen ground. I try to scream, but only snow comes out of my mouth.

A voice whispers from the sky, from the twin moons, from a mouth opening to reveal flares of lightning. Tophinghua.

"*I am not to be measured in half... Neither are you.*"

* * *

I WAKE WITH A GASP, COUGHING ICE FROM MY THROAT. I SHIVER. THE SUNNY weather of yesterday turns to a cold gray chill. Clouds blanket the sky, cloaking the tallest peaks.

I keep coughing, eventually retching and holding my stomach as my head spins. "Gods..." I rasp. I curl on my side. "Ahh, gods..."

The sudden chill, the altitude, grief, or perhaps simply the short hike itself, whatever the combination, I know this feeling. I'm getting sick again, dangerously sick. I pull back the sleeve on my left arm to find the red rash peppering the skin like an omen.

"No no... please..." Tears drip off my nose. "You have to get up. You have to keep going. Gods damn it, Thalon, you're almost there." And then what? *Can't worry about that now...*

Scrounging in my pack, I find a bottle of painkillers and take three times the recommended dose. I feel like I have an ice pick embedded behind my eye. I force myself to eat a handful of granola. I just need enough strength to make it to the air base.

Seven miles. The air base must be around the next bend. Just a little more...

I forget about the dancing lights and whale song. I almost forget about Azoto.

A cold, miserable drizzle descends, getting into my hair and lungs, making my chest ache and my clothes damp.

The path leads me down into the bowled valley, into a forest of red-barked trees. Their roots grasp the earth and stones like octopus tentacles. Yawning black scars in the trunks gape at me, screaming like my pain screams. Silent, agonizing.

I hear flute music. It floats around me, taunting me. Now I'm hallucinating for certain.

I make it to a small clearing and my pain wins. Falling to my knees beside a birch tree, my stomach heaves and I vomit a splatter of soggy oats and chewed up pills across the dead leaves.

*You're not going to die out here.*

A voice inside me whispers: *Yes, you are, and you deserve it.*

Sobs wrack through me between retches. Would that endless sleep be so terrible? I would never need to wake up broken, never have to remember I lost the Dusk Trials. And not just the Trials, I lost myself. I would never have to be a low skilled incompetent omelet. I would never have to remember my mother didn't want me. Tophinghua didn't want me. I would never have to mourn Azoto or fear being used as breeding stock by the Temple of Brosk because I was too fucking stupid to read the fine print. I would never have to be the wretched Aalgur Thalon again.

I don't fight my tears. Defiance is exhausting. Surrender is easy...

I look up at the sound of rustling and meet a face. A furious, feral face. Lines, like wood grain, mottle her skin, and her gold eyes glare at me.

At first, I see a carved statue, something left along the path to frighten travelers, perhaps. A hiker's scarecrow. But then she moves, a lithe creature on filthy bare feet. Dark curls fall around me as she leans over to inspect me. She holds a clay flute in one hand, tall, lean body rigid in surprise. Her tufted tail flicks, as if finding me the most repulsive slug. She's a huldra.

Something familiar stirs in my belly, a terrible, twist of foreign magic.

"Kvell…" I wheeze. It's all my feverish brain can come up with. Of course kvell didn't make me sick, I was sick before the Duskingr ever landed.

The huldra's nose wrinkles as she looks between me and the granola splatter. Her scowl deepens. She pulls headphones off her ears, like the kind pilots wear.

"Air base…" I can't finish my question, I end up retching instead.

The huldra sniffs at the vomit and leans away from me. Her tufted tail swishes. She grimaces and walks a full circle around me.

"Air base?" I croak, spitting out oats.

The huldra doesn't answer. She hops from foot to foot and then reaches both hands overhead. She brings her hands to her belly, taking a harsh, audible breath. Her hands form shapes, snapping from gesture to gesture. For a moment, I think I see the air distort around her, like heat waves rising from a sunbaked street… and then the girl stoops and lifts me, pack and all, across her shoulders as if I weigh nothing.

"Air base…" I moan, powerless against her.

The huldra's strong hands hook around my thighs and an arm. She jogs through the forest.

My head lolls. The huldra doesn't feel hollow at all, my feverish mind thinks. Her strong bones and sinews hold me in place. I feel the breath woosh in and out of her lungs as she jogs. Then, she slides me down onto a warm stone floor.

Colors sway around me and I blink to clear my eyes. Sweeping ceilings, stained glass, glorious wrought iron lanterns. The entire Temple of Brosk could fit inside this single room. Is this the air base?

I do nothing but lie there on the warm floor as the huldra girl's dirty feet pad away. It feels so good to lay here, to not do anything. To decay, fall apart, finally.

"Vespald, what is this?" A low, husky female voice approaches. I hear a harsh breath, a hiss. "Yes, I can see it's a sick selkie. Looking for the air base, you say?"

Forcing my eyes open, I watch the huldra, Vespald, communicate with an older woman by making different shapes with her hands.

The old woman takes a knee beside me. Scars rake down one side of her oak-bark face and the points of antlers gleam with silver bands in her flaxen hair. Her hand cups my chin and I realize her other forearm is missing.

"Selkie girl, look at me." She physically turns my face to look at her. "I am Illuet Yew of Ingfalla. What business do you seek here?"

Illuet? Not the Illuet from the Dusk Trials...

"Tophinghua didn't want me..." I whisper.

The Illuet's face creases in distaste. "You're lost, selkie girl." She places her single hand over my eyes. I slip into a painless, peaceful darkness.

# TWENTY-FOUR

I promised Ashling I would show her the sea.

Ashling cried at first, face pink and puckered. The roar of the waves frightened her. But then, I changed my shape for her, let her cling to my fur, and soon she giggled and splashed in the shallows. I turned sixteen as she approached her first year. Momma worked afternoons, and so I'd often jog home after school to play with her.

Ashling took to the water with a natural ease, soon crawling right for it without hesitation or fear. I knew the sea called to her, just like it called me. The same blood pumped through our hearts. We were both daughters of the Dread One, pelt or not.

"What on earth are you doing? Aal, no! Get her out of the water now!"

I startled at the raw edge of my mother's voice, dropping Ashling from my back. I shifted and grabbed her, lifting the squalling baby into my arms.

"Out! Now!" Momma waded in up to her knees to snatch the screeching Ashling from my arms.

"We were just playing!" I sputtered, climbing the beach to take my sister back. "I've taught her to float! She's very safe with me..."

"She's a baby," Momma scolded. "You can't just drag her into the water with you like that! She'll get sick or worse! No more of this, Aal. No swimming, no water. None of it."

Comforting Ashling's wailing cries, my mother walked her up the riverbank and away from me, leaving me seething and leaking angry tears.

* * *

Forbidden from playing with my sister in the water, I resorted to playing with her on land. She loved my soft sea lion shape. I'd use the shower to put on my pelt, dry off as best I could without hands, and then roll around with her on the upstairs carpet.

One day as we played, I set her with her toys and went to my room for something so insignificant, I can't remember now. I waddled right back to find her standing on the top step of the staircase. Our staircase on Scallop Avenue was long and steep and wooden with a tile floor below. Ashling wobbled on her sausage legs. She slipped...

Honking, I dove for her, snatching her arm in my mouth and pulling her back from the edge. I tasted her blood on my tongue. I barked and screamed until Pappa ran in from chopping firewood.

"Gods in the sea, Aal, what did you do to her?" Pappa grabbed a towel to cover the teeth marks on Ashling's arm. "You bit her!"

I kept barking, trilling, trying tell him: *She was going to fall.* I tasted her blood in my mouth. I cried and blubbered, heart cracking in two knowing I hurt my perfect little sister.

Momma ran up the stairs. She snatched the sobbing Ashling and spun to me.

"What did you do?"

"She bit her!" said Pappa.

"You hurt my baby, Aalgur." Momma's teeth showed as she stood over me, face a mask of loathing. "What *are* you? You're an *animal*. A stupid, vicious animal. A beast. If we'd known the gods would give us you, I'd..."

I barked and shrilled. If only they understood what happened...

"Stop it! Stop making that sound!" Pappa swiped a foot at me. It probably wasn't meant to be a kick. Imagining it from his perspective, I was making terrible noises while his injured toddler cried. But I remember it as a kick. I remember him looming over me and corralling me back into my room and closing the door. Without hands to turn the slippery knob, or water to change my shape, he trapped me in there.

I screamed and barked until my voice wore out, and then I lay against the crack beneath the door. My parents yelled in the kitchen downstairs. I could feel the anger through my whiskers.

"It's little more than a scratch." A voice I recognized from the Temple of Brosk assured my parents. Why did they call a priest? Why not a doctor?

"She can't... there's no way she could *infect* Ashling?" asked Momma's voice.

"You know as well as I, it doesn't work that way," replied the priest. "Bacteria, perhaps, but nothing more."

Infect Ashling with what?

"The child likely resents the baby was born human," the priest continued in a louder voice. "You got what you prayed for, but understand, your daughter's a teenager and she might be acting out..."

*Got what they prayed for?* My ears perked and drooped.

I lay on the floor, unmoving, until my mother came and opened the door. She pointed to the bathroom. "Go make yourself into a person."

When I returned, body slow and heavy, both parents waited for me, Ashling nowhere in sight.

"You can't play with her anymore when you're like that," Momma began the lecture.

"She was going to fall..." I tried. I folded around a hole in my stomach, I felt like I got shot with a cannon ball.

"She's not like you. She's not an animal..."

"I'm not an animal..." I rasp, voice sore from screaming.

"What do you call that then?" Momma points to the pelt in my hands.

"I'd never hurt her... not on purpose..." My jaw trembled. "I love her..."

"Then act like it," said Momma.

* * *

My parents decided to move to Poppy City, on the other side of the Duskheim Mountains before my seventeenth birthday. I refused to leave the sea.

I wore my pelt as we said farewell, human shaped but still cloaked in animal skin, visibly inhuman on purpose. I cupped Ashling's sweet round cheek in my rubbery hand and leaned in to kiss her nose. "I love you," I whispered.

"I'm going to sail the Svall," I told my parents. "I'm the way I am for a reason, and I'm not going to waste that. I'm going to crew a Duskingr one day."

I don't remember what my parents said. Perhaps they said nothing at all.

I watched them take Ashling from me, off to fields and hills and children like her. I wondered if she'd remember me. I wondered if she'd listen, late at night, for the call of the sea in her heart.

* * *

Thalon...

The first thing I hear is my heartbeat. Then my breath. Then my own voice murmuring in confusion. A dim, orangish light glows around me. My vision blurs and clears. I lie on my back in a room made of glowing crystalline bricks. Lanterns in wrought iron sconces flicker on the walls and a spicy, earthy scent of herbs in hot oil brings me back to myself.

Being present feels terrible. I groan and move my good arm over the soft table beneath me. My head throbs, my neck and shoulders burn. I feel dried out and desiccated, like a slug baking on the summer sidewalk.

"Aalgur Thalon."

I blink at the sound of my name. Two faces look down at me. An old woman with skin like oak bark and flaxen hair. A feral younger woman with huge golden eyes. Her face looks like carved wood, perfectly sculpted, but those eyes bore holes through me. Illuet Yew and Vespald. Huldror. I've never been so close to one, let alone two.

"Thalon. You must be present for this," states Yew in her husky voice.

Looking down, I find myself stripped naked. Two towels lend a bit of modesty, one across my hips and the other over my breasts. The towels create shadows under my hollowed hipbones. For a creature who literally peels off her own skin, I've never felt so naked, so exposed.

Yew places her single hand on my forehead. The spicy, earthy smell clings to her hand, and she rubs it into my forehead, then the center of my chest. I can't fight her off, I can hardly move.

"I would have rather Lylok assist with this, so focus, Vespald." Yew cradles a hand beneath my neck.

Vespald leans over the table, sliding her long, herb-lathered fingers under the small of my back. She stares into a corner of the room, expression tight, a hint of teeth between grimacing lips. Her long curls dangle over me and make my skin twitch.

I feel the thrum of thyir move through my body and I yelp. It hurts. My own magic feels like thorns tearing through my bones.

"What are you... doing to me? Stop!"

"Thalon." Yew places her hand back on my forehead. "Your body is attacking itself. The inflammation prevents the thyir from stabilizing. You're dying."

Her words don't mean much to my feverish brain, but thyir does. Remains of my magic quivers, deep in my body. It pokes me like shards of glass.

Vespald makes several shapes with her hands.

Yew sighs, short on patience. "You brought her here, Vespald. Take some responsibility."

Vespald grimaces. Focusing, she rubs her palms together and exhales a growling breath. She then places one hand on my chest and the other on my belly. Her touch is warm and firm.

"Breathe," orders Yew.

I take a deep breath.

Something squirms inside me, a ribbon of warmth shimmers between Vespald's hands and Yew's. I feel a series of pops in my chest and lungs, and the heat twists through my limbs.

"What is it?" My feet thump against the bed and my back arches. Nothing hurts, the ribbons don't cause pain, but I move like a marionette on strings.

"Breathe, girl," orders Yew. She holds me in place with her one hand and elbow stump. "The kvell was blocked. You need to breathe..."

"Kvell!" I try to scream, my voice little more than a hoarse whisper. I thrash and kick, my weak body quickly losing strength. Panic squeezes my throat. It *was* kvell. "Get it... out of me! GET IT OUT!"

Vespald grabs my ankles and presses them against the bed while Yew pins me down by the chest. Between Vespald and Yew, I am helpless and trapped. I still feel it. With every breath I take I feel hot twists of their cursed kvell slithering through my lungs and stomach. I weep, frail and pathetic. It's killing me. "Get it out..."

"It doesn't come out!" Yew leans down and grasps my chin. I have nowhere else to look but at her. "Look at me, beast girl. It's *yours*. That's *your kvell*."

I stop fighting, I stop breathing. The horrible soft warmth of kvell simmers down as I relax. I stare up into the deep angry lines on Yew's face.

"I... don't have kvell," I croak. "I'm a selkie... I don't have kvell..." And yet, there it is. I place my own hands on my chest and belly and feel the flutter of kvell for myself.

This isn't right. I don't know who, or what I am. A small, choked sob escapes me.

Yew makes a tired, disgusted sound in her throat. She places her hand over my eyes to push me down into sleep again. "Unfortunately, you very much do."

# TWENTY-FIVE

I wake up warm to a white blanket of snow outside. I lie beneath the weight of a down comforter, melted into the marshmallow mattress. I watch fat white flakes swirl outside a window.

Walls finished in heartwood, thick, double-paned windows, a hot pot of chai steaming beside me on a small dresser. I sit up at the smell of spiced tea, looking around the tiny room. Gevit and Blitz lie atop the dresser behind the tea service. Tiny ceramic pinch pots of cream and honey accompany the chai, as does a plate of dark, nutty bread, sliced cheese, and a tin of squid. I poke the bread. My finger sinks into its spongy warmth. Fresh from the oven. Someone just left this for me.

My pelt lies atop the comforter, spread out to keep me extra warm. The fur looks brushed and cared for, healthy and supple. I, myself, feel weak and aching, but sharper, clearer. Maybe I should worry about the food being contaminated with kvell, but I don't. I eat with both hands, tearing the bread into chunks and stacking it with cheese and tinned squid.

I pour cream into the tea, letting the warmth and honey infuse me. The huldror must have brought me here. Wherever here is.

When I finish eating, I crawl out of bed, unsteady on my feet. Someone dressed me in a loose shirt and pants of a warm knit. My face grows hot when I see they added underpants. Well, they did have me stripped naked, I suppose. Still, to be so helpless as to need strangers to dress me...

I open each drawer in the dresser, finding socks, towels, soap, and a selection of period care products. Everything smells clean and fresh. Is this some sort of inn?

In the bottom drawer, I find my pack and open it. My belongings are untouched. A hand goes to my hair. Someone brushed it for me. I feel exposed, completely at the mercy of others, and yet cared for.

Dressing in my own freshly washed pants and sweater, I realize my boots are missing. I put on socks and try the door.

It swings in revealing a dark hallway. The only light comes from a stone staircase leading up. I strap Blitz to my hip and throw my pelt over my shoulders, just in case.

From the bottom of the stairs, I smell fresh bread, sage, herbed chicken, and pine. I hold onto the wall as I take each step, legs weak. At the top, I find myself in a huge open kitchen with limed walls. Drying herbs and strings of sausages hang over triple sink basins and a giant pot simmers on the industrial sized range.

So, is this a restaurant? A lodge?

Hearing nothing aside from the crackle of embers, I move onward, through a stone arch. I limp into a space so large I scoot right back against the arch to get my bearings.

River stones form the walls between giant tree trunks. These same trees, hundreds of years old at least, form the cross beams in the vast ceiling. The wood and stone flow as naturally as if they grew there. The rafters must be forty, even fifty feet up, the room itself a cavernous space of stained-glass windows, smoldering stone fireplaces, iron chandeliers hanging from chains, and tapestries.

Tables and circles of couches or cushions suggest this space is used for meeting and conversing.

I hobble down the three steps into the recessed, stone floor. It warms my socked feet. Across from me, a Zahlek runescript forms a crescent moon beneath the wooden visage of Kvellsett, the Coyote Woman.

It's a temple of some sort then... but not just to Kvellsett. Each window depicts a god or spirit. Brosk carries His bone anchor over His shoulder. Fregnym shapes the stories of our lives on Their loom. Ryshvarad and Zandruik sing to passing ships from wave ravaged rocks. I see deities I don't know the names of as I limp through the space, people with curling horns and tentacles like squids on their backs, beings made from the Svall itself, stories I never learned. A trio catches my eye, a man, woman, and a canid creature with golden horns. All three of them wear masks and stunning robes woven with gold.

I shuffle in a slow loop around the huge room. Gentle incense flavors the air.

A long table against a wall holds bowls of pebbles, chips of crystal, and bundles of herbs, offerings or ritual instruments. I trace one finger around the lip of a bowl as my eyes wander to a tapestry above the table.

In the middle of the tapestry, the spiny-sailed *Naudeleid*, Brosk's ice ship, hovers over a giant maelstrom. Fire, lightning, and bands of the aurora dance. To the right of the *Naudeleid*, sailing and rowed ships war against violent waters, and to the left, six Duskingr soar through the aurora. My hand reaches up to touch each Duskingr and the Zahlek runescript names, unreadable to me. Even farther left, Duskingr nest atop buildings that hold the ships like baskets made for single eggs.

Words in my own language catch my attention from a plaque.

*Dusking: To balance the threads of nature within the self.*

*Duskingr: A traveler of the Svall. One who performs the art of dusking.*

My head tilts. I've never heard these terms used like this before. A

Duskingr has always just been an airship, not a traveler of the Svall. And what is *dusking*? To balance the threads of nature within the self... A look around the wall and table for further information yields nothing, so I continue on.

And then, I face Her. An entire twenty-foot window dedicated to Tophinghua and Tawkthalon. Light from the white snow outside turns Tophinghua into a shadow against an angry orange sky. Huge arms up-reaching in triumph, Her eyes glow like twin moons, each tooth made from a spear of silver glass. Tophinghua, Name of the Storm, the Dread One, reads a bronze plaque. Patron of Warriors and Victory. God of Thyir Itself.

I smile despite my situation. The glass artist depicted Her with nude breasts. *Ha!* Finally.

Then the shame creeps in, like a mold eating its way out from my ribcage and into my limbs. I took Her as my patron and fell in battle. She rejected my sacrifice. The weight of looking up into Her glass eyes crushes me.

Beneath Tophinghua in the window stands a proud, dark skinned woman in golden armor. A fur drapes from Her strong shoulders and in Her opposite fist She carries a radiant spear of glowing blue ice. Tawkthalon, Daughter of the Dread One.

The shame deepens. My hands go to my belly as I feel an unusual stir of warmth there: *kvell*. I am infected with kvell.

"Is that my curse then? My punishment for dishonoring you?" I mumble, voice heavy with sadness, not anger. "Kvell makes me sick. How can I possibly have both kvell and thyir in my body?" I look up at Tophinghua again, emboldened. "What does it mean, to contain both?"

"You aren't special," says a voice behind me.

I wheel to see Vespald leaning on a broom not three paces behind me. Her headphones ring her neck, and her hair sticks out of its messy bun.

She blinks her intense eyes. "We all have the potential for both, but most people don't like that."

"You—you talk?" The huge room swallows the squeak of alarm in my voice.

"Yes. I talk." Vespald twists her hands around the broom handle. She wears overalls and a wool sweater, feet bare and calloused. The skin on them, like her hands and face, looks like wood grain. The wildness of her brows, the intensity of her stare, and the lithe sincerity of her posture make me feel judged and found lacking.

"I talk," Vespald repeats. She makes her eyes larger. "Vesp."

"Vesp?" I take a step back toward the tapestry to square up my posture.

"My name. I'm Vesp."

As she speaks, I see the flash of sharp teeth and her tail snaps from side to side. Metal rings near the tuft of her tail flash in the ambient light. Funny, I always read the huldror had bovine tails but with her predatory teeth and luminous eyes, it comes off as far more lion-like.

"Oh... My name's Aalgur Thalon... just Thalon. So why do you do the hand thing?"

"The hand thing?" repeats Vesp in a deadpan voice. She takes one hand off the broom handle and makes a shape with it.

"Yes, that..."

Vesp's eyes narrow and then widen and her tail thrashes more. "This is also talking."

"Oh..." I decide against asking more for now. I feel flustered and cornered, unsure how she snuck up on me.

"Oh," repeats Vesp. Her cat eyes travel up to the Dread One behind me. "It is true? You took Her as patron in the Dusk Trials?"

"I... yes." My mouth feels dusty.

Vesp might be a hair taller than me, but she's certainly no older. Huldra or not, I need to get a grip. Letting her intimidate me in front of Tophinghua... maybe I *am* just an incompetent omelet.

"Hmm," says Vesp. She widens and narrows her eyes.

"Is the older woman here...? Yew?" I ask, tongue sticking to my gums now.

"Illuet Yew left for the Parliament. There is a special meeting because sailors died."

Just hearing her words feels like taking a fist to the chest.

Vesp sweeps the broom twice over a spot of floor and then props it against the wall. "She left before the storm and will return after. I am acolyte to Priest Lylok. Do you need anything right now, Thalon?" She stares at me.

"Actually, is there someone who can show me around? I don't even know where the toilets arc..."

"There are seven toilets..." Vesp begins pointing. Then her head snaps back to me. She stares, eyes fixed on the center of my forehead. "Do you want me to show you the toilets? I can show you other things, too." She leans forward, head tilted.

I lean away from her. She said something about people having the potential for both thyir and kvell. I pray this isn't some cult situation. "What is this place, exactly?"

"This is Ingfalla Shrine. We are in Ingfalla Forest and this is the Ingfalla Huldreby."

"*Ingfalla*, got it."

"Yes. Ingfalla from the Zahlek *Ingfalleshk* meaning: whim of the divine. As the mountains and forests are their whims, so too are we." Vesp recites the information and blinks at me.

"Sure... So... what is it for? Are you... healers?"

Vesp takes a step nearer. "We could only help you, not heal. You are very sick."

I grimace. "So, it's... not just all in my head?"

Vesp rocks forward and back on her feet. "It is in your head. But it's everywhere else too."

"Heh," I chuckle. But then my mouth gets a bit dry again. "You helped... but do you know what it is? Is there a cure?"

"I don't know." Vesp holds up empty hands and then links the fingers together in an odd chain. "I am still learning. Illuet Yew should return soon. Maybe Priest Lylok will know."

Vesp stares at me. I stare back. Her lips twitch a little. A sneer?

"Illuet Yew told me she watched you fight. Your thyir shattered. They couldn't wake you up..." She states each sentence as if reading it off a shopping list.

I have no idea what to make of it or her.

Vesp perks up and claps her hands. "Come on, I will show you the toilets. Is it time to go to the water? I can show you the hot springs, too."

"Hot springs? Gods, yes..." Cult or not, my carcass could use a hot soak.

Vesp makes a few odd shapes with a hand and then the unmistakable *come this way*, motion. She leads me through the enormous central chamber of the building, past the kitchen and down a hall of more doors like mine, perhaps bedrooms. She points out bathrooms as we pass, telling me which ones have the best taps or leaky toilets.

"This one doesn't flush right," she points. "Be warned."

I keep my distance, just in case. She's hard to read. But I'd like to think if I was in danger, the huldror could have thrown me off a cliff while I was unconscious. I keep my eyes sharp for signs of Gadvig's black suited goons.

Vesp motions me through another stone arch and into a mudroom. Shelves hold folded towels, robes, and a laundry basket.

Glass windows in the mudroom open onto wooden decking. Vesp opens the doors and the familiar tang of sulfur bubbles in. A gushing spring cascades through travertine pools, billowing steam in the winter air. She beckons me out onto the decking, where wooden steps lead down into the pools.

Vesp points down and recites information. "Only the pools with steps are safe. If there are no steps, they are too hot. Stay by the deck or in the creek, that is best." Vesp points at a sign depicting a thermometer and simply the word HOT written on it. "A visitor went climbing on the terrace once. He boiled alive. Very sad." She says this in the flattest voice before turning to face me, stare intense. She leans forward on her toes.

"You were so ill," states Vesp. "Your thyir is dim and your kvell is stuck. It must be long past time to change your skin. I will leave you."

"Long past time?" I pause halfway out the door to the springs.

Vesp blinks, serious. "If you spend too long in your human form, your mind becomes that of your beast self..."

"*Beast self?*" I shrill. My cheeks heat up. "Beast self? I change my shape when I want to, there's no time requirement... Is that what you think about us? That we're just... beasts? Besides, I *can't*. My thyir is *broken*. I'm broken..." Somewhere in my rant, the tears snuck up on me. They stream down my cheeks, hot and furious.

"I thought... I thought..." Vesp's hands make quick motions in the air and her face turns red too. "I've never met... I don't know how you... I don't... sorry..." Spinning, Vesp hurries away so fast I'm surprised she doesn't catch her tail in the slamming door.

I stand there, unsure if I feel embarrassed, offended, or guilty. Still dripping tears, I stagger back to my room. And promptly get lost.

Trying to get ahold of myself, I stumble into the grand hall. Since our tour, it's filled up with huldror of all ages. Gentle music plays, and the small crowd moves through slow, precise motions, lifting and lowering a single foot, pushing out with a hand, some kind of slow dance. They all stare at me as I stumble in.

"Does anyone know where I can find my boots?" I stammer.

Tails flick in annoyance.

A woman shushes me.

The huldror whisper, pointing to the pelt in my arms. I scramble out of the grand room as quickly as possible. By the time I spot the staircase to the basement, I'm sobbing. The tears come so easy now, since, well, everything.

Finding my room, I fall into bed and lay there crying like some homesick pup. I oscillate between crying for Azoto, crying for myself, and crying because I wish I were with Hans right now.

*Beast self.* The term replays in my mind. I curl tighter under my pelt. That is something my parents might have said. Something they probably believed. That at my core, I'm nothing but an animal who sometimes wears a human face.

# TWENTY-SIX

"Hello. You need this." Vesp announces after rapping her fist on my door. She glares at me, face sharp, eyes wide. She holds a steaming tea bowl in her wood-patterned hands.

"What is it?" I ask from bed. It's the next day and the drizzly slush outside matches how I feel.

"Medicine," replies Vesp. She stares at my forehead. A silence unravels between us before she elaborates. "It contains willow bark, turmeric, and other ingredients with anti-inflammatory properties. It should help you feel better. You will need better medication in the future."

I hold out a hand for the bowl and drink the bitter, earthy liquid while Vesp watches. She gives no further explanation, so I hand the bowl back.

Vesp rotates the bowl in her hands. "It is time to get up. You must do the kvellvahna."

"The... what now?"

"Kvellvahna. The art of activating and channeling kvell," recites Vesp, as if reading text off the wall behind me. "It is only through regular cultivation of the kvell within us that we may reach proficiency, as it is a fire easily reduced to coals."

I dip my chin. "To me, it sure sounds like kvell is making me sick. You're sure channeling it is a good idea?"

"Yes, I am sure." Vesp's words become clipped. Her tail flicks. "I felt your thyir myself. It is injured and your kvell is weak..." She looks at the ceiling, turning the bowl round and around in her hands. "Strengthening your kvell may help your thyir recover. You need to get up and practice. You seem very sad here."

I watch her stare at the ceiling. "How do you know anything about thyir?"

Vesp's eyes snap to me, then back to the ceiling. "My thyir is strong. I am good at channeling it."

I scowl. "Thyir is bone magic. Skin magic. Thyir changes our shapes. How do you even use it?"

Vesp taps her fingers on the bowl. "Time to get up, Thalon. They will start without us."

I consider telling her I'm too tired. It's not a lie. With a sigh, I follow her to the grand hall. About two dozen huldror gather around the crackling hearths. The huldror follow me with their eyes, and I stare right back. Tails swish over the floor and I narrow my eyes.

A clock chimes from the wall, and the huldror fan out from the fireplaces, picking spots on the floor. Vesp leads me off to the side and shows me how to stand. A few people step away from us.

"What am I supposed to do?" I hiss at Vesp.

"Follow me." Vesp hisses back. She then closes her eyes and breathes. One hand rests on her chest, the other on her belly.

I copy her. River-like music plays from somewhere, and I roll my shoulders, trying to relax. I can feel eyes on me though, judging me.

"Your hands are in the wrong places," Vesp whispers to me.

My eyes snap open, and I adjust my position. I raise my eyebrow in a question and Vesp shakes her head.

"Too tense," she hisses.

A growl underscores my exhale, but I try again to relax.

"Follow someone. Anyone."

No one follows the same instructions, I soon realize. Some people move only their hands in slow, laborious arcs. Some crouch and some balance on a single foot for minutes on end before bringing the other to the ground as if pushing it through mud. I catch a strange moment where a huldra switches feet and hovers, suspended in the air for a beat. My arm hairs stand on end. Kvell can defy gravity?

With Vesp frozen beside me, like she fell asleep on her feet, I shuffle to the back of the room where I can watch everyone and pick someone more mobile to follow. A wiry fellow seems to have a handle on it, so I mirror him. I sink into a low, almost grappling stance. Then I hold it.

Any minute now, I expect him to move. Soon, right? He has to move at some point...

He doesn't.. He rests, easy and peaceful in his excruciating low stance, like he's sitting against a wall.

I sweat. My legs tremble. The huldra man simply balances, muscles relaxed, in this horrible pose.

Finally, just about the time I feel my weak knee about to buckle, he moves. He sinks even lower to the ground. When I try to follow, my knee does buckle, and I thud to the warm floor. Heat flushes my face as the man looks over his shoulder at me before continuing to do nothing in his deep, agonizing stance.

I glance around for someone else to follow, someone easier... aha. A rotund fellow catches my attention, by far the thickest huldra in the room. Copper jewelry bands his tail and he wears his shaggy, graying hair in a sloppy bun. He moves from position to position, meaty fingers spread and relaxed.

Old and fat. An easy mark. I balance on one foot as he does, resting my ankle over my knee and more or less sitting on the air. Despite being chunky, my easy target moves his body with an effortless grace, as if maneuvering through complicated shapes and patterns costs him nothing at all. I mimic him, arms following circular arcs, spine bending and twisting, balancing on one foot at a time...

Sweat trickles from my brow to my chin. My legs shake. I stagger out of the gathering room and into an empty hallway, one hand over my mouth so I don't vomit in front of everyone. I end up on my knees leaning against a wall and breathe through the nausea. My sweat plinks to the floor.

Gods, I haven't thrown up from a workout since I was a teenager. And bested by the fattest person in the room, no less! What a shipwreck. What an omelet...

My pathetic heart still beats while Azoto... I squeeze my eyes shut.

"Why are you hiding?" Vesp pokes her head into the hallway. "We are only starting."

"Starting!" I shrill. I lower my voice to a snarling hiss. "Starting? This is ridiculous!"

"It is not. It is a dance," states Vesp, as if this should help.

I used to be a good dancer, a competent ts'kmet. Heat rises from my chest to the roots of my hair. "That isn't a dance! Ha, give me a sword, an axe, whatever!"

To my horror, the fat old huldra makes his way around the wall and takes a knee beside me. "Most battles aren't fought with swords or axes, anymore." He offers me such a kind, encouraging smile, it must be fake. "I'm Priest Lylok and you must be Aalgur Thalon."

Vesp folds her arms. "She doesn't want to do the kvellvahna."

I grit my teeth. "Because it's terrible and stupid and how in the depths is it supposed to help me?"

Vesp's tail swishes from side to side. "You won't get better at it if you don't do it."

I glare up at her. She glares back.

"I think we're getting off on the wrong foot here." Lylok pats a calming hand towards Vesp. "While my pupil is right, keeping your kvell healthy will lower the inflammation in your body, stressing out over it is not the way either.

"You're a fighter, aren't you, Thalon? A Dusk Trials champion?"

"Not anymore." No, the true champions fell into the fucking ocean.

"You're used to challenges and struggles... which this doesn't have to be. Let's just get you started with finding some stillness and breathwork. It doesn't have to be a fight."

Vesp gives me huge, round eyes from over Lylok's shoulder.

"Vesp, can you lead her without making her feel like this has to be a fight?"

Vesp's nostrils flare, but she motions with her chin toward the grand room.

"Remember, just breathe and be still," encourages Lylok. He follows us both back to the floor.

Be still? What good could that possibly do anyone? I stand, balanced, hands over heart and belly. I sigh.

Something unseen and unheard catches Vesp's attention and she suddenly whisks off into the shrine like a gust of wind.

"And there she goes," sighs Lylok. "That's alright. Remember, Thalon, we're starting with breath. Just breath... go ahead and take a deep breath with me... inhale... that's it, fill your lungs as full as they go..."

My attention zigzags as my ears catch a whisper.

"...What a weirdo."

My attention homes in like a harpoon. Are they whispering about me?

"That's rude. It's sad..."

"Not sure why they keep her around..."

A scowl etches into my face. They're whispering about Vesp, not me. I may know very little about Vesp, and she may be weird, but she carried my broken ass out of the woods...

"Brought that beast girl here..."

I catch the tail end of a sentence.

"Are we having a conversation?" A sharp and pointed glare from the round priest Lylok shuts them up.

*Beast girl...*

I take a deep breath. I take another one. A moment ago, I was considering crawling back into bed to lick my wounds. Now, I stay in this stupid pose out of spite.

* * *

AFTER THE EXCRUCIATING HOUR OF KVELL-WHATEVER, I HOBBLE MY WAY INTO a hot spring and grumble out my displeasure where no one can overhear me. It was supposed to make me feel better but my muscles shake, my head throbs, and a queasy knot sits in my stomach. Whatever. At least I'm not in bed.

Naked in the water, I inspect the splotchy rash on my left arm. It appears to be fading again. But for how long? What will set it off next time? What did Yew mean about my body attacking itself? How long will this go on before it kills me?

And how in the world is kvell, dirty, thyir-breaking kvell, supposed to help me heal?

*It's yours...* I remind myself and feel gross just thinking the words. *Yeah, and look what it got you...*

Steam pours from the river. Melting snow trickles in weepy little streams. There's no point in trying to make it to the air base with the weather like this. I suppose I'm stuck here. At least I'm not locked in, even if they did take my boots.

On my way back to my room, a looming figure blocks my path. Illuet Yew's pronged antlers scrape the hallway ceiling and I notice she has cloven hooves instead of feet. With her oak-bark skin, gleaming eyes, and double canine teeth, she seems more huldra than the huldror, ancient and wild and heavily scarred by a mysterious life.

"Thalon." Yew brushes a bit of slush from the embroidered sleeves of her robes. "I see you can walk."

"I... well, yes," I stutter. Should I bow or kneel? I don't know the expected respect protocol for an Illuet. As much wilderness as she is person, I feel compelled to acknowledge her station. "I'm out of bed…" I add, feeling like an absolute omelet.

"Good." Yew exhales and her impressive posture stoops, exhaustion deepening the lines of her face. "Then move along. The air base you seek is not far."

"I… what?" A knot tightens in my belly. Am I not wanted here?

Yew makes a flicking motion with her one hand and rests it on the back of a decorative chair. "You have no business in this forest, selkie as you are. Since you can walk, you can continue to the air base where you will intercept other people like you, I am sure."

I am speechless. She might as well have slapped me across the face.

"What is the meaning of sending my student away without my acknowledgement?" asks the calm voice of Lylok. He waddles around a corner. He smiles up at Yew, not intimidated in the least.

*Student?* I blink.

"Student?" Repeats Yew in a voice as level as a flatlined heart monitor. "That is a *selkie*, I would remind you. A sick selkie unfit to crew the Duskingr…"

"We can't all be fit to crew the Duskingr, Esteemed Illuet." Lylok's eyes close just long enough to add emphasis to his statement. His posture remains relaxed, fingers hooked behind his back, belly round and prominent. "But, you said so yourself, like our own Vespald has learned a knack for her thyir, this young woman has quite pronounced kvell. Not only will training help her recover some vitality, if she can learn to harness both elements in harmony…"

Yew's lips draw back over her sharp teeth. "And there it is. The empty wishes."

"Empty they may be, Illuet, there is no shame in wishing."

Yew makes a disgusted sound in her throat. "Do as pleases you, Lylok. Waste your time how you like. You have until Midsommer to demonstrate results. But make certain the girl earns her keep. And bathes. Gods, do selkies reek." She stalks away, hooves clicking on the stone.

"Will do." Lylok finger-waves at Yew's back before turning to face me. "Hello, student!"

"I'll... I'll leave," I sputter. "I know when I'm not welcome..."

"Nonsense!" Lylok shakes his head, eyes gleaming. "You have so very much to learn!"

"She... hates people like me!" I jab a finger after Yew.

Lylok bobbles his fluffy head. "I'm absolutely not defending her inexcusable racism, because, frankly, eww, but consider it in context. Up until a few months ago, Yew served on a Duskingr as Illuet. She'd served for decades alongside your people. Recently, she was injured. She now struggles to channel her significant kvell without a helping hand... a literal hand... which ticks her off to no end.

"Parliament voted her into retirement for being 'unfit' to sail. So really, she's as unfit to sail as you and she resents it."

"I'm still not welcome," I reiterate.

Lylok folds his arms. "Do it out of spite then. You know about spite."

I do know about spite. But it would be nice to feel wanted.

"I want you here. I want to train you," offers Lylok, as if reading my thoughts.

"But... why?" I pull over a decorative chair and sit on it.

"Because I see potential in you, Thalon. And I also see a spirit in need of healing."

I hunch over and stare at the floor tiles. "So, I'm a pity project."

"Not in the slightest. You are a tough, dedicated young woman who fought hard for what she wanted, and the world knocked you down. You deserve to see all of who you can be."

"Sure," I mumble, not convinced.

*I don't have time for your shit, Thalon,* Lexija once said. Why should Lylok?

At least if I stay here, I don't have to contend with Gadvig's henchmen and the Temple of Brosk pup factory.

"You'll get right to work," Lylok dusts his hands. "You'll be expected to carry your weight. Much like a Werkhaus, we exchange some labor for room, board, and spiritual expansion. I know you're sick, so you'll only be asked to do what you're able. For now, you may accompany my student, Vespald, in tasks throughout the huldreby. You've already met Vesp."

Only then do I notice Vesp lurking behind Lylok. Her eyes seem to glow in the dark hall.

"We've met, yes."

"Good. For the rest of the day, I need to attend to projects in my shop, so you two will need to occupy yourselves."

"Fine..." I keep staring at the floor.

"Good." Lylok nods, turning on his heel. "I will see you both later then."

I stay where I am, scooting a bit of gravel around with my toe.

"Well." Vesp twists her fingers together.

"Well, what?" I ask.

"Well. Let's get started."

I'm not sure I want to get started. I'm considering making a run for it. "Let me have my boots back, and it's a deal," I say.

# TWENTY-SEVEN

Turns out, my boots had been left in the grand entrance to the shrine the whole time. With everyone else's footwear. I wasn't special, as Vesp pointed out.

Vesp eases me into tasks one at a time, starting with sweeping. That's all I do for a week: sweep halls. Right back to where I started, swabbing decks, sweeping halls, what's the difference?

At least the work keeps my mind distracted from Azoto. I already performed her death ritual with Hans, but the scar left is slow to heal.

But then, as the weather mellows, Vesp starts me on bread delivery. Bundled in my canvas coat, I follow the crude map she gave me, limping from home to home and leaving paper bundles of bread on the doorsteps. Vesp usually sets me on a task, makes sure I'm not going to pass out or puke on it, and then leaves to do her own work. I notice she often wears her headphones plugged into a flat, glassy rectangular device from the Otherside. She bobs her head to music only she can hear.

Task by task, I begin exploring Ingfalla.

Houses built from quarried stones, river rocks, and wood form a vaguely horseshoe-shaped downtown. Several streets lead off into the thick, murky woods like spokes from a wheel. The horseshoe forms a partial ring around a huge, open-air gathering space. Tree trunks have been carved into images of Kvellsett, the spirit of decay and rebirth, Fregnym, the weaver of stories, gods I don't particularly relate to. Except for the decay part, that resonates.

On my first delivery trip, which consists of a single street, I catch my breath on a stone bench. I look up at the shrine itself as I do. The mammoth temple creates a clearing in the towering red treetops, allowing for a glimpse of the Duskheim spires beyond, frosted with snow. Tree trunks twist like arthritic fingers atop the shrine, balled up and knotted. It looks like the trees are still alive, but sickly or dormant. The trees look like they should be holding something, like there should be more shrine on top for them to cling to or...

"Oh!" I gasp out loud. "Oh! That's where they land the Duskingr! The ship fits on top!"

"Not for a long time," remarks a passing villager, tail swishing. He hurries by before I have time to ask questions.

"Yes, the Duskingr used to land at the six shrines." Lylok answers me with a smile and nod, as if pleased to receive a question.

He sands a bowled object in his hands, some sort of mask maybe. His open-air workshop sprawls around us. Leather work, woodwork, clay and small metal jewelry, Lylok seems to dabble in everything. Masks line the rafters. Are they Illuet masks? Does he make the masks for priests of kvell?

"The Duskingr dock at the air bases now, since they belong to Parliament. The Karrvossians used to care for the ships, but that too is obsolete. With no one to dusk, we can't tell the treetops to moor the ships. You can see, our shrine is rather..." Lylok wiggles his fingers as he searches for the word, then simply twists his fingers together like the trees atop the shrine.

"There's that word again: dusk, dusking…"

"Ah, yes." Lylok dampens a cloth in a bowl of water and uses it to smooth a rough spot on his project. "The duskingr, the people not the airships. They were masters of both thyir and kvell. With both elements held in equilibrium, they were able to unlock great power. Bend the trees, move the ice, select specific destinations on the other side of the Svall. I'm sure you've heard about it."

"Ah, yes. The children of the Ingvu used to move the ice, they say."

Lylok smiles. "Indeed they did. I like to imagine what that was like: to move the ice and bend the trees… to walk in the Svall. I like to tell Yew I'm going to see it before I die. Dusking. Someone is going to figure it out again. She hates hearing that. Oh, you should see her face, Thalon. All pruned up like this…" He puckers his face.

I smile. A part of me wonders if that's why he's taken such an interest in Vesp and I, if he thinks one of us might emulsion our cream and olive oil magics right into the impossible. I hope that's not the case. I don't want to let anyone else down. *Dusking? Get real, Thalon.* It will be a miracle if I ever change my shape again.

"Do you prefer that? Thalon? Or do you have a nickname?" asks Lylok.

I snap back to the moment. "I've… gods, I've just gone by Thalon. I don't know, it seems to fit…"

"Thalon, child of Tawkthalon. A lovely name and it suits you. I know we haven't worked together a lot yet, but when you're ready, I am the Master of Kvellvahna. I think you will grow to appreciate it."

I hide my surprise. A master of the kvell-whatever? I wonder how hard this kvellvahna can be if the master is so round. Who am I kidding? He leaves me in the dust. Maybe I should shelve that mindset.

"You will benefit from both the praxis and lore of the kvellvahna, this is clear to me. But we will only start when you're ready. For now, just step into group practice when you feel up for it."

"Ah... alright?" I shift my weight from foot to foot. "How will I know when I'm ready?"

Lylok meets my eye over his ambiguous project. "Trust. You will know, and you will let me know."

With a heavy sigh, I return to my cubby. Gone are my days of training with the most elite fighters in the land. Now I'll be learning the infuriating art of sitting on air and not puking with chunky grandpa.

Nonetheless, when I am certain Yew isn't watching, I begin joining in the group sessions of the kvellvahna, whether I like it or not. If moving the nasty kvell around will keep my body from eating itself alive, it's a price I can afford.

* * *



Signed and sealed, I drop my letter in the town's single post receptacle. The checkpoint had scared Hans more than seemed reasonable. No one expects him to be a broodmare for the Temple of Brosk, I'm not sure what he knows that I don't. I hope he and the Caravan made it through. I wish they'd be in Poppy City before Midsommer. Patience was never my greatest gift.

* * *

I don't know what to make of Vesp.

It doesn't take me long to catch her in the act of leaving food and tea for me. When I ask her to stay and eat with me, she shakes her head and backs out of the room, tail flicking. She helps me get started on tasks and then goes off on her own as if Yew is right and I smell or something.

Once afternoon chores are finished, I take myself to the hot springs for a dip. Cooked, I rough up my hair with the towel before wrapping it at my waist and crossing the shrine to my room. The tall ceilings, the stained-glass windows depicting glowing landscapes of the Svall, the ice ship of Brosk, and the Coyote Woman tending her crops. I pause to bask in the quiet, comfortable glory. My fingers trace over an image of a selkie or an Ingvu, I'm not sure which, turning a cresting wave to ice. Ah, what that must have been like. To control the thyir in the water...

Vesp stakes me in place with her furious eyes from across the room. She stares at me with such intensity, such venom dancing in her wilderness hair, that I freeze, pinned as intended. Her cheeks flush and her tail thrashes. My cheeks redden as well, ashamed to be looked at in such a way and not sure why.

Stalking down the steps, across the shrine, and up the steps on the other side, Vesp throws her own coat around me and pulls it closed over the chest. "You'll catch cold, Thalon."

Hooking my arm, she hauls me back to my room. "With your hair wet like that... you're just getting... getting not sick..." All but throwing me into my room, Vesp patters off on her bare feet and vanishes into the shrine.

Alone in my room, I run my hands over my own ribs, my hollow belly. Does she find me repulsive? Or was it just as she said, that I would catch cold?

Only after dozing off do I pop back awake with a realization. The huldror don't change their skins. Maybe I shouldn't walk around with my tits out.

* * *

I begin joining the communal meals, keeping to myself, not speaking to anyone. No one speaks to me, either. That's fine, I don't need any more lip service about beast girls. The only huldra who waves or offers greeting is chunky old Lylok, who I've been avoiding. I'm not ready to learn the kvell-whatever, not in earnest.

Vesp stalks into the hall with muddy feet and her headphones over her ears. I raise an eyebrow at her feet. No wonder the sweeping never ends around here. She flutters around the table like a moth, unsure where to land, looking everywhere but at me until the moment she does, then her stare hits me full force.

I blink at her, half-eaten roll in my hand, never sure what she might be thinking. At least by now I've figured out the stalking and glaring are features, not anger or poor performance on my part. At least, I hope not.

Her bobcat eyes pin me down. Accusingly, pityingly, what exactly?

"Hi," I say. "Good morning…"

Vesp slides her headphones down around her neck. "You can pick herbs?"

"Huh?" I pause, feeling stupid. "Can I pick herbs?"

"Walking." Vesp leans closer, tapping her Otherside device to turn the music off. The glass surface glows with shapes and colors. "We will need to hike. It is not far, but do you feel strong?" She cocks her head to signify a question.

Instead of answering the question, I exhale a loud breath through my nose, stand, and follow her tail to the doors. We'll find out if I'm up for it.

Outside a robin-egg sky sprawls above us. Already the first few butterflies have burst from their chrysalises, and the streams warble over stones polished by a thousand winters. I stop to stare at a butterfly alighting on a yellow bloom. Aside from a few sneezes of snow, we sort of danced right past winter into early spring.

"You grew up here?" I ask as Vesp stalks up a trail leading away from Ingfalla. We hop a small creek, her bare feet pattering across a rotting log.

"No," is all Vesp says.

"Hey, what are these called?" I point out a moss-covered stone carved with Zahlek runes. I've noticed them inside homes when I deliver bread.

"Hearthstone," replies Vesp.

"Ah. What's that?"

"It is a record of huldror families. All huldror are tied to a hearthstone."

"Oh." I inspect the stone beside me, picking moss out of a rune and tracing my finger over it. "Is yours nearby?"

"No." Vesp's tail flicks and she turns her back to me. "I am not part of a hearthstone."

I open my mouth to ask more but shut it as she walks away. If she wants to tell me, she can tell me, I decide. I follow her.

At first, I imagine I will hate hunting for herbs. My leg aches, my arm twitches as I limp after Vesp's long stride. But as we stoop beneath brambles to sniff fresh green sprigs or wander in slow, pensive steps along riverbanks, I relax. I breathe in the cool, fresh mountain air. I admire the heavy, sleepy greens of the forest, ancient and slow where we are fleeting and finite.

"Hmm." Vesp frowns, tail zigzagging back and forth. She squints at the trunk of an oak tree.

"Hmm?" I look at it as well.

"This shouldn't be here." Vesp points out a crack in the side of the oak.

A black, gooey ooze bubbles out, forming balls the size of fishing floats. Black baubles pock over the forest floor and splatter the small, nearby field with patches of gray, dead grass.

"What is it?" I ask, picking up a stick and poking a black boil. I recoil as it pops into a cloud of dust.

"Rot," replies Vesp, still scowling. "I will tell Illuet Yew."

"Is it bad?" My nose curls at the fetid smell. I almost gag. Whatever it is, my body sure hates it.

"It is bad when there is too much. There is too much here. We will need to burn this hill."

"Burn it!" I blurt.

Vesp turns to me, face blank. "Yes, burn it. We burn the forest every year. Different pieces of it, not all at one time. Fire keeps it healthy. The trees like fire. Do you see the big red trees? They only make seeds if there is fire."

With that, Vesp continues on her way. I follow, backing away from the black cloud as it settles to the forest floor.

We walk in silence for nearly an hour. Not a tense silence though, a rather comfortable one. Neither of us speaks, but Vesp doesn't put her headphones back on either.

Then, she thrusts a cluster of leaves under my nose, eyes big and bright. "Mint!"

"Oh…" I take a leaf and sniff it, then bite it. It reminds me of Kindling's Eve, of laughing around a fire and drinking cocoa. I grin.

Tail flicking, Vesp leads me to other herbs she knows, as well as the bark from a tree growing beside the stream, which she has me peel with Blitz. When Vesp spots a cluster of green mushrooms growing beneath a log, she pops some into her mouth. She passes one to me, leaning closer as if sharing an indulgent secret. It tastes of the earth and the smell of fresh rain.

A huge, unexpected grin splits Vesp's face. She sticks out her tongue to reveal it stained florescent green. I can see a faint glow inside her mouth.

"Ha!" I cackle, sticking out my own tongue.

We search and pluck little morsels here and there, and search some more. I find a quiet joy in looking. More than once, I sit down beneath the brambles to disguise my tiredness from Vesp. The treasure hunt takes more out of me than I'd care to admit, but for some reason, I don't want it to end. While I rest, I scrounge for the green fungus and share my trove wordlessly with her. The tuft of her tail flips over when she eats them, the copper rings on it catching flickers of sunlight. Our conversation becomes nibbling mushrooms and sticking our tongues out at each other.

We stop to drink from a spring. "Do you see the thyir in the water?" asks Vesp.

I look up at her from my cupped hands. "No? Should I?"

Vesp shrugs. "I was just curious if you could too."

"Wait, are you saying you can *see* thyir?"

"And kvell, yes. Though, it's not seeing really. Not exactly with my eyes. You had so much kvell knotted through you in the forest when you were sick. It was my first time seeing someone like me," she admits. "I don't meet a lot of people who can understand or want to try."

I'm not sure how to respond, so I keep to myself.

Our baskets fill and we turn back for Ingfalla.

"Oh." Vesp tilts her head over and stalks around a fallen birch. She pokes it with a bare, muddy toe. "We could use this. For repairs after the snow. There was damage."

I use Blitz to sever the crown of the tree. I then plunk down beside it to catch my breath. I pat the trunk like I might pat a dog. "We should come back with a group. Six or seven of us should be able to carry it..."

The rest of my thoughts fall out of my mind. Vesp hands me her basket. She prances one way, dances another, and lifts the trunk onto her shoulders as if it weighs nothing. Steadying the trunk with a hand and keeping balance with her tail, she resumes her way down the path. A shimmer surrounds her, blurring the ground with each step.

When I stay planted in my disbelief, she looks back over her shoulder for me, a smile in her eyes.

"Kvell," she says. And then, she vanishes.

"Vesp!" I startle.

The tree still floats in the air. Her gold-green eyes blink open. If I squint, I can almost see her outline.

Vesp reappears. "Thyir," she states. Still holding the tree, she walks toward town.

Mouth ajar, I follow in her muddy footsteps.

# TWENTY-EIGHT

The first thing I do back at the village is hunt down Priest Lylok.

"I'm ready. I think I'm ready, Lylok. Priest Lylok. Sir."

"Ah!" Lylok takes off a welding visor and sets aside his latest project. He gives me a huge grin. "I didn't want to rush you, Thalon. We all move at our own paces, especially with the magic of breath. But I'm so excited you're ready to begin! What was your 'aha' moment?"

"I saw Vesp pick up a tree. A whole fucking *tree*!"

"Ah yes. That's on point for her."

"No one told me kvell could make you strong!"

"Naturally! I'm sure we huldror have plenty of misconceptions of thyir as well. Especially if we learned them from Yew, the gods bless her."

I pull up a stool to sit but Lylok trots outside instead.

He motions me to follow. "Why don't we practice in nature today? Unseasonably nice weather for it." Lylok leads me out of town to a semiprivate clearing upstream from the hot spring pools.

Did he take me here so villagers wouldn't gawk at me? Did he do it because he knows their stares make me uncomfortable?

"Now, you're a skilled fighter. Yew was even begrudgingly impressed with your Dusk Trials fights." Lylok faces me in a loose, easy stance. He motions for me to follow him, rolling my shoulders and shaking out my arms and legs. "Coming to the kvellvahna from a background of combat might not feel like home for you at first, but once you adjust, you may find the two skills complement, rather than contradict. Much like thyir and kvell. We like to talk about our magics like cream and olive oil, as if no one has ever created an emulsion before." He cackles. "The metaphor stops there lest we make mayonnaise! Well, I suppose that usually has eggs..."

I don't get it, but his cheerfulness is contagious. "Alright, so I don't understand this at all..." I copy the swaying motion Lylok adopts, weight transferring from hip to hip. "I'm a selkie. Using kvell will damage my gods-gifted thyir... or so I grew up hearing. How can I possibly have kvell of my own? And for that matter, how can Vesp use thyir? And if we can use both, why don't we? I don't understand how any of this works anymore..."

Lylok weighs my questions before answering. "Vespald is an excellent example. It is not so much that Vespald *can* use thyir, it is that she *does*. As you said, you selkie folk hold to the belief that kvell injures you, drains your magic. We huldra see the thyir as returning us to beasts, detaching us from the intellect and discipline needed to channel our kvell. We used to wield magic of a much stronger sort, but I am sure you have heard the adage: Now the ice moves for no one, the trees do not answer, and the Svall obeys no master."

"Yeah." I sink to the ground as Lylok dusts a spot for himself and leans into a side stretch.

"Both us huldra and you selkie folk used to dusk, but we don't trust ourselves anymore. I can't even use my own thyir besides a trick or two. It takes an openness to it... like Vesp has. Like you might have some day."

I puzzle through this. "But... isn't there a chance it's true? That the kvell broke my thyir and made me a cripple?"

Lylok's face softens. "Before we continue, I'm setting a gentle boundary. You may not call my student a cripple, Thalon."

It takes me a moment to realize he means me. "I *am* a cripple."

"You're a person living through a unique challenge."

"Call it whatever you like, how do you know kvell didn't do it?"

"Because thyir didn't make Vesp see the world as she does, despite what anyone might say. Channeling your kvell is helping you to heal, not harming you. And if you embrace it..."

I follow his lead, raising my arms to the sides. "I hope you don't expect me to do the dusk thing."

"I expect no such thing. I ask only that you learn what you can from me."

I have nothing to say as Lylok guides me through a few more stretches and then waves me back to my feet.

"You are a student of kvell now, and I am a teacher. Cultural rifts must be set aside in the pursuit of practice and understanding."

"Sure," I reply. I follow him into the first steps of the kvellvahna.

* * *

I practice the kvellvahna every day that week. By the end, I wake up ready to get to work, ready to face the day.

That's when I realize, despite not being able to channel, or even access my own kvell, moving it around in the stupid dance helps. The rash on my arm, the pain, even the grief, fades. I feel better. The horrible kvellvahna works.

I dive into it as I dove into my training for the Dusk Trials. I commit to it. This delights Lylok, who I, in spite of myself, begin to warm to. Chunky grandpa or not, he meets me where I am and pushes me just enough but never too much.

The kvellvahna becomes the center of my days, the hub around which I place other tasks. Day by day, my balance improves and my muscles strengthen. My kvell practice goes from once a day to twice as my stamina improves. Then, as life flows through my veins in a way I forgot it could, I pepper short kvellvahna work between tasks and before bed.

"The kvellvahna isn't a race, Thalon." Lylok reminds me as he notices my enthusiasm. "Trust the process. Believe in the strength you already have."

Race or not, I devour it. I might still suck at it, but it gives me strength, and so I crave it. Like Katch, like hope, I crave what makes me feel better.

"Interesting how one arm is more afflicted than the other," remarks Lylok.

We all sit in his workshop together, him, me, Vesp. She copies Zahlek runes from a dusty tome and Lylok fits a stiff black leather bracer over my left forearm and wrist.

"What is this? Armor?" I watch him tighten and adjust the leather before taking it off me and snipping the straps to the proper lengths.

Opening the leather tube, Lylok shows me metal sewn on the inside. "I noticed your arm pains you. There must be nerve involvement of some sort. This brace will hold it in place, and the copper will help ease the pain."

I scowl at the brace. "So, I'll look even more like a cripple."

Lylok sighs. "I thought we agreed, you don't get to say such things about my student."

"I *am*..." I let him strap the brace to my arm anyway. I flex my hand. I stare at it and turn my arm. To give him credit, if someone didn't know the purpose of the brace, it just looks like a cool piece of black leather armor with tooled Zahlek runes. The pressure and support feel... good.

"A cripple and an imbecile, what a pair of students," deadpans Vesp. Her tail swishes over the floor.

Lylok rolls his eyes with such force his head goes with them. "Not you, too. Literally, the worst obstacles between you two and your goals are powerless little words. Thalon is not a cripple, Vesp is not an imbecile…"

Vesp levels her eyes on him. "I can't read."

"You can *now*. And you can read *Zahlek* to boot. So you were a little late, that does not an imbecile make."

"Weirdo then," snips Vesp. She snaps her book closed. She bounces her fingers in the air. "There is no use pretending I am not."

"Fine. Weirdo. We like weirdos here. You're a weirdo, you're a weirdo, I hope you've noticed by now, I'm a weirdo. I mean, come on. Just, *come on*. Can you picture a world without weirdos? Just an entire continent of folks with sticks up their butts like someone whose name begins with *why* and ends with *eww*? Kvellsett bless her but imagine it."

I snort, then laugh out loud.

"*Eww*," chortles Vesp.

I run my good hand over the brace, admiring the workmanship. Lylok invested days if not weeks into this. I suppose if I'm going to be a low skilled incompetent omelet, at least I can look cooler doing it now. My fingers find a skinny tube sewn into the palm and wrist. There appears to be a spike of bone sewn in. "Real boning, huh?"

"Something I've had laying around. Not sure if it was a hairpin or a tool for nalbinding, but it said it needed to go with you, and so there it is. It came from a selkie sailor long ago. And now, it's yours. A bone for bone magic. A point of focus, if you will."

I squint at a faded Zahlek rune on the bone and then turn my arm over. It really does feel better.

"So, Zahlek. Is it cool?" I ask Vesp.

Her eyes snap to me. "Oh. Is it cool? *Oh*. Did you know that Zahlek was the language spoken by realm travelers? Some say, it was given to them by the gods. Did you know the noun conjugates for place in time rather than the verb?" She leans in my direction, tail flicking.

I click my tongue. "Bold of you to assume I know what any of those words mean."

Lylok hops up and dusts his hands. "Come on you two. Let's see how Thalon's new brace helps her out."

* * *

The brace does help me. It keeps my wrist from popping and my hand from twitching. It also looks cool.

I sweep the floor of the grand room one afternoon. Incense floats in the huge, open space. Vesp plays her clay flute in her room and the distant music follows me.

I pause and look up at the stained-glass window of Brosk. Kneeling, I set the broom aside and offer my hands in gratitude. When I got sick in the forest, I figured that was it, the end of Aalgur Thalon. In that moment, I'd hoped it was. And yet, here I am.

Brosk looks down at me, eyes glowing in the afternoon sun outside. I'm not sure what I'm supposed to do. I feel better, but then what? What's my goal?

"What am I meant to do?" I ask out loud.

What do I want? What is my life supposed to look like now?

*You deny my daughter*, Brosk said to me in a fever dream.

But how? I cross the room and trace my fingers over the plaque on the wall.

*Tophinghua, God of Thyir Itself.*

I am of Her line, and yet, it's the magic opposing Hers that breathes life back into me.

"What do you want from me?"

The Dread One, like Brosk, says nothing.

* * *

Weeks pass and my health improves. Vesp and I go on more hikes together. We're silent together, but we start laughing too. My skinny, hollow muscles begin to fill back in. I bring Gevit to my private kvellvahna practices, using her as a weight while I move through infuriating postures. Infuriating they may be, I'm starting to get it. It's starting to make sense.

* * *

"I don't get it." I end my practice drenched in sweat. "I can tell it's helping me... But I can't do anything with my kvell at all. I can't even really tell it's there most of the time."

Lylok throws a robe around my shoulders. "You have to want it, Thalon."

My nose wrinkles. "I *do* want it. How could I *not* want it?" Maybe because it scares me, even now. It scares me to deny Tophinghua.

"You're right, Thalon, the dance will keep your kvell from stagnating. But to channel it, you have to want it.

"You can't just want strength, speed, or health even. You have to want the part of you who can use kvell. You have to welcome it as not just as a part of you, but a loved part of you."

I shake my head and growl air through my teeth.

Lylok fetches two wooden staffs and tosses me one. "If you've got some frustration, let's work through that before we part ways."

I catch the staff in my right hand, twirling the wood, pleased by the balance. My left hand slides into place, the wrist sturdy in the leather brace.

An incompetent omelet I may be, I will not be bested in combat by chunky grandpa. I take a low stance, keeping the staff crossed over my body and on guard. I shake my robe to the forest floor.

Lylok keeps his fluffy robe on and darts in. He takes simple steps, efficient and controlled motions. I block his jabs and step to the left, careful not to cross my feet, eyes on his body, not the stick. I feign low and swipe high. He rolls my staff to the side. I lunge in for another strike, and this time, a light tap lands on my upper arm.

Lylok circles me, relaxed. Why is chunky grandpa landing blows on me? How is that fair? My breathing grows heavy.

We keep at it, trading blows back and forth until a soft tap lands on my calf.

Frustration mounting, I swing for his shins only to have my staff rolled to the side. His staff taps my hip.

"You're good, Thalon. A good fighter." Lylok steps back to indicate we should stop.

I growl and throw my robe back on.

Lylok leans his staff against a tree. "In a fight, I don't doubt you'd prove formidable. But we aren't fighting, and the very thing that brought you victory in combat works against you now. Not every learning experience is a battle, even if we hold weapons."

"That makes no fucking sense!"

"It does though, Thalon. You're fighting yourself as much as fighting me. All the foundations of kvell can be found in your fighting background, but the trick is, you must stop fighting it. It's been with you all along, just like your pelt."

"I still don't get it..." I sink down and lean against a tree trunk. My head thunks back against it. "It's not a fight, but it is a fight. It's in me already but I have to want it... drag me to the depths, Lylok, can you hear yourself?"

"I do my best to," replies Lylok. He folds his arms behind his back and gazes off over the river. The sulfurous steam rises through the evening. "You will need to turn your practice inward, Thalon. You'll need to find what wanting your kvell means to you. It may take some time, but only you will be able to answer that question. No one can do it for you.

"You're progressing well though. Your enthusiasm is admirable. Be gentle on yourself." He leaves me with a smile.

I let Lylok get a head start before I limp down to the shrine and those glorious warm springs. In the water, I float, staring up into the fingery branches of the trees. To think, someone long ago shaped the trunks to hold the Duskingr. How did we lose so much of ourselves?

I'm not sure who Aalgur Thalon is anymore. I'm not sure what she's supposed to do. But I admit, it does feel good to find part of her again.

# TWENTY-NINE

My luck runs out. I don't notice until it's too late.

Spring roars into Ingfalla as a torrent of snowmelt, birdsong, and explosions of flowers. We're only in the second week into Ithnamarsh, weeks before lunar Spring. Yet Spring it is.

I'm catching up with Vesp. Sure, I still limp, my arm's messed up, but my stamina is on the mend. The mannerisms I originally took for standoffish from her are just that she doesn't always put on the expected facial expressions.

I'm learning I can seed conversations by asking Vesp about things she likes, especially if I ask about music or Zahlek. She animates, talking with her mouth, her hands, swaying from foot to foot, eyes shining. She lights up and comes alive. I love it.

One week, we've been working to repair a damaged roof, but the wind picks up. The trees rock and crack as the wind rises. Vesp pulls me by the arm. From the safety of the shrine's covered deck, we watch the trees whip and branches fall.

"Nope, nope…" mutters Vesp. She sways from side to side, as if mimicking the trees. She spins to me. "Do you want to go play in my room?"

I blink, a little confused by the childish wording. "Sure…"

Vesp tracks her muddy feet through the shrine, washes them in the hot spring, and then leads me up the stairs and to a small, deeply lived-in room.

Vesp has her space adorned with moss, twisty sticks, and colored glass bottles. Bookshelves hold record sleeves as well as books. Clay flutes dangle from improvised hangers. I assume she means to take out cards or a board game, but she hands me a book instead.

"You will like this book," states Vesp. She fiddles with her Otherside device.

I hardly notice the book, my attention drawn to the Duskingr posters on the walls. Paintings of all six airships. A lump rises in my throat when I notice the official Dusk Trial champion playing cards on her desk.

My good hand grips my bad arm. My painted face is in there somewhere. So is Azoto's. Gods, I still have my own set of playing cards in the bottom of my pack.

I can feel Vesp's eyes drilling into me. My attention returns to the posters. "Vesp, did you try out to crew the Duskingr?" I ask. "How do huldror compete anyway?"

"We used to all compete together in the Dusk Trials. Selkies would swim the Gauntlet, huldror would compete in the Fletching, and then the top competitors from both sides would fight in the Blood Spire. That was a long time ago." Vesp picks up the cards and slides them into a drawer. Her cheeks color and her tail flicks. "I entered the Fletching this year. Crewing a Duskingr would give me access to their history and runes… which is what I want. I am an excellent shot with bow and rifle. I placed in the top percentile for agility and athletics. I can read and write Zahlek. But I too am deemed unfit to crew the Duskingr at this time." She squeezes her fists so tight her knuckle bones stick out. Then she points to a chair. "Do you want to sit there?"

"For what?"

"To read," states Vesp. She untangles the cable for her headphones.

I have no idea what I'm expected to do, if we're going to play something or not. I take a seat and flip the pages. The book is illustrated, the people talk in dialogue bubbles like a newspaper comic. A character holds a great sword. Alright, I'll bite…

"What do you want to learn about the Duskingr?" I ask.

Vesp looks right at me. I can feel the intensity of her eyes. "I want to know how they sailed through the Svall."

I look up from the book. "You think someone on them today would even know that? Didn't Illuet Yew serve?"

Vesp inhales audibly through her nose. Her tail flicks. I get the impression there's more to it, but when she doesn't elaborate, I don't pry.

Something catches my eye. I sit up straight and point to a worn record sleeve poking from the bookshelf. "Is that from *Divine Jubilee*?"

Vesp snaps to attention and snatches the record. "You know *Divine Jubilee*?"

"Yeah, I fucking do." I lean forward. "What is that?"

"This is the music!" Vesp slips the record free and places it on a record player.

I fall back in time as the familiar melody begins to play. That old fable of the worm creeping down from the mountain, a slithering beast hiding in the river.

"Oh… oh wow. I love *Divine Jubilee*. I went to it when I was younger…" My imagination strays to blue dresses and dancing chest to chest with Azoto. Her smile, her laugh, gone forever and yet preserved in this song.

"Did you know that the composer for *Divine Jubilee* also composed the stadium music for the original Dusk Trials?" asks Vesp.

"I… had no idea. I didn't realize there was a composer…"

"Oh." Vesp sets her device and headphones aside and scoots closer to me. "Oh. Did you know that *Divine Jubilee* was inspired by the Karrvoss Caravan? They used to do dramatic reenactments of Ruhnsvalla history and legends..."

And, like Lylok said, there she goes. I shut up, fold my legs under me, and watch her bloom. She walks circles around the room to show off curios and clippings about the carnival show and its influences. I like to hear her talk, I enjoy how deeply she loves what she loves, and how shamelessly she loves them. I ask questions when she pauses just so she can narrow in on the details. By Krescean, the girl knows details. I don't know how anyone could ever think she lacked intelligence. Sure, she's unusual, but what do I care?

Eventually, Vesp talks herself out and scampers off to make us chai. I end up flipping through the illustrated book and then devouring it over said chai. With *Divine Jubilee* playing in the background, Vesp lies on her bed and takes notes out of a big, old book of Zahlek. I watch the tip of her tail flop back and forth and sip my chai. She made it exactly how I like.

While we never actually play anything, somehow the day slips away. I end up doing over an hour of frantic kvellvahna after everyone else goes to bed, just to make up for the sessions I missed.

* * *

The next day, we're back at it, repairing the roof. Holding nails in my mouth, I scoot around on hands and knees, pounding them in.

That's when I notice the problem. Halfway through driving a nail, a wave of dizziness falls over me. The shock of each hammer blow rattles the bones of my neck. My teeth start to ache.

*You're still healing,* I tell myself. *Nothing to worry about... just need to finish up this last bit here...* the hammer flies out of my hand, bounces off the roof, and narrowly misses Vesp's bare toe.

"Yikes!" yells Vesp from the ground. "You alright?"

"I'm alright!" I push myself up to sit and realize that no, I'm not alright. It all happens so fast. I sway, try to catch myself, and my arm buckles. "Seagull su—!" I roll right off the roof.

"Ah!" yelps Vesp.

I crash down on top of her. She tips backwards and we land together in the dirt.

"Ahh... Vesp..." I grunt.

Her sinewy body twists beneath me. She grunts too. Her tail smacks me in the side of the face. I can't seem to figure out which way I'm lying. Face up? Face down? Sunlight stabs my brain through my eye socket.

I must have passed out for a moment. I blink my eyes open to find Vesp shaking me, face contorted, tears and snot dripping off her chin. She makes a soft, high keening.

"Vesp..." I croak. Huldror circle us, murmuring. How long was I out?

Vesp makes symbols with her hands and presses her knuckles into her temples. She rocks slightly, her tail twisted around her shins.

"Vesp..." *Did I hurt her? I landed right on her...*

"What did you do to the selkie?" asks one of the spectators.

*She didn't do anything!* I try to shout. I make a gurgling sound instead.

Vesp hisses at the speaker. She places a hand on my chest and another on my belly. My kvell twists, writhing in response to her upset and frustration. My body flops like a puppet. The dizziness wins and I puke all over the side of someone's flower boxes.

Vesp gasps. She tries to place her hands on me but one of the huldror grabs her arm.

"Leave the selkie alone. What have you done to her?"

Vesp twists free with a snarl. She makes angry, choppy motions with both hands but does not speak. Tears streak her face.

Someone scolds Vesp. "Use words, girl!"

Two more huldror try to pull her away from me.

"Stop..." I moan. *What's going on?*

The people around me chatter, voices rising. The sound pounds in my head and I screw my eyes shut.

What's wrong with Vesp? Did I hurt her? I open my eyes to find her still making gestures at the people around us and at me. A woman tries to take Vesp by the wrist.

I try to push myself up. I need to get her away from these assholes. "Gods damn it Vesp, just talk to me!"

Vesp's hands go still. Her lips quiver, and she opens her mouth. She bites down on her knuckles.

The moment she goes still, the gawkers try to pull her away from me again.

Vesp growls. She shows her sharp teeth. Dragging my good arm across her shoulders, she lifts me and carries me away from the onlookers. Without the assistance of kvell, she grunts and gasps under my weight. She hauls me up the steps of the shrine and into Yew's study.

"Please... talk to me..." I wheeze. "Please... Vesp... I'm sorry..." *I'm so sorry I'm like this. I'm so sorry I'm a broken, disgusting mess...* I find that I, too, can't get words out.

Setting me on the floor at the foot of Yew's desk, Vesp makes several aggressive hand gestures at the Illuet.

Yew stands and leans over me. Her eyes track up to Vesp then back to me. "I see you've undone all my good work, Vespald."

*That's not true!* I want to say. I dry heave a little. Yew looks down on both of us with revulsion.

Yew leans over Vesp. "It's no wonder why your parents threw you through the Svall."

I hear a sob escape Vesp. Her bare feet charge out of the room and away through the shrine. Yew picks me up like a snotty toddler and walks me to the healing room. Grief and rage splinter through me. All I can do is moan.

"And she wonders why she is unfit to crew a Duskingr," says Yew.

* * *

"AND JUST LIKE THAT, YOU'RE BACK TO SQUARE ONE." YEW PLACES HER HAND on various parts of my body, reading my energy.

I lie on my back in the room made of glowing salt bricks. Again.

"It wasn't Vesp..." I whisper.

Yew says nothing. Her touch eases the discomfort and I find my voice.

"I need medicine. They had machines from the Otherside in the hospital..."

"Your body is hurting itself, selkie. Not even the people on the Otherside can cure this type of affliction." Yew speaks in a neutral tone, but her words sink into me like talons. Straightening, she inhales air through her teeth. "I need an extra hand. Don't go crawling off."

She stalks out of the room. She left a bucket on the floor for me to puke in. The pain in my head stabs so angrily, I almost need it. I was doing fine and now I'm back here. Valmut's face appears in my mind, strong, assured Valmut. I used to think I could be like her. What a joke.

Yew stalks back in with Lylok in tow. If I didn't know better, I'd think they were two different species. One so tall, lean and simmering, the other short, portly, and brimming with concern.

"Oh Thalon..." Lylok takes my good hand and squeezes it. He looks up at Yew. "What happened to her?"

"Who can say. Your idiot student was involved." Yew covers my whole face with her palm.

Kvell squirms and twists inside me. Lylok places a hand on my belly. The pain and sickness begin to ease.

Lylok keeps his peace for several minutes before speaking. "Vespald is not an idiot, Illuet."

Yew doesn't acknowledge him. I feel fuzzy and warm on the inside as the healing takes effect.

Yew withdraws her hand. "A selkie sickened in body. A stray sickened in mind. Your students are examples of mixing magics, not exceptions." Having said what she wanted, Yew stoops to get under the arch of the door. Her hooves click down the corridor.

Lylok huffs.

I roll my back to Lylok, tears trickling over my face. "Why am I sick again?"

"Overwork, stress, worry…" Lylok's hand rests on my upper arm. "Thyir is strong, it can burn a cold right out of the body… but it can also burn you…"

"But I've been practicing the kvell… the kvell thing! I do it as often as I can! Why isn't it helping anymore?" My voice pitches up into a whine.

"Ah…" Lylok places his fingers on the back of my skull. His hands are cool and comforting. "That… might actually be the problem. You're pushing too hard. You need to be gentler on yourself, Thalon…"

"I'm *trying*! I must be doing something wrong… I must have made a mistake…"

Lylok cuts off my sniveling. "Thalon. Listen to me. It's not your fault. You didn't make a mistake, you're not being punished. Heck, you're not even cursed. Bodies are weird and sometimes bodies do strange things, especially bodies who have put themselves under a lot of stress."

"Stress? I'm just trying to live!"

"Yes, and I think you're working way too hard at it. You're different now. Not less, just different. You can't be cured, but your condition can be managed, as you've experienced. Medicine, rest, and then, balance.

"You have to slow down." He squeezes my shoulder. "You can't win health in battle. You have to kindle joy. The ache in your heart will only give the sickness strength."

I stare at the salt wall, sniffing snot back up my nose. How does he know my heart still aches?

"Your thyir is strong but broken, your kvell sits stagnant in you. Your heart hurts and you try to bury the pain in work and purpose."

I curl tighter.

"You need to learn that you don't have to push through." Lylok sits on the edge of the table. "Thyir is bone magic. It moves through the spine, the joints. It gives power over hidden elements: Ice in the water, wind in the air, and allows us to change how we appear in the world.

"Kvell is breath magic, in the lungs and belly. Where thyir is the push, kvell is the pull. The heat of the fire, and sap in the trees. Kvell holds deep strength."

"Vesp uses both," I mumble. "She's not sick like me…"

"She's not. But she's still afraid to reach for her full potential."

"What Yew said…"

"Yew is cruel, Thalon. Injured and cruel. There is no excuse for it."

So, she hates me and Vesp. "Vesp didn't hurt me…"

"I know she didn't."

She didn't hurt me, but I hurt her. More tears spill from my eyes. "Lylok, why does she do those things with her hands?"

"It was her first language." Lylok makes a few symbols with his hands, gladdened by the change of topic. "She struggled with speaking verbally. Her mother taught her to sign Ketja. She still struggles to talk, especially when upset."

I frown. "She talks just fine. Gods, she never shuts up."

Lylok smiles. "Then she feels safe with you."

And I repaid that by falling on her. Incompetent Omelet.

Lylok gets off the table and sets a blanket over me. "You need to rest for now, Thalon. I'll get you some painkiller."

* * *

I take the pills he brings me and lie on the bed. I'm right back where I started. I'm cursed. Broken. Not enough. Never enough…

*Stop it!* I push myself off the bed to my feet. I use my sleeve to wipe my face clean. *Stop this nonsense! Where has it gotten you, Thalon?*

I may be sick, but I'm sick to death of feeling good for nothing. My legs shake, so I use the wall and my good arm to limp my way around the shrine to Vesp's room.

I can see the problem clearly now. The problem wasn't that she couldn't talk. The problem was, I couldn't understand.

Impeded as I am, I do the best I can to stomp to her door. I bang my right hand on it.

"Vesp! Vespald!" I holler. I seethe, afraid if I stop growling, I'll burst into tears. I hurt her...

I hear snuffling from inside and push the door open.

Vesp curls in the corner of her bed, wrapped in a comforter.

She stares at me, sharp teeth out, eyes huge, pupils narrowed to feline slits. Her hands twist together over her heart. I can't tell if she is going to cry too, or pounce on me and tear my throat out with her teeth.

I don't particularly care. I haul myself in and slide onto the other side of her bed like a seal. A seal, not a sea lion. Sea lions have some grace on land, thank you.

"Hurt you..." she whimpers. "Hurt you... I'm so sorry... so sorry..."

"You didn't hurt me, Vesp. But we have a problem. I don't understand you." Kneeling, I offer my hands to her, as one offers them to Brosk. "I want to understand. I want to learn your language. Please show me."

Vesp's face contorts with something very near anguish. She crawls to me and takes my hands in hers. Her hands are warm and calloused like mine.

Vesp brings one hand to her lips and then tilts it to me. She lifts my own hand, the weak one, to my lips. Her gold eyes look into me. "Thank you," she whispers. She repeats the gesture one more time. "Thank you."

# PART THREE

## THE ICE MOVES FOR NO ONE

CHAPTER

# THIRTY

Spring transitions into a warm, cheerful summer in the Ingfalla Huldreby. Day by day, week by week, I feel more like myself again. We fall into patterns of gentle kvellvahna, Ketja practice, and as my strength returns, play sparring between Vesp and I.

On one such day after the kvellvahna, Lylok asks me to meet him in his workshop in an hour. As I let myself into the shop, I just about have a heart attack when Vesp leaps out from behind a rain barrel.

"Surprise!" she cheers.

"Surprise!" I sputter. Well, I am surprised, that's for sure. "What's... what's the occasion?"

"Your birthday, silly!" Vesp drags me inside where a beaming Lylok waits beside a cake. Vesp points to the rune painted atop the frosting. "That's your name in Zahlek!"

"How... how'd you know it was my birthday?" I stammer. I trace the rune with my eyes. It's not quite like what I paint on myself before battle, but I can't point to the differences.

"It's on the Dusk Trial cards," says Vesp, bopping my shins with her tail.

Lylok passes me a knife and plate. "It's important to remember the little milestones, Thalon. Happy twenty-six."

I can't help myself, I tear up a little. I made it. Maybe, just maybe, in spite of everything, I'll keep making it.

Vesp grins, the fluff at the end of her tail resting against the back of my calves. We share the cake. We share smiles and laughter too.

Midsommer's fast approaching, and with it, the end of my time here. But Vesp and Lylok are right. I need to take time to remember joy.

* * *

*I SEE THEM. TO YOUR LEFT... MOVING CLOSER...*

Vesp crouches beneath the crown of a toppled oak. She uses a bit of thyir to blend herself into the greens and shadows. All I can see are her hands and gold feline eyes.

*How close?* I sign back.

*Thirty meters... twenty-five...*

My heart races. I hope our adversaries can't sense it.

I breathe in and breathe out, sweating in the mid-Ingvrushar heat. I carry no weapons and wear no armor aside from my arm brace.

My attention narrows to Vesp and only Vesp.

*Hold...* She keeps her palm perfectly still as her fingers make the word. *Hold... NOW!*

I spring from my tree stump hideout, tackling the first of two huldror. She yelps and scrambles, caught off guard and off balance. Her companion grapples me from behind. I use his momentum, rolling forward, throwing him over me. I land on top of him.

The huldra makes an *uff* as air rushes out of his lungs. The girl leaps on me. We scramble and grapple in the dust.

The huldra hooks her tail around my ankle like a whip and pulls my foot out from under me. She steps as I stumble, channeling kvell and using it to shove me to the forest floor. I hit hard. Stars pop in my vision.

"Think you can beat us at our own game, sea dog?" The girl grins, delight glistening on her teeth. She straddles me, holding me down.

I kick and buck, unwilling to go down so easily.

The girl grabs my legs and the boy holds me around the upper arms. The huldror pair laugh as they lift me.

"Sea dog," they tease. "Beast girl. Your weak ice-bone magic can't help you here."

Jokes on them, my magic's useless anywhere.

They laugh and carry me off like a freshly felled deer. "Now to get their trove..." muses the girl. "I bet the screwball put it in a tree. She always puts it in a tree... Your friend is very 'creative,'" smirks the girl.

"Pretty funny, huh?" quips Vesp. She strolls into the clearing with a casual sway in her hips. She carries a polished wooden ball under one arm. When she has the attention of my captors, she lifts the ball to her ear and shakes it. Goodies rattle inside. "Put her down. You lost."

"What!" The girl drops my feet.

The moment my boots get purchase, I drive backwards, crushing the boy against a tree trunk. He makes a satisfying *eheh* sound.

"Next time, don't let yourselves get so distracted," I suggest. I help Vesp crack open the ball and get to the candy inside. I pop a hazelnut chocolate into my mouth. "Mm."

"You two cheat," grunts the boy, rubbing his shoulder.

I hold out my braced arm and let my head fall forward a bit. "Yeah. We have such an advantage. Here..." I toss them both chocolates. They shuffle off, grumbling.

Vesp lowers her mouth to my ear. "They think we are easy prey."

"And that is their weak spot. Come on, let's go get our trove before someone finds it."

"They won't," Vesp grins and shimmies her hips. "I hid it in the shrine. In the fireplace. Up the chimney. The rules don't say anything about the trove needing to be hidden in the woods."

I shake my head. "Screwball."

Vesp swats my calf with her tail. "Beast girl. Are you feeling alright though? You put up quite a fight. You were the distraction. I didn't mean for you to actually *fight*..."

I take stock of myself. Over the past several months, I've been able to recover some stamina and strength. I take it slow, infuriatingly slow, introducing activities a few minutes at a time. My arm's not right, I walk with a limp. I get better and then get ill, but not deathly ill. I'm learning the rash often appears down the inside of my bad arm before my symptoms escalate. An indication to rest. I'm a skinny, gaunt ghost of the woman who fought in the Blood Spire. But I'm here, playing summer games with Vesp. In spite of everything, I'm still here.

"I think that's about as much fun as I can handle," I say. "No reason to overdo it. How was my Ketja?" Vesp and I work on Ketja daily, the language of hands.

Now that I have a basic knowledge of the language, I'm surprised we don't learn it for combat or loud environments. It would be fantastic at dance and fighting tournaments.

*Better every day! Even your tired hand!* Vesp signs to me. She always uses the sign for *tired*, for my bad hand. *Sometimes I can't tell if you're asking a question or not though.*

*I'll work on that...?* I add questioning emphasis to the end of my sentence.

Vesp gives my calves another smack with her tail.

Inside the shrine, Vesp heads straight for an empty fireplace to retrieve our trove. It's just another wooden ball that we filled with treats from the kitchen for the Tree Pirate Game. Much like Pirate Trove us selkie pups used to play. I rub my arm as Vesp stands on tiptoe, and then uses her arms and legs to climb a few feet up into the chimney.

I watch her tail swing from side to side. I grin. Along with the kvellvahna, I've been teaching her hand-to-hand combat. Someday, she's going to hand me my ass. I'm fine with that.

Vesp thumps back to the hearth with sooty feet and hands. The ball bounces down with her.

"Vespald, Thalon." Priest Lylok approaches us from across the grand hall, three scrolls tucked under his arm, a laden basket in the other. He sets the basket down and claps his hands, holding them out until Vesp tosses him a candy. "Glad to see you are bountiful pirates. When you've sickened yourselves with sugar, come help with the Midsommer pyres. After that, Vesp, you meet Priest Halvra down in the lower meadows for ritual review and, Thalon, please deliver the cherry tarts this afternoon."

"Yes, Priest Lylok." We incline our heads. The moment he turns his back though, we shove hazelnut candies in our mouths. Grown women we may be, with summer festivities thick in the air, I at least, feel the playful spark of a pup. Vesp shimmies her shoulders and catches a candy in her mouth. We make eye contact and giggle.

*Go?* Vesp asks me.

*Go,* I agree.

* * *

I try not to think about Midsommer, even as I help build the pyres.

We construct huge ones of dry brush to ignite on Midsommer's Eve. I understand the pyre at Midwinter, the rekindling of Brosk's fire, but I admit I don't quite get the significance of the summer counterpart. Regardless, dancing around three roaring bonfires sounds promising. With Midsommer mere days off, I have nothing to show for my training. Nothing to convince Yew I'm worth keeping around. I practice the kvellvahna daily but am no closer to channeling kvell than when I arrived. I suspect as soon as the celebration ends, Yew will send me packing.

And then what? Where will I go? What will I be strong enough to do? My eyes drift to Vesp. What will life look like without her?

"That's good enough for today, friends." Lylok announces once our pyres stand about seven feet tall. "We'll need to decorate them and fill them with offerings, but that should happen the day before the rituals. Don't want critters moving in. I can't speak for your palate, Thalon, but I'm none too fond of roasted wood rat."

"How dare you rob me of such a delight," I deadpan. I turn to Vesp. "See you at dinner?"

"See you. Don't forget, the eclipse tonight. We're going out together." She winks.

My heart and stomach both do something a little odd at the reminder. I stare after Vesp as she whisks away to ritual practice.

Shrugging it off, I return to the shrine for my delivery assignment.

* * *

*"...We're seeing tensions mounting outside the Parliament chambers as talks of the transcontinental railroad continue. Emotions run high!*

*"Wait...! This just in. I'm getting breaking news from off the coast...! An unprecedented naval confrontation in the South Sea Svall! Is it pirates? A foreign navy? Or something mysterious from the Otherside? As always, this is Reporter Kelpie and you're listening to Kelpie Live..."*

I switch off the radio on the kitchen counter. Reporter Kelpie always sounds so intense, so worked up and theatrically breathless, she wears me out. Filling my basket, I continue my delivery course.

A long, purple twilight sets in while I finish my deliveries. We aren't far enough north for the sun to never set, but we are far enough for the days to lengthen. Dropping off my last bundle of cherry tarts with a squealing huldra child, I start back for the shrine. I take my time to enjoy the warm smells of dried grass and the seesawing of crickets and other night bugs. I try to accept that soon I may have to say goodbye to this place... to Lylok and Vesp... There will be other beautiful places, other kind people, right? Maybe I'll finally hitch a ride with Hans again. The Caravan should have worked its way down the eastern side of Ruhnsvalla by now. They'll be setting up camp in Poppy City. His letter to me should be arriving any day now...assuming he made it through that stupid checkpoint. My shoulders droop.

As far as I am from the sea, from my home, from my life... I find, I don't want to leave. At least not yet. I feel like I'm not done here.

At the steps of the shrine, Vesp waits for me in a long, breezy dress. She wears a crown of elk antlers over a thick, loose braid. The twilight clings to her, setting shadows in the curves of her torso and flow of the dress, glowing in her feline eyes. Those eyes find me and she waves.

It's a hot night, but I'm sweating more than I should.

I climb the steps and look down at my trousers and sleeveless shirt. "Should I... I mean... I think I'm underdressed..."

"You're fine. We're just going to sit on the ground, silly." Vesp takes the basket from me. Jaunting to the kitchen, Vesp returns to me with a fresh basket, tail weaving under the dress. The long dark tuft on the end brushes the floor.

*Shall we?* she signs.

I hold out a hand for her to lead the way.

All through the huldreby, small bonfires glow, folks gathered around to eat their candies from the pirate game.

Vesp carries the basket in both arms. She leads me up a path beside the creek, picking her way between jagged points of marble in the wash of silver moonlight. We continue onto a spine-like ridge of stone. Bowled valleys dip down on either side of us, carved by glaciers eons before. The trees thin. Vesp takes a seat against the trunk of a pine, affording us a view down over Ingfalla. The fires wink below. It reminds me of my first night here, half out of my skull and hallucinating whale song.

Vesp spreads a small towel on the earth and removes nutty rolls, cheese, and a tin of fish eggs from the basket. Last comes two tea bowls and a small bottle of hard cider.

"Did you know, the dark moon is the time followers of Kvellsett commune with the dead?"

I reach for a roll. "I did not know that." I pick a single nut off the roll and chew on it. My heart still aches for what I wish I'd said to a certain dead sailor.

Vesp pours us both cider and turns to face perpendicular to me. "I suppose I should reach out to Hildre. That would be kind of me."

"Hildre?" I ask.

"Hildergulda," replies Vesp. The end of her tail flips over as she sips the cider. "She was from here. She died in the Duskingr training accident."

"So... you knew her?" I ask, unsure why Vesp seems guarded.

Vesp's eyes sweep out over the valley and she curls her tail around her feet. "She was a priestess in Ingfalla, and good at it. We participated in the Fletching together. She was deemed ready to crew the Duskingr." She turns the bowl round and around in her hands. "She had my respect for her work. Where I struggle, her steps were sure and true."

I sip the cider, focusing on the crisp, dry bite.

"But?" I prompt.

Vesp looks down. Her fingers claw around the cup. "Two of the sailors were from Vatska. Did you know them?"

I take a breath, not ready to return to these feelings. But Vesp hardly talks about herself. I want to know more, even if the price comes with discomfort.

"I knew them both, actually. But Azoto Seppanen..." I drain my cider and pour another.

"Azoto. She was your friend?" asks Vesp.

I exhale through my nose. "We were friends, yes. But then we became more than friends... and then I messed it up so bad, we couldn't even be friends again. It was my fault. All my fault."

"I'm sorry," whispers Vesp.

My spine rounds and my shoulders sag. "Me too."

We drink our cider as the crickets chirp and whirr. A ruddy smudge begins to slide across the moon.

"I know they're safe," Vesp murmurs. She reaches for a roll but doesn't eat it. "I know the gods will care for the sailors and guide them."

"Do the gods ever talk to you?" I ask. "Since you want to be a priestess..."

"Not if Yew has her way, I won't. But yes, I see the Mountain in my dreams, sometimes. I hear Her whisper." Vesp's claws pierce the roll. "She tells me that I stand in my own way. I don't know how to make myself different than I am."

The tin of fish eggs makes a loud snap as I open it. Vesp uses a claw to take one for herself.

Setting down the bread and fish egg, Vesp moves closer to me. Her arm presses against mine. "My parents didn't throw me through the Svall, you know. But they did lose me to it. We lost each other. I'd give anything to have them back. Mom taught me Ketja, Dad too... I was... *wanted*. It felt so good to be wanted... even as I am. And then they were gone."

I'm not sure what to do, how to comfort her. I place my hand on her back and she exhales. I feel her relax. There is no hollow in her back, of course. All I feel is warm girl, trembling as she begins to cry.

I know Vesp enough to understand she works hard to hide her feelings. She hides them away where we can't see them. But now, as the moon descends into darkness, she cries, long painful sobs.

"I never knew I was different until I came here. Before that... I was just me. But now... I am always so much. Too much." Vesp puts her hands over her face.

"It was *Hildre* who taught me that... who told me it was me. The world wasn't backward, *I* was. Too loud, too quiet, I cared too little, I cared too much... She taught me I was the problem..." She trails off. Her eyes stare into the eclipsing moon.

I shift position so my hand rests on her shoulder, my arm almost around her but not quite. Her body feels warm and strong, powerful and wild. "You're not too much," I say.

Vesp takes a shaky breath. "I want to be your friend, Thalon. I want you to be my friend too. But I know I'll be too much for you... if you know the real me."

I blink. I can't help it, I burst out laughing. "Gods, Vesp. I'm ill, not demented. I *am* your friend. We *are* friends. You're my *best* friend."

"But you don't *know* me..." Vesp protests. She turns to face me. "I spend so much energy making sure I say the right things and make the right face and do the right things with my body and don't hurt anyone with my magic and..."

I place my hands on both of her shoulders. The red moon gleams in her eyes. "Then let me get to know you. All of you, the real Vespald. I want you to feel safe being her with me."

Vesp stares at me, expression wild and unreadable. Her hands float in the air and then settle onto my forearms.

My heart warms my ribs. "I want you to know the real Thalon, too," I say. "Unfortunately, I'm still getting to know her, myself."

"We can get to know her together then," croaks Vesp. Letting go of me she settles at my side, our arms pressed together.

I glow on the inside. Her kvell shimmers against mine. I don't resist it, I'm not afraid of huldror anymore. I place my hand on her shoulder again, and together, we watch the moon go dark.

* * *

Lylok and I train, but my focus wavers. The day after the eclipse, a shipment of mail arrived, no letter from Hans included.

"You're heart's not in it. Why don't we shelve the lesson for today?" suggests Lylok. He holds a practice staff, as do I. We often move between kvellvahna and sparring and back again, now that my health has stabilized some.

I push my sweaty hair out of my eyes. "If I don't have something to show for myself, Yew is going to make me leave." I sink back into a ready stance.

"You have your health," Lylok points out. "You have shown great improvement with the kvellvahna."

"Somehow, I can't imagine she'll find either noteworthy." I bat at his staff and receive a smack on the shin.

Lunging in, Lylok sweeps for my feet and I leap away. I sway with his blows, letting the force of them roll off me, past me. I move well, almost dancing, and then he taps me on the shoulder with the staff.

"You have to envision it, Thalon. You have to see what you want."

I huff and take a defensive stance. "I'm seeing you on your ass, if that's what you mean."

"I mean with your kvell. Your goals. Your wishes. You need to be able to see yourself achieving what you want."

I scowl and circle Lylok. "What I want is impossible."

"Even better." Lylok circles opposite me. "If you can envision the steps to an impossible outcome, you can take those steps. Maybe not all of them, but at least one. So, see it. Close your eyes and see it. Here, I'm unarmed." He leans the staff on against a tree.

I close my eyes. I see myself apologizing to Azoto.

I see myself, strong, healthy, healed. I see twin moons and a storm rising. I see lightning crackling between enormous teeth. I see myself appeasing Tophinghua.

I see Vesp. Grinning, laughing, her curls floating on blue and violet light...

I shake my head and open my eyes as emotions rise through my chest. "It's... it's impossible." I force a breath. "You're right. You're right. We can shelve practice for now. I'm... not present."

"Do you want to talk?" prompts Lylok. He takes a seat by a tree and motions me to do the same.

I sit beside him. "I'm not sure there's much to say. Last night in the eclipse, Vesp and I talked about people we've lost. My ex-girlfriend died in the Duskingr accident. I fucked up what we had.

She was there for me anyway. Now she's dead. It should have been me…"

"Now Thalon, that's not true," replies Lylok. "But I understand your pain. Each life we lose takes a piece of us with it.

"But death is a beautiful part of life. We are temporal, finite. We never know how much life we get, that's why it is such a gift to live it."

"But why her and not me?" I pick the needles off a sprig of pine. "If I had been stronger, if I hadn't been sick… It could have been me on *Ursul*…"

"And then it would be her mourning you," replies Lylok. "And we would have never met. I would be poorer without you as my student."

"Ha…" I want to believe him, the key word being *want*.

Lylok motions to the shrine. "You should rest before Midsommer. If you enter the ritual with an open heart, you will surprise yourself."

The past few months have been a gift, a gift that will soon end, I know. But I nod, hoping that if I do as he says, if I see what I want in my mind, I can make it true.

CHAPTER

# THIRTY-ONE

Midsommer arrives. The longest day, the shortest night.

Lylok leads us through the final preparations. The kids of Ingfalla spent the last week weaving dried flowers into ribbons that we now drape around the pyres. Offerings of food, messages, prayers, and burnable trinkets fill the pyres. The set of three stand in a triangle, so tonight's dance can weave between them. Each one marks an offering to one of the major gods: Fregnym the Maker and Weaver, Ithnaan the Unmaker, and Brosk, Shepherd of Souls and God of the Sea. Little altars are set with candles for the other gods: Tophinghua and the Ingvu, Kvellsett, the Dust Ghost, and many more I don't know. The carved image of Tophinghua depicts a powerful yet obviously female figure. It feels good to see Her recognized. Weird the huldror would get it right.

We dress the tables in green and orange fabrics and set out baked goods from the shrine. I have a vague idea what tonight might bring. Something about dancing, drinking, but also duels. I'm not sure what Lylok means by duels, but I suppose I'll find out.

I spend the hours leading up to the ritual helping Lylok waddle in huge vats of green liquid. Vesp circles the entire village with a priest, blessing the corners of every cross street. I try to focus on the here and now, centering each task as it presents itself. Melancholy weighs my steps, a river stone in my belly. When I got here, I'd have never imagined mourning my departure. Yew hasn't spoken to me, but I doubt she'll tolerate me longer than necessary.

When Yew tells me to pack, should I set off for Poppy City? Ashling will be eleven years old now. Would she even remember I exist? My shoulders shrug up to my ears. As much as I'd like to see Ashling, I don't want to see my parents more.

Lylok and I lower the last vat of liquid into a base. He fans his face. "We're all set here, Thalon. Get yourself some dinner and your dancing clothes. You'll know when the party starts. Follow the music."

"I'm not sure I'll be dancing," I say.

"Nonsense." Lylok claps me on the back. "The fires get hot, so dress accordingly."

* * *

I don't have dancing clothes, so I settle on tight gray pants cropped at the knee and a compression bra. Sitting on the floor, I use a ballpoint pen to draw my fighting runes on my bad arm. Lylok said duels, right? My fingers rub the ever present ache in my left arm. Who am I kidding? I shouldn't be dancing, let alone dueling. Last time I fought, I almost got decapitated next to a pool table.

But still...

A drum beat rises from the village below. My head turns toward it. The beat swells and quickens, fast as the hooves of running deer. Strapping on my arm brace, I head outside.

The sunset paints the wispy clouds pink and orange. The huge, ancient trees become deep purples and blues. The candles in the village square twinkle like a night sky. Flutes join the drums.

The music gets into me, the drumbeats revving my heart and

infecting me with a breathless excitement. *Something is coming,* it promises. *Come closer... it's almost here, and you don't want to miss it...*

Hopping off the porch instead of taking the stairs, I hurry into the village, wading through laughing, smiling huldror. They seem to have come out of the woodwork, quite literally. The humble village swarms with people. Children run wild, pinwheels in their hands, clay flutes squealing and honking.

"Why are her eyebrows so fat?" A little girl asks her father. She jabs a finger at me. "Where's her tail?"

"Shh, don't point," hisses the father.

I shake my head and continue to the music.

More musicians join the song by the minute. Some even bring sleek, glassy Otherside technology. The song metamorphoses with each new sound. Folksy, woody tunes adopt a wild, mechanical edge. It builds in me like a draft of mead, leading me in, gripping me in a dry-mouthed excitement. I haven't felt this way since I stood on the beach with my fellow competitors, or faced Erik in the Blood Spire. The difference is, tonight, I have nothing to lose.

Almost six months have passed since I accidentally stumbled into the huldreby. Tonight, for the very first time, they show their hollow backs. I startle and do a double take as a woman walks past, shirt open in the back to reveal a gaping darkness. My eyes follow her, then move to Lylok as he pours himself a drink.

Lylok waves when he sees me and raises his mug to me. He wears a half mask of a bear, intricate tooled leather and bits of wood. When he turns his back to me, it is like looking into a bottomless pit.

The huldror aren't hollow, I know that from putting my arm around Vesp, but they look it. Just as the huldror skin resembles bark, wood, or river rock, the hollow back is an illusion. Gradients of blacks and grays give the appearance of a deep, deep chasm, deeper than a hollowed tree. A cavern to some other world. I can't tell if the hollows are natural parts of the huldror or tattoos, but the illusion raises the hairs on my arms.

So enchanted am I by the hollows and the music, I only half hear

Illuet Yew and Lylok give their opening greetings. The music doesn't stop, so neither do I. It moves me around at its whim. Then, in a gust of heat and a pungent musk of smoking herbs, the pyres erupt into flames. The fires gnaw and twist and grow in strength. So too does the music. Around me, the dance begins.

I scuttle to the side to observe, expecting something organized, like the ts'kmet. The huldror shuffle around, feet light over the bare, raked ground, some following the gallop of the drums, others the slower strains of flutes.

For a time, I simply observe. Lylok waves until he gets my attention and motions for me to join the dance. I make good and sure there is no rhyme nor reason to it before shuffling into the crowd. I let the current pull me in a huge circle around the three blistering bonfires.

Lylok orders the bonfires stoked hotter. The fires whip and moan. I thrum with the spirit of the night along with my huldror neighbors, moving my body through the falling embers. The enchantment goads them to circle and clap and kick up their heels. It smolders through me, too. I let it catch and kindle. As the night deepens, I search the crowd. Where is Vesp?

My eyes snap to Yew in surprise, drawn to the neon green glow of her antlers. She meets my eye and grimaces. Her teeth glow green. Glancing around, I notice green light peppering through the dancers. Huldror pour cups of glowing liquid from the vats Lylok and I carried in earlier. The liquid glows with violent phosphorescence.

Navigating through the crowd, I find a cup and pour a little for myself. A sniff reveals the earthy tang of Vesp's mushroom treat and the volatility of alcohol. I take a sip of the pleasant drink, but decide against that for now. I want to keep my head for the time being. I crave the momentum of the music and the free-form dance. Tonight, I just want to wash away the sense of loss. Loss of Azoto, loss of myself, loss of my place in the world. Tonight, I just want to be in the music.

I incorporate myself back into the dance. Dust and sweat,

burning herbs and timbers, we are all caught in the endless spiral of the night. As the year forms her wheel around the sun, so too do we form ourselves around the fires.

The night takes me over. It wakes up the beast in me. The huldror might poke fun at her, the beast girl, but tonight, she revels. They would do well not to laugh, the night awakens the beast in them as well. We sweat and grunt, skin slick from the heat, bodies bumping and sliding into each other. The drums holding a frenzied pace now, a breathless, primal tempo. We circle and circle, endless and free. We need not be anything here, we need only to move.

Then it begins. Two dancers break from the circle and step to the midpoint between the three towering fires. Mouths split open in green-tinged glee, or aggression. Two men, serious and sinewy. They begin a different sort of dance.

They move around each other, the steps partially from the kvellvahna, partially improvised. Their arms sweep, sharp teeth flash. Tails slash and feet stomp. Chests graze each other and slide apart. We of the circle keep moving, but voices hoot and cheer, attention drawn to the battle.

As the duel continues, I wonder how a winner might prevail. But then, one dancer takes two quick steps into the air, the force of his kvell slowing his descent to the ground. A wave of heat throbs up the fire behind him with a bone-rattling rumble. The circle whoops and cheers and his opponent bows. The loser returns to the circle while the winner paces between the bonfires.

Ah, so it is a duel of kvell.

A challenger approaches the winner, and the cycle begins again. After three rounds, the spectacle of fluttering the fire with kvell loses its novelty and I return to the primordial drive of the circle dance.

Time loses its meaning. I stop three times to guzzle water from urns and splash it over my head. Slicking my short hair into a tail at the back of my head, I return, letting the dance overpower my thoughts and feelings, letting it take me out of myself. The motion limbers up my body. I've spent the last six months building my stamina, and the dance feels welcome. The dance feels like home.

Voices catch my attention. Whispers in ears, a giggle here and there.

"Surprised she held her own like that..."

"I didn't think the imbecile could even use kvell..."

"Look at her though... what sort of dance is that?"

I turn toward the bonfires to see a tall, willowy shape, all sweat and sinew and wild hair pulled into a twisted braid. Vesp pours green wine into her mouth and swishes it before spitting it into the pyre like liquid fireflies. Leaning forward, she growls, tongue out, daring the next challenger.

I freeze, mouth ajar, eyes about to roll out of my skull. She is terrifying. I can't look away.

The boy who lost the Pirate Game to us stalks out. Confidence glossing his motions like a sheen of oil. He dances as the other duelers danced, expressive but measured, strong and grounded. Vesp, however, spins and leaps and dodges. Someone near me snickers at her antics, but it becomes a gasp as Vesp's pyre blazes up in a gust of unexpected wind.

Recognizing his defeat, the boy backs away from Vesp and into the circle. He does not give her the bow of respect.

Vesp paces like a restless puma, claws curled, tail thrashing, waiting for a challenger. Her mouth glows as she grins.

*Fight,* say her hands. *Fight, fight...*

"I don't want to beat her," blusters a man next to me. His companions try to shove him forward. "I don't want to upset her... she's crazy."

I lock eyes with him. He looks away as quickly as he can, mumbling.

Vesp wears baggy pants cuffed right at the ankles and a scrap of cloth floating over her chest. The black chasm of her back is a pit into which any one of us might fall if we look at it too long.

She simply stands now, waiting. Her eyes blaze in the firelight, streaks of glowing green stain her chin and chest and fingers. She is wild and the huldror pretend to mock her. I know better. I know she scares them.

A group of friends try to shove a huldra boy toward Vesp. He fights them off. "I don't want to mess with that!"

"Don't want to make her cry?" coo his friends.

One of them snaps his teeth. "Afraid she'll bite?"

Their laughter gets under my skin like mosquito straws.

I don't think, I do. I shove my way through the young men with a sneer on my lip. "Seagull sucking, chum-gutted cowards," I say. I step into the heat of the pyres.

Vesp faces away from me, her hollow back a gravity well. The wood patterns of her skin feather around the chasm, giving her the appearance of a tree trunk, through which I glimpse a world of darkness. I take another step, and another. The music shifts, something mechanical joins with the skin of the drums and the throaty flutes. I feel it in my chest and belly, a tightening of strings, a quickening of the circle dance.

Vesp feels it too and turns to face her challenger. Flames shine in her gold eyes. She smiles, face darkening as she bows into my shadow, mouth aglow like Brosk's, teeth florescent and hungry.

*What am I doing, she's going to eat me alive...* it is the last thought to enter my mind before Vesp lifts and stomps her foot. A ripple travels through the air between us, raw, wild kvell. The beast in me sees the beast in her.

*Dance,* her hands smack together, turning the sign into a command. *Dance!*

The dance puppets me. Six months ago, I mourned beside a different pyre, believing I would never dance again. Tonight, I feed my body to the dance and let it consume me.

*More!* orders Vesp.

She throws herself into her own dance. An unseen side of her emerges, the masks come off. She powers herself through aggressive leaps and predatory lunges. She lets the cultivated image of herself fall beneath our feet and surrenders to the music. I can't tell if she controls it or if it controls her. They merge together, Vesp and the music, a part of the night I cannot hope to match, and yet I try. I try to catch up, to keep up, to feel what she feels, to be as free as her.

I hop and kick and toss my hands in a feral mess of motions. There is no wrong or right, only the pace set by Vesp that I must keep. My breath comes in heavy gusts now... I must.

The visceral core of the music drops down to a dark, primordial rhythm. It throbs through us. Vesp lands from a leap on her toes and fingertips. She stalks me on all fours and springs as I dodge. Her glowing teeth laugh, her eyes sing. Are we predator and predator, or predator and prey?

The music rises, only to drop lower to a tectonic throb. I stomp into the beat. Suddenly, half of me flails, aimless, while half of me bursts into the powerful steps of the ts'kmet.

Vesp's face twists with a hungry delight. *Dance!* she orders.

*I am!* I sign back.

Her next step brings her up to me, naught but a slip of air between us. A thrash of her arm places it beside me. As the palm rolls over, she pulls on my kvell.

*More!* signs Vesp, teeth set in a grimace or in glee, something between.

My kvell crackles and swells under her influence. The thing us selkies fear...

*Harder. More. Dance!* Vesp's eyes shine and her claws flash. Her hands pull at my useless kvell.

Every breath I take becomes a desperate gasp. My legs kick out, my boots stomp into the clouds of dust. Sweat splatters around us.

I bring Vesp into the ts'kmet, trapping her as she traps me. I hook my legs around her body, elbows bent to bring my hands behind her head. Yet not a single part of us touches, save for the beads of our sweat.

Vesp leans in, looking down at me. She slides her hands up the curve of my back. The heat of her body burns, but our skin never touches. My kvell writhes.

Vesp balls her claws into fists and my kvell loosens, it unfolds.

I inhale in shock. "Oh…"

Intensity builds in the music. It pushes me faster, awakens the warrior sleeping in me. We dance face-to-face and then back-to-back, moving ever and always counterclockwise, twisting against the motion of the crowd, winding us tighter and tighter.

"Huh…" My exhales sharpen, my kvell simmers. It rises through my chest, tingles in my arms.

*Dance!* orders Vesp. She steps back from me. *Dance!*

Cut loose from her proximity, I stagger, I gasp. The kvell in me shimmers and twists. It isn't Vesp manipulating my kvell, it's me. Breathless, I try to push it down, try to get above the rising swell of heat and static electricity. I fight, I struggle. It's too much…

*You have to want it…*

The kvell flares, I can't hold it down.

Vesp locks her eyes on me, mouth aglow, teeth sharp and shining. *Dance!* demand her hands.

I surrender.

A guttural, desperate sound comes from my mouth as kvell burns through my body. I give in and it gushes out, rolling up the flames behind me in a ripple of raw power. The veins rise to the tops of my muscles as the kvell flows through me. Mine. It's mine. I am the fire.

*Yes!* Vesp's hands rise over her head as she calls her thyir. The pyre behind her bursts into a wall of shocking blue. *Yes!*

The dance pulls us back together. In the throes of our magics, neither of us claims victory just yet. We sweat and gasp and step and kick. Vesp's long spine curves as I lean over her, chest so very close to mine. My sweat splashes on her tree-ring skin, and then she backs me up, mouth aglow, claws weaving spells around me. The heat and kvell and thyir shimmer and simmer and spark.

*See me,* signs Vesp. *You see me.*

*Yes,* I reply. I can't look away.

Illuet's Yew's eyes burn into me. I feel them from across the clearing. I can't care about her right now. My world has narrowed to *dance* and *Vesp*.

I feel it approaching, the point at which I will have no more to give. With each step, kvell rises through me. I close my eyes, letting it incinerate me. A sparkle hangs on each exhale, a suggestion of silver. I give myself to the night, to the dance, to Vesp. I am running dry, but I am also something new.

The three pyres swell with heat. Streaks of green and blue climb into the sky...

The circle dance crashes in around us, pulled in like a breaking wave, each dancer adding to the magic. The fires howl, like we poured magical petroleum over the flames. Each and every huldra brushes against me, kvell on kvell. I am but one of so many.

# THIRTY-TWO

My limbs grow floppy and slow as the power disperses through the night, fluttering away like the sparks from the flames. I feel it in my breath and in my bones, a warm buzzing, a deep satisfaction in my chest and belly. As our duel ends, I find us propped together, cheek to cheek, Vesp's hands on my hips, mine clinging to her naked ribs. My fingers slip on her sweat. The music pounds, yet all I hear is the ebb and flow of our breath.

*Tired*, signs Vesp. *You're tired. Let's go now.*

I nod and let her pull me out of the spell.

As we leave the circle, the quiet night rings in my ears. I lean on her for balance, steps dizzy and uncertain. I think I overdid it.

Luckily, Vesp holds me up, leading me straight through the shrine and to the bubbling creek. She snatches towels and drops them on the deck beside the pool. Turning her back to me, she strips from her sodden garments and leaps into the water.

"Oh..." I stagger a little and strip as well, shambling to the next pool up.

"Where are you going?" calls Vesp.

"You... don't you want privacy?"

"I am in the bubbles!" she scolds and averts her eyes as I slide in.

A light catches my eye in the darkness, a faint green glow. It radiated from inside my arm brace, which I left on the deck. When I reach for it and flip it over, the glow fades. My left arm has a slight glow as well. Some of the phosphorescent wine must have gotten in the brace. Losing interest, I settle into the bubbles.

A huge, lazy grin takes over Vesp's face. She lets her head fall back on the wooden deck. *You found your kvell*, she signs, using the lovely swoop of the fingers for *kvell*.

"I... guess I did..."

"Hmm," Vesp hums. Her body floats in the bubbles, nakedness forgotten. For a long time, she simply lies there, and I lean back against the decking across from her.

Ten, fifteen minutes of burbling creek and cricket song later, she adds: "Had fun with you."

"Me too," I mumble, mind and body slow and dreamy.

Vesp smiles. Her bobcat teeth still glow a faint green.

"What did you see? When we danced. Could you see our thyir and kvell?"

Vesp hums. Her smile widens. "They danced together with us. Fire, ice, breath, and bones. You called your kvell and it answered. Maybe you will see them someday too." She rolls her head to look at me through her lashes. "What do you think? Am I too much for you?" she asks.

"You could never be too much for me..." I mutter. It's true. "You're just right."

With my head resting on the decking and my body floating in the warm, bubbling water, I feel myself start to drift between my thoughts like a wayward iceberg. Vesp dancing, her glowing mouth, her feral eyes...

Light flashes through the sky and I blink back to the present. The light dances and shifts, blues, greens and violets. It's coming from farther up the mountain, away from the celebration.

"Vesp?" I put my feet on the riverbed and hold onto the deck, ready to jump out if needed. "Vesp, are you seeing that?"

"Oh that?" Vesp turns her head just long enough to glance, then goes right back to floating. "That's just Kaldur Lake. It does that."

"*Does that*?" I echo.

Vesp squints her eyes open. "Yes. A current of Svall runs through the mountains. Kaldur Lake happens to sit right on top. When it erupts, you can see the Svall beneath."

"Oh." I settle back into the water. "So that's a normal thing…"

"Mm-hmm."

"Huh. I think I saw it my first night in the mountains… thought I had brain damage."

"Hmm," Vesp grins.

Using Vesp's reactions as my compass, I again close my eyes and let my mind wander.

"They say the lake is haunted," Vesp continues in a low, sultry voice. "Ghosts crawl from the waters they say. Shadows of those forgotten. Voices whisper on the lights…"

"Thanks, Vesp," I yawn. "Just what I need. Haunting."

"You need bed, is what you need." Vesp floats to me, facing the deck as I lie on my back. She doesn't acknowledge my bare chest, so neither do I. "I will mix tea for you. Something to help you sleep. It was… careless of me to push you so hard."

"That was the best thing that's ever happened to me." It's true.

"Hmm," sighs Vesp. "Me too. But now, go to your room and I will meet you there." Closing her eyes, she turns away from me, affording me the privacy of her culture.

Even as I wrap in a towel and head into the shrine, the warm afterglow of our dance goes with me. I did it. I channeled kvell. All I can think of is her.

* * *

I wake up late, sore, and my bad arm throbbing. Vesp knocks and lets herself in with a tray of tea and breakfast. We sit together on the bed to share it. She sits cross-legged and picks her food apart with both hands and the mannerisms of a raccoon.

We eat and drink tea in companionable quiet until a rap on the door announces another visitor. We both look up as Lylok shuffles in, expression stern, revealing nothing.

Vesp snaps up straight and I sweep crumbs off myself, self-conscious about getting caught so very near my fellow student. And so messy.

"Illuet Yew requests the three of us in her office," states Lylok. He steps out and waits in the hall for us to join him.

Vesp's huge gold eyes roll to meet mine. She twists her hands together. Looking to get this over with, I stand, strap Blitz to my thigh and toss my pelt over my shoulders. Falling into step behind Lylok, we follow him to the tall, dim office.

Deeply stained wood paneling lines the walls and books cram the shelves to the ceiling. Yew sits behind a well-organized desk, claws making a pyramid on her desk. Her ancient eyes rake over us as we enter.

"Aalgur Thalon." She says my name like it tastes bitter. "You had until Midsommer to demonstrate aptitude and respect for kvell. As Priest Lylok so graciously reminded me, you have done such. The bare minimum. Even so, you have fulfilled the aforementioned criteria."

I straighten my spine. "Does that mean I can continue my training with Lylok?"

"For now," concedes Yew.

Lylok clears his throat and steps up beside Yew's desk. Even sitting, she still towers over him. "Vespald. Thalon. Illuet Yew agrees with me: You have both demonstrated that you are ready for a task of greater impact."

I glance at Vesp. She widens her eyes at me. Task of greater impact?

"Huldror families on the western slopes have neither conducted their seasonal burns nor responded to messages from the shrine." Yew traces a claw along the woodgrain of her desk. "Lylok and I agree, it is time to send someone to check on them."

Lylok holds up a finger. "A task assigned to apprentice priests and priestesses."

Yew's face looks like it wants to melt off her skull. Her next words sound like they burn her tongue. "Indeed. This task falls to apprentices in the priesthood. Vespald, I promote you to the role of apprentice to Priest Lylok."

Vesp's tail tuft bristles like a bottle brush. She covers her mouth and hops from foot to foot.

Yew takes a sharp breath like she dropped a brick on her foot. "Aalgur Thalon, as a tournament fighter of some skill, you may be her apprentice warrior. I entrust you to guard her."

I straighten further. "Yes… yes ma'am."

Yew flicks her hand toward the doorway. "Be gone now. Lylok will brief you."

We make it down a single hallway before Vesp screams and stomps her feet. She drags her fingers down her cheeks. "Apprentice! Apprentice! Ahaha!"

Lylok beams, arms folded behind his back. "You've both earned your titles. That was some noteworthy magic last night. Now, let's go take a deeper look into the situation at hand."

# THIRTY-THREE

"This is the Ingfalla shrine and the huldreby." Lylok points to illustrated buildings on the map. We lean over it on the workbench in his shop. In the illustrations, a little Duskingr ship sits atop the shrine. The tall, regal trees cradle the black vessel. Five other shrines pepper through the jagged peaks of the Duskheim Mountains.

Lylok's finger traces down the Shastaar River to a trail, across a ridge, and to the mouth of the Erling River. He circles the slope of a mountainside.

"Here's where you'll be headed. It's not terribly far. Yew could absolutely walk it, but she won't."

My eyes track north to the illustrated Boreackt. I hope the Karrvoss Nomads made it safely to Poppy City. I hope my letter from Hans gets here soon. I need to know he's okay.

Lylok circles our destination again. "Two families live on the western slope, Family Frell and Family Hemlock. Frell and Hemlock have tended their slope for four generations without fail. Now, we haven't been able to get through to them. Which is where you two come in."

Vesp's tail swishes over the floor. "What are we to do when we get there?"

Lylok makes an 'X' on the slope with a pen. "See if you can find them, poke around, get a feel for what's going on, if anything. Honestly? The radios probably just crapped out and they couldn't be bothered to check in. They chose to live so far from the huldreby for a reason. You're just going to confirm that, nothing more. It's a long day's walk there. You'll need to camp for a night, or even two. I trust both of you to use your judgement."

Vesp and I glance at each other.

"Vesp, this will be your first assignment as apprentice priestess. You've demonstrated the mastery of ritual and proficiency in both kvell and thyir worthy of this responsibility."

Vesp dips her chin, eyes round gold moons in her face. "Thank you, Priest Lylok."

Lylok smiles and turns to me. "Thalon, despite both your heritage and disability, you have learned to channel your kvell. You are worthy and capable to act as warrior guardian to my priestess, are you not?"

I swallow. "Yes, Priest Lylok, I hope so."

"You can stop calling my Priest Lylok now." Lylok rolls the map. "Be gentle with your kvell, Thalon, as you are learning to do with yourself. While I recognize you have your struggles, I won't coddle you nor treat you as lesser than you are. You won your place on the Duskingr and while the threads in the Tapestry have led you down a different path, there's plenty of work to be done."

"Yes, Priest... yes, Lylok." I swallow my pride but allow it to bring me the slightest of smiles. His plans for Vesp are clear, she will be a Priestess of kvell someday. I wonder what he plans for me, if anything. I hope he has something in mind.

All the same, I'll take what I can get for now. Graduating from shrine gopher to warrior feels like taking the first breath after a long, deep dive.

Perhaps I'm not such an incompetent omelet anymore.

*We'll see about that*, chides my thoughts. I don't even know if I can still fight...

*Of course I can. What was last night if not a fight?*

I blush and rub the back of my neck. What indeed.

"Are you... coming with us?" asks Vesp. I can't tell if she sounds hopeful that he will or won't.

Lylok shakes his head. "No. You're ready to do a little hiking and camping without parental supervision. Now, you two weirdos, pack and make haste. Day's not getting any younger."

Vesp scampers out, but Lylok places a hand on my arm before I can follow. He beams, wrinkles happy little canyons around his eyes. "You grew up in a world where kvell was poison. A selkie using kvell as her own, it was an impossible thing. Last night I saw you call passion into the bonfires. I saw you embrace yourself as you are. Remember it. Remember how that felt, to touch the impossible."

"But it... wasn't impossible, was it?" I tilt my head, a bit confused.

"It was impossible. It was impossible, and then it wasn't."

* * *

Vesp and I walk along the top of the world. Stone spires hold up the glassy blue orb of the sky. Dry bushes make a *hush, hush* sound in the warm breeze.

We travel in silence, that comfortable, safe silence I have grown accustomed to with Vesp. We never need to fill it, never talk just to talk. She hums a little now and then, smiling and in grand spirits.

The trail leads along the face of a spire. The Blackberry Hills roll below us like little dumplings, all the way to the glittering crystal edge of the sea. In an absolute sense, I am not so far from home. But I am also in a distant and strange world, so very different from my little bubble in Vatska.

Do I miss the sea? Do I long to slide beneath the waves again, to spread my flukes and fly through the water? With every heartbeat. And yet the ache has dulled. With the dance of Midsommer still glowing in my belly, I instead look toward what this body might still hold for me. The selkie girl of Vatska could never have channeled kvell, that possibility did not exist for her. What might I become without my self-imposed limits?

I pause in a field, watching Vesp's tail sway behind her as she walks. A ripple passes through the grass. I turn a circle, allowing myself to feel gratitude for the day, the moment. My heart beats, my lungs breathe fresh mountain air, I get to stand here in this field at the top of the world. The first time I set foot in the Duskheims, all I could do was mourn what I had lost. While I'll likely never regain everything, it warms me to stop for a moment, to soak in the beauty around me.

Vesp turns and smiles. I grin and skip through the grass to catch up.

The sun sinks. Vesp measures its distance to the horizon with her hand and consults our map. She then leads us down a fork in the trail into a thicket of gnarled, pock-marked oaks. "We are a mile or so from the slope..." Vesp's attention snaps to the ground. Black bubbles of mold creep along the tree roots, branches. Leaves fester with boils.

"Oh yuck." Vesp wrinkles her nose. "They truly haven't burned here. It needs it."

"You've said that more than once. What do you mean by burning?" I ask. "Wouldn't burning just... destroy the forest?"

Vesp motions for me to follow her to a trickling creek. "The forests are made to burn on their own. Lightning strikes, they catch fire. It purifies them, cleanses the ground, and tells the seeds to sprout. But, we live here too and don't like our houses and shrines burning down."

Finding a satisfactory location, Vesp drops her pack and pulls out the tent. "We burn small plots at a time. It keeps the brush and dander under control and the old trees healthy. The big trees, the old trees, they need fire. We care for the forests, they care for us. But as you can see, this forest has not been cared for..." She indicates dead mounds of brambles, crispy dry branches and rotten trunks. "We will need to be careful if we build a campfire tonight, lest the sparks get ideas."

"I'll take your word for it." I drop my pack as well and help her pitch the tent. "I don't really know how forests work."

Vesp catches my eye over the top of the tent with a smile. "You will."

"If this part of the forest hasn't been cared for, what do you think happened to the huldror?"

Vesp shakes her head. "I have no idea, Thalon. But we're here to find out."

* * *

THAT'S NOT YOURS, RIGHT? I ASK.

Vesp's fingers snap together in a definitive, *No.*

Vesp and I crouch beside a boulder, peering down into an industrial compound. Rows upon rows of crops cover the hillsides surrounded by metal structures painted the same brown as the dirt. Some are enormous and hooked up to generators and strange systems of black panels.

The compound is off the trail and the buildings are tucked among the oak trees. Hikers could easily miss the whole thing. But I bet it's visible from above, by airship.

I can't think of the sign for 'grow' so I ask: *What plant, do you think? Food?*

Vesp shrugs and shakes her hands.

The Erling River cuts a swath right through the fields. The river flows under the fence. An arm of the river diverts through one of the largest buildings and out the other side before slithering back into its parent stream. Something Hans said flickers back to me, something about farming at the mouth of the river...

People move around in the compound. In the half hour we've sat here, I've counted ten in total.

*Could the huldror work here?* I venture.

Vesp shakes her head, unsure. *I don't know what* here *is.*

*We should go and see.*

Vesp points a claw to the heavy chain link fence. Razor wire loops along the top. *Why?*

*Animals? Bears?* I speculate.

*Why farm here? Why not there?* Vesp points down to the Blackberry Hills.

Why indeed. Why farm way up here in the middle of nowhere?

I sit up. Something squishes under my palm. "Suck a seagull…" I spit, shaking goo off my hand. The mold is in the grass and I've sat right in it. It bubbles from the ground like tar.

"This stuff isn't toxic, is it?"

Vesp shakes her head. *Only to plants.*

"Come on," I whisper, wiping my hand on my pants. "Let's just go say hi. Maybe the folks in there know where the huldror families went. It doesn't look new… they might know something."

Vesp glowers into the compound, tail bristled. Her eyes trace over steaming pipes, perhaps some sort of refinery. She chews on her lip.

"Come on," I coax. "Let's go say hello."

Vesp stays silent as we walk down the hill. We make no effort to hide or snoop, striding right up to the locked metal gates.

I look at the razor wire and down the fencing. The breeze carries a musty, sweetish smell.

My focus snaps to attention as two men in brown coveralls approach us.

"You lost?" one of the men calls to us.

I take stock of them: strong, active physiques and utility knives. Human most likely. The man on the left strikes me as generic. But the one on the right jerks now and then, a little too quick, a little jumpy. He unsettles me. If it comes to blows, I'll need to fight fast and dirty...

*Get a grip, Thalon, no one's fighting.*

"You two alright?" the man asks again. His eyes flick to Gevit across my shoulders.

"Yes." Vesp straightens her posture, expression intense, focused. "We are looking for the Frell and Hemlock families. They were living on these slopes..." She trails off to see if the men will offer an explanation.

One of the pair shakes his head. "There're no families here."

"Ever?" asks Vesp.

The man shakes his head. "Did you see any houses?"

"We did not see houses..." Vesp's fingers twist together. Her eyes snap from man to man. "What are you growing?"

"It's a sugar beet farm." The twitchy guy hooks his thumb over his shoulder.

I squint at him. There's something about him that sets me on edge... but I can't put a finger on it.

"Sugar beets..." repeats Vesp. "Sugar beets. Why are you farming sugar beets in the huldror woods?"

I watch the men. They don't become confrontational, but they do shift their posture just a little, a hint of defensiveness.

"I can't say anything for the huldra, you're the first we've seen. This farm's property of Spindel Co."

Spindel, the soda pop. Ah, sugar, soda. But why in the mountains? Why so far away from towns?

"What do you mean, property?" asks Vesp. Her cheeks flush and her tail snaps from side to side.

"Company owns it." The man on the left seems puzzled, but the one on the right shifts his weight with impatience.

Vesp looks to me and back to them. She hooks her fingers into the fencing. "You can't *own* the woods. The woods cannot be owned. This is the huldror wood. It is our responsibility to care for it, and now there is too much mold..."

"Look, lady, there're no huldra here," says the man on the left.

"But there… *were*," stammers Vesp. Her fingers curl into fists. She shakes the fence, just once, just enough to send a ripple up the chain link. "Where are the huldror now?"

"There're no huldra, no tree folk, just this godforsaken farm in these godforsaken mountains…" The man on the left takes off his hat and wipes sweat from his head.

"It's not yours, is it?" Twitchy guy takes a step closer to Vesp. "Are you from one of those families?"

*Yes,* I sign, thinking on my toes. How could they prove it one way or the other?

Vesp misses the hint though, furious eyes pinned on the men. "No."

"You own this land then?"

"No… you can't own the forest…"

"Then I don't see a need for this conversation to go any further."

Vesp takes a breath and growls.

I step up beside Vesp and rest a hand on her back. "Why is Spindel Co. farming sugar beets all the way up in the Duskheim Mountains? We're a long way from like… roads."

"That's not my business," replies Twitchy Guy. "Didn't you see the 'No Trespassing' sign? We could detain you and have you arrested."

Well, that took a turn.

"Nobody's trespassing, we just had some questions." I put an arm around Vesp's waist, applying enough pressure to signal it's time to go. Three more people approach from the camouflaged buildings.

"Well, you have your answers," replies the man on the left. "Have a nice hike now."

I pull Vesp back. She keeps her eyes fixed on the gates as I march us off into the woods and out of sight.

*They know… they know…* Vesp signs over and over.

"I can't say what they know or don't know… but what in the

depths is Spindel doing farming sugar beets all the way up here?" I say this as much to myself as to her.

*It's not... not theirs!* Vesp signs, motions stiff and furious.

"I know, but Vesp... we can't do anything about it. We're here to investigate the missing people..."

"They know..." Digging her claws into her hair, Vesp snarls in frustration. Spinning, she stomps into the trees, leaving me alone on the dirt path overlooking the guarded compound of sugar beets.

## CHAPTER
# THIRTY-FOUR

Vesp stomps into our camp like an atmospheric event. Twigs and leaves cyclone around her and her raging kvell. I catch a glimpse of it, a sparkle on the air.

"Vesp..." I begin, a little lost as to what, exactly, got her so worked up. Sure, the farm is weird and frustrating but...

Spinning to face me, Vesp hits me with rapid fire Ketja, hands sweeping and snapping through the air. I catch bits and pieces like: *Lylok and Yew entrusted me with... handling situations... speak for me...*

"Whoa, Vesp," I hold up my palms. "You're going to need to slow down, I'm not that good..."

Vesp bares her teeth and hisses a deep growl between them. Her tail snaps.

"Do you want to talk it out or walk it off?" I ask, offering her two favorite methods of processing difficult situations. She's got one up on me and punching walls...

*Walk,* Vesp snaps the sign at me.

"Want me to go with you?"

*No.*

"Wait," I reach for her before she can vanish into the woods.

Unhooking Blitz, I offer her handle to Vesp. "Be safe. If you're not back by supper, I'm coming looking for you. And I'm an idiot out there in the woods, so be back."

Accepting the hand axe, Vesp does exactly as I expect and vanishes.

Sighing and clicking my tongue, I set about playing house. I unroll the bedding, build a fire ring and sort through our camping food. The dancing last night and the hike today have my body aching, so I take my time heating up a can of soup.

The salty allure of the soup floats through the clearing when Vesp returns. Handing me Blitz, she plops down into the dirt, eyes red-rimmed and turned away from me. She wraps her tail around her feet and sniffles, wiping her nose on the inside of her collar.

"Are you alright?" I ask. Leaning over the pot, I stir the soup like a witch tending a potion. "Want to talk it out now?"

Vesp sniffles more and nods, but then says nothing. I serve us both soup and take a seat across the fire from her. Somewhere in the distance, coyotes yip and yowl.

"This was my first assignment as apprentice priestess... and I can't even do it myself." Vesp's voice rasps. Her posture droops, tail wilting. She moves her spoon around in the soup, scooping up chunks of meat and letting them plop back in.

"I am... incapable," she speaks into the bowl. "I know Lylok sent you with me because he knew I wouldn't be able to handle things on my own... wouldn't be able to say the right things... and he's right!" Vesp huffs. Her claws bite into her wooden bowl. "I couldn't have handled that by myself. And it was talking! Just talking to two strangers!" Her rising emotions send a crackle through the fire. I watch the sparks to make sure they don't reach any dry leaves.

I stir my own soup and take a bite while I gather my thoughts. "You know, Vesp, I don't think that's being fair, to you or me. For one thing, neither of us had any idea we were going to walk into a Spindel Co. beet farm, if that's what it is. How are you supposed to prepare for that? And also, I'd like to think I'm not just here as a mouthpiece.

"But for another thing, why's it bad if we work as a pair? Seriously. The crew of the Duskingr are paired up just like us: selkie and huldra. They work as teams, four of them per ship, right?"

"It's not the same thing..." Vesp looks down at her feet. "I was not deemed fit to crew a Duskingr..."

"Yeah, well, we're a club, I guess," I slurp my soup. "But Vesp, our country's not even run by one person. Ruhnsvalla's managed by the Duskir Parliament, not a monarch or anything like that. We're meant to work together. Sum of our strengths not our weaknesses and all that..."

"Thalon. You don't get it, you don't understand..." Vesp finally looks up from the bowl. "I'm too much, I'm too... too..." She makes claws in the air around the bowl, as if she can simply tear the word she needs out of the air. "Thalon, I'm from the Otherside. I was born on the Otherside..." She looks away from me again, face darkening, tail tightening around her shins.

I blink at her. Alright, fair game, girl. I didn't expect that. "Oh. There are huldror over there?"

Vesp shakes her head. "No. Mom was sent over. Banished. She never said why." Setting down her bowl, she wipes her eyes, dust mixing with her tears and leaving muddy streaks. "But she loved my dad... they loved each other and me. But he was human and I... I'm from that other world..."

I take a moment to process this information before responding. "I'm not sure I follow. Why does that make you feel incompetent in your very first assignment? Which you *didn't* mess up."

Vesp shakes her head. She looks so tired, so defeated. "I'm just... never going to cut it. As hard as I try, as much as I practice, my mind will never work like other people's and I'll never be from Ruhnsvalla. I'll always be an Othersider... some idiot who wandered in from the Svall..."

I give my head a shake. "I'm not sure how that matters, to be honest. Your mind works fine, and who cares where you're from?"

"They used to be so cruel to me." Vesp curls up tighter, fingers finding a stick and peeling the bark from it.

"Well, whoever they were, they're assholes, they don't matter, and now you're an apprentice priestess. So ha. They can suck seagulls."

"Hildre was chosen to crew the Duskingr over me, even though she was younger..." whispers Vesp.

*Yeah, well, now she's dead,* I bite my tongue before I speak. Instead, I circle back to the topic at hand. "You did exactly what needed to be done today. You learned there's a Spindel farm, you learned the huldror are who the heck knows where, and you got to see in real life, that people can suck in lots of different ways. You did well."

Vesp smiles, a weak, heavy smile that soon melts away. But she picks up her bowl and continues eating, so I join her. For canned soup, after a day's walk, it does the job. I debate sharing my own feelings about losing my ability to shift, breaking my thyir, washing out of the Dusk Trials... falling in battle with Tophinghua as my patron... But I realize I don't really need to say it. It happened. It sucks. I can't fix it and it's not Vesp's problem.

"So... if your parents are on the Otherside, how did you get here?" I ask, hoping it's not a difficult topic.

"They didn't throw me through, if that's what you're worried about. No... it was my fault. I was just a little girl." Vesp's gold eyes take on a dreamy glow from the fire. "You can't see the Svall on the Otherside, but I could feel it. It was fourteen years ago this summer. I was twelve, listening to music, I had my headphones on, and I felt it pulling me... calling... like a whisper on the back of my neck. And I just..." She holds out her empty hands and signs the last words, *Walked through.*

"And... you can't get back?" I venture.

She shakes her head. "I have no way to control when I'd end up. Perhaps long before my parents met, or were even born.

Perhaps long after they have died..." Tears well up and spill down her wood grain cheeks. "Without dusking, I can't control when to go, and I could never get back to here and now... But, Thalon... I would give anything, *anything* to see them again. I love them so much... and I know they love me... But the ice moves for no one, the trees do not answer, and the Svall obeys no master... Not for a long, long time."

* * *

I stare into the black abyss of the tent ceiling. I can't kick my own ass out of the cycle of frustration. I want to ball my fists and scream but feel powerless. Not only had Vesp gone to bed sniffling, but a suspicion gnaws at me. I can't get it out of my head that not all is right with the sugar beet farm.

I mean... sugar beets? In the mountains? Why not in Vatska with our farmlands? Somewhere close to roads, to trade and infrastructure? Why the middle of absolutely nowhere? And the razor wire? I cross my arms and grind my teeth.

Vesp rolls over and rolls again, ending up on my side of the tent. I go still as stone as her rump rests against my thigh. Shoving herself in her sleep, Vesp's back presses against me, and then, oh no, the tip of her tail twists around my ankle. I hold my breath, afraid to exhale, afraid for my heart to beat too loud.

Vesp settles in, peaceful and cozy.

I allow myself to breathe again but can't seem to get my heart to slow down. My insides squirm and flutter as if I swallowed live minnows. The feeling of Vesp's long body and delicate warmth, the stink of pine and sweaty girl, I sigh.

Vesp just snuggles in closer beside me, breathing soft. I start sweating. It's a warm night.

I stare into the black ceiling. What am I supposed to do?

Vesp hums in her dream and rolls to face me. She lays her arm over me, like I'm a stuffed animal. I make myself breathe through the pulse in my throat until I relax. Vesp stays where she is, so I put my arm around her too.

I feel the magics between us, the soft kvell of our breath, the deep thyir in our bones. I feel the feathery edges where our magics touch and mingle, like the Midsommer dance, only soft and fragile.

A honey-sweet warmth blooms through me. I smile into her tangly hair. Suddenly, I couldn't care less about sugar beets. My entire world focuses down onto the rise and fall of my arm as Vesp breathes. I smile in spite of myself. It feels so good to be wanted, even if it's just in a dream.

* * *

I wake up alone in the tent at dawn. Outside, I hear the fire crackling and Vesp humming to herself.

I hope it's not weird that we cuddled. That's not weird, right? I hold a breath and count to ten before stretching and yawning, making enough noise to alert her that I'm awake now.

"Good morning." Vesp gives me a finger wave as I crawl out of the tent. She offers me a steaming mug. "I brewed tea. There are anti-inflammatory herbs in yours. We've done so much these past two days, I am worried you are getting worn out."

"Thanks. That was thoughtful of you." I take the tea and sip it, trying to play it cool. She probably doesn't even remember. *You're overthinking it, omelet.*

Spears of sun stream in from the east, promising a sweltering day.

"Food." Vesp indicates the hard-boiled eggs we brought, a tin of fish, dried fruit, and jerky.

I take an egg and crack the shell with the backs of my knuckles. Vesp paces while she eats, selecting a strip of jerky and walking, one contemplative step at a time, around the fire ring. When she finishes a strip, she begins the process over, completing another circuit around the clearing while she eats. I don't get it, but it's cute. She reminds me of a butterfly unsure of which flower to land on.

I wonder if she knows we spooned a little. A chip of eggshell goes flying as I poke the egg a tad too hard with my fingertip. Gods, we're just getting closer, she's finally getting comfortable taking off her masks around me, showing me the Vesp she doesn't show anyone else... if she knew, would she put the masks back on?

And what about our official arraignment as priestess and warrior? I didn't sign any paperwork, but that sounded rather professional to me... perhaps hopeful thinking on my part, but still. I've got something... well, something that doesn't suck going for me. She trusts me. She's opened up to me. I would love for our friendship to grow into more...

*More what, omelet?*

"What are you thinking about?" prompts Vesp, tail flopping one way, then the other. She looks at me through her lashes, sinking her teeth into a peeled egg.

"I, um... I'm thinking about this egg..." I shove it into my mouth with part of the shell still attached. It crunches between my teeth. Yes, I am, in fact, an incompetent omelet.

"We have salt and pepper for that." Vesp holds the shakers out to me, and I fight through a hideous blush. *Way to make it weird, Thalon.*

"I'm grateful for your support last night, Thalon." Vesp takes another bite of egg and pokes the fire pit with a bare toe. "I can be... a lot. Thank you for not running away..."

My eyebrows skew. "I have no intentions of running away."

"I hope that is true..." murmurs Vesp. She pokes the rock with her toe again and then stoops to pick it up.

"What kind of rock it that?" I ask, hoping to steer the topic toward something harmless.

Vesp rolls the stone in her hands so I can see the Zahlek runescript chiseled into it. "This was a piece of a hearthstone. From a huldror home."

I jump to my feet and take the stone as she gets on her hands and knees to investigate further.

"Could this be from those families...?" I grimace. The runescript has no dirt inside. There's no moss or lichen...it hasn't been outside of a house for very long.

"Thalon..." Vesp tugs on a pile of brambles, revealing shattered wooden planks beneath. She squints at the ground and then crouches to whisk the leaves away with her hands. Her fingers slide into deep, symmetrical imprints: tread marks.

"Tractor," whispers Vesp. Her claws sink into the dried earth. "Fresh. After the rains..."

"Not more than a few months old," I add.

Vesp nods and straightens. Her feet follow the tread marks up the hill. Now that I see them, they're hard to miss. When we reach the top of the hill, we can see the tracks make troughs through the grass. They lead right to the sugar beet farm.

I return to camp just long enough to fetch Blitz and Gevit.

Looks like we'll be doing some more talking.

CHAPTER

# THIRTY-FIVE

*Shipment?* Vesp signs to me.

*Looks like...* I sign back. We again peer down on the compound from above. This morning, workers use vehicles to drive crates and barrels to something hidden by the trees.

*We need to talk to...* I struggle for a sign I don't yet know. *Important person. Inside. Not worker.*

*Agreed,* nods Vesp.

But how? We wait and watch. I count nine people out working. I even recognize the odd mannerisms of Twitchy Guy from yesterday. One man in particular catches my attention, a figure on the smaller side, hurrying from location to location with a frantic, unusual gait. Too fast, too jerky, like one of the automatons from *Divine Jubilee*. A snag of unease sits in my belly. We need to talk to someone in charge, but how? What if they don't let us in? Should we break in?

Furthermore, if they used tractors to demolish huldror homes and lied about it, how dangerous are these people?

"Let's go ask," I whisper. I motion for Vesp to slip back behind the ridge as we approach. I lead us all the way to the bank of the Erling River.

As we snoop closer, we get a better view. Workers load the crates and barrels into the hold of a large, silver airship. For a moment, the bottom falls out of my stomach as I mistake the vessel for the *Cloudberry*. But no, same class of vessel, different color, different ship. Using an airship to get goods off the top of the Duskheims...not so weird, right?

Vesp and I creep along the fence toward the gates, me crouched in the thick, dry hay, her turned nearly invisible with thyir. Something feels off. I can't say what, intuition has never been my gift. Could have something to do with smashing houses...

A muffled voice cries out from inside the compound. I snap a hand up to tell Vesp to hold. What was that? I strain my ears, focusing past the gush of the river and back-up beepers. There! A voice in distress.

"This is illegal! You can't do this! Let me go, let me GO!" The voice yells. It's coming from inside one of the long, brown buildings.

Vesp and I make eye contact. Without a word, we slip into the riverbed and under the fence. Whoever built the fence didn't plan on people using the river to get under it. Leave it to humans to be afraid of getting wet.

We wade under the fence and creep along the chain-link. We stay low to the ground and out of sight until we reach a long metal building. We wait, crouched in the weeds, until I'm certain none of the workers are inside. The upset voice has gone quiet.

On my signal, we slip from the grass and through the unlocked door. Once inside, Vesp and I pause with the closed door to our backs. Long, blue fluorescent lights run in two rows down the ceiling of the single, continuous room. The space feels huge but also cramped. The diverted stream from the Erling cuts a trough down the center of the floor, covered in metal grating. Vats, like plastic wine barrels, line one wall, connected by tubing and gauges. Oil-drum-like plastic containers crowd the high shelving. Pallets of chemicals and other equipment cram the space, and a sweet, burnt smell wrinkles my nose. It's... familiar.

My head snaps to a small figure tied to a pipe in the wall. A figure with greenish hair and hazel eyes overflowing with frustration and fear.

"*Wavern?*" I sputter. I dash to them and pull the gag from their mouth. I use Blitz to sever the ropes.

"Thalon! Thalon! What are you...? How are you?" Wavern wheezes and coughs.

They shake like a bush in a hurricane and I sit them up and check for injuries. Fresh blood trickles from their nose and one eye is turning purple. A few feet off, a gray mass I recognize as their Otherside note-taking gizmo lies in about seven pieces, stomped to ruins.

"Wavern... what in the depths...?" I begin but Wavern crushes me in a fierce, desperate hug.

"Thalon, by the gods, all the gods, how did you find me?"

"Cashing in that Thalon favor punch card, I guess..." I try to give Wavern a smile of reassurance, but it's more a grimace of confusion. "What in the depths are you doing here?"

Wavern takes a breath, a hand to their chest. "They're... oh, Thalon, it's so much worse..."

*They're coming!* signs Vesp. She attempts to blend into the metal wall. Footsteps and wheels approach.

I scramble, holding little Wavern like a child as I look for places to hide. I won't fit behind the vats, the crates are too...

The door opens and two men enter, pushing and pulling a dolly of glass containers filled with a cloudy gray sludge. The man pulling stops to gawk at us, and I recognize him as Twitchy Guy from yesterday.

"You—you can't be in here! How did you get in here?" demands Twitchy.

I shove Wavern behind me. Vesp fails to vanish into the wall and stands there, unsure what to do.

"You have my friend," I state. I keep my voice firm. What are we up against? "We're taking them back."

The man pushing the jars steps around the dolly. He flips out a box knife and points it at Vesp. Small and wiry, scraggly hair and untended beard, watery little eyes and yellowed teeth. I'd know him anywhere, even out of context. Vesp backs away from the knife.

"Cortland!" I blurt. "Cortland?"

Cortland snaps his head to me, a sneer showing his discolored teeth. For a moment, I don't think he recognizes me.

"Thalon," he states. Then he laughs. "Some nerve you've got, showing up here. That's the one, Tam. Almost lost me the partnership."

Cortland chuckles, then cackles. The other man, Tam, finds the situation much less amusing. "You're all trespassing on private property."

"Boss'll handle it." Cortland takes a step closer to Vesp. "But who are you? You're one of those dirty tree cows, thinks they own the place."

Vesp's mouth falls open. "Cow?" she stutters.

"They were here yesterday, the selkie and the tree cow," states Twitchy... Tam. His voice grates on me... I know it from somewhere...

Something clicks for me, something Cortland said. My limbs go slack. For a moment, my knees threaten to buckle.

"You... you bet against me." Blitz dangles, limp at my side. He'd been talking with Tam that evening on the *Cormorant*...

Cortland scoffs. "Yeah, and look what you did, almost cost me big time, Thalon. But you came through there at the end..."

I brace my good arm on a barrel beside me. I take deep breaths, as if Cortland had punched me in the sternum. He never had faith in me, never believed I could succeed. All this time, I thought I'd let him down...

Cortland says something that I don't hear. Next thing I know, he has Vesp's arm in his greasy hand, the box knife in the other. The little glint of metal draws my gaze, the silver edge so close to Vesp's wrist. The thinking part of my brain turns off.

One stride closes the distance between me and Cortland. The

next quick step pivots my body, winding it up for power. I throw a punch that cracks into Cortland's jaw with a wet pop and splatter of spit and blood. Sheet metal wobbles as he bounces off the wall. I spin Gevit off my shoulder and swing her around.

I don't stop, powered by numb fury. My body follows the rotation of Gevit and I step in. I slam the handle of the axe into Tam's stomach and catch his chin on my knee as he doubles over.

"You son of a bitch!" I spin back to Cortland.

The pathetic bone-bag crawls backwards from me on the floor. My fist curls into the front of his shirt and I lift him just enough to throw him down again. I have so much to say to him, about the double shifts, sludge eels, the speech after speech about taking pride in my work... maybe even to ask him what in the depths he's doing here... but all that comes out is: "*Fuckwad...*"

I never meant anything to him. Not a gods damned thing.

Three more people stampede into the room.

"Ah!" Yelps Vesp. Her initial shock flips to action.

She grabs and trips a worker mid-stride and lands atop her, wrenching an arm behind her back as the woman yells and groans. Just like I taught her.

Wavern ducks and covers their head as I sweep Gevit's blades around. The two new men yell, leap away, and leap back in, ready for a fight.

But so am I.

Gevit makes a slick whisper through the air as I bring her around and drive the pommel right between the closest man's eyes, snapping his head back. Tam grabs me from behind. The moment I feel his grip, I pin his arms to my sides and fall to my knees. His body crashes over me and onto the concrete floor.

I should fight like I fight with Lylok, smart, not hard. But I am livid and snarling. Smart is not activated.

I roll with the momentum, already lunging for the next enemy. He ducks Gevit and clips my jaw with a fist. It's enough to stagger me off-balance. He swings again and I block with my left arm. The brace absorbs much of the force, but the shock still blinds me with a jolt of nauseating pain.

Quick stepping back, I swing Gevit through a diagonal arc to create space between me and my opponent. The blade cracks into something above my head. It sticks. That gives Tam the break he needs to kick me in the stomach.

It takes all I have in me to keep my grip locked around Gevit and pull her free as I fall to my knees. The force of my fall slices Gevit right into the top of Tam's boot. It bisects his boot and foot completely in half down the midline. *Holy shit...*

He screams.

From above, a thick, sweet smelling goo splatters down over me. Brackish liquid streaks my arms and gets in my eyes. The smell, the taste, sugar and rot...

Thoughtless panic takes me over as I find myself covered in Katch. I slip and scramble. For a single breath, I lie on the dusty sand floor, looking up into the blinding lights and a stadium of people, every single one of them watching me lose. Watching me fail. Watching me break into a thousand unrepairable pieces.

But then I'm on my feet again in a blue lit building covered in Katch and holding an axe. Tam screams from the floor, foot squirting blood. Cortland has Vesp's head pulled back by the hair. That snaps me out of the flashback.

I kick Cortland as hard as I can in the chest. He sprawls to the floor and I roar.

The door crashes open and seven more workers charge in. Four of them hop the handrail of the ramp and rush me. Blades slinging blood and Katch, I swing Gevit, slicing a forearm, smashing a rib. I use the axe to create space around me, a cushion of safety as I back up. Step-by-step, I move down the center of the warehouse. Yet another man races in. I see knives, cutters, shears. We're outnumbered.

I hold my adversaries off with Gevit, staggering one woman back with a pommel strike to the jaw, sending another sprawling with an elbow in the gut. I can taste the rotten sweet smell of Katch on my tongue. My chest and belly start to burn. We have to get out of here...

I look past my opponents, they've pushed me twelve yards or so from my friends. I look just in time to witness something I will never unsee.

A large man holds a work hammer in his fist. He steps, he channels his significant strength through the metal head. It crushes into little Wavern's sternum and keeps going, as if to sink all the way through their body and out the other side. Bones snap, a muted, wet sound. Wavern's eyes go wide. Then they flop backwards into a crate and crumple to the floor.

*No...*

Vesp shrieks. She leaps onto the man's back. Reaching around, he grabs her by the hair and throws her into a stack of barrels. Vesp staggers up and falls. She tries to pull herself up again and leaves bloody handprints on the barrels. Rage takes her. Screaming, she slams her weight into huge man again. Using the strength of her kvell, she lifts him, runs with him, throws him to the floor. She ploughs on, climbing his body and slamming his head into the stone.

Her display of raw aggression and magic gives my attackers pause. They gape in awe and fear. Vesp leaps, claws sinking into soft flesh. She is fury, she is terror, and then two workers snatch her by the tail. They pull her off their coworker and hurl her into the wall. The sheet metal bows and smacks her to the concrete.

Vesp screams, wrathful and terrified. She scrambles, but the big man is up. He knocks her back into the sheet metal again. Her blood seeps down the metal wall.

We aren't getting out of this...

Gevit's blades drip in my hands. She is too heavy to lift. There is no action, no thought, simply defeat and despair. There is nothing for me, nothing to be done.

These people are going to slaughter us.

Something tugs in my chest. My breath catches. Vesp's hand reaches toward me for a moment, a single moment, and falls to the concrete. Her dazed eyes find mine. She reaches out to me with kvell. It pulls me and my thyir answers. Her desperation meets my despair.

The buzzing blue lights of the warehouse tilt around me. Something inside me snaps, like a levee breaching. Gevit weighs nothing in my hands now. In the garish blue light, the blades of my ancestors' axe shine, hungry and eager.

The hot summer morning chills. I breathe in, I breathe out. My breath steams in the air.

Chaos pinwheels around us. Voices shout and scream. I don't know who is where or doing what, or if anyone is taking a swing at me. My world is Vesp. The scene beside the barrels slows. It becomes a painting. The huge man lifts his hammer. Vesp's eyes lock on me. The hammer rises over her head. The weight of the tool hinges at the top, poised for the downswing...

Vesp's kvell flares hot. It pulls me like an invisible string. My boots carry me forward onto the grate in the floor. Below me, through my feet, I feel the little stream, the flow of water. Outside, it meets the Erling River. It flows for miles, through mountains, to Vatska. It flows into the ocean. It joins the ice of my ancestors, the song in the sea.

I see the waves in my mind. The waves, the cold, the ice. Even with my sickly thyir, I call for the sea. The sea answers.

I step. I step again. I hear nothing, nothing but the trickle of water below my feet and waves crashing far away.

I plant my foot and reach for that trickle. I don't think. I let Vesp pull me, I let whatever she needs climb through my body from the water. I surrender to her like I did in our dance. The sea rises through me, up through my feet, into my lungs and bones and blood. It rises to answer Vesp's desperate call.

The head of the hammer begins to fall.

Gevit lowers as I arc her back. My muscles flow through the motion they have taken ten thousand times, the motions my foremothers took ten thousand times before me. The same motions that cracked open a barrel of Katch and split Tam's foot in two. This time is different. This time when that heavy ancient blade circles, when her weight swings down, I let her go. I give her to Vesp.

And whatever Vesp asked for, whatever she needs, flies with Gevit.

Blade over handle, Gevit spins through the warehouse, wood stained from the sweat and oil of countless hands, splattering Katch and blood. The faded, worn out runescript flares in the blue lights, and she glows like a star. She impacts a metal support beam over Vesp's head.

Shards of steel explode as Gevit shatters. Metal sprays outward through the warehouse. The workers jerk and stumble as the metal pierces them. The huge man steps backwards with a shriek, his hammer clatters away. The workers shrill and stumble.

I see little of it. I float for a moment, suspended on kvell, then my foot comes down and I run. I leap over Tam and plough the man with the hammer onto the floor.

Vesp crawls to Wavern and scoops their limp form into her arms. Her eyes find mine, mouth open and wordless. My boots skid on the slick floor. I search for Gevit, but Gevit is gone, splintered, impossibly, into oblivion. The shards of her shimmer across the floor like ice crystals.

I pull Vesp and Wavern up, Blitz snapping to my good hand. We've bought a moment. We have to get out of here...

"That will be quite enough of this nonsense," states a loud voice of authority. Next comes the unmistakable racking of bolts in precision rifles.

I freeze. Vesp freezes. Bodies roll and moan, bristling with axe shrapnel, most of it little more than skin deep. Tam keeps screaming and moaning, blood spurting from his bisected boot.

Double doors at the back of the building swing wider to reveal a pair of armed security in black suits. Their rifles level on us. Behind them, dressed in an exquisite silk suit with high-waisted pants, buckskin flight gloves, and a coat draped over her shoulders, stands Edyta Gadvig.

I face her, shaking, dripping, and gasping. Staring down the barrels of the rifles, I lower Blitz to the floor and hold up my hands.

Gadvig inspects the scene, expression impassive and unimpressed. Her gray eyes settle on me and narrow. "Miss Aalgur. A surprise indeed. I did not realize you were still alive."

# THIRTY-SIX

I stay crouched, my good arm acting as tripod. My bad arm curls around the boot print on my stomach. I tremble, gutted and flimsy under the deadly steel mouths of the rifles. Each breath I take stabs pain through my ribcage and the sweet, oily Katch trickles down my back. The smell of it makes my mouth water and my stomach churn.

Vesp crouches beside me, the crumpled form of Wavern in her arms. I can hear Wavern making tiny, wet sounds with each breath. My guts twist, the warehouse flickers, and my left arm shakes.

Gadvig's eyes rake over me. "Miss Aalgur. When you didn't report to your assignment at the Temple of Brosk, we feared the worst." Her eyes move to Vesp. "And you are...?"

Vesp's breath hisses. She stumbles over her words on the first try but manages to croak: "Vesp—Vespald. Priestess. Ingfalla..."

"I see," replies Gadvig. "You and Miss Aalgur, and this... troll. I assume you work together?"

Either the world wobbles or I do. My only goal is to get us out of here alive. I think as fast as I can, which is a tall ask. "Yes. We're here on behalf of the Seppanen family. At their request. We're expected to check in tonight."

Evoking the Seppanens sends a flicker over Gadvig's face. Irritation? Disgust? It vanishes too quickly for me to tell.

My spinning mind tries to tally up our situation. Gadvig of Headwaters Distribution... okay, that tracks. Sugar beet farms for Spindel Co. sure... Black puddles of Katch pool at my feet. I slide my gaze across the concrete to the moaning Cortland and Tam attempting to staunch the bleeding.

Why is there Katch here?

Two more armed men in black suits enter through the door with the ramp, stepping over the metal splinters, all that remains of Gevit. Did... Katch corrupt the metal? How did she explode like that?

One of the men gathers up the scattered remnants of Wavern's Otherside device and brings it to Gadvig. She gives it a look but doesn't touch the pieces. Leaning in, the man whispers in her ear.

Gadvig holds up two fingers and he steps behind her.

"They know..." wheezes Wavern, each word like gravel. "They know everything. Spores, eels, soda..."

Whatever Wavern means to say ends in a wet cough. Droplets of blood fleck the floor beneath them.

Gadvig tilts her chin. "I'll help you with that, little troll. We manufacture Spindel's proprietary vitality enhancer in this facility. The unique properties of the spores in these woods travel downstream and form a symbiote of sorts with the cove eels. Something new is formed, something unique. We refine the improved eel venom in this facility. And yes, little sleuth, it is in the soda. It is the best part of the soda. You can tell Lars all about it. No secrets here."

My brain struggles. They put drugs in the fucking soda?

"This is... Katch!" I sputter.

The competitors in the Dusk Trials were testing positive for a chemical, Wavern said. We all had Spindel in our rooms... so no one would notice when a sponsor gave us something stronger...

Gadvig gives me a level look. "And what exactly is Katch, Miss Aalgur?"

My hands curl into fists. The knuckles of my left hand crackle, swelling.

Vesp straightens and finds her voice. Her tail thrashes. "Parliament will never stand for this!"

Gadvig gives her a slow, deliberate blink. "Child, I am the Parliament."

Vesp and I freeze. What?

Droplets of Katch and blood lift from the floor as Vesp's kvell rises with her anger and she stomps her foot down. She uses the back of her hand to wipe a streak of blood off her face.

"This is... wrong. This is... criminal." The floating blood looks like black pebbles in the weird blue light.

"There is nothing remotely criminal here, Miss Priestess. Our proprietary substances are not illegal. They aren't even regulated. Now there's a thought," replies Gadvig. She flicks two fingers, and the black suits lower their rifles. "The only criminal act of the day is your trespassing. That *is*, in fact, a criminal act."

My brain is still several exchanges back, rattling around on sludge eels and drugs in the soda pop. The spores infect the eels, the eels make the venom that gets turned into the drugs... fire in the forest kills the spores... But the families who burn the forest are gone...

"Why did you sponsor me in the Dusk Trials...?" I ask, but even as the words leave my mouth, I begin to see a glimpse. Owned soldiers. Crew of the Duskingr who answer to Headwaters...

Valmut...

*Kip.*

"Community investment." Gadvig gives me a soft smile, eyes crinkling and head tilting just enough to imply she finds me an idiot.

But why? What does control of the Duskingr get her? Surely, she could buy newer, faster, better airships for her distribution nonsense. Why control the oldest relics in Ruhnsvalla?

"We have nothing to fight about, Miss Priestess, Miss Aalgur. Even you, little troll. Not a single unlawful action has occurred today, except for the three of you breaking and entering onto private property. To what end, exactly?" She looks at Wavern, who clutches their chest and belly. "Contaminate inventory?" Gadvig's eyes move to the moaning Tam. "Incite violence and injure employees?"

"You kidnapped my friend." I show my teeth. I can taste the Katch on my tongue, even though I'm certain none of it got in my mouth.

"No such thing occurred here," insists Gadvig. "The troll was simply being detained until proper authorities might be called."

"You... can't do this. You *can't*..." Vesp balls her hands into fists, but I can hear the quaver in her voice growing. "Where. Are. The families?"

"Where you hollow folk go or don't go is at the bottom of my concerns," replies Gadvig.

I meet Gadvig's gray eyes with mine. "But you know, don't you?"

Gadvig takes a single, casual step closer to me. "Do I know what backwoods tree dwellers do when their land is purchased through eminent domain? No, Miss Aalgur, I assure you, I do not." She lowers her chin, eyes still on mine, posture relaxed. "We are in the wilds here, undomesticated lands much akin to the open seas. Accidents can happen."

A chill settles in my belly, my lips feel numb.

Vesp's voice hisses on the edge of a sob. "You can't do this... you dishonor yourself before the gods..."

Gadvig doesn't move her eyes from me as she speaks. "I can, Miss Priestess. If the gods object to my business model, they can take it up with me themselves. I don't deal in intermediaries."

Gadvig gives me a pleasant, generous smile. "We are done, Miss Aalgur Thalon. You, your priestess, and the little troll may go for now." She motions to her two suits. "See them out, won't you?"

The black suits don't aim at us again, but I feel the muzzles of the rifles watching us like falcons.

Gadvig's voice follows us. "Give my regards to Lars, won't you?"

We walk out the gates under the hungry rifles.

"Keep walking," says a black suit. "Don't turn around."

We do, we keep walking. Vesp cradles Wavern in her arms.

Gadvig didn't exchange a single blow with us, and yet I feel hopeless in our defeat.

* * *

"I can't believe her…" Vesp stomps into camp, Wavern cradled to her chest like a child. "How can… can that woman be on the Duskir Parliament?" Vesp screams. She tears open the tent and places Wavern on the edge of our nest. "She's neither a huldra Illuet nor a selkie Chief! She… she… Argh!" She digs her claws into her hair.

The flare of her kvell pulls at me. My own magic stirs in answer. Thyir or kvell, it's hard to tell. I stumble and sway, jittery like I just downed a quart of espresso.

Katch. I have to get the Katch off me… I pull off my outer clothes, using them to wipe myself clean. Angry red welts have already appeared on my left arm, spreading up from under the brace. My joints crunch with a dry, sandy pain. I feel drunk and distant. But not distant enough to miss the horrible whistling sound of Wavern's breath.

"W-Wavern?" I stagger to the tent and sink to my knees.

Wavern's eyes squint open, a drop of blood slides from their nose. How bad did that man hurt them? I take hold of Wavern's buttoned shirt and tear it open. The sight of the injury brings bile to my throat.

The hammer crushed a pit into Wavern's sternum. Huge purple bruises spread from uneven ribs. It's not just bruising, it looks like internal bleeding… this is bad… gods, this is so bad…

My breath makes a *huhh-huhh* sound in my ears. We have to get Wavern to the hospital… or the shrine. They don't have a day… how do we get them there?

"Thalon..." Wavern take hold of my hand. "It's okay, Thalon..."

I grip their hand. "It's not fucking okay..."

"Thalon listen..." Wavern's breath squeaks as they reach into their pants pocket and press an orange keychain into my hand. "You have what you need... in the south sea... everything." Wavern fights to hold their eyes open. "You are... all you need. Make them pay."

The breath in their broken lungs whistles and falls silent. Their chest doesn't rise again.

I don't move. I can't move. "Wavern?" I give their shoulder a shake. "Wavern?"

This isn't happening...

Vesp's hands cup Wavern's crushed sternum and broken ribs. Hope shines in her gold-green eyes. Then it fades. Her fingers feel for a pulse, and I watch the hope die in her.

More than that, I feel it. Her hope shimmers on her kvell, and I feel it snuff like a candle flame. The smoke of despair fills us.

I can't speak, but I form the words with my lips. *No. No, no...*

The smoke fills me, clouds me, overflows. My fingers claw into the earth. The forest swims around me, fire fills me, the dry leaves beneath me shiver as my rage swells, kindles, bursts. A roar tears my throat, the beast in me claws her way out.

I stand and turn toward the sugar beet farm. I am one woman with a hand axe. I don't care. They won't stop me. They won't stop me until I've torn their farm to ruins and I lie lifeless in the rubble. I don't care if they shoot me down before I reach the fence. I am the force to reckon with and I must try.

*Tophinghua be with me,* I pray. *Mother, guide my blade...*

I take my first step and my knees buckle. My time hitches, sputters. One moment I am here, one moment I lie in the arena looking up into the spotlights.

I fall with a thud into the dry, rotting leaves.

CHAPTER

# THIRTY-SEVEN

I walk out of a charred forest onto the starlit beach. Brosk's fire waits for me.

I walk to the fire and sit in the sand. The fire crackles but the heat can't warm me. I am so tired.

Brosk is not here.

My body falls back into the sand. My vision wavers. Out in the waves, a figure turns toward me, a darkness without stars. Eyes open, twin moons. Orange flames crawl at the edges of thundercloud hair. She takes a step toward me, then another...

* * *

THE THROB OF MY GALLOPING HEART FILLS MY EARS. MY EYES OPEN LONG enough to see Vesp's bare feet pounding down the trail, my useless body across her shoulders.

Where is Wavern? We have to go back for Wavern.

Wavern is dead.

That's not right. That can't be right. It can't...

The gusting sound of Vesp's breath fills my ears as she runs.

* * *

My body burns as strong hands lay me on the table in the salt-block healing room. Those strong hands touch my face, my belly, my wrists and ankles. So many hands.

"It's killing her," I recognize Lylok. "Whatever they did, her body can't take it..."

*Finally,* I think.

Hands grip my face. My eyelids flutter. The familiar, feral eyes bore through me. "I won't let you," growls Vesp. "I won't let you die."

Vesp's hands hold me, Lylok's join her. Then I recognize the cool, raw power of Yew. She pours her kvell into me, lashing my soul into my flesh and cooling the blistering heat of the Katch.

"We can help her, but she must also help herself," says Yew.

"You have to stay," whispers Vesp's voice in my ear. Time must have snapped again. She and I lie alone on the bed in the salt-block room now, her sinewy body linked around mine.

*I don't,* I want to say. My mouth doesn't move. *I've failed everything I've tried to do. I've lost everyone I've cared for or they've left me. I will never be enough. Let me go.*

*You have to,* I imagine her voice, a dream from some other place and time, some distant shore to which I will never sail. *I was alone before you. Now, we are more... We are more.*

* * *

"We prepared Wavern's body. We've sent them on. They can rest now."

I lie in my room. Vesp sits on the bed, feet leaving dust on the comforter. Bandages and scabs cover her hands and part of her jaw.

Days have passed. I sit up, I hold a cup of tea in my right hand and sip the bitter liquid. I am alive and yet, on the inside, I am dead. Worse than dead, I am worthless.

"Illuet Yew is on her way to Parliament. She will do what she is able to do." Vesp's voice carries no confidence, her bountiful curls hang limp around her face, like the tresses of a weeping willow.

*It's my fault.* It's my fault Wavern is gone. I got them killed.

Sitting up, sipping tea, is all I can manage. My eyes close and Vesp stays with me. Her warmth presses into me when I shiver, her fingers comb the agony from the back of my neck and skull.

In the dead of night, Vesp leaves me. The room turns cold. Frost crusts over the window.

I try to breathe and can't fill my lungs. Something presses down on me, crushes me. My eyes open to find myself held tight beneath the coils of a mammoth beast. The body twists and rolls, impossibly huge, big enough to swallow a ship, and yet contained inside my room. It crushes me, covered in dark and light gray fur.

Eyes like twin moons look down at me from the beast's face. A leopard seal. Saliva shines as She shows me Her teeth.

Then, the leopard seal splits open, the fur peels away. A woman's face leans over me, big as the ceiling, big as the sky. The skin of Her face mottles from dark to light. Her hanging black hair falls around me. It is thunderheads, it is acrid, it is smoke. Licking hot flames crawl up the ends of Her hair and Her eyes pin me. Her lips hold a soft, human curve, Her teeth crackle with lightning.

*Mother,* I whimper. *Mother, let me die.*

Her lips pull back, Her mouth opens far too wide, too sharp, too infinite. Tophinghua's voice rattles through my lungs and bones.

"What are you?" She asks.

* * *

Two weeks pass and I can limp to the toilet on crutches. I come back to the world like a badly tuned radio, fading and crackling. I improve, I regress, angry red blotches cover my arm, belly, and one side of my face. It's different than the first flareup where I stayed in the hospital, but I'm still in that limbo state, still untethered between life and death, even if I can hobble around.

Vesp and Lylok work in tandem to heal me, but their magic can't touch the crater inside me. Wavern's death tore it wide and raw, but if I'm honest, I've carried it since long before I met them.

I sit in bed and finally flip through the Dusk Trial trading cards. I see Azoto, Rawl, and Aalgur Thalon. I look into the face of the woman I'll never get to be again.

"Thalon, let's go and sit in the garden," Vesp crawls up beside me as I lie in bed. Her fingers trace over the back of my neck and she plucks the cards from my hands. Picking a little tin of salve off the dresser, she rubs a bit over the rash on my cheek.

"Thalon," Vesp states my name like an order. "Thalon, you need to get up."

I stay where I am. She can pick me up if she wants to move me that badly. "Why?"

"It is like when you first came here. You are sick and sad and the sadness makes the sickness worse. And that makes you even more sad."

She's right. I was like this before. Things got better, things felt right. And then, wouldn't you know it, fate dragged my entire existence right back to the depths again.

"Thalon. You can't stay like this. This isn't what you are."

I roll to look at her. "What am I, Vesp?"

Vesp stares through my pupils, right into my ugly heart. I expect her to say something thoughtful and meaningless. "You are a stubborn, depressed woman and you smell."

I blink at her. My mouth cracks open. "Well... you smell too."

"Not like salty sea dog. And I have never been to the sea. I am using speculation."

I take a breath. It makes an audible sound on the exhale.

Vesp's posture droops. "Thalon. It isn't your fault."

This gets me. The yawning emptiness in me sizzles. "It *is* my fault, Vesp. You were there. I started that fucking fight." The crackling anger catches fire. I sit up, heart thudding in my ears. "If I had just gotten Wavern out of there, if I hadn't let my fucking pride get in the way... It's my fault they're dead, Vesp. So many things are my fucking fault."

Vesp holds her ground. She leans over me. Her tail flicks from side to side. *It is not,* she signs. *They... they stole our land. They are stealing our people. You did the best you could.*

"And it wasn't enough." I push myself all the way up and throw off the covers. "I am never enough." And now I know, I never will be.

Tears rim Vesp's huge feline eyes. She presses closer still. She signs the shape for my name, the name she made for me in Ketja. She makes the sign again. *She is enough for me.*

The fury breaks and crashes out of me. I press the heels of my hands to my forehead and sob. "I shouldn't be here! Why do I keep surviving? Why do I keep living, if you can call this living, when everyone who means anything dies? I am worth nothing!"

Vesp flashes her teeth in an angry hiss. I don't care, I grab for my crutches and drag myself up. My balance wavers and my hip slams into the dresser. The pain bites through my entire side but more than that, Wavern's ugly orange star keychain sails to the floor. It cracks in two.

I hobble around to gawk at the remnants. The last stupid plastic reminder of one of the best people in this miserable world...

"Oh..." Vesp scrambles to the floor. She lifts both pieces and holds them up. "Oh... did you know it was a storage device?"

I hold onto the dresser to stay on my feet. "A... a what?"

"This can hold information," Vesp turns toward me so I can see it. "Remember Wavern's electronic typewriter? The people in black suits broke it. But whatever was on the typewriter could be on here. There... there could be an entire library inside of this."

The horrible, lying twinkle of hope sparks to life in me. Is there a way we can help? *You have everything you need,* Wavern said. They didn't mean that literally, right?

"Can you... get it out?"

Vesp traces a claw around the rectangular lip of the device. "I do not have the cord for this. But someone in a city might. Yew told me they sell Otherside tech in Adlervik..."

"Are you saying that Wavern's kitchen eel shit might be in there?"

"It could be. We won't know until we take the information out. It might even work with my music player."

"Could someone in Ingfalla have what you need to do that?"

"I don't know..." Vesp clicks the keychain back together and hands it to me. "I will check."

# THIRTY-EIGHT

Vesp spends two entire days scrounging every nook and cranny of Ingfalla for the right type of Otherside cord. Even though she eventually slinks back to my room in defeat, the keychain did the trick. It gave me a goal. As Wavern once said, I'm a girl of goals.

It gets my ass out of bed and my thoughts off feeling miserable about myself. I'm still miserable, sure, but now I must become a raging menace for Gadvig. I can die after that.

Unfortunately, my body didn't get my heart's memo and after hobbling around and attempting a round of simple kvellvahna, I'm back in bed, head spinning.

Vesp hovers in my doorway. "No luck. In good news, we can get what we need. Lylok sent word to Yew to bring us the right cable from Adlervik." She looks me over from head to foot and scowls. "You don't look very well."

"How dare you," I quip.

Vesp helps herself up onto my bed, dusty feet and all. "You sound more like yourself but..." Her fingers spider over my face and down my neck.

The sickness has become a different flavor now. My lungs feel tight, my stomach knotted and skin hot.

Vesp places a hand on my brow and pulls back the covers to set the other on my belly. "Oh, Thalon... you're not alright... The Katch is still hurting you."

"I've been worse."

Vesp doesn't reply at first. She scowls. Her fingers cup around my ribcage. "Your thyir is... different."

I blink my eyes open. "Different how?"

Vesp shakes her head. "It's just... different. Not like your baseline... I am not sure how to balance it to your kvell. I see them... they are angry inside you..."

Vesp's round, intense eyes look through her lashes as if she can read my thoughts on my forehead. She leans closer, her curls fall around me. "You should try putting on your pelt."

A tremor moves through my bones at the thought. I don't remember how my own thyir felt, how the shift changed my body from one shape to another. "I can't..."

Vesp leans in to read my body with her hands. They touch my back, my belly, the pulse at the side of my neck. Her breath stirs my hair. The curve of her lips floats beside my face. My arms prickle into gooseflesh.

"Try," she whispers. She slides off the bed and rifles through the dresser. She hops right back, my black pelt folded in her arms and transfers the bundle to me. She drags my arm across her shoulders. "Channeling your kvell during Midsommer changed you. Let's go to the water and see." Hooking an arm under my knees, she lifts me.

Being held like this changes me too. I feel... what do I feel? When was the last time someone carried me so tenderly?

*Gods damn it and gods damn me... she's so strong...* My eyes dart sideways at the angles of her jaw. *So pretty...* Fuck that. Vesp isn't pretty. She's powerful. She's fierce. There is no one else like her... Weightless in her arms, the crater inside me fades deeper, crusts over. My resolve tightens. My body remembers our dance...

She carries me to the hydrothermal river, the steam a moist whisper in the summer night. Crickets wail under the waning moon.

Vesp sets me on the edge of a pool with my feet dangling into the bubbles. Embarrassment overpowers my physical discomfort. "Vesp… if I'm going to try this, I'm going to need to take my clothes off."

"Mm-hmm." Vesp turns her back to me. The tuft of her tail makes little sweeping motions over the wooden deck.

The pounding of my heart crawls up the back of my throat and into my ears. It has nothing to do with a fever, and everything to do with Vesp. Sweat slides down my ribs from my armpits. *We've been naked in the creek before! Pull yourself together, dumbass!*

"Tell me when you're in the water," Vesp speaks into the dark woods.

Using my good arm to strip, I shove my clothes aside and slide into the hot water. Reaching up, my hand hesitates on my pelt before pulling it in after me. For a moment, I do nothing but float. My pelt floats with me, familiar and yet alien, as if it belongs to someone close to me, but isn't truly mine. *Don't get your hopes up, Omelet. This isn't going to work.*

"I'm in," I say.

Vesp shimmies out of her pants and drops her vest. She slides into the water facing away from me. With bubbles up to our chins, she walks right up to me. I'm not ready. I'm too ready. I hold myself as still as possible as she inspects me, resisting the urge to reach out and let my fingers brush her skin. A few days back, I wanted to curl up and die. Now look at me, queasy, feverish, and aroused. What an omelet.

"Can I read your magic again?" asks Vesp, eyes almost furious in their intensity.

I nod my head. "Yes."

Vesp's long, strong hands press to my belly, then slide around to my back. Amid popping bubbles, I hardly feel the magic as she tinkers around with it. I feel other things though. Her hands slide up my ribs and under my armpits. In the hot water, so very close, so very naked, the breath in my mouth turns cold. I can't swallow, I can't think.

Her face so near mine, I would need only to tilt forward on my toes for our noses to brush. Feral curls splayed over the water, Vesp looks down into my eyes.

"You are ready," she murmurs.

"Yes..." I whisper back.

Vesp places her hands on either side of my face, her thumb brushes the edge of my lip. My mouth opens, just a little, hopeful... She shoves me under the water.

I snort water up my nose in surprise and shift.

My fur folds around my skin, bonding to it, becoming me. My bones flow from one shape to the other. My joints pop, tendons and ligaments stretching and shortening. I whine as the shift finishes, the sleek black body of my birth floating to the surface in agony.

But that pain fades as the shift completes. I did it. My thyir! My pelt! I pop my head out of the water and bark out a peel of laughter.

"Ah!" Vesp stumbles back, slipping under the surface and then shooting up, laughing too. She claps her hands, laughing and laughing.

I laugh with her, then I dive. I zip up and down the river, flying between the cold stream and the hot vents, flukes propelling me like wings. Blind in the darkness, my whiskers read the gushing water, showing me boulders and banks. I swoop back to the pool, to Vesp. My whiskers paint me the shape of her, her long, slender waist, the curve of her hips, her tail flowing with the current.

Floating up, I lie on my back with my flukes spread like wings. Above me, the black trees claw against the stars. I breathe in and breathe out, feeling the crackle of my thyir and the warm flow of kvell. They flow past me, through me, with me.

Vesp's hand pets the fur along my side. Our two magics blend.

"Pretty," murmurs Vesp. "Soft..."

Her hands run the length of my side, and I follow the touch. My body slims and lengthens, fins splitting into legs, aquadynamic body molding back into my skinny torso and broad shoulders. I make it to a human shape and stop. I leave the pelt as part of me, my skin from the neck down covered in fur, my arms and shins rubbery and dark, nails blunted claws. I don't dare split myself in two again. I've lived divided for far too long.

"Hmm," hums Vesp, hand still on my side. Her other hand rests on my belly. "Yes. That is better. I can see it. Can you feel it?"

"Yes." I float in her arms. The sides of my webbed feet rest against her calves. Perhaps I still feel a touch of fever, an ache in my bones. Those discomforts fade against the glow spreading through me. My pelt... my kvell, my thyir... *her...*

I lift a hand from the water and push wet curls from her face. I let the backs of my fingers slide down her cheek on their return to the water.

*Say something! Say anything!* One part of me yells. *Don't wreck this! Don't make it weird!* Yells the other.

*You're both naked!* Wails a third.

"Vesp, I..." I start to say, but I can't finish it. Frustration pins my tongue. She's my favorite person in the whole world and I don't want to ruin that by being...

By being me.

"Vesp, thank you," I whisper, voice thick and husky. I look down, where my black fur merges with the black water beneath the stars. "This is me."

Vesp's hands lift my chin so I must look at her, so that she fills my horizon and my sky. "Yes," she whispers.

"Yes," I whisper back.

Vesp's hands stay on me, one hand on my belly, kvell swelling beneath her touch, one hand on my spine, feeling the flow of thyir. Two magics in harmony.

I feel the kvell in her. I am not attuned to it as she is, it feels as new to me as the smell of the forest did on my first night by the lake. But my fingers reach for it, resting on her waist.

Our magics brush together, two wild creatures sliding past each other in the night, close enough for fur to ripple against fur…

Vesp's hands circle my waist and she pulls me up and closer. My hands don't know where to go. She pulls me closer still. Her fingers travel from my spine up to cradle the back of my head. My heart pounds, her heart pounds.

I feel every place our bodies touch and the kvell running through each breath we take. It sizzles where we touch, electric and warm and safe. It flares as Vesp cups my face and rests her forehead against mine. Does she feel it, too? She must.

Her hands travel back down my sides and I gasp, breath silvery, shimmering. It must be steam, perhaps I am seeing things…

"Thalon," murmurs Vesp.

"Vesp…" my voice rasps.

"You need to rest now. You are tired and sick…"

Protests build up in the back of my throat. I don't want this to stop, I want it to go further… but she's right. The shift gutted me. As she helps me from the water, I collapse to all fours, limbs trembling and weak.

"Ahh, seagull sucking shitty luck…" I spit.

Vesp spins into a robe and kneels to towel me off, rubbing my fur and roughing it up. "You were able to shift. Your luck is better than sucking seagulls. Unless, seagull sucking is a good thing?"

"Heh, no."

"Hmm." Vesp smiles.

When she has me dry enough, she half carries me back to my room and tucks me in like a sick pup.

*Right back*, signs Vesp, and slips out.

I lie on my side, still shaking, still simmering. The gods drag me to the depths, I've fallen hard… and for a huldra.

*For a woman*, I correct myself. *For a beautiful woman of magic.*

Vesp pops back in and closes my door, a little jar in her hand. Knee walking onto my bed, she rolls me to my belly and scoops a finger full of ointment from the jar.

The ointment smells of camphor and wintergreen and tingles on the skin as she massages it into my neck. Her fingers search out the knots in my muscles, squeezing and stretching them. I melt into a blob of fur.

"Sleep now, selkie girl," she breathes into my ear.

I don't need to be told twice.

# THIRTY-NINE

I wake up in the warmth of my own fur. My thick, dark pelt covers my chest and belly. I gasp and hug myself, relishing the texture of my webbed hands and blunted claws. My bones may ache, but magic flows. Thyir and kvell. Neither is strong, but both live in me. I am whole.

Stretching, my arm bumps into a warm body. I open my eyes to see her lying beside me. My hackles raise.

*Vesp.*

She sleeps curled against my side, hands squeezing a rumple of blankets. She wears nothing but the robe from the hot spring.

I lie as still as I can. I know how I feel about her, but what does she feel for me? Am I a trusted friend and companion? Or does she too want something more?

As if hearing my thoughts, Vesp flutters her eyes open and stretches like a cat. She rolls her shoulders and flops her tail around before raking her claws through my fur.

"Hmm," hums Vesp. Her hands slide over my ribs, following the warm kvell beneath. "So soft..."

A grin brightens my face, I can't stop it. She cuddles back up with me and I wrap my arms around her. For a moment, I can step back from grief. My focus narrows to the supple warmth of Vesp's skin and her earthy scent, the musky smells of a lived-in body. A sigh lifts and settles my chest. I close my eyes, content to draw the moment out as long as we may.

The knock on my door startles us. Vesp holds still as a wooden statue, the end of her tail bristling like a bottle brush.

Lylok's voice comes through. "Thalon, when you're up, there's something at the post for you. And if you happen to see Vesp, send her my way, will you?"

"Will do!" I call.

Vesp holds her breath until the footsteps vanish into the shrine and then rolls her eyes up to meet mine. We both giggle, covering our smiles with our hands.

"You heard him. I need to get up and find Vesp." I pat her back. "The wily mink could be anywhere."

"Mink," echoes Vesp. She stretches again, sits up and tightens her robe. "Mink, mink, mink."

There are so many things I could say to her. "I didn't realize you... would stay the night..." I trail off.

"I needed to make sure you were alright." Vesp's gaze bores into me, serious. Leaning over the bed, she rakes her claws through my hair.

I swallow a squeak in my throat. *Don't you dare, Thalon.*

Vesp holds my gaze. "You need to get up. You need to find Vesp. Better hurry, she could be anywhere." Hopping away, Vesp slips from the room like a brisk breeze.

What is she saying to me? Everything? Nothing?

How will I fuck up this time?

*No, no, you don't get to do that, Thalon,* I scold myself as I dig through my drawers in search of garments that will sit nicely over my fur. *You don't get to manufacture problems. See what you want, just like Lylok said...*

I'm sure Lylok meant something else.

* * *

THE SWEET, COZY MOOD DIES AS SOON AS I HOBBLE MY WAY TO THE MAIL outpost. The single worker gives my fur and rubbery hands a long stare before handing over an envelope. I expect a letter from Hans, but it's my letter to him from half a year ago, returned. A blazing red bindrune stamp of the Duskir Parliament covers the front.

My hackles bristle, my claws bite into the paper. "What does the Parliament stamp mean?"

"It means the post box was closed and the letters were undeliverable," replies the bored worker.

I spend the next hour locating the address in Caldera to write Hans a new letter. I keep the returned one. It feels like a warning.

* * *

A FEW DAYS AFTER THE OMINOUSLY STAMPED LETTER, I STIR INGREDIENTS together for brownies in the kitchen. I can sit while I do it, and I get all the eggs into the bowl without incident.

Vesp paces, stopping to smash walnuts when she passes the cutting board, but otherwise distracted and restless.

When she finally finishes the nuts, I shove the dish into the oven. "Hey, Vesp. I think we need a change of scenery."

Vesp's eyes snap to me. She waits.

"We're spinning our wheels a little... at least I am. There's not much we can do about anything until Yew gets back..."

Vesp leans closer. Her tail flicks over the stone floor. "Camping? Kaldur Lake? It's not too far... I can carry the gear. The moon is full..."

I wipe my hands on my pants. "Meet me back here when the brownies are done."

* * *

An hour later, we set off together beneath the scorching sun. We climb from the valley and along the ridge. I wear Blitz on my hip. I miss Gevit but my heart doesn't mourn her. She had the most warrior death imaginable. I try not to dwell on other things I've lost. I can't go back, I can only go forward.

We follow the path I once wandered, cold and sick and heartbroken. My fingers brush the tree Vesp found me under. I was a lost girl then. Maybe I'm still lost.

I burst out laughing when I see just how close the shrine and Kaldur Lake are to each other. Up a hill and around some boulders. A few short miles. The granite shores hold the water like cupped hands, reflecting blue sky and gathering clouds. Chipmunks dart between the scattered sugar pines.

Setting down our packs, we savor the day. We walk a lazy circle around the lake and wade in the chill, salty water. As evening approaches, we build a cozy camp.

The lake mirrors the boulders and fluffy pink clouds. We skip stones over it, and I break out a bottle of mead. The heat of early autumn cools as the clouds roll in, lush with the scent of coming rain.

Vesp sits on a log beside me, her shoulder touching mine. Her tail whisks over the pebbles behind us. Without a word, Vesp unwraps the brownies as if revealing a sacred treasure. We both enjoy a piece with our mead. It reminds me of our first walk together, looking for herbs in the woods. When I finish my brownie, I dig a box from my pocket. Inside are my Dusk Trial trading cards. A selkie woman grins and flexes, face painted and absurd. She's not me, not anymore. Vesp watches as I feed cards, one by one, into the campfire.

Vesp's tail flips over. She dips her chin and looks sideways at me through her lashes. "I have a gift for you. Now seems right. But I worry it will make you sad."

My muscles brace and I force them to relax.

Bottom lip between her sharp teeth, Vesp lifts her hand from the pocket of her dress and offers it to me. When her fingers open, a gleaming shard of polished steel sits in her palm. She turns her hand, dangling the bit of metal on a leather thong. The smooth, rounded edges hide that it was once splintered and raw.

*G-e-v-i-t*, Vesp spells the word to me with her hand.

Sad is not what I feel, but the tears come anyway. They spill down my cheeks as Vesp fastens the necklace and brushes back my hair. Placing my fingers on my chin, I offer them to Vesp in thanks. Her eyes narrow to happy crescent moons.

Our silence continues, the evening deepens.

"So. Anything you'd like to do tonight?" I ask.

Vesp's eyes move over the twilight water. "Dance," she whispers. "I feel powerless right now. I hate that feeling. I hate grief and I hate waiting. I want to feel what I feel when we dance." She turns her face to me. "Do you feel well enough?"

My heart picks up tempo. I consider myself. Remnants of rash still pock my bad arm, but they're on their way out for now. "I do."

Vesp watches the dark water for a few beats before taking out her Otherside device and a set of speakers. The music starts, a bouncing, rollicking melody, rolling over the water.

I can't help it, I tap my foot. Vesp grins.

"Will you show me the ts'kmet?" she asks. She stands and sways with the beat.

The full moon swells over the horizon and stains the gathering clouds yellow and ripe. I reach for Vesp's hands. "It would be my pleasure."

Soon I'm grinning too. "The basis of the ts'kmet is a strong foundation. Every jump, kick, and stomp are built up from the balance and stability of your stance..."

We begin, me guiding Vesp through the first basic motions. My hands settle on her hips as I explain the stance. She never stops smiling. In a way, the ts'kmet and the kvellvahna are not so different. Many principles and motions exchange between the two, just at different speeds. I wonder if both dances arose from a single source long ago.

I teach Vesp the very basic side steps and how to hook our legs around each other's bodies. I show her how to tap the bottoms of our feet together.

Tail swishing with excitement, Vesp turns up the wild music.

"This is music from the other world, my world. You can pick songs if you like. There are thousands inside."

My head bobs. The spicy flavor of the popping, driving mix reminds me of Vesp. I can see her as part of the world that made this music. "This is perfect."

Vesp faces me, expression serious, stance balanced and coiled, as if poised to step into combat against me. The bass thrums in my chest. We face each other. Vesp lifts a foot and lowers it with intension and kvell.

*Dance*, she orders.

And we do. I start slow and conservative, reviewing the basics of the ts'kmet for myself as well as her. Gone are the days of my mastery of it. But then I loosen up and shake out. What use do I have for mastery out here?

Vesp alternates between mirroring my ts'kmet steps and slipping into her aggressive, free-form motions. She throws her arms, letting the music move her at its will. I let myself follow. I surrender to the rising moon and cold splash of water beneath my feet as we drift into the lake, to the thudding of our hearts and the harsh exhales of our breath. We need not be anything but ourselves out here.

My body feels flimsy still, so I treat it gently. I'm not trying to win, I just want to be myself and be with her.

The music evolves and intensifies, climbing through us and between us. Kvell and thyir awake in us. Vesp steps in, her leg makes a bold hook around the back of my thighs. In traditional ts'kmet, she would make the contact and then let go. My arms would hook around her without touching. But we aren't dancing just the ts'kmet. She uses the hook of her leg to press the length of her sinewy body against mine. My webbed hands grasp her back. Her ribs expand and contract under my fingers, her sweat a tangy scent.

We spring apart, then loop back together, and spring apart again. The bass drives us deeper into the water. Up to our calves, we stomp through it. Our thyir and kvell spill out from us, a spiral at the center of which we dance. Water droplets hang in the air around us and our campfire flares green and blue.

Then, something changes, as it did on Midsommer's Eve. A unity tethers us. When my next step splashes down, the ice in the water reaches up to me. A shimmer runs through me.

I shudder and the tether snaps. A sigh escapes Vesp. Her eyes close as she falls back into the music, swaying. The ice in the water recedes.

Again, the music metamorphs, and soon our tether of magic rebuilds. We circle and stomp, arms grasped around each other, legs kicking, intertwined. We gasp and pant and sweat. Our opposing yet complementary magics merge and drive and push us...

Vesp's fingers splay and flutter with the notes of the music. My eyes catch words hiding in them.

*Want*, suggest her hands, *you.*

I spin and kick and land on all fours. I'm imagining it. We leap and stomp, and her gold eyes lock on mine.

*Want*, grasp her hands, *you.*

My hackles rise. *We're dancing, friends dancing... don't see things that aren't there, Thalon... don't wish for things that...* I think.

*Want... you...* say Vesp's hands. She jumps into a spin, falling in slow motion as kvell ripples through her. She lands with her eyes burning the question into me, droplets suspended in the night like crystals.

*Yes*, my hands say back. *Yes, yes...* If it was a mistake, if she didn't know she was saying it, what can I lose?

On the next beat I find myself stepping backwards up the shore. Vesp's mouth presses to mine, her hands digging and hungry in my fur. My hands reach back and catch our weight as we tumble onto the picnic blanket. I make an incoherent grunting sound, a beast girl in spite of myself. Gasping, I kiss her back.

Vesp's hands grasp my jaw. She kisses me, kisses deep into my mouth, my sharp sea lion teeth and her bobcat fangs. I dare not think, I dare not breathe. My arms encircle her, my webbed fingers slide down her spine. Her breath quickens, her hands pull me up by the thighs, pressing my back to the shore of the lake. My legs squeeze her hips and her tail twists around my ankle, holding me here and now.

Thyir is in me, kvell is in me, and something else, like Brosk breathing sparks through me. The only sound I hear is the song of the crickets and the wet sounds of mouths and teeth and tongues. The music has stopped.

I inhale her. We gasp together, laugh nervously and dive back in. Our hands follow kvell and thyir. The two magics crackle from us, through the lake at our feet. I feel the water, in me and in her, the ice of my ancestors. A shiver of cold and heat spreads between us as our hands reach deeper. Our fingers search for the intersections of thyir and kvell. We dance a different dance between unseen bonfires. And the magic soars.

My thyir is hers, her kvell is mine, flowing between us, twining and roaring, flames charring us from the inside out, my head thrown back, each breath gray and shimmering with frost.

Behind us, the lake comes alive with dancing lights. We barely see it, we see only each other.

To think, we once believed our magics do not mix.

Forehead to forehead, we drink in the night, stars in the sky, stars on the water. We fall into those stars together.

THUNDER GRUMBLES OVER THE MOUNTAINS. WAYWARD RAINDROPS SMACK the roof of our tent. Vesp and I lay nested together, cozy and content as a sigh. The splat of a raindrop stirs me. I smile at Vesp's warm body pressed to me, her tail looped around my leg. There is nothing I want and nowhere else I would rather be. I am grateful for my life now, even if it's hard sometimes. I fall back to sleep still smiling.

The night splits open in a cataclysmic crash. The world blasts white as lightning strikes a pine beside us. We shriek and reel, blind and deaf for a moment. We fall from the tent in a tangle of arms and legs and a tail. We shriek with giddy laughter at the charred, smoking tree.

"We should probably head back to the shrine. You know, before the lightning decides we look tasty," I say.

Vesp nods and signs: *Good idea*. The end of her tail bristles.

My fingers fumble as I buckle on my arm brace and Blitz. Vesp tosses her wrinkled dress back on. We meet eyes and blush.

Zigs of white electricity suture the clouds overhead. Dawn stains the horizon, bright licks of orange reaching up beneath the clouds. The light reflects on the water of Kaldur Lake, spattered and wrinkled by drops of rain.

I think nothing of it and neither does Vesp. And then she freezes, leaning on the rolled tent. Her pupils shrink to slits as her eyes reflect the brightening dawn. "Thalon..." she hisses, "Thalon. The light..."

"I know. It feels like we just went to sleep..."

"No." Vesp turns me around by the shoulders so I face the orange glow. "No. That's west. That's..." her voice falters.

A murder of crows spins, screaming from the brightening horizon.

It's not the sun rising.

My breath catches in my throat. A deep ripple passes through the earth and air, a stirring of primal kvell and thyir, a thrumming of divine power.

Vesp's hands begin to shake as she signs one word over and over.

*Fire.*

# FORTY

Vesp and I stand and look.

Tongues of flame crest the ridge. They growl, gulping the wind and devouring the dry, autumn forest. The fire roars like a beast, thundering through the ground and sky. Cracks ring out like gunshots as entire tree trunks snap. Birds take flight only to fall from the air as heat overtakes them. Even down by the lakeshore, the flames transform the night into a dazed orange panic. My knees turn to jelly.

A few weak raindrops hit my face. They do nothing to the fire, nothing at all. The fire doesn't know they exist. It is a beast of its own, growing and spreading, insatiably hungry.

On the far side of the slopes, a flash illuminates the smoke. The rumble of the explosion reaches us after. A series of pops and flares of light follow. Toxic fumes rise into a plume and are swallowed by the inferno. So much for the sugar beet farm.

Balls of burning debris hurl from the crest of the ridge, igniting everything in their path. It spreads faster than the birds can fly and faster than we can run.

"We have to go, we have to go!" My voice has gone scratchy and breathless. I grasp Vesp's arm.

Lightning detonates like a bomb. It creates a shadow in the smoke. A figure, standing from a crouch. As big as a mountain spire, a rising pillar of destruction in a ravaged sea of flame. I don't wait for eyes to open. I know who it is and so does Vesp. We abandon everything but our memories of the evening and run.

We run with everything we have, feet pounding down the trail, smoke belches over us and heat presses at our backs. The fire screams and thrashes, spitting vengeance and annihilation. It rolls in a deep, guttural roar. The roar becomes a laugh.

Vesp pulls me by the hand. My limp slows us but fear gives me borrowed speed. We leap down switchbacks and skid in dry leaves. When we plunge into the huldreby, the fire glows like a sunset on the windows of the shrine.

"Wake up! Wake up!" Vesp screams. She hits gongs and bells as she passes them and the walls of houses.

"Fire!" I hobble through town, making as much noise as I can. "Fire! FIRE!"

Huldror stumble from their houses in disbelief and confusion.

"There's no fire," someone gripes. "Get yourselves back to bed..."

"Crazy girls," grumbles another.

Then someone screams. A horn trumpets from the steps of the shrine. Panic takes hold of Ingfalla. There is, very much, a fire.

"Wake up!" I holler, ripping open the doors. "WAKE UP!"

The fire hasn't crested the hills around our valley, but it spits out meteors of flame. A projectile arcs over the ridge and lands beside a home on the outskirts of town. The wisteria vines disintegrate into fire.

"Water! Water..." I stagger to a halt in disbelief as flames burst through the windows of the cabin from the inside. A wall of heat desiccates my skin, my eyes. The house goes up like waxed paper.

Two thoughts war for control of my mind. *We have to get to safety. We are all going to die.*

Lylok rushes from the shrine in his nightclothes. "Inside! Everyone, into the shrine!"

The stone shrine, of course! I spin. Sparks land atop the ancient structure, smoldering in the twisted, dry trees on top. The blossom of hope wilts in me. The shrine will burn too... it's already burning. I sink to my knees.

*Get up*, a voice inside me orders. I do. I stand.

A second cabin bursts into flames. The roar of the fire drowns the screams of anguish. My face is numb with shock. Smoke belches, flames repaint the world. How did this happen? When will I wake up from this nightmare?

I look up into the inferno, mere minutes from town. There is nowhere to run, nowhere except a shrine made of trees as dry as paper. I look up into the stadium and see faces watching me fall. The stadium, the Dusk Trials, they feel distant, meaningless. Burning manzanita rolls down the hillside and into the river. Wherever it rolls, new fire pops to life.

Snapping Blitz from my thigh, I wade into the river and start swinging. I cut brush and pile it so the fire won't have ladders to jump the river. That's the hope at least, that the river will somehow stop it. But then, mid-swing, my breath catches, axe a useless little tool in my hand. I look up.

The fire crests the ridge. However tall the trees are, the fire reaches three times that into the sky. Two points of light blaze like lighthouse beacons. The light falls over me.

She looks down and I look up into Her eyes. The twin moon eyes of the Storm. She is here, the Dread One. Lightning cracks between Her teeth. She is here, as Brosk said.

And this is not a dream.

I stand taller. I face Her. I face the fire. I fill my lungs and roar.

*Laughable*, I can almost hear the inferno say. It falls like fireflies into Ingfalla.

Her power surges from Her, thyir so vast and pure, it could disintegrate me. But I feel kvell too, so sharp it becomes lightning. A primal mix of both magics, all magic. She is everything and there is no escaping Her.

It is one thing to pray to a god or to take Her name for your own hopes of victory. It is another thing entirely to stare into the face of a god and see that god stare back. I am nothing, I am no one and...

And yet.

The river flows past my legs. The Shastaar River, a distant vein leading, someday, to the heart of the sea. The ice of my ancestors laps at my calves, always there, always taunting, a song I cannot sing. I look up, up into the face of Tophinghua. She is no god of thyir. No, She is thyir, She is kvell. She is not to be measured in half...

She looks down at me, waiting.

"Thalon!" Vesp screams. She runs for me as huldror scramble, buckets of water in their hands. She grabs me, but I don't move, I can't move.

This is Tophinghua. This is my God, my Mother... I have never truly known Her.

"We need water!" gasps Vesp. "We will die without the water..." She crumples at my side, a tiny scream lost in the roar of the angry god.

The water.

The ice stirs in the water. I feel it in my bones, in my heart, in me, in Vesp...

*The ice moves for no one.*

Reaching down, I take Vesp's hand and pull her up. I hold her here with me as the fire rains around us. I drop Blitz and take her other hand. I tear my eyes from the fire until I see Vesp and only Vesp.

"Vesp..." I whisper. "Help me..."

The sea spat me out for a reason. Whether a truth or a comforting lie I choose to believe, She spat me out for a reason. That reason is now. That reason is *us.*

"I know," I whisper. "I know what She wants." Saying those words aloud chills my skin.

Vesp's eyes stare past me into the unstoppable. Tears stream down her face. She nods. She feels it too.

Our fingers slip together, we cling to each other, and then we step. We step, we push out with kvell and pull in with thyir. We wade into the river. A dance, both practiced and improvised. The raging wildfire becomes our music. We let it move us at its whim. Our feet splash, the water quivers. I surrender to Vesp and she surrenders to me. Ash paints the ground and streaks our faces. We pour sweat. Together, we offer ourselves to Tophinghua.

The water of the Shastaar River shudders and skips. We need more…

"Help! Help us!" wails Vesp. "We need everyone! Anyone!"

Fear tingles over my arms as nothing happens, as no one answers. But then someone does come. Lylok charges for us, face grim with determination.

"We have to go, we…" Lylok's voice vanishes into the roar of the fire. His hand hovers over my back, his mouth opens in shock, then a livid, wild joy.

Another priest begins to protest, going so far as to grasp Vesp's arm and try to wrench her away. His eyes go wide in shock as well. "What…? What is that…"

"HA!" cackles Lylok. He wastes no time. Falling into a strong stance behind us, he channels kvell directly into us. He turns to face the shrine and hollers: "EVERYONE! ANYONE WHO CAN! TO THE RIVER!"

And they come, the huldror, weeping, frantic, gentle folk staring up into their own unmaking. Lylok uses one hand to pull kvell from the huldror and the other to pour it into us. "Everyone!" he crows, feral, delighted. And they begin to follow.

The sheer breadth of the huldror's kvell rolls through us, with us, out of us. Just like at the bonfire, the kvell grows with their numbers, building, intensifying. The thyir in me, in Vesp, in the water and fire, it leaps and twists to match it. I pant heavy breaths of snow-white frost. My body shakes, my sweat freezes my fur into crystals.

The Shastaar River jumps and spits. It snatches burning leaves from the air and pushes back the smoke. With each new huldra, the power of the river swells. I feel the sea, I feel my home in the water. I feel the ice in me.

Of all of us, I am the weakest. But I can open myself up to this, to them. I can connect us to the water.

The water sings through me, the ice sears my heart. I let it in. My pelt clings to me and my teeth sharpen. So much power, untapped and raw and burning through us... It will consume us all...

What do I do with it?

I grit my teeth, my resolve wavers. What am I thinking? I'm going to get us all killed...

The river shakes, I shake, Vesp beside me weeps, trying to keep her focus.

"Do you see it?" Lylok whispers in my ear.

I shake my head, I don't have the breath to answer.

"You have to see it. You have to see what you want."

My head turns toward the shrine. The silhouettes of children huddle under the eaves. The twisted trees atop burn bright now.

Houses burst into flame as Tophinghua reaches down, reaches a hand toward the shrine.

*What I want is impossible.*

*Even better.*

"I can't..." I gasp.

Lylok places his hand on my spine, the bones that betrayed me, and holds me steady as my knees grow weak. "You are the daughter the Dread One intended. You must."

I look up into the inferno that is Tophinghua. I will never have enough to match Her wrath...

"We're here with you," Lylok speaks to me and Vesp. "Don't be anything but you. She is enough. We're all here together. You're not alone. We're here."

I sob but I stop fighting myself. With the village at our backs and the inferno gnawing down the mountain, I let the ice guide me. I lift my hands, Vesp lifts hers. We share the same breath, the same heartbeat, the same terror. We lift our hands. The river lifts with us. The water flows up the banks and over the feet of the huldror. It pushes bubbling fingers up the knoll to the foundation of the shrine. Water crawls right up the walls like centipedes. It flows down the streets and into the surviving houses and shops.

I breathe in fire, I breathe out frost. The wall of flames generates its own wind. It hits us like a battering ram, knocking us back. We plant our feet, each of us practiced in balance. Kvell rises through the huldror like the Midsommer dance, it tells the river where to flow.

Water pushes up walls, coating the shrine and village. It steams and hisses, spitting as the flames fall like dying butterflies.

Groaning and snapping, the trees of the shrine shudder. The trunks splinter, straighten, unfold. Fresh green buds burst from the gnarled branches and the fire scatters into beads of rising golden light. The shrine of Ingfalla blooms.

*What I want is impossible...*

Tears stream down my face and freeze into icicles on my chin. *I can see it, Lylok...*

The ice may move for no one, but we are more than *one*.

I turn my hands over, and as one gives thanks to Brosk. Vesp mirrors me. With every shred of kvell and thyir, spite and love in my body, I close them into fists.

A shock ripples through us, the river, the air. A moment of absurd, obscene silence falls. In that silence, I draw a breath and look up into Tophinghua's terrible eyes.

"I AM YOUR DAUGHTER!" I roar. *I am enough.*

The river turns to ice. Silver and frost encrust the shrine, the homes. White angry steam billows as the fire collides with ice. The steam swallows us, all of Ingfalla.

A wave of blue and gold rolls up the wall of flames. Tophinghua throws Her head back. Her laughter peals through the night. Then,

She looks down at me. "*YES*," She says. "*YOU ARE. AND NOW YOU BEGIN TO SEE.*"

She smiles and steps back into a wall of rain.

✳ ✳ ✳

THE RAIN TRAVELS OUT OF THE WEST, OUT OF THE SEA, A TORRENTIAL WALL of water. It pours over the unstoppable fire, two acts of the gods colliding. Hot steam rolls through the forest as fire and water fight for dominance. At Tophinghua's whim, the rain begins to win.

The shrine glows like a beacon, flowers blooming in the branches of the tall, proud trees.

I don't know how long we held the river up, how long we were duskingr. It ends suddenly and I collapse like a felled sapling into the riverbed. I lie in the pooling mud and see nothing but rain. My life blurs, a chain of events sifting together and out of order. I see moments of my existence.

I hold Vesp's hand, beautiful twists of silver in her curls, my own fur flecked with gray. We are old now, we have lived such lives.

I lie on my back, staring into the lights of the stadium the day I lost everything. *Get up*, says my voice. *Get up…*

I hold Ashling for the first time, so small and fragile. My flukes flail in desperation against a doorknob I cannot turn. *You're an animal…* says my mother.

Vesp lifts me up from the ruins of my life and carries me on her shoulders into the next.

*What are you?* asks my mother.

*What are you?* asks Tophinghua.

*This. I am this.*

For a moment, we were duskingr. And then the moment ends. My time aligns, and I am back in the mud.

Vesp slips down beside me. Rain dumps over us, steam gushes from scalding wood. I turn my head until Vesp is all I see, until she is my horizon.

*What I want might be impossible, but I can see it. I can see it now.*

Knee deep in the mud, old Lylok turns a slow circle, lifts his hands to his face and weeps.

# FORTY-ONE

It began and then it ended, as we all do. The fire consumed many houses in the huldreby. Many more were spared. The rain lasts an entire week, remaking the forest in its image. Trees topple, roots burnt to cinders. Without those roots, portions of the slopes slide away.

Not a trace of the rot remains in the western side of the huldror woods. I can't imagine any part of the sugar beet farm survived. I suppose the gods took it up with Gadvig, as she'd suggested. Up the mountain from Ingfalla, Kaldur Lake arcs and crackles with light from the Svall, unsettled by the upheaval of primal forces. The lights dance in the night.

The displaced huldror gather in the shrine like scattered leaves, scattered but collected, and little by little, we pull ourselves back together.

My body paid a heavy toll for the ice we called, and for that week of rain, I do little more than sleep. I don't fight it this time. I give myself permission to hurt and then heal, however that looks. I may never be well, never what I was before, but Vesp and I have found something new, or something old, perhaps, and that is strong enough. The Thalon of Vatska could have never moved the ice.

Watching the village, I see memories of myself, of such an unexpected fall. And in that, I see in this community that which I could not see within myself. They come together, what might crush one person, they hold with many hands. They unite rather than flee. They see the whole rather than the broken pieces. Because we are, as Lars Seppanen once said, more than one.

Yew returns to the ashen forest and blooming shrine. I watch her sink to her knees in the mud, stricken, devastated. She gazes up at the shrine, the trees tall and open, like a hand awaiting a Duskingr to land. Yew's Coyote Woman mask falls beside her.

"Dusking," states Yew, as if the word tastes bitter. Her eyes pass between Vesp and I. "Duskingr..."

Vesp looks to me, then to Yew. She intertwines her fingers through mine and nods.

"Duskingr," I echo. I turn the word around in my mind. It does not feel earned, not yet. *Duskingr.*

Yew's tail flicks. Her eyes fill with tears and without another word, she stalks away.

⁎ ⁎ ⁎

Lylok summons us to his workshop. A large wooden chest sits on his bench. "Vespald, Thalon. I knew this day would come. I wasn't sure what it would look like, but I knew."

Without another word, Lylok opens the chest. From a bed of velvet, he lifts a mask.

Priest Lylok looks into the empty eyes of the mask, expression soft. "The hermit thrush. An unassuming creature with the most enchanting of voices." Eyes bright with pride, he offers the mask to Vesp. "Daughter of the earth. Priestess."

Vesp takes it in both hands, tail fluffed, eyes huge. She stares at the eyeholes, enraptured, until she snaps back to herself and bows in gratitude.

I move to embrace Vesp but Lylok stops me with a gentle hand. Shaking his head, he lifts a second layer of velvet to reveal another half-mask. This one is painted gray and mottled, the bottom edge a row of vicious teeth. A leopard seal, like Tophinghua.

Lifting it, he inspects it for a moment before extending it to me. "She saw you and you saw Her. Despite everything, you saw yourself. Remember how that felt, Aalgur Thalon, to see an impossible thing. Daughter of the sea. Priestess."

My hackles raise. I accept the mask. I am not worthy of it. But I damn well will be.

Lylok takes a breath. "There is so much to be done. With Parliament. With our peoples. With Ruhnsvalla. With you."

Taking my hand, Lylok turns my palm up. Lifting Vesp's hand, he places it over mine.

Vesp and I hold our masks, our hands. Our eyes find each other, two surprised strangers meeting on a wild path once more.

Lylok beams. "We are stronger together."

* * *

Vesp and I stand together on the ridge, valleys of forest to either side, blackened and leafless. Night falls. The fire revealed the Ikthvar air base in the distance. A red beacon roves like a lighthouse. We stand in silence as a Duskingr airship lowers to the base, a black dagger in the gloaming sky.

To our other side, the waters of Kaldur Lake dance with the light of the Svall as if it delights in Tophinghua's destruction.

We wait until night deepens and the spotlights at the base turn off. We walk in silence back to Ingfalla. No voices, no music, no crickets. The quiet feels off, foreboding.

"Something is happening..." says Vesp. We pause, listening. Vesp points. "At the shrine... I see lights..."

I see them too. The villagers cluster at the shrine, lanterns in hand.

A knot tightens in my belly. Something has changed... I feel it in my breath and bones.

Voices whisper, frightened, alarmed. Someone weeps.

We push through the crowd.

Two bodies lie beneath the eves of the shrine. Are they injured? Are they dead?

Two more figures stand beside Illuet Yew. Battered, bleeding, remnants of uniforms dangle from their limbs. Lylok wraps them in blankets.

An enormous gray man holds a hand against his cracked and bleeding tusk. Dried blood cakes his chin.

A short young woman stands beside him. One eye is swollen shut. Portions of her lush hair have been burnt to the scalp. And yet, she holds herself with dignity and reserve. She keeps a comforting hand on her companion.

Rawl and Azoto.

*Azoto...*

My breath leaves me. I slip down to my knees beside Vesp.

Azoto's eyes look up, meet mine, meet me where I am, on hands and knees. Her mouth opens.

*Thalon...*her lips shape my name. Her eyes are black and full of ghosts.

"How..." I manage.

Yew turns her ancient face toward the mountain and the black shadows of the trees. Blue and violet light sways behind them, taunting, delighting.

"They came out of Kaldur Lake," she says.

# GLOSSARY

PEOPLE

·Aalgur Thalon: AWL-ger THAL-in (she/her)
  ·Anton Gill: AN-ton GILL (he/him)
  ·Ashling: ASH-ling (she/her)
  ·Azoto Seppanen: AH-zo-to sep-AN-en (she/her)
  ·Bently Kane: BENT-lee KAHN-eh (he/him)
  ·Blake: (he/him)
  ·Bryr Klashek: BREYE-er KLASH-ek (she/her)
  ·Cortland: (he/him)
  ·Dr. Belkis: BELL-kiss (she/her)
  ·Edyta Gadvig: ed-EET-ah GAD-vig (she/her)
  ·Elren Johanson: EL-ren yo-HAN-sen (he/him)
  ·Erik Leivara: ER-ik LEI-var-ah (he/him)
  ·Hannahlesh: HAN-ah-lesh (she/her)
  ·Hans: (he/him)
  ·Hermon Sokolov: HER-men SO-ko-lov (he/him)
  ·Hildergulda: HIL-der-GUHL-da (she/her)
  ·Jalmari: YAH-mar-ee (he/him)

·Jess: (he/him)
·Kelpie: KELP-ee (she/her)
·Kipper Arnfins: KIP-er ARN-fins (he/him)
·Koshkarl: KOSH-karl (he/him)
·Lars Seppanen: LARS sep-AN-en (he/him)
·Lexija: LEX-ee-yah (she/her)
·Luka: LOO-kah (he/him)
·Lylok: LIE-lock (he/him)
·Rawl Kane: RAWL (rhymes with crawl) KAHN-eh (he/him)
·Signe: SIG-nah (she/her)
·Tam: (he/him)
·Valmut: VAHL-moot (she/her)
·Vespald: vesp-AHLD (she/her)
·Wavern: WAVE-ern (they/them)
·Willawesk: WILL-ah-wesk (she/her)
·Willits: (he/him)
·Wilk: (he/him)
·Yew: (she/her)
·Zynk: ZINGK (unspecified)


## THREE PRIMARY DEITIES

·Brosk: BROSK, God of the Sea and Shepherd of Souls (he/him)
    ·Fregnym: FREG-nim, the Weaver, the Maker (they/them)
    ·Ithnaan: EETH-nahn, the Unmaker, Goddess of Death (she/her)


The Ingvu (ING-voo)
    Children of Brosk
    ·Krescean: KRESH-ee-an, the Shipwright, the first Ingvu (he/him)
    ·Tophinghua: tope-FING-oo-ah, God of Storm and Strife, also called the Dread One, the Dread Hurricane, the second Ingvu (she/her; in religious writings often: he/him)
    ·Volier: voll-EE-eer, the North Wind, the third Ingvu (he/him)

·Ryshvarad: REESH-vah-rad, Ice of the Sea, Patron of Lost Souls, twin of Zandruik (he/him)

·Zandruik: ZAND-rook, Snow of the Glaciers, Patron of the Defenseless, twin of Ryshvarad (she/he/they)

## THE DUSKINGR AIR FLEET SHIPS

·*Greshkah:* GRESH-kah

·*Jagdahl:* YAG-doll

·*Kullkesh:* KULL-kesh

·*Machtesh:* MAHK-tesh

·*Ursul:* ERR-sool

·*Vhran:* VRAN

## MISC.

·Blitz: a hand axe

·Boreackt: BOR-ee-act, the Mountain (she/her)

·*Cloudberry*: (she/her)

·Duskingr: DUSK-ing-er or DUSK-ing-AIR.

NOUN: a rigid sided airship, one of the original realmships built by the Karrvoss Nomads. One who travels the Svall.

To dusk, dusking, VERB: to hold both elements of nature in harmony within the self.

·Duskir: DUSK-eer

·Gevit: GAH-vit, an old battle axe

·Illuet: ILL-oo-et, a High Priest/Priestess of kvell.

·Karrvoss, the Karrvoss Nomads: KAR-vahs, nomadic machine builders from the realm of Karrvossha.

·Ketja: KET-yah, a signed language

·kvell: KVELL or KFELL, magic of breath

·Kvellvahna: kvell-VAHN-ah, a ritualistic dance or practice to move or channel kvell

·Kvellsett: KVELL-set, Goddess of the Harvest and Decay, also called the Coyote Woman or Coyote Mother (she/they)

·Naudeleid: NAH-da-lied, the Ice Ship of Brosk (she/her)

·Tawkthalon: tahk-THAH-lon, adopted daughter of Tophinghua (she/her)

·thyir: THEER, TEER, or in Old Zahlek: THEE-reh, magic of bone.

·ts'kmet: TISK-met, a cultural selkie dance.

·Svall: SVALL of SFALL, the barrier between Ruhnsvalla, the Otherside, Karrvossha, and all other Realms, whose names have been lost.

·Zahlek: ZAHL-ek, a dead language of gods and time.


## PLACES

·Adelaide: ADD-el-layd, a city in inland, southern Ruhnsvalla

·Adlervik: ADD-ler-vik, capital city of Ruhnsvalla

·Blackberry Hills: mountains along the western coast of Ruhnsvalla

·Caldera: inland city in southeastern Ruhnsvalla

·Coven Cove: a sheltered cove in northern Vatska

·Duskheim Mountains: DUSK-heim, tallest mountain range in Ruhnsvalla and home of the Boreackt

·Erling River: AIR-ling

·Ikthvar Airbase: ICK-th'var, a Parliament run airbase in the Duskheim Mountains

·Ingfalla: ING-fall-ah, a huldror shrine

·Kaldur Lake: KAHL-door

·Movaska: moh-VAH-ska, a mining town in northern Ruhnsvalla

·Poppy City: an inland city in eastern Ruhnsvalla

·Ruhnsvalla: ROONS-fall-ah

·Shastaar River: SHAS-star

·Shonoda: SHOW-no-dah, a huldror shrine

·Tannenburg: TAN-en-berg, a coastal city in eastern Ruhnsfalla

·The Otherside: a realm directly across the Svall

·Vatska: VAT-ska, a once thriving selkie seaport, home of the Dusk Trials Arena

## DAYS OF THE WEEK

·Broskstag, Kreshtag, Nadeltag, Sturmtag, Volltag, Ryshtag, Zandtag

## MONTHS OF THE YEAR

·From the beginning of the year:
Fregnymarsh, Ithnamarsh, Broshkar, Alkar, Ingvrushar, Druskall, Thyirshrall, Vhrandahl, Machtahl, Kullvre, Arkosre, Kvellsettre.
·By Season:
Spring: Broshkar, Alkar, Ingvrushar
Summer: Druskall, Thtirshrall, Vhrandahl
Autumn: Machtahl, Kullvre, Arkosre
Winter: Kvellsettre, Fregnymarsh, Ithnamarsh

# Acknowledgments

It takes a village to tell a story, I believe that with my whole heart. I may be the fingers on the keyboard, but there would be no book without the support, patience, and love of that village. I doubt I will capture all of you on this page, so please know, if you are in my life in any way, you helped.

My deepest gratitude to Meagan Friedman, who chose to take a chance on this tale and then kicked absolute ass on every aspect of development, revision, and bringing out the best in me as a writer. To Meagan and everyone who has worked with Quills and Cosmos to bring this book to life, I offer my hands to you as one offers them to Brosk.

To every teacher, mentor figure, heck, even doctor who encouraged me to write and keep writing, you did it! We won. To Micah Perks who is always there for me, to Charlie Jane Anders for her kindness, to the incredible writers and friends who have said: keep going. Y'all, it's happening! To Sarra Cannon, your positivity helped me believe.

To Kathryn Lee, for showing me how it feels to hold my own book in my hands. You have given me a priceless treasure.

To Nina, Mim, and Colin, you three are the pillars in my life. Without you I am no one, wandering the pines. I wake up every day blessed for each of you. To Elec the Mage who always believed, and to Luci my biggest fan and cheerleader: I couldn't do this without you. I don't say it enough, I am grateful every day for you.

To R.A. Salvatore, the first author to write me back, scimitars high! To Simon Sylvester, who brought my love affair with selkies to life.

To Ronan Harris, Eivor, and every person who creates music, you write the heartbeat of other worlds.

To Till. You know why, you freak.

To Popo, Sow, Nalani, Hobbit, Troll, Ruby and Mar, and all my family, thank you for supporting this less-than-typical dream. To Tom, I love our phone calls.

To Niall Keogh for transforming my hideous scribbles into the Anchor of Brosk and giving Tophinghua her teeth.

To the archeologist who allowed me to pay my respects at the actual grave of the Birka Warrior. You unknowingly set things into motion that could not be stopped.

To Cody Harbottle, who gave me the voice of the Mountain.

To the wonderful folks and veterans at the Moffet Field Museum for walking me through the ins and outs of airships with enthusiasm and patience. I asked so many times what would happen if an airship was hit by lightning/fire/magic missile/the hand of a god. You gave me answers for each.

To you writers wondering if you should tell your stories. If not you, who?

And lastly, to libraries. May we never be denied them.

# About the Author

Arlo "Zven" Graves (they/them) grew up in rural California mountains surrounded by nature and all the magic it contains. They're lucky enough to live in their childhood community, in a once abandoned cabin.

Zven lives with a condition called mixed connective tissue disease; think a cousin of lupus. After a particularly bad flare up in 2020, Zven realized how much they wanted to see chronic illness represented in the fantasy adventure stories they loved reading, to see characters find purpose and fulfillment, even without a magical cure.

Zven has a degree in creative writing from the University of California Santa Cruz. Their short nonfiction, *Gerald: a Memoir,* won the Stories That Need to be Told 2023 grand prize, and their debut novella, *Black Rose*, is out from Graveside Press.

Find them online at www.arlozgraves.com.

threads.com/@arlozgraves

instagram.com/arlozgraves

goodreads.com/Arlozgraves

amazon.com/author/arlozgraves

bsky.app/profile/arlozgraves

mastodon.social/@arlozgraves

# ALSO BY ARLO Z. GRAVES

Black Rose

Stories That Need to Be Told 2023

Rogue Waves: A Dragon Soul Press Anthology

Beautiful Darkness: A Dragon Soul Press Anthology

# CONTENT WARNINGS

(Emotional) child abuse

Attempted suicide (drowning, ocean)

Violence

On page character death

Blood

Depression

Fantasy world racism

www.ingramcontent.com/pod-product-compliance
Lightning Source LLC
Chambersburg PA
CBHW030736310726
48969CB00005B/1235